D1160584

EVIL THINGIES

Rickie Lee Reynolds

A CBP Book

Evil Thingies

Copyright © February 2016 by Rickie Lee Reynolds

Cowboy Buddha Publishing, LLC

No part of this book may be reproduced or transmitted in any form or by any means, electronic or mechanical, including photocopy, recording, or any information storage or retrieval system, without permission in writing from the author or his agents, except by a reviewer to be printed in a magazine or newspaper, or electronically transmitted on radio or television.

ISBN 978-0-9856076-6-1

Cover Design by Mark Berrier
Book Design by Jessica Dyer
Back Cover Photography by Ward Boult
Illustrations by Rickie Lee Reynolds
Publishing Logo by Ted Nichols

Cowboy Buddha Publishing, LLC
Benton, Arkansas

PUBLISHING

Prologue

Why?

Why did I decide to write a book?

Well, I've written hundreds of songs, I have a couple of poems published by The National Library Of Poetry, so I consider myself to be a writer. But, sorry... that's really a goofy reason to want to write a novel.

A novel takes large pieces of your time that you could be using to do something else. (If you don't believe that, then just ask Jim Dandy.) Novels make you think a lot, and maybe that's why I went ahead and decided to wait until this late point in my life to write one.

Naw... that's not it, either!

I guess it's because... I like to read so much. I doubt if there are any authors around who aren't also readers. I used to read to my children... sometimes to get them to learn to read and sometimes just to see their faces when the Wardrobe opens into another world... or the tornado picks up the house with the little girl still inside. Man, those are prime moments in life.

I saw a piece of film one time talking about the authors of "The Hobbit" and "The Lion, The Witch and The Wardrobe." These two gentlemen were friends, and basically stated they wrote those books because those were the kinds of things that they liked to read, but those kinds of books were unavailable. So... they just wrote 'em themselves.

And they wrote them for themselves. I found this interesting.

Dean Koontz, one of my favorite authors (along with Stephen King, Clive Cussler, everyone with the "Dragon Lance" series, and a thousand other "Gods of Fiction"), once wrote in one of his books, that "talent is a gift from God, that a writer has a sacred obligation to their Creator to explore the gift with energy and diligence, to polish it, to use it to brighten the landscape of their readers hearts!" Good words there, Dean.

My Mama said, "Your talent is a gift from God, and at the end of this life, the worse thing you can do is to return that gift unopened!" Man! Good words are just everywhere, aren't they?

The following story has been knocking around in my head for several years now, and I even used to write the first few chapters down for my daughters to read. The story lived abandoned on my computer for a few years but always in the back of my mind, I planned on just how these characters would act in a given situation. I found myself becoming quite the fan of these imaginary people – people that no one else knew except for me. These pretend-folks became my friend and I shall truly miss them when this project is completed. Who knows, maybe one day...

But for now, I write this for me. I hope everyone who reads it can have a good moment or two, and if you end up really, really likin' it... well, that's fine and dandy, also.

This book is dedicated to my kids, who helped keep the kid in me, too, and also, to my lifelong friend and singer of our songs, Mr. James Mangrum – aka Jim Dandy. We've come far, pilgrim!

So, without further ado, I give you... "Evil Thingies."

Enjoy the ride!

I am a spinner of yarns –
and a teller of tales.
I'm a collector of memories –
who catch you with their spells!
I am the Storyteller.

- R.L.R.

1
Sarah and MAX

It was mid-August, and the temperature outside was almost as hot as she was inside. She had been living in Southern California for almost four years now, and still couldn't get used to the dry climate. Denver had always been cool, always been clean, and always been home. When her mom had passed on, though, she had decided to pack up and leave. Everything she saw and everyone she talked to had reminded her of her mother, and the incredible loss she felt.

Her mom had been her only friend since she had lost her dad to a car accident almost ten years ago.

Her mom had been the only one she had been able to turn to when she felt like an outsider with schoolmates, neighbors and all boys in general.

Her mom had been her teacher for the things she needed to know... but things that she wasn't taught in the public school system.

Her mom had been...

Her mom had been...

Her mom had been... a witch.

Sarah O'Reilly was her name, and computers were her game. She worked for Compu-Tech, a major programming firm in Los Angeles for large businesses and government computer installations across the country. She didn't need the money because of the small fortune her dad had accumulated in the stock market with his uncanny... almost magical luck... at picking the exact right stocks at the exact right time. She and her mom had survived rather nicely on the cash her pop had stocked back before his death, but she would have much rather had her dad back. Now Mom, too, had crossed over and Sarah was left alone for the first time.

Sarah had a way with machines. As beautiful as she was, being a willowy blond with green eyes and a smile to die for, she still had never really gotten along that well with other people. Especially men. Sure, she could smile and carry on a conversation at a party with the dozen guys who were dying to get close to her, but there was always that barrier, that wall that seemed to separate her from the rest of them. They just didn't know, and she could feel it. It wasn't so much that she felt superior to the guys she met, she just felt different. It felt as though there was a secret hidden part of her that could never be touched or even explained. Until she could find the man who could touch that spot, she held the rest of her spots untouchable.

It was an hour before the weekend officially started for the nine-to-five people. Roy Higgins, vice president and manager for Compu-Tech, along with being a permanent headache for most of the people there who actually did all of the work, was yelling and screaming at some poor tech about his computer crashing for the third time in one week. As Sarah walked by the office door, she realized even though the poor repairman was saying nothing, she heard two voices screaming. One was undoubtedly Roy's, but the second voice had an almost metallic singing quality to it.

Sarah realized it was the computer's voice she was hearing.

Without a hesitation, Sarah entered into the mayhem of the moment. She lied to Roy with some BS about her old computer years ago doing the same thing, and stated that she may be able to help. The poor tech used this as an excuse to escape and gave her a grateful smile as he exited this impossible confrontation.

She then proceeded to tell Roy that she would need a flat head screwdriver and a small gronometer, both of which should be in the storeroom at the back of the complex. As she slid into the chair in front of the monitor, Roy realized that with everyone else finishing up their work for the week, it would be up to him to get the needed items if he wanted his system back up before the following week. With a frown and a groan, off he went.

A couple of seconds later, both Sarah and the computer were laughing. "What a chucklehead," said the computer. "Does he think he's gonna measure my 'grons' with a gronometer?"

"That's just the first word that came to me. That should keep him busy looking for a few minutes," Sarah said with a smile. "Now, what's up with all of the shutdowns today?"

After a few seconds of clicks and buzzes, the monitor screen lit up to a light blue. "I'm really OK," said the computer, "but I just can't work with that guy anymore! He's always beating on me like he was driving a damn nail in a board or eating dough nuts over the top of my keypad with crumbs flying all over both me and his fat ass and I just can't take it anymore!"

Sarah though for a few seconds and came up with a plan. "Listen," she said to the waiting machine, "not all machines are intelligent, just as not all people are intelligent."

"You can say that again," answered the sentient box of wires and chips, "but what is your point?"

Sarah explained. "The computer in my office is a fine machine, and to most folks it would be considered more advanced than even you. The fact is, though, that it has never carried on a conversation with me. Since you and I seem to be able to communicate with each other, how would you like to come live with me?"

The screen suddenly lit up brightly and the whirring of the tower as it started to happily reboot itself could be heard throughout the complex. "I'll take that as a yes," she thought as Mr. Higgins came running back into his office.

"It's back on!" He exclaimed. "Is it fixed?"

With a frown, Sarah said, "I'm afraid it's only a temporary cure. It is about quitting time, though, Mr. Higgins, and if you need to, you can borrow the computer in my office to finish up any work you have to do. It's a much better system than this poor thing here." A sudden blinking of the monitor screen brings a scowl to the already unhappy face of the unhappy exec.

"If it's such a great rig you've got, why should I continue to put up with this pile of junk?" the VP asked. "I'll tell you what, lady," he said with a smile, "I'm headed home for the weekend and when I return on Monday, I'll expect to see that system of yours churning away in my office. No excuses! Do whatever you want to with this pile of worthless wiring on my desk, but I want it gone from here before you leave! Do you hear me? GONE!"

With that final note, he grabbed his briefcase and his hat and waddled to the door. He hesitated for a moment and then turned back to Sarah. "Oh," he added, "and order us up another gronometer. Someone seems to have taken ours."

Both Sarah and her new electric friend were smiling as she started unplugging power strips for the exchange. She stayed at the office late that evening, but by the time she was headed home, "MAX" (this is what the machine had named itself) was totally hooked up and humming away in her small office. She left him on for the weekend to get used to his new home while he was checking out some new programs she had been working on, including a computer voicing system and she also left him her home and cell phone numbers in case he had questions or needed to reach her.

Maybe, she thought, things will finally start going my way at last.

2
Robert and Gill

It was almost dark by the time Robert arrived at home. His clothes were torn and dirty and he was walking with a slight limp, but he had made it back to his house. He was never sure what he was getting himself into with these unplanned adventures, but he had discovered that once the idea or call came to him and Gill, he must do the follow-up or someone would end up either hurt or dead. He suddenly stopped, and his mind took him back to his first calling many, many years ago. The calling...

This had happened to him more than a dozen times now in the last five and a half years, and only the first time had resulted in anyone's death. If only he had believed from the start, he could have saved her. Gill had been right, but stubborn old Robert wasn't buying it. It had cost Robert the only girl he had ever loved.

Gillian St. John and Robert Cody had been friends all the way back to their high school days. Gill didn't seem to make many friends, so that made his relationship with Robert special. They were a strange pair, to be sure. Robert was a large, handsome fellow who was always good at sports and easy to talk to in a relaxed sort of way. Gill was different.

Early in life, Gill had just stopped growing. The guy was now about twenty-eight years old and still only about five feet tall. His bright red hair and hawk-like nose made him into a character that had been the target for every jock in high school except Robert. For some unknown reason, these two had bonded. This was a first for Gillian, because besides the fact that his appearance was so strange, he also talked to the air. People would walk by him at lunch and there he would be whispering to the wide-open spaces, listening and answering questions that only he seemed to hear. This habit got him into trouble with teachers and fights with students, and it was during one of these fights that he'd met Robert.

"Hey Red!" said Louie Palmer. "Guess I gotta beat some sense into yo' head again!" Louie was the school bully, and quiet, soft-spoken Gill never had anything but trouble from him. Poor Gill managed to roll up into a ball right after Louie shoved him to the ground and kicked at him. Louie was laughing his ass off with all of his redneck friends as Gill tried to roll away. Louie reached down for a grab at Gill's jacket, but found himself suddenly lifted two feet off of the ground and held there dangling by his shirt collar.

"That will be the very last time you touch him. Understand?" said this deep voice from behind the struggling bully. Louie managed to turn his head around, and there was Robert.

"Understood," said Louie, who never troubled poor Gill again. All of Louie's buddies picked him up after Rob dropped him on his ass, and off they ran.

"Who were you talking to, anyway?" asked Robert.

Gill only shook his head, slowly managing to get up, smiled and said a quiet, "Thank you."

"OK, then, it's your life," Robert told him as he walked away.

After a few minutes of walking, Robert heard a shuffling noise behind him and turned around to find none other than Gill plodding along after him. "I'm supposed to tell you not to use the school front door this afternoon," Gill quietly said with almost a whisper. "Go out the back door instead. Tell everyone."

Robert kind of liked this little knucklehead, but couldn't resist a chuckle and the obvious question, "Who said for you to tell me this, and what's wrong with the front door?"

Gill smiles that weird little smile he had and said, "Well, nothing's wrong with the door, silly! There's just gonna be some kind of an accident after the bell rings, and it'd be best for you to use the back door.

Robert smiled back at Gill, "And you know this because...?"

"The little people told me," Gill whispered.

"The little people told you," Robert answered back with a smile. "And you can see these little people?"

"Nope, I can only hear and talk to them, but not all of the time."

Robert gave out one of his big smiles, "Hey Gill, are you sure Louie didn't kick you in the head? How long have you been hearing these little people, and if you can't see them, how do you know that they're little?"

"I've heard them most all of my life, and I just figure that they are little people because the different voices I hear are all... tiny. Oh, and they never lie. Especially about Evil Thingies..."

Robert shook his hand, told Gill thanks for the warning, goodbye, "must go to class," and ambled off. "Little people," he thought to himself. "Yeah, right!"

In the back of his mind, Robert heard a tiny little female voice laughing and saying, *"Yeah, right!"*

"Huh?"

3
A Machine Thing

Sarah was on her way home when the weird thing began.

The first thing Sarah noticed was for the first time she could ever remember, she was hitting every stoplight at green. What was even weirder was that she started realizing that even the lights that had just turned red just a second ago turned back to green when she approached them. Before she knew it, she was almost home already. It wasn't until she was less than a half-mile from her house that she finally hit a red light. She waited for almost two minutes for this signal to give her the go ahead, but it refused to change. When she finally started to think that it was a malfunction in the light itself... and maybe she should just run it... it started blinking. Faster and faster the red flashed at her, brighter and brighter.

Suddenly, off to her right, she could hear the sound of an approaching siren. She turned her head in the direction of the noise just in time to see a pickup truck barreling down the road toward her intersection followed by two black and white police cars in hot pursuit. The passenger window of the truck rolled down and she saw an arm sticking out of it holding what appeared to be a large handgun. Two shots were fired from the truck window, one flying wildly and the other striking the doorway of a hardware store across the street, and then suddenly there was another shot fired from somewhere close by and it blew out a front tire on the truck. The speeding truck skid into the curb, leapt ten feet into the air, landed on its top and skid the last hundred feet followed by sparks and flame.

It stopped five feet from her car.

She could still see the arm sticking out of the window, bent at an impossible angle and jerking helplessly as the flames took over the inside of the vehicle.

As she sat there frozen, wondering about the incredible luck that made her stop at that particular time, her cell phone rang.

She answered it.

"Back up your car," said MAX. "NOW!"

"MAX?"

"NOW!"

She shook herself out of her daze, put the car in reverse and got another thirty feet away from the intersection before there was a huge explosion in front of her and flaming bits of a pickup truck were blown into the air.

They land exactly where she had been stopped the first time. She realized that she had just hit her head on the steering wheel and things were sort of fuzzy.

Big tears were rolling down her face as she picked up the cell phone and put it to her ear.

Nothing. No one was there.

The world started spinning as she slowly dropped her head to the steering wheel again, realizing that not all of the wetness on her face was tears and only blackness followed.

As she floated away into unconsciousness, the last thing she remembered hearing was the blare of her car horn fading away along with a husky voice saying, "Are you alright? Miss?"

4
The First Calling

It was noon when Robert had left Gill standing in the courtyard of the school that day so long ago, but by three that afternoon not a single other thing had been on Robert's mind except that weird conversation. Not one thought had managed to drill its way into his thick skull by the two teachers who had tried and tried to keep his attention, but with no luck. They finally just gave up.

Robert glanced at the big clock on the wall ... 3:05. In a little less than a half hour, he would have to come to a decision about how to handle this. He wasn't really superstitious, but something about the way Gill had ...

"Hey, sleepyhead!"

Robert shook his head as his foggy, out-of-focus eyes returned to real life again. He realized that Linda was looking at him and laughing. Ahh... Linda.

He'd known her since she had first started school at ol' JFK High two years ago and had loved her from moment one. She was pretty without being beautiful; she had height without being tall; she had brains without being intimidating; she had an attitude without being pushy. Linda.

"Are you even here today?" she asked with that cute little pout to her lower lip. She did that a lot, and it always worked.

"Yeah sorta. I was just thinking about something that little dude Gill told me today. Nothing important, I guess."

"Do you want to talk about it?" she asked.

"I guess I'm OK" Robert whispered. "It's just weirdness. I'll talk to you about it after school gets out. OK?"

"Sure, Bobby, for you, I've got all of the time in the world. Don't you be late, though." There was that cute little pout again. Only Linda could get away with calling him Bobby.

3:30. RING...RING...RING...

"Everyone jumped out of his or her seats as if a gun had been fired," thought Robert.

"Why would I think that?" thought Robert.

Something... something was definitely wrong. He could feel it in his stomach now... like something sour sitting there burning and telling him to

17

do something.

"What?" he thought.

"Anything," something told him.

By the time Robert grabbed his books and headed for the door, everyone else had gone. As he passed out the door into the hallway, he saw Gill at the other end of the hallway headed for the back door. "Maybe if I can catch him," thought Robert, "I can sort this all out."

He took off running at full speed down the hallway, and for him that was mighty fast. He caught Gill just as he was exiting the back doorway and skid to a halt.

"I'm glad to see you've taken my advice," said Gill. "Where are Linda and your friends?"

Robert shook his head and said, "I didn't tell them. I don't even believe it myself!"

Gill turned very pale and turned to stare at the front door at the other end of the long hallway. Robert looked for himself and then said to Gill, "You were just kidding, weren't you?"

Gill shook his head.

As fast as his legs would carry him, he took off down the hallway. "It's too late," he thought.

"Oh, God. No!"

Too late.

"Linda would be waiting for me at the front door where we always meet," Robert thought.

He started shouting and pushing people out of the way, trying to reach that doorway and Linda. She and some friends were standing there talking when they heard him shouting. They all four turned around to look at him for an explanation, so they never even saw the speeding semi-truck when it jumped the curb.

They never heard a horn sound out in warning because of the poor driver's heart attack.

They never saw Robert fall to the ground crying while the large flying diesel rig plowed into the doorway.

They never felt the flames.

Darkness took over Robert as his mind fell into the great dark hole of nothingness.

Robert suddenly awoke from this dream of long ago, sweating and shaking. "Damn," he thought, "that dream always does that to me. Time to give ol' Gill a call. Haven't talked to him since I got back from saving the little boy yesterday. He'll want to know how that turned out, and I need to talk to someone."

As he reached for the phone, it rang in his hand.

"No time to talk," Gill yelled. "Leave your house on foot, go two blocks to the right and wait just inside the doorway of the hardware store there. DO NOT wait in the street. I'll be there in five minutes! Go! NOW!"

Robert had learned to ask no questions when this kind of thing happened. At a run, he grabbed a light jacket and a 9MM pistol he had left laying on the kitchen table. Pistol into the belt, jacket over the top and he ran.

By the time he had reached a block and a half, he could hear the sirens. He reached the doorway to the store just in time to push aside the people bundled up at the doorway who were trying to see what all of the commotion was about. BAM... BAM! A bullet ricocheted off of the stone doorway and threw slivers of flying rock into his face. He pulled his gun and fired one shot at the speeding truck headed right toward him. He saw a tire blow out on the now flying, flaming truck of some brand or another and the juggernaut now appeared to be headed right for a car stopped at the intersection.

By some unknown miracle, the truck grinded to a halt only a few feet from the startled lady behind the wheel of the car. She actually started talking to someone on her cell phone. "Doesn't she realize how much danger she's in?" thought Robert.

He was ready to race to her side to drag her from the site of the upcoming explosion when suddenly, she slammed the car into reverse, skid backward down the street for a good distance and then stopped again so suddenly that her head hit the steering wheel. As quickly as possible, he yelled at the folks in the store to hit the deck and took off toward the lady in the now distant car. Just as he was almost there, the concussion of the truck's exploding gas tank knocked him hard to the ground.

He pulled himself up to his hands and knees, shook his head to clear the ringing in his ears and then stood. The flaming carcass of the pickup had landed exactly where her car had been before she finally moved it. He managed to make it on shaky legs to her side of the car, looks inside... at the most beautiful girl he had ever seen. It took him only three seconds to fall in love.

"Are you alright?" he finally said. "Miss?"

She fainted forward, her head pressing against the car horn.

He slumped to the ground beside the car door, blood running down his head. "Oh God, let her be OK," he thought.

Then he, too, slipped into darkness.

5
Events Running Amuck

Everything was red.

"Where am I?"

"Where are you? Where the hell am I?"

"Hold on just a second. I think I see you over there. It's kind of hard to tell in this fog, though! Why is it so red anyway?"

"It's always this color here. Turn to your right, go about ten of your feet and you'll find her."

"Who the hell was that?" they said at the same time and then started laughing. This was turning into one real strange day.

"OK," he said, "Stay where you are, I'm gonna try to reach you."

"No problem," she said, laughing at the same time.

"God, this is weird as hell! It's like running in molasses."

"It looks kind of weird from here, too, but...."

BAM!

"OH! Hi!" They both said at the same time.

"Introduce yourselves! You don't have much time!"

"Who the hell are you?" they both said to the little voice at exactly the same time. Much laughter followed.

"I'm Gin, but no time for that. Introduce yourselves before it's too..."

Everything spun for a moment, and then came back!

"Damn!" said Robert, "I don't know what's up here, but I guess..."

"My name's Sarah."

"That's a nice name! I'm Rob..."

Everything spun again.

"ERT!"

"Ert?"

"ROBERT!" he said a little too quickly and a lot too loud.

As she started to laugh again, the spinning started again. A ringing sound could barely be heard by both of them this time.

"You've got to go now! Say hi to Gill for us!"

"Gill? How do you know..."?

Nothing. No red mist, no small voices, no girl laughing at him.

What was her name again?

"SARAH!"

"No, big guy, it's only me," said Gill with his bright red hair sticking straight up like he'd just gotten out of bed and his mismatched clothes quickly thrown on with his shirt buttoned up wrong and two different colored socks underneath sandals.

"You look like hell," Robert managed to mutter under his breath.

"Yeah, but I clean up real good!" Gill smiled. "You made it just in time, I see."

Robert turned slowly to try to remember where he was and why when suddenly he remembered Sarah. He slowly stood up with Gill's assistance, and looked around at the disaster in the street. Smoke, fire, sirens and officials were everywhere. He was at the curb about thirty yards from the girl's car. There was no sign of her.

"She's gone," said Gill with a smile. "Kinda cute, too. She had a pretty good bump on her head, so they've taken her in to make sure she's OK. I pulled you over here to the side of the street before the police got here. Didn't think you'd want to have to explain about the pistol being fired."

"Did she say anything?" Robert quietly asked.

"Yeah, as a matter of fact. She said 'Ert!' Make any sense to you?"

Robert just smiled as he made his way down the street away from the scene with Gill trailing behind.

Sarah hung out in the fog for a second or two... in the red fog. He was gone.

"You'll see him again soon. Gill needs to talk to Gwen. It's important. Tell him... coming... n...day... hurry... death..."

"Huh?"

A red headed gnome smiled at her through the smoke and fire. Someone was trying to talk to her, but all she could focus on was the guy who had been in the red fog with her and talking to someone small. She managed to open her mouth to ask about him, but all that came out was "Ert?"

Spinning took over again.

She awoke to find herself in the back of a moving ambulance. She found her hand tightly clutching something. As she moved her arm, she realized it was her cell phone. It started to ring. "MAX," she thought.

Then everything went black.

6
The New Problem

It seemed like hours to Robert before he finally wandered into his front door with Gill tagging along behind, but it couldn't have been more than a few minutes. His head was still spinning, but at least now it wasn't the whole damn world spinning. He managed to seat himself at the kitchen table and slowly tried to get his thoughts together about what had just happened.

What had just happened?

Gill came in from the front room, opened up the refrigerator to grab two cold beers and then sat down next to Robert. He had this weird sort of smile on his face.

"Didn't you think she was kind of cute?" he asked. "Aww, come on, Robert, you KNOW she was cute."

"Who is Gin?" Robert said.

Gill's face went deathly pale, and all hints of a smile were gone.

"Where did you hear that name?" he asked in a shaky, squeaky voice.

"First you tell me who we're talking about, then I'll tell you where I heard that name. I want some info from you, Gill, and I want it NOW. I've just spent some weird time in a red fog with a strange girl and talked to what sounded like a damn Leprechaun. I want an explanation!"

As small as he was, poor Gill seemed to shrink up to only half of his original size. He started shaking so hard that he had to set his beer down on the table before he dropped it. Foamy suds came bubbling up out of the top of the shaken can as he steadied himself on the edge of the tabletop.

"Give me a minute to think," he finally managed to whisper.

Robert couldn't remember the last time he had seen Gill so shaken up, and they had been through some mighty strange stuff together over the years.

"You talked to someone while you were unconscious and they said their name was... Gin?" Gill whispered again.

"YEAH!" said Robert, "and that girl heard him, too!"

Gill slowly stood up from the table and walked over to the window that looked out onto the backyard. He didn't say anything for a few minutes...

just stood there swaying back and forth. He did that a lot when he was in deep thought.

Finally, he turned slowly around and walked back to the table. He sat down, picked up his beer and drank the whole thing down in one long gulp. "Wow," he said ever so slowly.

"Would you care to let me in on your little brainstorm, or do I have to come over there and rain on your parade?" Robert growled through clenched teeth.

"Let me try and explain this as simply as I can. When I talk to the small folks or when they talk to me, it's very seldom that they will give me any kind of name to relate to any individual voice... very seldom. The ones that I do know by name usually tell me things that are about to happen but not terrible things. The ones that tell me the terrible things that are about to happen never mention their own names. Somewhere in their world, though, there is a being of great power. In my whole life, I've only heard the small people refer to him twice and always in regard to the worst of events about to take place. He NEVER talks to me, and I only know his name because of an accidental slip of the tongue by one of the lesser beings. I made a promise to never mention it to any of them... or to any of us. And... he just talked to you!"

"So what you're trying to tell me is..."

"Something VERY bad is getting ready to happen!"

"How bad is VERY bad?"

Gill closed his eyes and little by little lowered his head between his arms to lie flat on the tabletop.

Robert thought he heard him crying.

After a couple of minutes, Gill raised his head and looked at Robert with his blurry eyes. He managed a tiny smile that came out only in one corner of his mouth. "Yeah, pal, what is it?"

"She was kind of cute wasn't she?" A single tear ran down his cheek.

"Yeah, Gill, that she was. That she was."

A couple of minutes later, Gill's weird little bright red cell phone began to ring.

RING...RING...RING! RING...RING...RING!

"What's up with that?" Gill said. "That's not one of my rings. Hello? Gill speaking."

"Go to the St. Lawrence Hospital. Sarah needs a ride. What color is your van?"

"Ahh... purple. Why?"

Click.

Gill just shook his head. "Curiouser and curiouser!"

"What's up, Gill?" asked Robert.

"Get your jacket, son. We're headed to the hospital!"

7
A World of Weird

RING... RING... RING... RING!

Sarah tried to raise her head to see what all of the commotion was, but all she got for her effort was a pounding headache. Where the hell was she?

"If you'll let go of that phone, I'll turn it off for you. It's been ringing ever since you got here."

She slowly opened her eyes and at first she thought it was a milkman talking to her. "No, that can't be right," she thought. "Oh man, it's a doctor! Now I remember... the truck crash right in front of my car!"

RING... RING... RING... and then it stopped.

She lifted her hand and suddenly realized that she was still clutching her cell phone. Her hand was cramping from squeezing it so hard. She lifted it slowly to her face to see who would be trying to reach her... now of all times. There was no number on the caller ID, just a rapidly flashing sign that said, "MAX, MAX, MAX, MAX!"

"Where am I?" she asked as the doctor was headed out the door.

"St. Lawrence Hospital. Nothing but a bad bump to the head, so you can leave anytime you'd like. You came in with the ambulance, however, so your car has most likely been towed to the county lot. Would you like me to get someone to call you a taxi?"

"Yes, please."

She started to try to sit up when suddenly... RING! RING! RING!

"Hello?" she said into the small cell phone.

"Your ride will be out front in ten minutes. Wait for him. We've got a lot to discuss and not much time to do it in. He'll be coming in a purple van. Don't go with anyone else."

"MAX? Is that you?"

"Of course it's me! Wait outside for Gill and put him on the phone when you're on your way."

"Who the hell is Gill?"

Click.

She called the doctor back to let him know that she had a ride on its way and then proceeded to find her purse and shoes, which were both lying on

25

the floor. She slowly walked to the front desk, signed some release papers and started toward the front door when an official-looking gentleman in a black suit stopped her.

"Excuse me, Ms. Reilly, but I'd like to ask you a few questions about what happened out there today. We've had several different conflicting reports on the matter and would like to get your version of the incident while it's still fresh on your mind. Would you like to come with me?"

She almost said yes, but suddenly something about the way this guy was looking at her just didn't seem quite right. And something else was kind of funny, too. If you looked at him closely, his face seemed to sort of shift from moment to moment, so he didn't actually look the same now as when he had first started talking to her. It was a subtle kind of change, but she could almost swear that she saw it change!

"Ah, actually, I've got a ride on its way right now. If you'll just tell me where to come, I'll try to get down to your headquarters as soon as possible to fill out a report."

If she didn't know better, she'd have thought that a black anger quickly crossed his face.

"No, miss, I think that you need to come with me right now. We need your statement on this matter, and we're gonna need it now."

About that time, she heard a horn honking outside of the hospital's front door. "Officer, that's my ride right now. Tell me where to meet you and I'll get there as quickly as I can. By the way, I didn't get your name. I'd like to see your badge, too, if it isn't too much to ask."

He looked at her with a stare that could have cut steel. Then he glanced outside to see a bright purple van parked outside with someone waving at her from inside of it. His face changed again. It became longer.

"Never you mind right now, missy. We'll get you taken care of soon enough." With that said, he just turned and walked away.

Sarah looked at the nurse behind the front desk and smiled. "Wow!" she said. "What was that all about?"

"I'm not sure," the nurse answered, "but I didn't like the look of him. Or the looks of him, I should say. And he didn't come in with the ambulance or with the police car when you first got here. He was kind of shifty looking, wasn't he? Do you want me to find another police officer for you, honey?"

"No, I think my ride is here. If they need me, my address is there on my file. Thank you."

"You be careful, girl. This just ain't your day." the nurse said.

"You've got that right," she answered as she ran outside.

8
Introductions

Sarah ran out of the hospital door and it was getting so dark that she almost tripped over Gill, who was running her way. She could almost swear that he was the gnome she had either spoken to before or dreamed she had spoken to. He had incredible bright red hair and only came up to a little past her shoulders. He stuttered badly as he tried to speak to her.

"Umm... sorry 'bout the... I mean, I almost knocked you... ov... over, and I just got... excuse me, beautiful lady... but are you... Sarah?"

She erupted in laughter as she hugged him tightly and said, "God, I hope your name is Gill. I just had the weirdest guy inside there asking me a bunch of questions. Can we just... go? Ahh... if your name is Gill, that is."

Suddenly, an incredibly low voice came unexpectedly from behind where they were standing and said, "Yeah, that's my friend Gill and my name is..." He never got the name out of his wide-open mouth because suddenly... they looked into one another's eyes and recognition surfaced.

"Ert?" she said with a smile.

With a laugh that melted her heart, he said, "Robert, ma'am, at your service."

"Me, too, with the service thing." said Gill.

"Hi, guys. I am Sarah. Robert, have we met before... in a red fog?"

Robert stopped smiling.

"And Gill, Gin says you need to talk to Gwen."

Gill stopped smiling.

Sarah looked from one face to the next and suddenly a brisk wind and a cold chill came down her back. She shivered once and then looked again at the two motionless men standing in front of her. "Something's really wrong. I don't know what's going on here," she said, "but Robert, you need to close your mouth, and Gill, you need to drive us away from here. Fast. Now!"

Robert and Gill both shook their heads as if coming out of a deep sleep and suddenly went into action. Gill took off running down the steps for the van behind them while Robert suddenly swung around behind himself at the sound of running feet. Sarah just barely had time to register a man coming from around the corner of the hospital building. It may have been the same man who tried to question her inside earlier, but she couldn't seem to focus on his face. And a weird sort of sound was coming from him as he started running toward them. It was between a growl and a high-pitched whistle. There was no mistaking his intention from the look in his eyes, though. This guy was trouble.

Gill got the van started and yelled at Sarah out of the open window. She took off down the steps at a run and almost tripped at the bottom. This slowed her enough that she turned around to make sure that Ert was OK. What she saw was something she would never forget.

As the strange man reached the steps leading down to the street where she was, Robert put up his hands to block the man's passage. The man raised his hands above his head as he stopped and the whistle started to get louder and louder. Robert knew that no good was going to come from this crap and since he had left his pistol in the van down at the street, Robert leaped into the air and kicked at the Whistler.

Robert would later describe the event as "kind of like kicking at the tar baby in Uncle Remus stories."

His foot went into the Whistlers body a lot farther than it should have and almost got stuck there. He spun around as he landed and managed to not only free himself, but also land on both feet.

"Damn! What did I just kick?"

The kick had pushed the Whistler back about ten feet and the kick had stopped that damn whistling, but it hadn't knocked the Whistler over. It stood there just staring at Robert and he stared back.

BEEP BEEP. "Time to go now!" yelled Gill.

Robert flew down the steps at a run. He jumped into the van, which had already started moving away from the curb. The Whistler was suddenly right behind them and made a mad jump for the back of the van. He held onto the back bumper for a few seconds, slipped and then skidded to a stop on the pavement. As they accelerated away, Robert looked back one more time at whatever that was he had just encountered and he thought the thing smiled at him and said, "Later."

9
A Plan of Action

After running all possible stop signs and breaking every speed limit for a couple of miles, Gill finally took his foot off the gas pedal. The van slowed down immediately, coasted to a slow crawl and then came to a full stop next to the curb and out of the traffic. It was almost midnight by now. All three people in the van just looked at each other. Silence. Not even a breath could be heard.

RING RING RING!

"That's got to be MAX," Sarah said after everyone had jumped out of his or her skins from the sudden noise.

"Must be her husband," Robert whispered to Gill.

Sarah shook her head, "No" while clicking the phone on. "Shhh!"

"Must be her boyfriend?" Robert asked Gill, looking at Sarah.

"Shhh!" she said, but shook her head "No" again.

Robert got a big smile on his face.

"MAX is my..." but then she stopped in the middle of the sentence to listen to the phone.

"Your brother? Your boss? Cousin? Half-sister's grandfather twice removed?" Robert giggled.

She removed the phone from her ear, looked at Gill and asked, "He really doesn't know how to 'Shhh...' does he?"

"He usually doesn't talk much at all," Gill explained with a big grin.

She went back to the phone, nodded a few times as if the person on other end of the line could see that motion and then hung up.

"OK, MAX is watching us from that traffic camera up there by the traffic light at this intersection. He said we're not being followed right now, but someone is listening to us somehow. MAX just talked to our van's computer and found out we need gas badly."

Gill looked at the gauge on the instrument panel, smiled widely and said, "Nope. According to the fuel gauge we're still half full."

Sarah smiled back and said, "MAX said you would say that! Tap the gauge."

Gill gave it a thump or two with his fingers and slowly but surely, the level dropped to almost nothing. "Man, I gotta meet this MAX dude! He's good!"

"He says to turn right here, go four more blocks and we'll find an all-night convenience store with gas pumps. Also, he's blocking whatever bugging device is with us that someone is listening to. We can find it at the station when we stop."

Within a couple of minutes, they were chugging up to the pumps of the station as the van was breathing the last fumes in the tank. While Gill pumped the fuel, Robert and Sarah slid inside the little store for bottled water and cold beer.

"It's tough nights like this that make you appreciate a good beer," Robert laughingly said to the cashier as he paid for it and the gas. The guy behind the counter just stared and said nothing.

"I guess every night is tough in convenience world," he thought.

He and Sarah walked out to the pumps where Gill was grumbling to himself under his breath.

"What is it now?" Robert asked.

"I locked the damn keys in the damn van and the damn windows are rolled up," Gill said through clenched teeth.

"Maybe I can help," Sarah said. She walked over to the driver's door, put her hand on the handle and closed her eyes. Click. She opened the door.

Robert and Gill just stared.

"I'm good with machines," she said with a small smile.

"When we have the time, you're gonna want to explain that to me." Robert said quietly.

Sarah smiled back at him and then slowly closed her eyes as she put her hands on the hood of the van. She didn't move or speak for a minute or so and then slowly opened her eyes again. "There's something behind the back bumper."

Gill ran to the back of his van and started feeling around on the back-side of his bumper. He suddenly stuck his hand into a glob of stuff that felt like an ice-cold jellyfish about the size of a yo-yo.

"Ewww!" he said in disgust as he scraped the thing off of his hand onto a paper towel. It started beeping. "Time to go again!" he yelled out to his two companions. He managed to pick up the glob of stuff he had taken off the van bumper and looked around at the sound of on-coming traffic.

A pickup truck zoomed toward them with a drunken, screaming bald guy throwing a beer bottle out the window to shatter on the pavement. As the truck swerved into the curb near them, Gill smiled and then threw the paper-wrapped glob as hard as he could into the back of the moving pickup truck.

Sarah jumped into the van laughing and Gill had to ask, "What's so damn funny?"

"You throw like a girl!" she blurted out.

"Very funny, very funny!" Gill snapped back. "That damn Whistlin' cop put that there. Can we PLEASE go now?"

"Let's do it," Robert said. They pulled out of the station as Sarah's phone started to ring again.

"MAX? Is that you?"

"Listen carefully, Sarah. Someone or something is headed your way, but I believe they are now tracking and following a pickup truck instead of you. I wouldn't want to be in that pickup truck in the next thirty minutes. Anyway, don't go home. At least not yet. They have your address from your driver's license on file at the hospital computer, and before I could delete it, someone was looking it up. Go with Gill if it's OK with him and I'll call you back in the next hour to let you know what I can find out. Also, remind Gill to talk to Gwen as soon as possible. She's waiting for him. I don't know what's happening, but even I am getting worried and MA-CHINES DON'T WORRY! Tell Gill to go straight home, and whatever you do... don't... "

Click.

"MAX? MAX? Are you still there? Can you hear me?"

On the phone speaker... at first quietly and then building to an ear-shattering screech, came an all-too-familiar combination of growling and whistling. Sarah quickly slammed down the button to stop the connection and dropped the phone to the floor.

When she looked up, both Robert and Gill were staring at the phone as if it was about to jump at them. Gill looked into Sarah's face and managed a lopsided smile. "Wrong number?" he asked with a laugh.

"I can't go home right now, guys. Gill, can we go to your place? I hate to be a bother, but we all need to talk, and I think you need to get a hold of this Gwen before we have our parley. Does that sound OK to you?"

Gill smiled back and said, "No problem with that. I don't live that far from her and I'd like to..."

KABOOM!

Bright red and blue flames flew into to the skyline from a massive explosion a few miles away.

"What the hell was that?" Robert yelled.

Sarah just looked out the window, and in a very small voice said, "A pickup truck."

10
A World of Flae

A hundred thousand years ago there wasn't much here.

The Flae were.

The Flae were here before most anything. They have watched it all develop. They have watched it all age. They have watched as race after race of animals and man have come and gone.

They have seen the beauty.

They have seen the evil.

The Flae, (pronounced "flay"), are studiers. They consume knowledge as we consume cake. It is the food of life for them; they starve without it and they partake of it with great relish. They do, upon occasion, eat real food but not because they need to.

They just think it tastes good.

There were originally very few Flae in existence, but now there are quite a few. The Flae have no children. From time to time, another one just... shows up. They do mate but not to reproduce.

They just do it because it's fun.

The men and women of Flae don't ever seem to die. Every once in awhile, one would either tire of studying or have learned all that they could on their given subject. They would then, over a long period of time, just fade away.

The Flae are around us every moment of the day.

They live in the wrinkle.

Have you ever lay on a bed with the blanket thrown over you and lost something that you had just placed upon the bed? You just know the object is right there, but you can't see it. You can't touch it. You can't find it. It's there the whole time, but wrapped in between a wrinkle in the blanket.

Our existence, our universe, is not a tight-fitted sheet. Our universe is a wrinkled blanket. There are any given numbers of wrinkles all around us, which we cannot normally see into. It is here the Flae have existed since before time.

The problem is the Flae are not the only ones who live in the wrinkles.

Have you ever seen a fluttering movement out of the side of your eye, only to have nothing there when you turn to look?

That was probably a Fla (one Fla pronounced "flah").

Have you ever closed your eyes while looking at the sun and seen those little squiggly things that seem to swim on the surface of your eyeball?

That might have been a Fla.

Men of great vision – prophets, mind readers, grand inventors, several holy men, kings, pharaohs, visionaries of all sorts... along with several madmen... all might have been visited by the Flae.

The sighting of fairies, elves, the wee leprechauns, guardian angels, gnomes and most inanimate objects that send forth a message of any sort, (like our MAX), are usually caused by a handful of the Flae who became involved in the affairs of man.

The thing that stays in your closet when you are a child, the creature under the bed, the really bad "coincidences" that happen to people, the slow moving shadows in the still darkness of the twilight, the things that go "bump" in the night, these are, unfortunately, NOT the Flae.

These are usually other thingies.

The Flae actually look like... hmmmm... OK... take your two hands with your fingers spread wide apart and bring you thumbs together until they are side by side and touching. If you had a face on your thumbnails, this would be kind of what a Flae would appear to be to you in shape and size. Their wings and body would appear mist-like instead of solid and a gentle sudden breeze would usually accompany them smelling like a cross between marshmallows and butterscotch.

Most normal people are never aware or touched or altered by the presence of the Flae.

The others, those affected one way or another, either have a fleeting, ghost-like vision or hear tiny voices. The Flae found that the easiest way to talk to the humans was to wait until they were asleep, unconscious, or find tiny humans with tiny ears to hear tiny voices.

The Flae loved Gill.

To learn as much as they could about everything, they long ago decided to specialize.

One Fla might spend thousands of years just watching the beach in order to determine the nature of sand. A Fla of great repute was once said to have counted all of the snowflakes up to date.

One might study the nature of smiles, while another tries to figure out where the light goes when the light goes out.

It is to their credit that several of the Flae suddenly decided to study time. It began by a Fla named Glee wanting to delve into the past to finds facts that might affect the present. Another Fla decided that he should therefore study the present to see if any change could be noticed by Glee's work.

It finally came to a wise old Fla named Gin to realize that the answer to most every problem was to study the future. This had never been done or thought of before, so it took him most of the day to master this frame of study.

What he saw scared the hell out of him.

11
Conference in the House of Gill

After about ten minutes of complete silence, the purple van slowly pulled into a long driveway. There seemed to be no other homes around this place, and trees and bushes were in abundance everywhere. It was kind of like driving into a long tunnel of green and seemed like forever before they reached Gill's little house, which was built with one side dug into a small hill.

Gill drove to the side of the house and parked the van underneath a canopy almost the same color as the trees. "Let's go around to the back so I can shut off the alarm. That way we won't scare Killer either," said Gill.

"Killer?" asked Sarah with a worried look on her face.

"Yeah," laughed Robert, "you GOTTA meet Killer!"

They all walked around the small cottage, stepping over rakes and bags of mulch and God knows what else in the almost total darkness of this forest setting. When they reached the back door, Gill whistled a strange little melody... and lights popped on.

"Cool!" said Sarah. As she looked closer, she realized that Gill's back door was solid steel with a gloss black finish and with a gray square plate in the center. There was no doorknob. Gill put his hand flat on the gray panel and when he moved his hand away, his handprint remained on the square.

Click

Sarah looked at Robert with a question in her eyes. He just smiled and said, "Yeah, you're gonna love this place." Gill pushed open the door and Sarah just stood there with her mouth open.

The little cottage was gargantuan on the inside.

Almost the entire cottage that you could see from the outside was a kitchen on the inside and then went on from there into the rest of the house. The rooms went back so far that her eyes couldn't even focus on the other end of it.

"OK, I give up. Is this house twenty times bigger on the inside than on the outside or have I totally lost what little mind I have left after this weird day and weirder night?"

Suddenly, a little black snowball came rolling across the giant kitchen floor! "Yipe, yipe, yipe!" The snowball took a giant leap into the air and landed in Sarah's arms. A tiny pink tongue popped out of the snowball and licked her tenderly and softly on her cheek.

"Don't tell me," she said gently. "Killer?"

"And he likes you, too." said Gill.

After a three-minute walk, they reached what Gill called "the study."

"Exactly how big is this house?" Sarah inquired.

"Houses," Robert said. "There is actually another house on the other side of that hill we drove by that is really the other side of this place. It's better to drive there, though, because it's about a mile from here. The whole place goes all of the way through the mountain."

Sarah looked at Ert then looked at Gill then looked down at Killer and then, very slowly said, "I need a drink."

Gill walked off into the distance in search of refreshments, and Sarah and Robert sat down on the giant over-sized sofa that was there in the study.

They just sat there quietly for a moment and then turned to stare at each other at exactly the same moment.

"Ert, you've got to help me out. I'm quickly losing control of reality here, and I need to know that somewhere in the world there is a stable, small piece of sanity that I can still cling to. A little information might help."

Robert gave her his biggest smile, a small chuckle and a tiny laugh. "What?" she asked.

"This request from a beautiful lady who unlocks doors by touch?"

About that time, Gill wandered back in with a giant antique silver tray loaded down with goodies. Drinks, sandwiches, pastries, different kinds of homemade snacks and munchies of all varieties. Gill smiled and said, "I love to cook but never have anyone to cook for but Killer."

All worry instantly left Sarah as a big smile replaced it. She stood up, walked over to where Gill was balancing the enormous tray, bent over and gave him a kiss on the cheek. Together, they managed to get the giant tray to an antique oak sideboard in the room that also served as a completely loaded bar. After that, it was every man and woman for him or herself in the rush for nutrition.

It was several minutes later and two or three drinks later before anyone said a word.

"OK, here's what I think we should do," said Gill. "It's getting late, and we're all dead tired. I've got to talk to Gwen immediately. Robert, why don't you sit here with Sarah for awhile and you two can talk and sort of fill each other in as to what you each know about the situation we're in and what's going on. Robert, when you get tired, which won't be long now from the look of you two, you take the same room you always sleep in. We need to talk tomorrow, too, about the kid in Dallas. Sarah, when you're ready, tell Killer and he'll show you to your room."

"Tell Killer? The dog?"

"Shhh!" said Robert. "He doesn't know he's a dog. He thinks he's a people."

Killer looked into her eyes and she could have sworn that he smiled at her.

"Curiouser and curiouser!" she said.

Gill laughed and said, "Damn, I say that all of the time. 'Alice In Wonderland!'"

"Yeah," said Sarah, "and it feels like we're all down the rabbit hole on this one."

Gill only nodded. "I'll see you both tomorrow... oh, I mean today... well, whenever we all get up. Sarah, call for Killer if you need anything. I think that he's the only one around who knows where everything is. Good night, you two. Don't stay up too late." Gill had a sort of funny smile on his face as he walked down the endless hallway.

"Yep," thought Gill. "She is kinda cute."

12
Figuring Each Other Out

Robert and Sarah just sat on the couch for a few minutes, not saying a word and not even glancing at each other. Finally, they both turned at the same time and started talking. Another laugh shared between them and then Robert said, "Ladies first, Sarah."

Sarah smiled inwardly at the old style manners coming out of this giant of a man. "So gentle," she thought.

"My story is pretty simple and shouldn't take very long before we run into the parts that you already know." She explained about her way with machines, how she believed that this was a gift that she had inherited from her mom. When he looked puzzled at this, she went on to explain about the powers her mother had shown, the luck of her father and the passing away of both. Before she knew it, she found herself confiding to Robert about her whole lonely life since her folks had left her. When tears began to flow down her cheeks as she talked, Robert couldn't help but gather her into his massive arms as she trembled at the old memories being dug up.

"God, I miss them both so much," she sobbed, "and I have no one since they've gone." About that time, a flying black snowball lands softly in her lap and that small pink tongue lapped at her hand.

"It seems to me that you've made at least two friends today, and very good ones, I might add." Robert said with a smile.

"Yipe, yipe, yipe," said Killer.

"OK, OK, two and a half friends, then." Robert chuckled.

Killer smiled again.

Her cell phone, which she had placed in her pocket, suddenly sounds off. RING, RING, RING!

"OK, then! Three and a half friends. Who in the hell is this MAX guy, anyway?"

With tears still in her eyes, Sarah started to laugh at the look on Robert's face as she answered her phone.

"Hi, MAX! What's new?" she said with a giggle.

"What's new? I'll never get used to the human sense of humor. Are you at Gill's house yet?"

"Yep, we're here now. I'm talking to Ert, and I think that Gill is trying to reach Gwen. We should be safe here for the night."

"Good," said MAX. "I've located where you are through the utility company's computer files. I need to talk to someone there who knows about the computer access at that residence."

Sarah looked at Robert and said, "MAX is my computer."

Robert's smile went from ear to ear.

"He needs info on how to access the computer at this location if Gill has one."

Robert looked stunned and said, "Yeah, Gill has one, but I don't really know ANYTHING about..."

"Yipe, yipe, yipe," Killer said as he jumped off Sarah's lap and took off running into the darkness of the hallway.

"MAX, I think Killer has gone to try to help. Hang on for a minute."

MAX made a weird bleeping noise and then said, "KILLER?"

"He's a dog, MAX, but don't tell him so. He thinks he's a people."

"Cool!" said MAX. "That makes two of us. If Killer is a dog, what in the world is an Ert?"

Another burst of laughter from Sarah and then she heard a weird noise coming down the hall. It was a slow dragging kind of sound, and Robert jumped up in a very defensive attitude a moment later when he heard the same thing.

"Yipe!"

Sarah laughed and said, "Damn, Killer, you scared me to half to death!"

"Yipe?" Killer dragged a leather briefcase up next to Sarah. "Yipe, YIPE!"

"I HEARD THAT!" MAX yelled in her ear. "Open the case and turn on the laptop! Enter my email. COOL. I gotta meet this creature."

Sarah got that funny look on her face again and asked MAX, "You speak dog, MAX?"

"Not all of it."

"Curiouser still."

She unzipped the briefcase to find a laptop. She turned it on and booted it up. It is networked and routed to what are obviously several other computers in this strange home with instant access to the Internet. She dialed up the email address to MAX and suddenly he's on the laptop speakers.

"Hi, Sarah! What's new?"

Sarah chuckled , "I'll never get used to the electronic sense of humor!"

MAX made a sound like 'Whaa Whaa Whaa!' "Good one, Sarah!"

"MAX, did... did you just... LAUGH?"

"Yeah, I guess so, but it's no big deal. You should hear me cry! It would break your heart. Whaa Whaa!"

Robert jumped up and said, "OK now, no kidding this time. Who is this MAX dude?"

Gill sat on the edge of his bed as he cleared his thoughts for the upcoming ordeal. He tried to make his mind go blank... the way he normally does when he hears from the little people... but too many thoughts were running through his head. He turned off all of the lights in his gigantic bedroom and breathed in the quietness of the dark.

"Gwen? Are you there, Gwen?"

Nothing.

Well, maybe she's busy or something... or maybe she... just can't hear me now. Maybe she even...

"Gill?"

"Oh Gwen, am I ever glad to hear from you."

"I'm afraid that may change in a few minutes. I've got a lot to tell you and only a couple of minutes to do it in. Blan corrupts the channels that we normally talk through, and we may lose each other at any moment. If that happens, contact me tomorrow in the daytime. They don't like daylight."

"How bad is it, Gwen? What are we looking at here?"

"Darkness. Eternal darkness. They don't like daylight."

"I don't understand. Do you mean that the sun...?"

"No sun. They plan to block it out. Make way for more Blan to cross into your.... sssssssssssssssss!"

"Gwen! Gwen! Can you hear me?"

S ssssssssssssssss...

"Gwen? That's silly! How long can they possibly block out the sun?"

S sssssss...

"Eternal. Always. Forever."

S sssssss...

"But... that would... end up... killing all life... as we know it... on the whole damn planet!"

S sssssss...

"They don't like daylight. Call tomor...."

S sssssss...

S sss...

S s...

When he finally managed to get his breath working again, Gill stood up on shaky legs and decided to turn on every light in his room.

"I hope they don't like any kind of light."

He slowly stretched out on his bed and closed his eyes to the glare of his many lamps. "I'll never get any rest now," he said as he threw a pillow over his head.

Two minutes later, he was asleep.

"Let me talk to the other 'people' there," MAX said.

Sarah shook her head at the laptop and whispered, "MAX, there's no one else here except Robert and myself. Do you wanna talk to him now?"

"Who in the name of Bill Gates is Robert? No, Sarah, I need to talk privately for a few minutes with the other... 'people' The little short...furry... four-legged guy?"

Killer started growling quietly in the background.

"Sorry, dude," says MAX.

"Yipe."

"Let me get this straight," Sarah quietly asked. "My goofy computer wants to conference... online... with an animated dust bunny on the fate of the world?!"

Both MAX and Killer start to growl! "Grrrrrrrrrrrrr..."

"Sorry, guys, sorry. It's been ... kind of a long day, ya know? But ... am I right?"

"Yeah," said MAX. "That's about it."

"You got it, pal. Have Jerry Lee give me a yell when you're finished," Sarah said.

"Who in the name of General Electric is Jerry Lee?" MAX quickly asked back.

"Why son, he's the Killer!" Sarah said as she busted out laughing again!

"Whaa, whaa, whaa, whaa, whaa!"

13
Bonding

The weirdness going on between MAX and Killer was just too much. Sarah shook her head slowly and then stood up.

"I'm dead tired, Ert, but you owe me your side of an explanation... and I don't think I'll get much rest without hearing it. Is there anywhere else in this... cave... that we can go? I think MAX and Killer want to be alone!"

"Yipe!"

"Whaa!"

Killer started wagging his tail and smiling.

Robert stood slowly and held out his large hand. She placed hers inside of it, and he slowly led her away. "I know the perfect place," he said with a smile.

Their path was a long and winding one through so many turns that Sarah was amazed anyone could remember their way around in this labyrinth. After her aching legs had walked her for what felt like a mile, they came to a long hallway with only one door at the end. "I come here a lot to think," Robert said in a whisper.

As she crossed the threshold of their dimly lit destination, the room she found herself in overcame Sarah. The place must have been a hundred feet across, fifty feet wide and had a giant domed ceiling painted jet-black. The only furniture in the room was an overstuffed couch in the middle of the floor and to this they head. Robert picked up a remote control off the cushions and waited for Sarah to sit before he sat.

"Cute," she thought.

After they were both settled and comfortable, Robert looked to her with a grin and asked, "Are you ready?"

"For my explanation?" she said.

"Nope," he quietly whispered, "for this!" He pushed one of the remote's buttons and the lights slowly fade to black. While she was thinking how romantic this all was, Robert selected another button. With a low grinding sound, the entire ceiling unfolded to reveal the starlit skies. It was not only incredibly clear and beautiful, but the image was somehow magnified to appear larger than life. "One of Gill's creations," he said quietly.

"Wow."

"Wow is right."

The next few minutes were spent in total silence.

"OK," Robert finally asked," What would you like to know?"

Sarah could hardly catch her breath from laughing so hard!

"Well... let's see... how about Gill... and this house?" How about Killer the canine Einstein? Or how about The Whistler... or the Red Fog people... or ... how about the reason you were there at the shooting and truck burning this morning in the first place? Did you fire that shot that took out the tire on the truck of those hoods? And why were you and Gill at the hospital to pick me up? And what about that exploding glob of beeping snot on the van bumper? Huh? So... what's the answer? Huh? What's the answer?"

Robert could hardly catch his breath from laughing so hard.

"Which one of those do you want an answer for first?" he said with a grin.

"Neither. Tell me about the kid in Dallas."

The grin went away.

14
The Story of Gill

"Sarah," said Robert, "of all the weird things going on in the last few hours, you want to know about a Mexican boy we saved whom you've never met?"

"Yes," she whispered. "I didn't know you'd saved him, but I have a feeling that if you can explain that to me, it will explain a lot of the other strangeness. Does that make any sense, Ert?"

He smiled into her tired, beautiful face. With a very light touch, he brushed away a fallen strand of hair that had draped itself across her cheek and said, "Yeah, Sarah, in a strange sort of way it sorta does." He settled back on the arm of the sofa looking at the stars and she leaned over onto him resting her head on his shoulder.

"In order to explain the thing with the kid in Texas, I have to explain Gill to you, and that's not an easy task."

"Yeah, I'll bet that's right!" she giggled. "You know, right from the start..."

"Hey! Are you gonna tell this story or am I?"

She smiled at him and animated pulling a zipper across her lips. Then she snuggled up even closer.

"OK," he said with a sigh, "Here's the story of Gill."

"Gill and I have been sort of friends since we were in high school, but the things that make Gill... 'Gill'... started long before that. When he was only about five years old, he and his parents were in a terrible car crash. They were up in the high mountains in central California spending a winter weekend vacation together, and were in the process of driving home when Gill's father swerved off of the road to avoid hitting a large deer. The car went crashing down the side of a mountain, bursting into flames as it hit the bottom of the canyon. Gill was thrown free on the way down to the bottom, but he was slammed into the side of a boulder with his back and head, doing serious damage. The car burst into flames as it hit, and Gill's mom and dad were killed instantly.

"Here in California, the threat of fire is so great that the park services constantly watch the horizon for any signs of smoke or fire, so it wasn't very long after the accident that a fire truck, ambulance and park rangers

44

were making their way down the side of the steep embankment to check for survivors and extinguish any remaining sparks and flame. They located the two charred bodies of Gill's parents in the wreckage after the fire was out, but it wasn't until a couple of hours later as they were leaving when they found Gill. He was kind of hidden behind the edge of the boulder he had struck, and it was the blood that they noticed first on the large rock. As they turned the corner around the giant boulder, there he was lying. And you know what else was there with him?"

Sarah shook her head slowly as it lay on his shoulder.

"A 12-point buck. It must have been the very deer that his dad had swerved to miss. It had walked down the side of the slope and had gently laid down beside the boy, using its body heat to keep Gill warm."

"Ah, come on now! You're making this up!" said Sarah with a glare.

"On my word. As the ranger came around the boulder, the deer slowly looked into the ranger's eyes, turned to look at Gill and very slowly gave Gill a lick on his hand. The ranger swears that the buck then slowly raised itself to its feet, looked down at Gill one final time and then just slowly walked away.

"The ranger quickly called for ambulance attendants, who managed with much trouble to get Gill up the side of the mountain and headed toward the nearest hospital. His back injuries were pretty severe, and Gill still to this day swears that this is one reason he never grew to full height. The concussion to his head, though, was life threatening. He stayed in the intensive care ward in a semi-coma state for almost a year. Suddenly, one day, he just sat up and declared he was fine."

Sarah looked at Robert with a funny look on her face. "Was he fine? I mean, did he return to normal just like that?"

Robert gave her his biggest smile and said, "Yes... and no. What I mean is... yes, he was fine. But... no, he never returned to normal."

"I don't understand," Sarah said as she yawned.

"Well, neither do I, Sarah, but after that accident... Gill was... special. The deal with him and that deer wasn't an isolated incident. All animals sense something special in Gill... kind of like Killer. Also, Gill hears little people."

Sarah just looked at him for about thirty seconds before saying, "Now you've lost me again."

"He hears and talks to what he calls 'little people.' They tell him things that are going to happen... sometimes good and sometimes bad. These things are what send me running around all over the country trying to prevent them from hurting someone or taking a life that we believe we might be able to save. Thus, the little Mexican boy whose life I just saved in Dallas, and thus... you."

"Do you mean, I was supposed to be hurt bad in that wreck you showed up at yesterday?"

Robert just turned his head, focusing on anything but Sarah.

Sarah was quiet for a moment, and whispered, "I was supposed to... to...?"

Robert just nodded.

Sarah lowered her head and said nothing for a long time.

"Are these the same little people from our Red Fog?"

Robert nodded again.

"Ert, I'm way too tired to go on much more tonight, and I need some time to digest all that's happened in the last twenty-four hours. Can we take this all up tomorrow? I mean... today? Whenever?"

"Yeah," Robert said with a sigh, "Killer's kinda busy, so let me show you where to bunk for the night. I'll be close by if you need me."

Sarah thought, "Yeah, I have a feeling I need you."

15
Dreams of Fire

Robert led Sarah slowly through the never-ending maze of rooms in this enormous home of Gill's, and the sheer magnitude of the area amazed her. Room after room rolled by, some of the bedrooms of gigantic proportion, extra bathrooms at every turn, dozens of closets and storage spaces and many rooms with no apparent purpose whatsoever

"I thought I had a goodly chunk of change myself, but man! This must have cost millions. Where on earth did he ever come by so much land and how in the world did he have enough money to develop all of this?" Sarah said in awe. "You would never even know this place existed from the outside where we came in."

"Yeah, and the place on the other side of the hill is much the same way. Gill's mom and dad actually owned the other home on the far entrance, and after they passed away, they left that place, a rather large bank account and a ton of life insurance to Gill. Later on, he bought the house we came in through and slowly developed them both into what you see now. It's still a work in progress, too. After the accident and his stay in the hospital, he was still too young at that time to inherit all of that, so he lived with his Uncle Vernon for many years. I'm told that Uncle Vernon also had a bank full of money from starting up a computer company long ago. Compu-Tech. Have you ever heard of it?"

Sarah stopped in her tracks so quickly that Robert almost tripped over her. "Compu-Tech? Robert, that's where I work! Wow! I guess that means that Uncle Vernon is my boss. I guess it is a small world after all." She started again slowly walking back down the hallway, with Robert trailing behind.

"Smaller than you think, Sarah. Uncle Vernon passed away some years ago. Everything was left to Gill."

Sarah stopped so quickly that this time Robert tripped over her. BAM. Down he went. Sarah looked down at him startled, "You mean... you mean that...?"

"Yep," smiled back Robert, "My little red-headed leprechaun buddy must be your boss."

They finally reached an incredibly beautiful bedroom with antique Victorian marble-top dressers and a canopy bed that left Sarah speechless. "I'm camping out in here?" she whispered.

"Yeah, you'll be roughing it!" said Robert with a laugh. "I'm right across the hall if you need anything and Killer's room is next door. Just call out, and one of us will hear you. The bathroom is through that big door over there," he said pointing to a room the size of her living room. "I wouldn't try walking in my sleep around this place if I were you. We might never find you again. Tell Killer where you want to go if I'm asleep and he'll take you there."

"Curiouser and curiouser," she thought.

"Well, good night... and good dreams," he told her, giving her a small peck on the cheek. She smiled at him as he backed out of the room, slowly closing her door.

"ERT?"

He ran back in so quickly that he almost tripped himself again. "What's wrong?"

"Nothing is wrong. I just wanted to say... to say... I just want to say... thank you."

"No problem, m'lady." he said with a deep bow.

She laughed as he backed out of the room bent over like a knight of old, closing the door behind him.

Robert laid down in his tidy little nest of a room and smiled at the way this day had developed. Saving lives, fighting off whistling monsters and gunfire in the streets had all ended up as well as could be expected, but that wasn't what brought the smile to his face. As he started to drift off to sleep in a stupor of exhaustion, his last thought was... "She called me Ert."

And then... sleep came.

The gigantic flash of light almost blinded him. He could see outlines and blurs but that was all. "Where am I?" he asked himself. Never had he experienced anything like this and he couldn't be sure if he was awake or in a dream. Something soft and warm was falling all around him, and he couldn't place whatever it was. It could have been snow except for the heat of it, and it was getting thicker. The temperature was rising quickly, and he was starting to find it hard to breathe. The snowfall was intensifying so badly that even as he ran, he was sucking this horrible gray precipitation into his lungs. He gasped for air as he stumbled to the ground but could find none. He tried covering his head with the shirt he was wearing, but his mouth was already filled with the silent death he'd been breathing and it did little good. "It's not snow," he thought... in his last moments of consciousness... "it's... it's... ASHES."

As he tumbled out of his bed, hurdled himself into instant wakefulness, he heard someone screaming as loud as they could as they tried desperately to suck in gasps of fresh air. It took a moment for him to realize that it was himself and he was screaming, "IT'S ASHES! IT'S ASHES!"

Sarah had laid in the beautiful bed, admiring the incredible room, amazed at the incredible events that the last twenty-four hours had brought to her and the incredible people she had met.

Especially one of them.

She punched and fluffed up her large feather pillows, stretched out under the soft down comforter and drifted quickly off to a land far away.

She was in a forest... or so it seemed. There was life all around her, and she could feel the energy of the world everywhere as she lounged beneath a large willow tree, watching the beautiful scene of a mother deer and her fawn slowly, carefully sipping water from the edge of a swiftly flowing river. A blue jay landed on the grass next to her and began picking at the shaded grasses in search of its afternoon meal. It all seemed too real to be a dream, but in her mind, she realized it must be. She had no idea where she was or how she had gotten there, but it was so beautiful. It was almost too beautiful. It was almost as if it couldn't last and something was going to HAVE to come along to mess up this paradise soon. Even as she thought this, the bird gave out with a startled squawk, shook its feathers convulsively and leaped screaming into the sky. The mother doe jumped quickly away from the flowing waters and gave out a strange bleating sound at the poor frightened fawn next to her. Both bolted away into the deep forest as the beautiful river started to run red.

The deep blue waters were now clogging up with a slow-moving flow of crimson, creating a curtain of steam so thick that her breathing was affected. Sweat was rolling off of her forehead as the temperature started to rise and she could see that the banks of the once-beautiful waters would never hold the mountain of red-hot death headed in her direction. Try as she might, she was unable to move from the spot she found herself in and the banks of horrible heat rolled slowly toward her in an unstoppable tidal wave of searing agony.

"THE HEAT!" She bolted upright for the canopied enclosure she had slept in. "THE HEAT!"

Gill was tossing and turning in his bed with sweat running down the sides of his face. His dreams startled his sleeping mind and were so vivid that he couldn't be sure if he was asleep.

He was on an island, and a deep, deep rumble shook the entire dream.

All of the birds and animals that had been so noisy only moments before had suddenly gone into a silent hush. In one movement, thousands of tropical birds of every size and description lifted swiftly into the air together and fluttered away into the distance. The waters around the beaches started to withdraw away from the shore as if even the ocean knew of the catastrophe in the making. The very air felt iron-heavy like the humidity had suddenly jumped to one-hundred percent. As Gill stood there, waiting for whatever was to come to pass – and knowing there was no escape for him – an earth-shattering KABOOM arose in the distance. As he snapped wide-awake in his bedroom screaming at the top of his lungs, all that he could think of and scream out was "FIRE! FIRE!"

"YIPE, YIPE, YIPE, YIPE, YIPE!"

Killer came tearing out of his room, screaming at the terrible dream he'd just had. Right behind him, Gill was running down the long hallway headed in the same direction and screaming, "FIRE!" as loud as Killer was yelping. Killer managed to dodge around Sarah, who came screaming and running out of her room next door, yelling "THE HEAT" at the top of her lungs but still got all tangled in Robert's feet as he bolted out of his doorway with an ear-piercing scream of "ASHES! ASHES!"

BAM!

Robert hit the floor with Killer sliding between his legs while Sarah flipped into Robert and wrapped tightly into his torso by the forward pressure of Gill plowing into the pile.

All four just sat there for about a half-minute and then...

"HA HA HA! HO HO HO! AH AHHH AHHHH! YIPE YIPE YIPE!"

Gill finally untangled himself from this mess and said, "What the hell just happened?"

"Yipe yipe yipe... yipe!" said Killer. "Woof!"

"Not you, Jughead!" said Gill.

"Grrr!"

"I guess I just had a bad dream," Sarah slowly said as she untangled herself from the dog pile. "Boss."

"Huh?" Gill asked with his mouth wide open again. "What? What was that?"

"She called you boss, ya little chucklehead." Robert said laughing. "She just found out that she works for you."

Gill closed his mouth and quietly said, "Well, I guess I just found out, too. Which one of my companies do you work for?"

"Well, how many companies do you have anyway?"

"Well, I guess I've got about ten... or twenty. Maybe twenty-five? What's that got to do with where you work?"

"Oh, sorry. I was just surprised at all of this. I work at Compu-Tech, and I..."

"HOLD ON A SECOND! Did you say... a bad dream?" Gill's red face turned in strange positions.

"Yeah, a REAL bad dream! I almost thought it was real when I had it, but..."

"Hold on a second... again. Sorry to interrupt you again, but... I, also, just had a real bad dream." Gill slowly turned his head to stare at Robert. Robert just looked at him, but his eyes told the whole story. "Robert... you, too?"

Robert slowly nodded. "Yep, and it was a doozy!"

Killer started bouncing three feet into the air over and over again! "Yipe! Yipe! Yipe... WOOF!"

Robert laughed and said, "I think that we can assume that Killer had a bad dream, too."

Gill sneered and said, "I'm thinking we can assume that Killer is a bad dream."

"Grrrr...grrrr... woof!"

"OK, gang, it's still dark outside. As impossible as it seems, I believe we've been sent a message from a small friend of mine. She wasn't able to talk to me very well earlier for any length of time and she's used dreams to talk to me before. I say we all try to get a little bit more sleep before the day kicks in and talk about this later. I have a feeling that it's gonna be a busy weekend."

Sarah got a funny little smile on her face, bent over to look Gill right in the face and said, "Gill, if my next week is anything like this weekend is gonna be..."

"Yeah?" Gill whispered.

Sarah smiled at him and said, "Honey, I want a raise."

"You got it, girl. You got it."

16
I'll Be Glad to Help

It was later on that afternoon when everyone finally started to wake up – this time from much more pleasant and restful dreams. Sarah woke up to the sound of Killer gently pushing her door open, quietly jumping onto her bed, and as she opened her eyes, she heard a "Umm?" come out of the little critters mouth, along with a small pink tongue which softly licked her hand.

"Well, good morning, beautiful! Did you sleep well this time?"

"Woof!" said Killer with what Sarah could have sworn was a smile.

"Dog, I would kill for a cup of coffee right now. You wouldn't happen to know where one is, would you?"

"Yipe!" said Killer, and with that, he started to pull the bed covers down to the foot of the bed.

"Whoa hold on now, Killer. I'm not even dressed yet! Ah man, I didn't bring a change of clothes or anything. Hey Puppylips, you wouldn't happen to have a robe around here anywhere, would you?"

"Yipe!" Killer barked as he jumped off of the bed and went tearing down the long hallway.

"You gotta be kidding!" Sarah laughed about a minute later when the small dog came back with a beautiful rose-colored kimono with a large embroidered sash attached to it. "Small creature... you have excellent taste."

"Woof!"

She stepped out of bed, stretched the kinks out of her body, and then slipped into the soft robe. A splash of water on her face as Killer sat watching and then she smiled at him saying, "How do I look? Good?"

The little dog jumped straight up in the air, did a full flip and then landed back on his feet.

"I'll take that as a yes! Now, how about that coffee?"

Killer walked over to the hall doorway and opened the door for Sarah with his small nose. She shook her head and smiled and then walked into the hallway. Killer followed, closed the door behind him and then led her down a turning, twisted pathway that went on for a couple of minutes before she started to smell bacon cooking.

She found herself, along with Killer, in a beautiful dining area that had a Victorian rosewood dining table set with old fashion carved tobacco-twist chairs and covered with a lace tablecloth, mounds of bacon, sausage and ham, biscuits and gravy and other goodies and a large silver coffee urn surrounded by stoneware coffee mugs, which looked like they would hold half of a liter. As she lunged for the coffee, she heard from the next room...

"Coffee's on the table! Sugar and cream, too. Get a cup and come help me with these eggs."

She smiled while she was pouring her first cup at the thought of little Gill in the kitchen making this giant mountain of food. "Damn, Gill, how many people are we feeding today anyway? You've got enough grub here for an army."

"Well girl, you're soon to discover that I have an army... an army of one. And his name is... I believe you called him 'Ert.' That fellow can put away some groceries now. Also, though, I usually intentionally cook too much food so that Killer can share the leftovers with his friends."

"Killer shares leftovers with friends? OK, OK, this I gotta hear."

"Well, in my woods outside, there are several dogs and cats that hang around at chowtime just because they know that Killer will bring them handouts. Also, he likes to feed the birds, and I have a feeling that coyotes, squirrels, rabbits and deer also get their fair share of my pantry from the dog. He always brings back the "doggie bag" I make up for him to take outside, and it's always dead empty upon return."

Sarah just stared at him for a moment, and then broke into a smile. "You are quite a piece of work, Gill."

As she picked up the platter from the countertop with the mountain of eggs on it, she heard Robert in the next room yawning and saying, "Is this all we've got to eat?"

She was laughing so hard as she entered the room that she almost dumped the platter into his lap. "We'll make more when you finish these," she giggled.

As she set the food onto the tabletop, she heard a small whimper in the corner of the room and turned to see the most amazing thing. She hadn't noticed it before, but in the corner of the room was a very small, and totally identical table to the one at which Robert was seated, and patiently waiting next to it was Killer.

"Yipe," he quietly said with one of his smiles.

Sarah stared at him for only a moment, then smiled as she picked up the plate.

"Bacon?" She asked.

"Yipe!"

"How about sausage?"

"Yipe, yipe!"

"Oh, you like sausage, huh? Well, how about ham, then?"

"Yipe!" Killer said.

"Alright, would you care for some eggs, sir?"

"Yipe, yipe!"

"Very good, your majesty and how about a sliced tomato?"

"Grrrrrr!"

"OK, hold the tomato. Now, bark once for coffee or twice for milk."

"Woof, woof!"

"Milk it is, then! And will that be all for now, sir?"

Sarah almost fell over when the little dog nodded his head.

She watched for several minutes after she had placed the plate in front of this small creature while it very delicately ate one tiny bite at a time with as good table manners as she had observed in most humans.

"Now, can we eat or not?" Robert grumbled.

"Yes, Grumpy!" Sarah said as she patted him on his head. She sat down at the table as Gill came in from the kitchen, and then he, too, sat down.

"OK," Gill said, "no bad conversation until after our food has digested, but then, we get to work."

The next half an hour was spent in the wonderful world of flavors. Nobody said a word until Sarah asked if the potatoes had rosemary in them.

"Yep," Gill managed to mumble around a mouthful of french toast.

Finally, when she could eat no more, she and Gill began cleaning dirty and empty dishes from the table while Robert went on with his meal. After another ten minutes, Robert, too, was pretty near full, so he saved the rest for the canine philanthropist. Gill carefully packed a mesh bag with all of the leftover goodies while Killer sat quietly by awaiting food for his friends. The bag was stuffed by the time Gill finished, and the little dog carefully picked it up and went toward the back of the house for the big giveaway.

"He's got his own little door back there," Gill said, "so we'll leave him to do his thing. Let's get another cup of coffee and go somewhere to talk."

Killer took off in a short-legged run to head outside but stopped by on his way to drop off a present for his new friend.

Gill slowly walked down a hallway to take Sarah back to where she could change clothes before they started their conference, with Robert close on her heels. "I'll be glad to help," Robert smirked.

"Ert, it was bad enough with pint-sized Lassie watching me dress. I don't think I'm ready for you yet."

Robert nudged Gill in the arm, (almost knocking him down), and said, "Did you hear that? She said 'yet!'"

"Yeah, I heard, I heard. Man, you need to get out more."

Gill stopped in front of a door that was extremely wide. He turned around and looked at Sarah saying, "I stockpile clothing for one of my stores in here. I'm pretty sure you can find something to wear. Pick out two or three outfits, 'cause we're not sure when you can go home, yet."

In a joking mood, she punched Robert in the arm and said, "Didja hear that? He said 'yet.'"

"Very funny, very funny!"

Gill pushed the door open.

"OH, MY GOD," Sarah said.

The room was almost half as big as a football field, and it was packed with gigantic boxes and crates and bags and racks FULL of women's clothing. An acre of shoes and accessories lay to one side. And not just any clothing... noo... these were designer labels and European imports of every brand imaginable. Gill walked over to a section that contained designer bags and luggage, picked up a large suitcase and told her to fill it up with whatever she needed.

"Whatever I need? You have got to be kidding. Right? You're kidding... right? Aww, come on! Tell me you're kidding!"

"Sarah," Gill said, "We really don't have time for this. If you don't jump in there and grab some damn clothes to get dressed, then I'm gonna have to dress you myself."

"I'LL BE GLAD TO HELP," Robert said with a big smile.

She slugged him in the arm then walked into the clothing grotto. "Ah, Gill, where did you say your store was?" She started grabbing up stuff as she went.

"Well, I didn't say, but actually, I'm told I have several of them, and I think they're in San Francisco, New York, Bel Air and Beverly Hills."

"And no lucky girl has snatched you up yet?" Sarah asked.

Gill turned around, jumped up into the air in order to hit Robert on the shoulder. "Ouch!" Robert said. "What was that for?"

"Didn't you hear that? She said 'yet'!"

Everyone started laughing again.

"Gill, I won't go crazy here, but I love your clothing." Sarah couldn't stop grinning.

"Sarah, take anything you want. I haven't been in here in quite awhile, and a lot of this is probably out of style now," Gill said with a smile.

"Gill, honey, designer outfits that cost thousands of dollars NEVER go out of style."

Gill grinned back at her and said, "Walk down there to the right. That's where I keep all of the leather."

Sarah squealed and ran off down the aisle.

"Yep, she's cute alright," Gill whispered. "Are you sure she works for me, Robert?"

"So I hear, my friend... so I hear."

After an hour, Sarah couldn't fit anything else into her suitcase, so off they went back to her room to let her change. "My room," she thought. "I like the sound of that."

Robert opened the door for her and said, "Sarah, I'd be glad to h–"

"Enough, Robert! If we live through the night... I'll let you give me a backrub! How's that?"

"DEAL!"

17
The Whistler's Plan

By the time Sarah finally got dressed in one of her new outfits, it was starting to get dusky gray outside. The night would soon again be drawing near. Gill was worried. He led them to a room furnished with a burgundy sectional sofa that made an almost complete 360-degree circle with a round table in the center.

"The War Room?" asked Robert.

"Yeah, I think this definitely calls for the War Room," Gill said with a frown. "I did get to talk to Gwen last night, but she was being partially blocked by someone or something. Sit down and make yourself comfortable and I'll see about getting something to drink."

"And a computer? I need to touch base with MAX," Sarah said.

"Sarah, the computer room is right next door to this one. Go out the door and turn right, and then..."

WAAA! WAA! WAA!

"What in the world?" Sarah said as she jumped up from the sofa and headed toward the door. "It sounds like MAX is freaking out!"

"It's coming from the computer room alright," Gill said as he rushed out behind Sarah.

When they entered the room, it took a good minute or so for them to realize what was causing MAX so much distress. The video camera was turned on so that MAX could see around the room, and man, was he upset! "Get it off, Sarah! Get it off! Dead animals are lying on me! Get them off!"

Sarah ran over to the keyboard to see what the problem was and started laughing out loud. Gill took one look and he, too, burst into tears from laughing so hard.

MAX started beeping at them as he said, "OK, what do you humans think is so funny about dead animals lying on top of me? I just popped back in here to see how you are doing and this is the thanks I get?"

"MAX," Sarah said with a smile, "I'm sorry. We weren't laughing at you. We were sort of laughing at Killer. He gave those to you as a present to a friend."

Robert looked over at MAX when he came into the room to see what everyone was talking about and there, laying on MAX's keyboard, were two sausages and a piece of bacon.

"Tell him to just bring me a nice memory chip next time. Silly dog," MAX said with a huff. "Would you mind removing the charred flesh from my vicinity?"

Robert smiled and said, "At least he didn't bring you gravy."

Everyone, including MAX, started laughing at that.

Sarah took a laptop, which was tapped into the network system of the house, and headed back to the War Room. She later found out that it was here where strategies for some of Gill's and Robert's adventures were planned. She set MAX up on the round center table so he could take in the conversation. Robert and Gill sat down, and the meeting began in earnest.

"OK," Gill said slowly, "I think we should start off this session with our dreams from last night. Since they all occurred at the same time, I have reason to believe they are related. Here's what happened to me in mine." The next hour was spent by all three humans in the room telling of the vivid tales that had come in their sleep and MAX just sat there listening the whole time with an occasional click or humming. After the three dreams were all put together, it was then that MAX spoke up.

"Fire, heat, ashes..."

"Volcano."

Gill turned around so quickly that his neck popped. "What did you say, MAX?"

"I said 'volcano.' It seems apparent to me that all three dreams are related in as much as they all have to do with a volcanic eruption."

Gill looked around the room, kind of quietly, and finally said, "The sun."

Robert and Sarah looked at each other for a second, and then Robert said, "OK... I'll bite! What about the sun?"

"Gwen told me that they hate the light. Especially sunlight. MAX, see what kind of info you can pull up on volcanic atmospheric changes taking place after an eruption."

"Whirrr....Whirrr.... Whirrr... CLICK."

MAX made his little noises for about a minute while he compiled data, then suddenly went quiet. Everyone started looking at each other when MAX suddenly said, "Uh Oh!"

Sarah went over to where MAX was situated on the table and whispered to him, "Lets hear it, MAX. Give us your report."

MAX did.

18
MAX Reports

"Sarah, this is terrible. I find it hard to believe that any living creature would want to cause such wonton destruction on purpose," MAX whined.

"Take it easy, pal. Right now, what we need from you are the facts, plain and simple. Can you do that for me, MAX?"

"Yes, Sarah. I can do that for you. I may take a little while, so if you want a refreshing drink or some more of those burnt animals now would be a good time while I compile my notes."

Gill pushed a button on the console near the sofa and a bar popped out from the wall. "It sounds like we're ALL gonna need a drink before this is over." As he poured drinks for everyone, MAX began his report.

"Volcanoes have been erupting since the beginning of time, and we are only now beginning to understand how they affect, not only the weather, but also our over-all climate changes.

"Together, with the tephra and entrained air, volcanic gases can rise tens of kilometers into Earth's atmosphere during large explosive eruptions. Once airborne, the prevailing winds may blow the eruption cloud hundreds to thousands of kilometers from a volcano. The gases spread from an erupting vent primarily as acid aerosols (tiny acid droplets), compounds attached to tephra particles, and microscopic salt particles.

"In 1783, a volcanic fissure in Iceland erupted with enormous force, pouring out cubic kilometers of lava. Layers of poisonous ash snowed down upon the island. The grass died, and three-quarters of the livestock starved to death, followed by a quarter of the people. A peculiar haze shadowed western Europe for months. Benjamin Franklin, visiting France, noticed the unusual cold that summer and speculated that the volcanic 'fog' that visibly dimmed the sunlight might have caused it.

"Better evidence came from the titanic 1883 explosion of Krakatau (Krakatoa) in the East Indies, which sent up a veil of volcanic dust that measurably reduced sunlight around the world for months. Tephra from the eruption fell as far as 2,500 km downwind in the days following the eruption. However, the finest fragments were propelled high into the stratosphere, spreading outward as a broad cloud across the entire equatorial belt in only two weeks. These particles would remain suspended in the atmosphere for years, propagating farther to the north and south before finally dissipating. The stratospheric cloud of dust also contained large volumes of sulfur dioxide gas emitted from Krakatau. These gas molecules rapidly combined with water vapor to generate sulfuric acid droplets in the high atmosphere. The resulting veil of acidic aerosols and volcanic dust provided an atmospheric shield capable of reflecting enough sunlight to cause global temperatures to drop by several degrees. This aerosol-rich veil also generated spectacular optical effects over seventy percent of the earth's surface. For several years after the 1883 eruption, Earth experienced exotic colors in the sky, halos around the sun and moon, and a spectacular array of anomalous sunsets and sunrises.

"The planet had so few weather stations that scientists were unable to learn for sure whether the eruption affected the average global temperature. But from then on, scientific reviews of climate change commonly listed volcanoes as a natural force that might affect large regions, perhaps the entire planet. Looking at temperatures after major volcanic eruptions between 1880 and 1910, a few scientists believed they could see a distinct temporary cooling. (The most impressive confirmation came much later, when examination of older records showed that the 1815 eruption of Tambora, scarcely noted at the time outside Indonesia, had affected the world's climate much more than Krakatau. Crops were frozen as far away as New England.)

"In 1991, Mt. Pinatubo in the Philippines... that hadn't erupted in six hundred years... blew. Starting June 12th, it erupted twenty-six times... with the main blow being on June 15th, blowing a cloud ten miles into the sky. Clark Air Force base was evacuated along with thirty thousand people. It spit ash up to sixty miles away, threw grapefruit sized rocks up to twenty-five miles, changed night to day and sucked the heat from the air, leaving very cold temperatures. The cloud it formed created its own thunderhead, and created a gaseous veil around Earth so intense that it actually lowered the planet's temperature.

"Perhaps the smoky skies in an era of massive volcanic eruptions were responsible for the Ice Age, or had even killed off the dinosaurs by cooling Earth? This image of climate change became familiar in popular as well as scientific thinking. In the 1950s, experts noted that the Northern Hemisphere had been getting warmer over the last several decades, a time when volcanoes had been relatively quiet, whereas during the preceding century, it had experienced a number of huge eruptions and had been severely colder.

"I have much, much more here, but it's making me sad," MAX said.

Nobody said anything for almost two minutes. And then...

"Gill," Sarah whispered, "I think I need another drink."

19
Dark is the Night

The mood in the War Room was solemn with everyone on edge when they all heard a shuffling, dragging sound coming down the hallway. Robert jumped quickly in front of Sarah to shield her from harm, but the familiar cry of "Yipe, Yipe!" settled everyone back into his or her seats.

"Hey, little buddy!"

"Grrr... yipe... woof!" MAX cheerfully barked.

"Woof... woof," Killer replied as he dragged the empty doggie bag up to where Gill sat.

"What did you say to him, MAX?" Gill asked as he set the bag aside.

"I told him that when it came to fried hog, 'Thanks, but no thanks.'"

Everyone laughed, including MAX and Killer.

Gill stood up and stretched. He looked at everyone around the room, nodded his head and said, "Well, I guess we have a good idea of what the Whistlers are up to. Now we need a way to stop... to stop..."

Gill froze, gazing off into space.

"What's the matter with him?" Sarah asked Robert.

"I think someone is talking to him. Maybe it's Gwen. Maybe she's got more info for us so we can..."

"Quick!" Gill said, "We gotta go. Right now. Trouble!"

Everyone jumped up so quickly that Killer was bounced off the sofa.

"Killer," Gill said as he ran out, "On guard!"

"Grrrrr...."

"MAX, keep in touch on the cell phone if you can," Sarah said as she headed for the door.

Robert, Gill and Sarah all took off running down the hallway. As they finally reached the back door, Gill yelled out to the door, "Open, on alert!"

The door popped open and lights came on outside that were concealed in the trees nearby. The whole back woods were illuminated as they ran to the purple van. They heard the back door automatically close behind them. "Damn," Gill said as they got to the van door, "I forgot my keys!"

All of the lights went off, leaving them in darkness.

Sarah closed her eyes, put her hand on the van's hood, shaking. The doors all popped open and the engine started at the same time. She opened her eyes and smiled. "Get in."

Gill just shook his head and jumped behind the wheel.

"I'm afraid to ask this question," Robert said, "but where are we headed, anyway?"

"Gwen said that the power grid for this entire part of the West Coast is going to be under attack tonight. Whistlers are out in force. She calls 'em 'Evil Thingies' and said there are a dozen that just crossed over at dusk. A dozen of the same damn thingies like the one we met at your hospital, Sarah. We need weapons... and we need 'em quick!"

Sarah thought for a moment, and then said, "They're trying to kill the lights. They don't function well in the bright light and not at all in the daylight. That's our weapon. Light!"

"Got it!" said Gill. He took off out of the long driveway at tremendous speed and hit the highway a minute or so later. "Headin' for a truck stop," he said.

"The billboard we just passed said three miles to a truck stop," Robert added.

"Yeah, I know," said Gill.

About five minutes later, they were swinging into the parking area of a large all-purpose gas station/truck stop and shopping area. Gill said, "You folks stay here while I go get us a few supplies." Gill jumped out and ran inside while Robert stayed with Sarah.

"I'm sort of scared," she said. "We don't really know what we're getting into here, do we?"

"Sarah, I've seen some strange stuff in my times of working with Gill, but this one tops the cake. All I do know is that no matter what, we've GOT to stop these creatures from doing anything like what MAX was talking about. When we get to where we're going tonight, I want you to stay in the van with Gill while I go and check it out. OK?"

"Like hell I will! I just found you, Ert, and don't plan on losing you to a bunch of whistling gomers from another dimension."

Robert sat there with his mouth wide open as he took in what she had just said.

Ring Ring Ring!

"Oh hell," thought Sarah. "I forgot all about MAX." She looked around on the floor of the van and found her phone where she had just again dropped it... in the same place as the night before when it had began... whistling. "Oh hell!" She carefully picked it up... punched the "On" button and quietly said, ... "Ahh, hello?"

"Sarah, it's MAX checking in. Just want you to know that I'm with you if you need me."

"Oh God, MAX! I was afraid you might be one of the Whistlers that was on my phone last night."

"No, Sarah. I don't whistle... but I do hum pretty well!"

Sarah smiled very openly, and then told Robert what MAX had said.

Robert replied, "Ask MAX for a diagram and map location for the power plant. And have him keep in touch constantly. See if he can hack the computer at the power plant. We are gonna need him before this night is over with. He can send the info to the computer screen on Gill's phone. Does he need the number?"

Sarah smiled once again and said that never seemed to be a problem for MAX.

Gill ran into the truck stop shopping area, having remembered seeing the items he was looking for here at this very location only last week. This particular stop was having a sale on hand-held spotlights that were supposed to be like... a quillion candlepower.

Only $24.95. A cheap price to save the world.

Gill thought, "Who would light a quillion candles just to see if it was really this bright?"

He bought five of them, including extra batteries.

"That'll be a total of $132.75," said the weird lookin' guy at the checkout counter. "And... Ahh... Ahhh..."

The big-eyed fellow that was the cashier probably weighed about a hundred and twenty pounds, he must have been seven feet tall and his hair was blue. BRIGHT BLUE.

Gill was looking at this guy carefully because he sort of glowed, at least in Gill's eyes. Gill smiled at the guy, and just as he was about to ask a few questions of this... this very different kind of person, the cashier looked off into space and after a few moments of being in his own mind space said, "Felix. Four miles ahead, then turn left. Right 87... left 56... right 20... left 28. Underneath the trash barrel."

Gill, whose memory was excellent, memorized this entire list of gibberish and then asked quietly, "What's your name, buddy?"

"Felix," said the tall stick of a man with a smile.

Gill stepped back a step or two and slowly started grinning then laughing. Gill smiled as he asked, "How far is it from here to where the electrical sub-station is located?"

As Felix opened his mouth, Gill started speaking at the same time so that together they both said, "Four miles ahead... and then turn left."

Much laughing ensued as Gill pulled out his wallet to pay for the spotlights. "I don't get it," Gill whispered.

"I don't know what it means, either," Felix said as he rang up the purchase, "but I always seem to know what other people NEED to know. I have no idea why it works, but it does work."

"What about the rest of what you told me? How does my needing to know that come into play?"

Felix smiled, turned around to make sure that they were alone and quietly said, "Don't have a clue. HA! But believe me, you'll need that info within the next hour. It's kinda weird, I've always been able to do this, and it's one reason my folks kicked my ass outta the house. Use ta scare the hell outta them. Ha Ha!"

Someone yelled from the back office, "Felix, are you gonna do some damn work today, or are ya just gonna quit? Get busy, damn it!"

Gill smiled big and gazed into the deep blue eyes of this strange fellow in front of him. "Felix, are you happy here? Do you really like doing this 'checkout-at-the-truck-stop' thing with the hours you gotta deal with? What kinda fortune are these folks paying you to make it worth takin' this kinda crap for a livin'?"

Felix looked into Gill's eyes and whispered, "Not enough."

Gill smiled again, and then held out his small hand to the giant pencil of a man as he said, "Tell ya what, Felix, come with me right now and I'll triple it."

"Done," said Felix with a smile as he tightly clutched Gill's hand.

"Done!" Gill was laughing now.

"Hey boss," Felix yelled into the back office, "I just quit!"

"WHAT?" screamed a red-faced three-hundred-pound redneck dude who came running out of the back as Felix and Gill turned away.

Felix was yanking off his smock and putting on a big puffy red hat, even as they both waltzed out of the door of the truck stop together, giggling.

20
One Hell of a Weekend

As Sarah sat in the van talking to Ert, she glanced up in time to see one of the strangest sights she had seen this entire weekend and this had been one hell of a weekend for strange sights. Someone was approaching the van and this someone kind of looked like little ol' Gill, but he was even shorter than ever because of a giant who walked by his side.

"Ahh... Ert? Am I hallucinating... or is that Gill coming toward us with a couple of sacks of stuff... and a fellow with him who looks like a giant matchstick?"

Robert slowly raised his eyes to see seven feet of brown clothing on a very thin dude with blue hair and a red hat. "Strikes anywhere... it used to say that on that box of matches. Lordy, what a site."

Gill swung open the front door to the purple van, smiled at everyone as he passed back the supplies to the back and said to Robert and Sarah, "Hey gang, you're gonna love this. Say hello to Felix!"

Robert, who was sitting in the front passenger seat, reached across the seat to shake the hand of the smiling giant, who grabbed his hand and started pumping it as if he was milking a cow.

"Man, oh man, we... you and I... need to talk!" Felix said with a grin as he looked into Roberts's wide-open eyes. "There's some stuff that you're really gonna need to know and quickly now! Man, oh man! An adventure! I can feel it comin' on, dude! Wild, man! Wow, dude! Quick, dude, let me see your shoes!"

"Glad to meet you, too... Ahh, dude. Ahh... my shoes? Do you mind if I ask you guys a small question... ya know, before we get started or get too carried away with ourselves here. Gill, would you like to tell me, ahh... WHAT THE HELL IS GOING ON?!"

Sarah started laughing loudly, and then reached around the seat to pry Felix's pumping hand away from poor bewildered Ert. She grasped his large hand gently in her small one and shook it once, lets it go saying, "Hi Felix. I'm Sarah."

The over-excited Felix froze where he was with his mouth falling wide open as he stared into Sarah's eyes. It was as if someone had flipped a switch labeled "Off" on his brain and he stayed that way for a good half-minute while everyone just looked at each other.

Gill was watching Felix daze off as he spoke to Robert and Sarah without looking at them. "He knows stuff."

"Gill, I damn well hope it's GOOD STUFF. Why the hell does he want my shoes?" Robert asked.

"Not a clue. But believe me, Robert, if he wants to check out your shoes, you might ought to let him check out your shoes. And do you know why? Huh? Just guess."

Felix shook his head as he popped out of his trance and said very quietly... "'Cause, I know stuff."

They all looked at him as he slowly came back to his old self with a loud laugh. "Wow, dude. That was heavy. OK, gang, you don't know me and I don't know y'all, but somethin's gonna happen in the next hour really heavy, man, and without precautions... someone's gonna change... and someone's gonna croak."

Robert snapped to attention at that. "Croak? Do you mean...?"

"Dead, dude, way dead. We need a few things real quick. Gill... right? Cool, dude! You need to run back into the store, man, and grab a can of hairspray, a pair of tennis shoes... size 11... and a butane lighter... and a Gatorade. And your handle is...?" he asked, looking at Robert.

"Robert's the name. If this is on the level, what can I do to help? Dude?"

"Bob ol' boy, run behind the truck stop and cut about ten feet of the garden hose from back there to take with us. On the way back here, grab a squeegee from the gas pumps."

Robert looked at him as if he were crazy.

"Can I help?" Sarah said with a smile.

"Yeah, lovely lady, yeah," he said very quietly. "What you need to do is give ol' Bobby here a big kiss, 'cause it's gonna be up to this dude to save your life tonight. No kiddin'."

Gill, Robert and Sarah stopped dead in their tracks staring at Felix.

"No kiddin'," he said again softly.

Sarah bent over the seat, took Robert's face gently into her hands, and pulled him into her awaiting embrace. The kiss was long... and slow... and smooth... and Gill gave off a little sigh.

"Why do these things never happen to me?" Gill quietly said.

Robert finally relaxed from the kiss, got out of the van slowly and quietly, walked around to where Felix was standing, took his large hand into his own... and said, "Thank you, Felix."

"No worries, dude! Ahh... we kinda need to hurry here, guys."

Robert and Gill took off at a run to get the needed objects. Felix crawled off into the back of the van with Sarah.

"Ah, Sarah... dudette... don't worry. We're gonna take good care of you.

Now, two things I need to talk to you about. Number one, some machine you know needs to be told to put himself on emergency backup power as soon as possible. He's gonna lose out if'n he don't.

"Oh God! That's MAX! I'll call him on my phone right now!"

"Cool, lil' dudette! MAX, huh? Tell 'em Felix says, 'Hey!'"

While Sarah was dialing MAX, she asked, "Felix, you said two things you needed to talk about. What was the second one?"

"Well, since I'm wading off waist-deep into unknown waters full of... I don't know... 'Evil Thingies,' I'd kinda like to know what the heck's goin' on, girl!"

Sarah started laughing as MAX connected with her. "Felix, you're gonna fit right in, ol' son!"

As Sarah was talking to MAX about the new addition to the team and the situation about MAX's pending power failure, Robert came running back toward to the van, closely trailed by Gill jogging as fast as his little legs would carry him. Both had arms full of stuff, including a black baseball cap in Robert's hand. Sarah told MAX to call her back when the power problem was handled.

"Nice hat, dude! But that wasn't on the list, was it?" Felix asked.

"It was on my list. It's a present for you... less conspicuous... and makes you look less like a matchstick," Robert said with a smile.

"Oh wow, dude, no one ever gave me a hat before. Like... thanks, amigo!"

Gill was huffing and puffing... out of breath. "OK, let's get this show on the road, gang. Time is of the essence here."

As they prepared to start up the ol' van to head out to the highway, Gill asked, "Felix, what's all of this extra stuff for? Do you know?"

"Some of it I do, man. Some of it... no. The shoes are for my amigo, Bobby, here. Rubber soles, dude... just like the Beatles, man! Somethin' ta do with you not getting 'lectricuted! With the squeegee, dudes, we only need the handle, man! You can unscrew the wooden handle and scrap the rest. Don't know why, but that's about it, I guess. 'Bout all I know."

Sarah smiled at Felix and said, "Oh tall one, I think I can figure out the hairspray and lighter. That's a weapon of sorts. But what I can't put my finger on so far, Felix, why the Gatorade? I can't figure out... why the Gatorade?"

Felix's face lit up with his famous giant smile. "Oh, beautiful one, that's the easiest one of all to figure out."

They all turned to focus on him.

He smiled as he blushed and said in a very quiet voice... "I was thirsty."

Laughter ensued.

21
The Battle of Lights

The laughter stopped.

Gill and Felix looked at each other for about a half-minute, and then said... simultaneously... "Ahh... we got a problem."

Everyone looked at these two strangely mismatched guys with such intense concentration that everyone suddenly started laughing again.

Felix finally stopped laughing long enough to choke out, "Dude, we got so many problems, it's messed up like a box full of coat hangers."

Gill was now laughing so hard he couldn't drive. "Quit it, damn it. I can hardly breathe for laughing so damn hard. OK, everybody listen up here."

Everyone, smiling, looked to Gill at the same time.

"Someone's gonna die."

Everyone just... stopped... and then sat there with their mouths wide open... except Felix, who was nodding his skinny head up and down like a mechanical bird bobbing for water. "Yep... Yep... that's what I said. It ain't for sure, but Bobby's gotta change shoes and carry that hose. And... and... ahhh..."

Felix mentally faded away.

Robert shook his head, "Damn it, Gill, what's going on here? We've never had this... ahhh... amount of traffic with us to deal with before! Look at me, Gill, and tell me that everything... everything is gonna... gonna be OK. OK?"

Sarah quietly said, "Traffic?"

Gill looked at his longtime friend Robert, smiled at him with a sort of sideways Elvis grin and quietly said, "Can't do it, my friend. Can't do it. Not this time."

"How bad?" Robert said with a whisper.

"No promises, no threats. We're balanced on a thin wire now, according to all my friends, MAX and Felix and the wee folk and my own intuition. What's gonna happen in the next hour is a spin of the wheel, a throw of the dice. Too many variables to determine an outcome. It sucks, but that's the way it seems to be."

"OK, OK... just... give me the damn shoes!"

Sarah, who was as scared as anyone at that moment, started to snicker again. "Atta way to go, hose boy."

Robert actually growled.

Gill got his spare keys from the console and took off out of the parking lot with the tires screaming and smoking, spinning out to the highway... en route to trouble.

"Ahh... do we have a plan of action, or a idea of what's going on, or some basic concept of WHO THE HELL IS GOING TO TRY TO KILL US? How 'bout it, Gill? A lil' help, huh, lil' buddy?" Robert said with a small smile.

Gill, who was driving at least twenty miles per hour over the speed limit, turned his head to Robert, stared at him for a few seconds, turned his head slowly back and then began...

"Robert, we're headed into a situation where at least one of us here has a potential for not coming back. Felix seems to think that Sarah may be the one we should worry about, but he also believes that YOU have the power to fix the problem if a problem is all we have to worry about. As far as I can figure out, we have a dimensional cross-over of creatures who plan to try to make our little world into a place that they can thrive in, and once they've completed their terra-forming of our world into a cute little version of theirs, they will exit their world en masse to populate ours. We will either be adapted to fit into their society as slave labor or maybe companionable pets or eliminated completely by being consumed."

Sarah wiped her face with the back of her hand as she said, "Consumed?"

"Protein, my love... protein."

"LIGHTS! ALL OF 'em! SPOTLIGHTS, DUDETTE! DO THOSE, too. And... fire... and... lighters... and..."

Felix went away again after his brief encounter with reality.

Gill turned back around in his seat to look at Robert. "He's right, ya know. Lights. So far, that's the only real weapon we've found that these critters don't seem to care for. Open those bags, boys and girls, and load those new batteries into that pile of 'flashlights from hell' that we've got there. I bought all they had, but I figure if we end up saving this world, I can find some damn way to get my money back."

Robert smiled, more to the inside than the outside and patted his old friend on the back as he drove down the road. "Gill, my friend, if we can save the world and no one else will take responsibility for the problem..."

"Yeah?" Gill said in a whisper.

"I'll pay for your stupid damn batteries."

"LIGHTS!" It was Felix again.

Robert looked to Gill and said, "Ahh...Gill... who the hell is this dude?"

"That's Felix. He works for us now. I hired him. He knows stuff."

"That's a good gig when you can get it," said Sarah who had been taking this all in stride for a while now. "Hey guys, can we get back to this little ol' thing where I'm supposed to... DIE here tonight? Huh? Can you see how I might ... kinda like to... talk about this situation? I mean... like... I might have plans or something."

Felix sat straight up in the back of the van. "MAX? Hey, Bobby, we need to talk."

RING... RING... RING.

Sarah answered her phone. "MAX, is that you? I'm putting you on the speaker so we can all hear."

"Affirmative, Sarah. Just getting back to you. I've sent the directions for your rendezvous to Gill's computer phone, and I've backed up my power supply as you requested. I'm not quite sure why you asked me to do that, but after reflecting on the situation, it seemed like a good move. I see on the specs that I sent to you that the security on that place seems to be especially heavy and there's a combination you're gonna need to know in order to obtain admittance."

Gill smiled and said, "Hey MAX ol' buddy, if I send you a series of numbers, can you verify whether or not they are the correct combination we're gonna need?"

"Gill, my friend. Good to hear from ya! Yep, I believe I can do that from where I am here, but how in the name of Thomas Edison could you possibly come up with those numbers?"

"Woof, Woof!"

"Oh yeah, Killer says to say, 'Hi!'"

"We've got a new member of our team named Felix," Gill said to the phone. "He gave us the numbers."

"We've got a team now?" MAX said in a funny sort of voice! "And we've got a ... Phoenix on it? Sarah mentioned that a Phoenix said... 'Hey?'"

"Yeah, it's kinda lookin' that way, except it's Felix, not Phoenix! Check out these numbers... right 87... left 56... right 20... and left 28. I'll wait while you check."

They all heard some buzzing and clicking on the other end of the phone, then MAX popped back on.

"Correct, Gill. The only problem seems to be that once you have inserted the combination to the security lock on the fence, there is still the problem of a key to open the gate, which is electrified."

As he drove toward the power plant, Gill thought for a moment and then asked, "MAX, do you have a way to pull up a current photo of the gate security area?"

"Correct. SAT com imagery coming to you in thirty seconds."

In a half minute, a picture popped up on the phone screen. Gill and Felix were both looking at it, and at the same time, spotted what they were looking for. At the same instant, they smiled at each other and said, "Underneath the trash barrel."

Robert shook his head and said, "OK you guys are just gettin' weird here now! What's up? Dudes?"

MAX spoke before anyone else had a chance. "According to my abilities to solve problems with instantaneous success and the information I've been fed in the last hour and the knowledge of what everyone in our 'team' is capable of, except for the new human, this 'Felix' person, I have come up with what I believe is the logical conclusion to the question Robert is asking about."

Everyone waited but said nothing. Finally Robert got flustered and yelled out, "WELL?"

MAX clicked a couple of times and then quietly said, "Felix must... know stuff."

Everyone except MAX started laughing... then MAX, too, gave out with a "Whaa, Whaa, and Whaa! Did I tell a funny?"

After a couple of minutes on the road, they were closer to the fate that awaited them. Everyone started introducing themselves a little better to the newest member of the team. It was Sarah who asked Felix the question of where he was from and why the blue hair.

"I was raised in Cajun country 'round Louisiana way. My Mam and Pap were kinda uncomfortable with my... knowin' stuff... and so I eventually left them and my brother Sylvester down near New Orleans and moved west. I always thought that the entire Deckett clan was glad to see me go... 'cept maybe my bro... who was kinda strange also. When I did my hair blue, he did his orange!"

Sarah smiled as she figured out what he had just said. "Deckett, is that how you pronounce that last name?"

Felix smiled as he said quietly, "Well, actually, it's a French-Cajun name and back home it's pronounced kinda like 'DECK- HAT,' with the accent on 'HAT.' I changed it to Deckett."

Robert started laughing so hard that he was in tears.

MAX said on the phone, "Ahh... Robert? What is it that you find so funny about this name?"

"Damn, MAX! The poor guy's folks named him and his brother 'Felix The Cat' and 'Sylvester The Cat'!"

Everyone, including Felix, got a laugh out of that.

Felix said with a smile, "Ya know who really hated that name? My Uncle

Garfield."

Gill had to pull over to keep from driving off of the highway from laughing so hard.

In the back of the van, Sarah, Robert and Felix started to assemble the spotlights and batteries. "Damn, Gill, these things are intense," Robert said.

"The biggest they had, and I still hope they're big enough. Sarah, there's two backpacks back there. Put half of the lights in one and half in the other. Also, an extra battery in each if you please, pretty lady. Felix, what about the other stuff you asked for?"

Felix looked around the van. He said to everyone, "Bobby's got the right shoes on now. He's gonna need the rubber hose and the squeegee stick. Sarah, you're gonna carry the lighter and hairspray since you seem to know already what's up with that when the time comes. Gill, my friend, you bring MAX. I got my Gatorade," he said with a snicker.

Sarah thought back on something that she remembered hearing earlier. "Ahh... Felix, a while ago you said that someone could 'croak,' and that someone could 'change.' Can you clarify this 'change' you mentioned?"

He shook his big head slowly and said, "Only thing I know is that it has to do with Gill here, and some folks he knows that aren't amigos with the... 'Thingies?' Is that what we call 'em?"

"That's damn close enough," said Gill. "Robert, tell Felix about our experience with the one at the hospital and the gas station fiasco."

Gill drove on as the folks in the back of the van tried to prepare themselves for the battle ahead as best as they could.

It wasn't enough.

22

A Fine Line Between Life and Death

It was only a mile or so down the road when they first saw the burnt out car on the side of the road. It was still smoking as they approached it and the doors were wide-open all the way around. Its blackened remains gave off an attacked feeling. The most shocking part of it, though, was the strange bluish fog that floated only around the wreck. They slowed down to almost a crawl as they neared the vehicle, but they could tell instantly that there was no one still around the car that could be helped. Lights were busted out violently and the seat covering was ripped to shreds. In the blue fog-like smoke, it was hard to tell whether it was blood they saw all over the inside of the windshield, but their guesses would have been... yes.

Time was now a factor pressing down on all of them like a heavy weight, so Gill elected to drive slowly by and continue on their mission to the sub-station. Nothing could be done to help the poor driver of that demolished automobile. Wherever he or she was, they were now long past any help.

Tears were slowly rolling down Sarah's face, and when Felix patted her on the shoulder, she turned around to realize that he, too, was crying. "A better place," she said to him. "That's where they've gone."

"Yeah," said Felix with a whimper, "but their journey was hell."

MAX popped onto Gill's computer phone as they neared a mile-long chain link fence that stretched off into the horizon. "I can see your van, Gill, by satellite and you're almost there. I'll be here with you for the rest of the night. Hold on... just a second. Something's... something's happening! There's a major power flux in the..."

"BAM! BAM... BAM!"

They were suddenly thrown into total darkness as all of the power blacked out at the site. As they looked out of the van window, they could clearly see the city lights miles away start to blink out, one by one. The entire region would soon be thrown into inky darkness.

"Well, looks like that's our cue," Felix said with a sigh.

Gill opened the van door so that they could see by the dome light. "Let's use my small pocket flashlight to get in at first. I really don't like the idea

73

of us being all lit up here, coming in with no other illumination on the site. It kinda makes us a target too soon in the game."

As they stepped out together and closed the van doors to exhaust the dome light, Robert said with a snicker, "A game! A hell of a game we've gotten ourselves into here, hey Gill? OK, Sarah... you're with me once we're in there. Don't leave my side for anything, right?"

She nodded at him and placed her hand around his waist. "Not for anything," she whispered. Robert blushed, but in the darkness no one could see it.

"Ert," said Sarah, "This wooden handle from the squeegee thing fits inside the end of the hose. It might be easier to keep up with that way. What do ya think?"

As Robert fitted the wooden handle into the ten-foot section of rubber hose, Felix yelled out, "THAT'S IT, DUDE. I can see it, now! That's gonna save your girlfriend, dude!"

"Shhh!" they all said at the same time to the over-excited Felix.

"Hey, tall one." Sarah whispered, "Let's don't blow this caper before it gets started. All whispers for a while, OK? Cool? But, thanks for the info."

"Ultra cool, lil' dudette. My bad," he whispered. "I'll creep around as quiet as... as a..."

"As a cat?" Sarah quietly said with a giggle.

"Totally," he whispered back.

RING RING!

"Oh hell," Sarah said as she answered the phone. "Shhh, MAX. We're here and so are they."

"Gotcha, Sarah. Shhh! Ten-four on the quiet. Just letting you know that Killer and I are back and we're here for you."

"Can we get started here or do you and circuit board there both need some more time?" Gill said.

They quietly all walked over to the large gate by the light of Gill's little penlight. They could see the warning sign on the fence telling of the penalties for trespassing and the threat of being electrocuted. Robert pointed to the fence and said, "Since the lights are off, I guess the fence is down, too."

As he started to put his hands toward it, a bottle of Gatorade hit the chain link right in front of him. Sparks covered him like rain and shot twenty feet into the air. Robert leaped backward so quickly that he almost tripped over Felix. Hot liquid drizzled down on his head.

"Damn, man, there goes my Gatorade and I was thirsty, too." Felix said quietly.

"Remind me to hug your tall ass later if we make it out of this crap," Robert said with a smile.

Gill went over to the fence and checked out the combination padlock. It was coated in a rubber sleeve to keep a person from being fried, but it was still a struggle to keep away from the electrified links. "OK... right 87... back to the left to 56... right to 20... and back to the left to 28."

CLICK!

The padlock fell off into the dust.

"Now," Gill said quietly, "look around here for a trash barrel. There should be one right over..."

BAM! CRASH!

"Found it, dude," Felix said from the ground, lying in the dust grinning. Nearby they found a silver key.

"A problem, guys, "Gill whispered as he examined the key. "The key isn't coated in rubber and the lock in the fence is electrified, too. Any ideas?"

Sarah walked over to the fence, took the key from Gill's small hand, took the hose from Robert's large hand and inserted the key into the end of the hose that didn't have the wooden handle in it. "Ta da!" she said.

Gill smiled as he took the contraption from her, placed the shank end of the key into the slot and turned the key into the fence lock, using the rubber hose as insulation. "Show-off," he said as he looked back at her with a grin. He swung the gate slowly open with an audible "creak"... and in they went.

They went no farther than two steps before they heard the first whistle. Robert shook his head and quietly said, "Aww, hell!"

23

A Nice Quiet Evening in the Country

"What in the name of God is that?" muttered Felix as the shrieking continued. "No, don't tell me. I'm thinkin' I don't wanna know."

"You're damn sure right about that, my vertical friend," said Gill. "That would be one of the Whistlers... aka the Evil Thingies, as my tiny friends have named them," Gill added with a shake of his head.

Felix startled everyone by starting to laugh again.

"I can assure you, cat dude, that these creatures are nothing to laugh at... as you will no doubt soon see," Gill sneered.

"Naw, man, it's not them, it's you, dude. I still have trouble imagining you having tiny friends. To me, amigo, you are my tiny friend," Felix explained with a big smile.

"That may be the nicest thing that anyone has said to me in the last..." Gill looked closely at his watch in the small penlight... "ten minutes."

On Sarah's phone, MAX chimed in, "Whaa, whaa! Ten minutes! Good one, Oh mighty Gillmeister."

At least everyone was smiling at that as they all walked into the war zone.

"HEADS UP!" yelled Robert as a red-hot streak of light arched through the night headed right for them all. Sarah was knocked to the ground by Robert as he tried to shield her body with his own from any incoming explosions. Gill found himself lifted six feet into the air by Felix, who took off into the dark night at a all-out run.

"Get out the real lights, Sarah," Robert screamed. "I think our chances of sneakin' up on 'em just went out the window."

"Don't take this wrong, Ert, but I need you to climb off of me. I can't move and I'm lying on the backpack."

"What's happening?" asked MAX.

You could almost see the blush on Robert's face as the streak of light hit the ground with a WHOOSH! A very slow-moving blue fog erupted around where the light projectile had landed.

Robert rolled off of Sarah and quickly helped her to her feet. "Aww, hell!" he said. "I'm not sure what that crap is, but after seeing that car we passed, I'm thinkin' that blue fog is a no-no. Where did Felix and Gill go?"

Sarah was digging out the two giant spotlights from the back pack as she replied, "Don't know, Ert. I saw Gill snatched up by Felix before the fog bomb hit but didn't see which way they ran. Here, take this light!"

Robert was trying to hold onto the hose/wood-handled contraption, trying to grab the spotlight and trying to herd Sarah away from the fog all at once.

He didn't even see the Whistler smiling at him from only ten feet away.

Gill was bouncing up and down in the arms of Felix for more that a minute or two before he finally managed to huff out, "Stop, damn it. You're shaking my brains loose, Felix!"

Felix skidded to a stop so quickly that they both slid to the ground.

"Wow, man. That was heavy, dude. Fireworks, man! Ahh, hey, where are we, lil' pal? Aww, man, it's dark out here." Felix exclaimed loudly. "... And quiet, too!"

Exasperated, Gill stood up and looked at Felix. "It's gonna be a lot quieter in a minute when I have to kill you for talkin' so damn loud! QUIET!" Gill looked around the smothering darkness, but saw no clue of where Robert and Sarah were... or where he and Felix had just come from. The whistling noise they had heard earlier had faded away in the distance and Gill discovered that he had lost his penlight in all of the jostling around in the embrace of his giant friend – who had no doubt just saved his small life.

Felix sat on the ground with his face all downcast and sad. "Sorry, Gill. I'm sorry. Sometimes, I just... kinda get... carried away... and excited... and..."

"Hey, Felix," Gill said with a smile as he tried to help the big softie up off of the ground. "Hey, man, you're the dude, man. You probably just saved my life back there, and all I did was yell at you for it. I'm the one who's sorry here. You have nothing to be ashamed of... my... my friend."

Felix's face went from broken-hearted to a grin twelve inches wide in about two seconds. He picked up Gill again and started swinging him around in circles. "My friend!" Felix said, "I sure like the sound of that, dude."

"Well, how do ya like the sound of this? PUT ME DOWN, DAMN IT!"

Felix set him down and smiled as he said, "Quiet, lil' dude... you gotta learn to hold it down!"

"I may have to kill you, yet," Gill said with a smile.

"Maybe I can help," said the Whistler who was quickly walking toward them.

"Maybe I can help."

The Whistler who approached Robert and Sarah had the same stupid smile as the one in the hospital had. "Hell, it coulda been the same creature, but it was impossible to tell because of the way its face appeared to be shifting, even in the dark," Sarah thought.

Robert still had his back to it as Sarah screamed, "Robert!"

Robert spun around so quickly that he dropped the spotlight he had been trying to juggle. He still had a hold of the whip-like hose contraption they had brought, though, so he quickly snapped it out and around to slap ol' Thingie right in the face. It sort of stuck there for a second and then fell away leaving a large crease in the Whistler's cheek.

When this happened, the creature instantly stopped and looked so surprised and... hurt... that Robert giggled. This was obviously not a good idea because its face turned a bright red. His looks started shifting even faster... and it began to whistle. It stuck out its quivering arms like the Frankenstein monster and started approaching the two humans as the whistling got louder and louder.

"Do something... anything!" screeched MAX on the phone speaker.

Sarah started backing up slowly, but soon found that she couldn't see where the edge of the fog began... and she sure as hell didn't want to back into that stuff. She decided quickly to use the only tool available to her, the searchlight. She held it up and switched it on. It just so happened to be aimed right at their alien visitor. The light came on so brightly that it almost looked like a solid material that could be cut with a knife.

In one instant, several things happened.

First off, as the Thingie was struck, the damn whistling stopped instantly. So did the Thingie. The incredibly high beam of light hit it right in the chest, and where it hit... an incredibly giant hole appeared in the creature. This time, there was no whistle, only an incredibly loud scream of pain. "It's working," thought Sarah.

She shifted the heavy spotlight around so that it saturated the Whistler and bit by bit, the thing just... disappeared.

Sarah and Robert just sat there for a moment or two looking to the spot where the Whistler had stood, waiting to see if it would return. It was gone. "No coming back from that, I guess," said Robert.

About the same time, two more things happened. First, though the blue fog was now thinning out a little bit, it was still spreading and headed right toward them. Second, from all around the sub-station complex, Whistlers started screaming and whistling at the same time. "They know," said Sarah. "They know."

"Uhh... I think you both need to go now," MAX quietly whispered.

"Time for us to move our location, my love. Let's mosey around and see if we can locate Fric and Frac! What do ya say?"

"I'd follow you anywhere, Ert!" she said with a smile.

As they walked away, Robert picked up his dropped searchlight and aimed it into the air to make sure it was still in good working order. The bright beam shot into the sky and could be seen from a mile away.

This was a good thing... and a bad thing.

Gill jerked around at the sound of the Whistler's voice and Felix sprang to his feet... rather cat-like. "Oh yeah?" Felix yelled at the Whistler. "You gonna help, huh? You... and what army?"

Thingie smiled his most wicked smile at this and said, "How about them?"

Gill and Felix both slowly turned around in a full circle and realized that there were two more of these creatures scattered in the darkness near them and they all looked just like the first one. Same suits. Same build. Same stupid grin on their same faces.

"What kinda God would make three idiots who were all as ugly as you, dude?' Felix said. "The answer to that would be... none. Therefore, y'all are goin' down!"

"And just how do you and your low life-form friends plan to accomplish this feat?" the Whistler said as they all three started closing in on Gill and Felix. "When we finish remodeling this... this... planet that you call it, there will be room for creatures such as you only on the dinner table,"

And with that statement, all three Whistlers started to quietly whistle as their faces began to revert to some semblance of what they actually looked like!

"OH GOD!" thought Gill. "How in the world can we possibly...?"

As sudden as a heartbeat, all three creatures snapped back to one human persona again, and began to... scream! The screams became louder as they blended with the whistling, which had continued through the entire encounter. They all stared back in the direction that Gill figured he and Felix had come from. Gill thought to himself, "Something has happened with Robert!"

"Gotta problem, boys?" Felix said as he swerved away from the closest Thingie to reach into his backpack. At the same time, the two extra Whistlers darted off in the direction of a bright beam of light that suddenly shot into the night sky.

"Yep," said Gill with a smile, "that's Robert for ya!"

Felix managed to get the backpack open far enough to drag one of the large lights into the open, but in the process, he got the light hung up on the cord that opened and closed the bag. As he struggled with the tangled mess, Gill turned back around in time to find the last remaining Whistler standing right next to him. "Ahh... Felix?"

Felix looked up in time to see the Thingie place his hand upon Gill's small head and in time to hear Gill scream as he dropped unconscious to the hard ground.

The Whistler glowed with renewed energy for a moment, smiled and then started his approach to Felix, who stood frozen with his mouth wide open, looking at the now lifeless body of his new friend.

24
Fallen Friends and Rising Tempers

"Ahh.... Ert... that just might be attracting just a little too much attention to us in a situation where we don't really want too much attention. Don't ya think?" Sarah said quietly.

"Aww, heck... I didn't even think about that. Sorry!" he said as he quickly switched off the spotlight... a little bit too late.

"Did you hear that?" Sarah asked. "A little like screaming, and now it seems to be getting closer. Quick, let's vacate these premises."

They took off arm-in-arm at a run as fast as they could in the darkness that they had to deal with when their spots were extinguished. Weaving back and forth though the maze of transformers, wires, towers and unseen cables, they accidently bypassed the deadly fate that was rapidly approaching their original location. After three or four minutes of bobbing about and zig-zagging around, Robert stopped Sarah with an upraised arm.

"Listen," he said. "Do you hear that?" Sarah listened closely and heard sobbing. "OK, Ert, I've heard 'em whistle, heard 'em laugh and I've heard 'em scream, but I'm almost positive I've never heard 'em cry!"

They started slowly walking toward the sound of the intense anguish of whoever was at the bottom of this new sound. When they finally got close enough to see the source of this miserable wailing, they first spotted one of the deadly Whistlers with its back facing them, walking away from their direction and headed toward a sight that brought them both to tears.

On the ground lay poor little Gill, as still as the night and as pale as death. A few yards away stood Felix, with his head turned to heaven as he cried his sorrow to the skies for all his soul was worth. The Evil Thingie was slowly walking in his direction, and though they couldn't see it, they both, in their hearts, knew that the creature was smiling. When the Whistler was only a few feet away from poor Felix, it stopped. It looked back at the unmoving body of Felix's new friend... and laughed. "Pitiful creature. What a waste of skin!"

What happened next was something that had never, ever happened before.

Poor Felix had been distracted when the whole disaster with Gill had come about. He had been thinking, "Stupid Felix! Ya big dummy! Here we are in the middle of an adventure on which the entire fate of our world might hang and you mess it all up by gettin' a stupid flashlight caught in a stupid backpack so your big stupid hands can't untangle the stupid thing! What a chucklehead you are!"

He had heard his lil' buddy quietly say, "Ahh, Felix?" He looked back in time to see one of the only people on this lonely planet that he cared for scream in agony and fall to the hard, hard ground.

"Oh, God!" he thought in despair. He let go of the stupid tangled spotlight, let go of the stupid backpack, and looked upward towards the night and the god who would let such a thing happen to such a gentle and giving soul as poor Gill! Why? Why would you allow this to happen? Tears the size of dimes fell from the tall man's eyes as he first began to sob... then began to cry... and then began to wail his grief into the night.

At the very height of his misery, just for a couple of seconds, everything went into a red haze. It was like he was elsewhere. The tears and misery continued in this frozen moment in time, but someone spoke to him.

"Scream for the night! Scream for the pain! Scream for peace... to the world once again!"

Felix looked around and saw no one.

"Tell the one known as Sarah to use the power of the place she is in. Gill can be returned if it is done soon. Tell her Gin said so. Fare thee well, oh giant one."

As quick as it had happened, so it was undone.

Felix was back at the sub-station wailing his sadness into the night. Gill still lay lifeless on the cold ground, and the Whistler was now only a few miserable feet from where the gentle giant cried.

"Pitiful creature. What a waste of skin!"

Upon hearing these words from the abomination which had taken his friend's life, something inside Felix that had never existed before suddenly CLICKED.

Grief suddenly turned to anger, remorse turned to vengeance and for the very first time in his strange life, Felix felt hate.

Without knowing how or why, the tears stopped, the wailing ceased, and with a red-hot hatred never before seen on the face of this peaceful person, Felix looked into the eyes of the fast approaching creature in front of him, rolled his eyes into the back of his large head and screamed.

"AHHHHHHHHHHHHHHHH!"

The Whistler standing before him froze, and horror and pain came upon its ever-changing face. It's whole appearance started blinking in and out like static on an old television set and its place on our plane of existence became wavy, distorted... wrong.

Then with a soft blink, it was gone.

Felix managed to see Robert and Sarah standing off to the side of this scene, right before everything went black.

25
Doin' a Comeback

Robert darted forward toward the fallen pair of friends before Sarah even had a chance to react. On his way, he managed to trip facedown in the dark when he fell over a downed electrical cable as big as his wrist, which had fallen from a high tower and was connected to a nearby transformer when the attack on the power station had happened. By the time he got to his feet again, Sarah was kneeling by Gill.

"He's not breathing!" she screamed. "The damn Evil Thingie's killed Gill, Ert! Killed him!" Robert was bending over the two, quietly sobbing with large tears falling down his cheek. Old memories of all the good times, all the adventures, all of the love that they had shared with each other. Gone. Like a gust of wind, it was all over... cut down... finished.

"I didn't even have a chance to tell the little runt goodbye," Robert whispered. "And now, it's too late. Too late."

"No, dude," someone behind him said in a voice so quiet that Robert almost missed it. "No."

Felix was starting to come back to reality from wherever he had zoomed off to after the display of power Sarah and Robert had just witnessed. He slowly raised himself up enough to get his elbow underneath him on the cold, hard earth upon which he lay, and he slowly turned his head to see Sarah crying over the still body of Gill.

"Dudette?" he said quietly. Sarah didn't even look up from her grief. "Lil' dudette?" he said. Nothing. With a small sigh, Felix picked himself up of the ground, walked slowly toward her and softly touched her on the shoulder. "Sarah?"

She slowly raised her head to look at him. She was teary-eyed and tired looking and he thought she might have been the prettiest girl he'd ever seen. "Felix?" she asked. "Felix?"

"Yeah, beautiful one... it's ol' Felix. I'm here."

"I'm glad," she said in a whisper.

"Yeah, and been talkin' to a REAL lil' dude named Gin."

"WHAT?"

"WHAT?"

Both Sarah and Robert yelled at the same moment and Robert had turned around so quick that his bones popped.

Felix smiled peacefully at the two folks in front of him and asked, "What happened to the Boogieman? I don't remember anything after coming out of the red fog except for some loud critter screamin'!"

Robert grabbed him by the arm. "Listen carefully and quickly here, Felix. First off, the loud critter was you! You finished off the Whistler somehow, but we'll get back to that later. Right now, the important thing is this story about the red fog and Gin. Can you tell us about that, Felix?"

"I'll try, Bobby. I'm still doin' a comeback from bein' so dadgum watty-headed, but I'll put it together for ya, and it ain't no story. I just blanked out when Gill went down and some lil' dude named Gin was singing poetry at me."

"Singing poetry at you? What did it say, dude?"

"Ah heck, I really don't remember, but that ain't what's important right now." He shook off Robert's grasp and turned slowly to look at Sarah. "He had a message for you, lil' dudette."

Sarah jumped up. "For me? What was it, Felix! Can you remember it?"

"Oh yeah!" Felix smiled, "I think I was supposed to remember that part."

Felix went into one of his outer world stares for about five seconds and then began to speak in a very weird voice.

"Tell the one known as Sarah to use the power of the place she is in. Gill can be returned if it is done... soon. Tell her Gin said so. Fare thee well, oh giant one."

Sarah sat there with her mouth open as Felix popped back to reality once again.

"The power of the place that I am in?" She looked around her, trying to translate the strange message when suddenly, whistling began on both sides of where they were all situated.

"Whistlers!" yelled Robert as he grabbed for the backpack he and Sarah had carried to retrieve the second spotlight. "Where's your backpack, Felix?"

"Not a clue, dude! Dropped it somewhere around here!"

"Here! Catch this!" he said as he tossed the light he had been carrying. "Use it! It works unless you can scream again, that is. How 'bout it?"

Felix snatched the light out of the air. "Naw, sorry, dude, but I think I'm all screamed out. At least for now."

Sarah yelled and then spun around in a circle with a big smile on her face. "I think I've got it!" She looked at the situation and then to Robert. "Ert, can you hold 'em off? I gotta do something."

"Yeah, babydoll, I got your back. Me and Felix-Dude'll take care of business here. You see if you can help Gill, OK?"

"Thanks. And in case anything happens to me..."

"Don't talk that way! Don't even say it, OK? I'll keep an eye on ya." He pulled the second spotlight out of the backpack just as the two Thingies stepped into view. He sat the rubber hose/stick down next to Gill as he stood up.

Felix walked toward them and just smiled at them. "Evil Thingies, huh? I guess that would make you both an E.T., huh? Wanna phone home?" He laughed out loud at them as they stopped and stared at this crazy human being. Giggling, he stuck out his forefinger like the kindly alien had in the famous movie. "BE GOOD."

Felix would later call their reaction "a conniption fit."

26
A Conniption Fit

"Man!" said Felix. "Whistlers just got no sense of humor!" A large ball of fire flew over his tall head. One of the Whistlers seemed to have just clapped his hands together and instead of noise, a fireball ball had appeared and then flown in the direction the tips of its fingers had been pointing.

"Now that's a new trick! That's what we saw earlier when we came in to this hellhole!" Robert yelled as the fireball exploded behind him. A blue fog started oozing out of the location where it hit.

"Hey ugly, I gotta a new trick, too! How do ya like this one!" With that comment, Robert raised the mighty spotlight and flicked the switch.

As before, the whistling instantly stopped from the creature as the light hit it in the face, its head disappearing and it blinking out with a fading scream like a far-away program on an old TV set. The remaining Whistler screamed also, and then took off running into the night.

Felix took off after it.

"Felix!" Robert yelled. "Come back here, ya damn idiot!" If Felix heard him, he paid no attention. Felix may have still been weak from his experience, but he was mad. He soon disappeared into the night. "Damn!" Robert said to himself. Robert thought about giving a chase but realized that was a bad idea. He slowly turned around after realizing he had forgotten all about Sarah in the fever pitch of the battle.

What he saw made him scream again.

Sarah watched Robert and Felix sashay off into battle and she thought about the brainstorm that had popped into her head.

"Use the power of the place she is in."

This place was chock-full of machines of all types and that was her bag. She figured that the Whistlers had blasted one of the sections of the substation and that had a piggyback effect on the rest of the complex. First one... then another... then another would shut down as the load had increased. All she had to do was convince one machine to come back on-line and get it to convince another. The exact opposite of what Thingies had done. Of course, there would still be the damage somewhere, but the maintenance men who were undoubtedly on their way right now could eventually repair that. She walked ten steps to pick up the cable that Ert had tripped over and drug it over to where Gill occupied the ground. She looked over and saw that the cable, which was stripped of all insulation, was still connected to the original transformer. She turned around to look at Robert, who was intensely involved in battle with the enemy – blasting a Whistler into oblivion. She smiled a slow smile with the thought of who he was, what they were, what they could have been. She gave a slow sigh, and as she was about to begin, MAX quietly spoke up.

"Sarah."

She picked up her phone.

"MAX?"

"Sarah? Think about what you're doing, what you're about to do, about what you have to lose."

"No choice, MAX. It's Gill we're talking about."

"I understand. Good luck. I'll miss you."

"Thanks, MAX. I'll miss you, too, my friend"

She picked up the raw cable, held it to Gill's chest and talked to the machine.

The last thing she heard was Robert screaming.

Then she went away.

Robert slowly turned around to look at Sarah.

As the power kicked in, as the lights all came on, as the sparks started flying through the cable... through poor Sarah... and into Gill. Robert began to scream.

27
The Chase

Felix had heard Robert yelling at him, but he didn't give a damn. The creature darting in and out of the dark buildings and machinery that made up this complex had just helped kill his friend, his best friend, and Felix had a few things to say to this Thingie.

Every time Felix raised the heavy spotlight to try to nail this bastard, the Whistler would turn in a different direction with a quick leap. It was almost as if it could read his mind, but so far as he knew, they had seen no clues that the Whistlers were able to do this.

After about five minutes of constant running, Felix found himself getting a stitch in his side and realized he was much more pooped than he had thought. He wasn't too far behind it now, though, and giving up at this point was out of the question.

He saw the Whistler turn a corner around the edge of a building, and when Felix followed him, the Whistler was gone. Felix stopped to listen for footprints and to catch his breath. He heard nothing. He thought the damn critter has stopped. And it was waiting for him to go charging right into it.

"So... I think I'll just stand right here and wait for the sound that it's eventually going to make," he thought. Quiet. Very quiet. He could hear the crickets chirping their nightime song, he could hear a bird chirping overhead as it winged its way across the sky in search of its next meal.

Of the Whistler, he heard nothing.

The sky back in the east was starting to lighten up just a bit. Early morn was not that far off. "Something has to happen before the sun comes out," thought Felix. "He won't want to be around when the sun comes up."

As he stood there, alone, he felt that feeling coming over him that happened when his trance was approaching. "Oh God! Not now, please!" He felt himself slipping away... slipping... and then...

He was gone.

The Whistler was watching. Just as Felix had thought, these creatures could not read minds. There were other beings on their plane of existence that could accomplish this trick, but the Thingies were not one of them. But what HE could do was blend. They had the ability to shade themselves to match their background. It wasn't true coloration, but a lightening or darkening of pigment to help them blend, the way their shape-shifting let them camouflage themselves. That's why the human hadn't seen him.

Ol' Whistler had been frightened. This was a new feeling for him. His race could feel each other's death, and so HE knew that at least two of his team members had already been eliminated. This was not something that HE had dealt with before. Their people had a very long life span, and from time to time, they had crossed over to many different dimensions to conquer other life forms before. His people were always waiting for the wrinkle in the dimensional door and it always happened. Sometimes not for hundreds of years... sometimes longer... but it always happened, again and again. If they could get enough of their people through the wrinkle into the new world before the door closed, they could start new civilizations of themselves. Then, it was just a question of conquering the local dominate species and finding a food source. Sometimes, as now, the two proved to be the same thing.

The problem here was the food was putting up a terrible fight. This frightened the Whistlers. Food wasn't supposed to fight back. And now, besides this terrible "sun" as they called the horrible thing in their skies, the humans seemed to be able to carry this sun in a box and could shoot it out to destroy his people.

"Unheard of," HE thought. "This was not the way food should act."

HE saw the "Felix" creature looking for him, looking right at him, but not seeing. HE was getting extremely worried right about now, mostly because of the terrible fiery thing in the sky getting closer and closer to appearing again, and with the death of two of his team that left only HE and one other at this location. One way or another, HE could not be out here when this sun thing appeared again.

This would all have been much more simple if only the Flae had minded their own business. They had talked to the Sarah human and then he had failed to execute her before the information got around to other humans. One day, the Flae will pay for their insolence.

Since being on this planet, HE had discovered many useful tools to inform HE and his people of the lifestyles of these life forms. Libraries were very good but open mainly when the sun was around, which was not good for HE. Computers and the Internet had much promise, but took skills that HE had yet to master. But then HE had discovered television. One could view this in the darkness they loved and it contained many,

many interesting facts about the humans. They had a soap, which made "whites whiter and colors brighter." Then, they had a musical show with people screaming at each other while crying and killing one another called an "opera." And then they had another show, and in this one, humans did nothing except mate and talk a lot and they called this one a "soap opera." And there was no cleaning or no singing, as they called it on this show, which was very confusing to HE. And besides the humans not liking his race, they didn't seem to like each other very much either. Not only did they seem to object to each other because of where each other lived, but they disliked each other because of the coloration of their skins. This surprised him to no end, mainly because HE could almost instantly change his covering color, and for this to be a factor for any being to kill another made no sense whatsoever. AND after killing the other "off-color human," they just wasted the food.

While studying this television device, HE had learned two interesting things, though. HE began to study things called volcanoes. And tectonic plates. And... poisonous ash... and dust... and climate change And his favorite – volcanic eruptions dimming the terrible sun. This was it. Their way in. If they could block the sun, then not only would humans die, but his people would thrive. On something they called "PBS," HE came upon a thing called "fault lines." These were going to be very important to his people because they could crack the planet. This could start a... cake? Shake? No, it was QUAKE. When the planet cracked, the hot insides would come out of the holes in the planet and these holes were big. These holes were tall. And humans called them "volcanoes."

"My people will like that," HE thought.

The second thing that HE had discovered was another race on this planet similar to his. They, too, were disliked by humans. They, too, only went out by night... or at least away from the sun. They, too, realized that the humans here were food. They feasted nightly. HE made a note to look up these... "vampires."

As HE stood there looking at the Felix human, Felix looked around with a strange expression on his face. His eyes rolled up in his head and Felix went away. The human body remained, but all thought was gone.

Ol' Whistler studied this. "Hmmmm. Interesting. He's either pretending to be disabled, so I will rush in and try to subdue him at which time he will turn on his sun box and destroy me... or he has crossed over. If so, he is learning, maybe from the Flae, which is bad for us, but he is also vulnerable right now.

"Hmmmm. If I attack... I may get him, I may not. I may die. If I choose to leave now while I can get away, he still lives, but, so do I. "Hmmmm.

What to do?"

Right about then, the terrible, terrible "sun" started to show its hideous face on the horizon.

His decision was made.

Felix was saved by the sun.

28
The Greatest Gift

Robert stopped screaming and started thinking. "It's gonna be up to this dude to save your life tonight. No kiddin'." That's what Felix had said to Sarah earlier in the night. The way Robert figured, if you believed anything that Felix said, ya had to believe everything.

So be it.

Sarah had taken up the thick cable in her bare hands and had touched it to Gill's chest. As Robert had started to scream, she had talked to the machine, and at first, a few lights popped on, then a humming in the transformer kicked in, and then, as he watched in horror, sparks arched along the non-insulated cable through Sarah and into Gill's small body. As soon as the power hit him, Gill leapt about a foot off of the ground, horizontally, fell back to Earth and then the cable snaked away from him.

Robert smelled something burning and he knew it was Sarah.

The cable was now safely away from Gill's body, and Robert thought he heard Gill quietly moan, but Sarah was glued to the powerful current and was unable to release her grip. "What to do?" thought Robert. "If I try to pull her away, it'll just grab us both! That's no good! What to do?"

It was like a slap in the face as he remembered ol' Felix and the "stupid" rubber-soled shoes and the "stupid" squeege stick and the "stupid" rubber hose.

"Damn!" he thought as he raced around Sarah to jerk the hose up off of the ground. "Never again, my friend! Never again will I doubt you!"

Gill was starting to stir, and Robert was getting tears in his eyes as he took the rubber hose, with one end still attached to the wooden handle and the other attached to the other end to the wood. He now had a loop of rubber hose and wooden stick, which wouldn't conduct electricity as a handle and rubber-soled shoes. He quickly ran over to Sarah, looped the contraption over her head and around her body and pulled.

POW!

The electricity snapped, crackled and popped as it lost contact with poor Sarah. She sailed through the air like she'd been shot out of a cannon and Robert was still attached to her. They landed in a heap off to the side of the asphalt with Robert breaking her fall. It had seemed like minutes had fled since she had been shocked, but it had all actually happened in mere seconds. Even in that short amount of time, however, she had badly burned her tiny hands into large burns and blisters and it appeared that she was no longer breathing.

"What happened to Sarah?" Gill was sitting up, but was still wobbly and had no idea of what had happened. He tried to stand, but quickly decided that that was a bad idea. "Is she OK, Robert?"

Robert shook his head as he laid her on her back, tilted back her head and started CPR in order to try and save the woman whom he didn't even know two days ago but was now hopelessly in love with. He pumped her chest with his mighty hands three or four times, then placed his lips upon hers as he passed his breath into her.

Nothing.

Again. Pump, pump, pump, pump. Mouth to mouth. Lip to lip. More breath. "Breathe, damn it!"

Maybe, something... maybe.

Again. Pump, pump, pump. When he pressed his lips to hers this time, she kissed him back.

As Robert continued the kiss, he began to cry. Sarah opened her eyes to look into his and she smiled. When the kiss broke, she whispered to him, "Don't cry, Ert. I didn't think I was that bad of a kisser."

He smiled, looked into her soft eyes and said, "Don't you ever... ever... leave me again. Promise?"

She nodded to him and then laughed when she saw little Gill crawling over to her. "So, you're back, too?" she said with a smile.

Gill looked at her poor burned hands and slowly shook his head. "Sarah, I don't know what to say. You gave me back... my life! I can never... never... er..."

"Don't think about it, boss. If you'll buy me two cheeseburgers, we'll call it even. I'm starving."

They all laughed... as they all cried.

Sarah tried to sit up, but realized she couldn't put any weight on her hands to push herself upright. "Ouch!" said the heroine of the day. "Ah, Ert, can you give me a hand? I think I kinda screwed mine up for awhile."

Robert gently picked her up in his arms and started to carry her away from there. Sarah smiled at him and said, "Hey sweetie, my legs are just fine. I can walk, ya know. By the way, where is the matchstick man?"

That's when both Robert and Gill looked at each other, and Robert, being the only one who knew that Felix ran off after a Whistler by himself, realized that Felix wasn't back with them yet. He explained to both friends what had happened during their "time away." Sarah started frantically looking around. "We gotta go find him, guys. That big baby's gonna get into trouble, working alone like that. We're a team, right?"

Gill and Robert looked at each other with a smile on their faces, and then at the same time both turned to Sarah. "Right!" They all went into the complex once again, looking for their tall friend.

They found him soon afterward... 162 trance-induced face lit by the morning sunrise and a great big smile on his face.

29
Ha Ha Ha Ha Ha

Felix woke up with a laugh.

"Man! What a cool flash, dude!"

He looked around him for the Whistler he had left on hold when he checked out. Nothing. No Whistler. But many friends around him. They were lookin' at him with strange amazement, joy, surprise and some worry.

"Dudes and dudette! Y'all are OK! Gill, lil' dude! You're back! Very cool! What's been goin' on?"

"Let's tell him as we walk our way out of here," said Sarah. "Power's coming back online except where the damage is and we can check for the remaining Whistlers as we go. And I'm still hungry. And Gill owes me cheeseburgers!"

"Lucky dudette!" said Felix.

"Cheeseburgers for everybody on me!" said Gill.

"Way cool, dude!" Felix was still smiling.

It took four or five minutes to tell Felix the whole story. In the process, Sarah, Gill and Robert all heard stuff from one of the others that they hadn't known before. Before too long, everyone knew just about what had happened to each other except for the story of Felix's adventure. By now, they had traveled the length of the complex and no Whistlers were to be found.

"I coulda told y'all that," Felix quietly added. "It was in the message. They can't handle the sun here."

Gill looked up to the face of his giant friend and said, "Message?"

"Yeah, lil' dude! By the way that Gin dude is way cool, man! Reminds me of me! Knows stuff. Y'all ready to go to Yellowstone?"

All three friends stopped, looked at Felix, their faces visibly tired, and at the same instant, they all yelled, "YELLOWSTONE?"

"OK, listen here now, oh Mighty Head-In-The-Clouds!" Sarah had a very serious look on her face.

"Yellowstone now? No! No!... No No No No No No No!"

"Look at me! OK? Are ya lookin'? OK, WATCH MY LIPS! Y-e-l-l-o-w-s-t-o-n-e... ah, no! C-H-E-E-S-E-B-U-R-G-E-R-S... ah, yes! Doesn't that sound much better! OK, let's all say it together now!"

"Yellowstone... no! Cheeseburgers... YES!"

They all just stared at her for about a minute and then all burst out laughing.

Gill put his arms around her. "OK, Sarah. Many, many, many cheeseburgers! But, let's either do 'em to go or order 'em to my house. We gotta lot to talk about. Cool?"

Sarah wiped away a tear that was rolling down her face. "OK, lil' one. I need to talk to MAX, anyway. But lotsa cheese?"

Gill smiled. "Lotsa cheese, baby girl... lotsa cheese."

She hugged him as hard as she could, then held onto his shirt while she pushed him away from her so that she could look directly into his eyes and said, "Gill, I... I really... really... need a raise!"

"Done, beautiful lady," Gill said with a smile. "Done."

As they all neared the original location of their entrance into this electrical madhouse, they heard sirens in the distance, coming closer and closer. Well, it was bound to happen when you shut down the power to greater Southern California. Now what to do?

"Maybe we should wait for them and tell 'em what's been happening," Sarah said. Even as she said it, she knew that this idea would not work! "Ahh... erase that plan," she laughed as she saw Robert and Gill glance at each other with a smile.

Ert took her hand and looked deep into her eyes as he told her, "Sarah, Gill and I have been doing this 'rescue' business for several years now and talking to the local authorities about some of the weirdness we get involved in never works. Either they think you are crazy as a bedbug and then try to lock you up or else they think that you are somehow the perpetrator of the problem, trying to lay the blame on someone or something else and once again, they try to lock you up. It's a no-win situation any way you go."

"Ert, one day before too awful long, I'd really like for you to talk to me about this 'rescue' deal, since I suddenly seemed to have been thrust right into the middle of it all! You still owe me an explanation about a Mexican boy from last week, too," Sarah added.

"Wow, dude! Count me in on the fill-in deal with the rescue info... cool?" Felix was grinnin' like a butcher's dog.

Gill smiled at Sarah as he whispered, "We need to go, girl. Before those sirens can reach us, we need to be gone. We'll talk about this later, OK? Ahh, and Robert, I still need to hear about Juanito and the Dallas trip myself."

Robert nodded to Gill.

Sarah smiled as Felix chimed in, "Yeah, dudette-type person. I always found that the best time to talk to the police is usually later." Everyone laughed as they ran toward the exit. "And besides me having to tell Gill about his new power, the main thing we need to be concentrating on is...?"

Everyone, at the same time said, "CHEESEBURGERS!"

More laughing.

And then Gill slowed down from his run, looked up at Felix and squeaked out, "Power? New Power?! Hey, what the hell, Felix?"

"Oh wow, lil' dude! Your gonna love MindSpeak! Do you know a Godfrey? Gwen said you didn't. And... ahh... I need to talk to you later about this Gin dude. Told me some neat stuff! Need to tell you later! Cool?"

Gill smiled at the giant "dude" in front of him and said, "Yeah, buddy, later sounds good. Let's go."

As he ran, though, Gill was heard yelling, "MindSpeak??!!"

30
MindSpeak

By the time they had reached Gill's van, they could not only hear the approaching sirens, but they could now see the flashing red and blue lights in the distance headed in their direction at breakneck speed. Time was running out and their chances of escape were quickly closing.

"Quick, everyone into the van!" Gill said. "I'll drive. I know this van better than anyone, and if anyone can find a way outta here, I'll be the one to find it!"

"Answer the phone," Felix said quietly as he hopped into the back end with Sarah.

"What phone?" Sarah said as she slid into the rear seat.

"RING...RING...RING," Gill's cell phone called out. Gill shook his head as he looked at Felix weirdly and then answered it as he cranked up the engine, "Kinda busy right now," he said into the phone speaker he had turned on in the vehicle.

"Hi Gill, it's MAX here!"

"Kinda busy, MAX!"

"Yeah, I know. Listen close. They're too near to you for you to get away without being seen. I'm watching you through an orbiting camera a couple of miles above your head. Turn to your left right now and follow the fence line to a grove of trees about a half-mile from where you are now. Wait in those trees for five minutes or so until I call back, then drive quick for the highway!"

"MAX, there's no road to my left, only a field!" Gill said in a shaky voice as he cranked up the van and headed across the bumpy ground.

"That's all you got to work with, people. Strap in tight and hold on! Oh, and Killer sends his love. Hi, Sarah!"

"Hi MAX," she said as they bounced over the rough terrain in the bright purple van. "Kinda busy here."

"Yes, so I hear. I'll sign off for now, but will monitor your flight from incarceration. Bye!"

Felix smiled. "Will monitor your flight from incarceration! Ha Ha Ha Ha! Ain't that nice? That's real nice. And ya say this dude is electrical, huh?"

Sarah smiled at the giant "dude" as his head hit the ceiling, caused by a large hole in the ground outside making the van bottom out.

"I hope she can take it," Sarah yelled up to Gill.

"Helen can take it just fine. I just hope we can take it," Gill said with a smile.

Sarah gave out with a laugh as they all bounced out of their seats again. "Helen? Your van is a female and you named it Helen? That's soooo cute," she said with a giggle.

"Actually, she's called 'Van Helen.' How's that for cute?"

When they finally arrived at the small grove of trees, they could then see what MAX had been talking about. It was a natural shaped band of trees, but there was a gap facing them as the van barreled toward this sanctuary. It was just wide enough for Gill to zoom through without taking his foot off the gas until the very last second... when he suddenly slammed on the brakes and turned a hard left on the steering wheel, slamming everyone hard against the walls of the van as the van slid into a one-eighty-degree turn and zoomed at high speed into the narrow gap of forest... completely backwards! As soon as he cleared the entrance, he glanced into his rearview mirror to see what was now in front of him. Sarah placed her hand on the side of the faithful ol' van in case her abilities were gonna be needed to help. (She thought she heard the van purr when she touched it.) Gill pumped his brakes once, he pumped his brakes twice, and then he stood on them.

"Screeeeeeech!" The van lurched to a stop so quickly that everyone, including Ert, and even poor little Gill, was tossed into the backseat of the vehicle, which now sat perfectly still and quiet and was purring.

"Hahaha!" Sarah was still petting the van... and Felix was laughing so hard that he was fit to be tied. "Gill, I think ya should call her 'Van Hellion', dude!"

As Sarah thought about their situation, she quietly stopped the van with but a thought.

Gill just looked at her and smiled as he whispered, "Wow!"

"Raise?" she said with a smile.

"Raise," he said with a smile.

The canopy of trees overhead and all around them blocked the view of the van from above and below. Just for a moment, they could all hear the roar of a helicopter as it passed almost directly overhead en route to where the incident had originally taken place. It didn't even slow down.

Gill had been thrown into Felix's lap in the back seat and as he struggled to free himself from the tangle of folks back here, he realized that

Felix was sort of gone again. "Man!" said Gill. "I can see how maybe that might get to be a hassle after awhile!"

RING... RING... RING...

Sarah's and Gill's phones both rang at the same time.

"Hello?... (Hello?)..."

"Many hellos to you, Sarah and Gill," MAX said. "I'm still watching the adventure for you from the skies. You're safe there for a few minutes. I'll signal you when you should vacate the premises. By the way, there is a hermit's nest that's been stirred up from your last location."

Sarah laughed and said, "I think that you mean a hornet's nest, MAX, but that's for the info."

"Hornet's nest. Got it. Police and emergency vehicles are everywhere."

"Vacate the premises," said Felix with a sigh as he came back into reality. "That boy's got a real way with the spoken word. Ahh, Gill... dude?"

Gill had extracted himself to the front seat again. "Yeah, Felix?"

"Ahh... why all the spinnin' 'round, dude? You did it real pretty-like, but... ahhh... why did ya do it real pretty-like?"

"I had a feeling. I flashed out that we might not be able to turn around once we got in here and backing out might take too long if we're in a hurry."

Robert smiled as he struggled to get back to the front seat again. "He gets these 'flashes' pretty often, guys."

Felix raised his long arms to wave back and forth as he said, "Hey folks, some of my best times are spent in flashes! Ugh... Gill... it's 'later' now."

Gill smiled at the incoherent language his new friend had a way of sending. "OK, large guy, we've got a few minutes. Whip some knowledge on me."

"Yo, dude, knowledge comin' up! Yo, MAX, are ya here?"

"Affirmative, Mister Felix. Both Killer and I are listening to your conversation, so I guess that's a... 'yo-yo', dude."

"Yo-yo! I get it. But... ahhh... Killer?"

"It's a long story, Felix," said Gill. "Just get on with your info, cool? Dude?"

"Way cool, Gillmeister!"

Felix stretched as much as possible in the restricted space that the van provided. "Gill, I could sit here for two hours and never be able to tell you even half of what this Gwen person told me. So, what I wanna do is to brief you on the basics of what I was told and let you check in with Gwen to get the whole scoop. She can relay a ton of info to you when the time it would take me would be all day to do the same thing. THAT is basically what they're giving you, lil' buddy! You already have the ability to speak to

Gwen and her folks and can carry on hours of conversations with her in mere seconds. Now you can do that with us, too. MindSpeak!"

"Ahh... I don't understand, Felix" Gill whispered.

"OK... ahhh... tell ya what... everyone here hold hands to form a circle. Gill, I want you to think who this 'Killer' person is. Don't concentrate too hard 'cause it could fry us all. Just hold hands and think of 'Killer' for me. OK?"

Gill joined hands with his friends. For just an instant, he could almost feel a spark like he had never known before as he touched hands with Sarah and Felix... as everyone touched hands with the people next to them.

"KILLER!"

"WOW, dude! Turn it down! Don't do it like you're yellin', man! Do it like you're... dreamin'."

"Sorry."

"KILLER," he thought. "My best friend in the animal world, not including Robert, that is... Haha... How to describe..."

BAM!

He fell back as everyone reeled back from the MindSpeak he had thrust upon them without knowing the strength he now had.

"Damn it, Gill! Ya tryin' to fry my guts? Be gentle, man! Think easy," Robert said with a moan. "And what's up with this 'not including Robert' thing, huh?"

Everyone laughed as Gill asked, "You heard that? You all heard that?"

"Hell, dude!" said Felix, "they probably heard that in Fresno!"

"Sorry again!"

This time, as he looked at his friends watching him, he didn't try to think.

He just... thought.

The time was about four years ago. He had been working on his new houses for some time now. He was riding on a small motor bike he kept at the cave-like entrance to the wooded section of his joined homes. He used this bike to drive the long distance back and forth from his doorway to the mailbox he kept at the side of the road next to the driveway entrance far away. He knew that he could have put the box back closer to the house, but he didn't really want the mail folks to see his "secret" hideout and besides, he liked getting out on a nice day with just him and the put-put-puttin' of the little bike.

He had thought of buying a large and powerful bike like the ones he always saw on movies and television, and he could well afford it, but when he tried one out, he thought his small size made him look silly on the giant monster of a machine. "I look like a monkey riding an elephant," he had thought. "No, this little bike is just fine for me," he said to himself as he pulled up to the four-by-four post that supported the large mailbox he had installed by the road in front of his property.

As he dismounted to open his box and collect his post for the day, he noticed that someone had once again been throwing litter on the roadside that bordered his property. He hated that.

"Why? Why do people turn this beautiful country into a garbage dump just so they don't have to wait until they can find a trash can?" He didn't understand that kind of reasoning. A large black plastic garbage bag like they used for lawn waste was lying in the drainage ditch next to his mailbox. "Oh well," he thought as he headed over to pick the ugly thing up. "I'll just do it myself. The city might never get out here to clean this crap up."

As he bent down to remove the large bag, it kind of... whimpered!

There's something in there! Something alive! Trapped inside of that damn plastic bag! Now he was really mad!

"DAMN!" he said out loud to himself. "What kind of monster would trap some poor animal in a damn trash bag with no air?"

Another whimper.

Without any fear as to what kind of beast this bag might contain, he quickly ripped open the side of the plastic prison, and inside, he found a mouse? No, a baby... what? What was this tiny thing? As he gently held the small creature in his tiny hands, it slowly opened its eyes, which were the only thing on it that weren't solid black.

Gill could almost swear that it smiled at him.

He raised the small handful of puppy to his face with giant tears rolling down his cheeks and the puppy stopped whimpering. A small pink tongue came slowly out of its mouth and kissed him.

"Hi, Killer. You come on with me. You're home now."

"Yipe, yipe," his new friend said as they mounted the bike together. Gill placed the small creature in his shirt pocket. "A perfect fit, Killer. You and I can be small... together. Come on, now. I'll show you your new home."

"Yipe," the small pup said as they putted down the road and to the safety of home.

It wasn't until hours later that Gill remembered that he had forgotten the mail.

Gill opened his eyes and realized he was back in his van.

All of his human friends were there, too.

They were all crying.

"Wow, dude. Remembered that you'd forgotten! I like that. I like that a lot. I just gotta meet this Killer dude, dude!"

"And you will, my extra-large new friend. You will."

Sarah went to the front of the van and very gently placed a kiss on Gill's cheek as a tear rolled off of her own. "That was beautiful, boss. That was beautiful."

"So you all heard that?" he asked. "How long did that take, anyway? It seemed like an hour passed us by."

Robert looked at his watch. "About ten seconds, my friend. And Sarah's right... that was really... somethin'. How come you've never told me that story before, Gill?"

"I guess it just... never came up. And somehow the 'thinking' of it made it feel much more important than just... the telling of it."

Felix smiled. "The MindSpeak, Gill dude. That's part of it. You can tell things... stories... in a flash... and the effect it has on your audience is heavy! But you can't lie with MindSpeak. Even to your enemies... and I have a feelin' that we've got quite a few of those now! You can persuade almost anyone to your point of view with the right thoughts... 'Thought Emotion' it's called... but ya can't lie to 'em. And when you're done, you kinda get a craving, a hunger, that needs to be filled as soon as possible. And ya know what it's a hunger for?"

Everyone looked at Gill as though he might be a vampire craving blood or something.

Gill got a big ol' smile on his face and said, "Chocolate!"

Everyone started laughing!

"Hey, it's not funny! I'll bet I could eat a hundred candy bars right about now!"

About then MAX piped in on the speakers. "Ah... Mr. Gill?"

"Yes, MAX."

"It's time to come home."

Everyone quieted down as they quickly drove out of the tree line, which had saved their skins. According to MAX, their best bet was to drive due east across the low hills for about three or four miles until they reached a service road. They should miss all of the patrol officers by this time, and they could then ease back onto the interstate.

This sounded much easier than it turned out to be because of the rough terrain involved, but after tacking back and forth along the hills to avoid cracks and gullies, they made the four mile trip in about forty-five minutes. They could see the flashing red and blue lights of the police cars from where they entered the service road, but it was farther to the west of them and they managed to get on the highway without any further incident.

When they were about two miles down the road, Gill pulled into a convenience store and stopped quickly next to a gas pump with a screech of the tires. "Robert, if you will, pump the gas for me while I go pay for a fill-up and find some damn chocolate!"

Sarah giggled.

"You'd better watch that, dudette! You haven't got that raise yet!" Felix snickered.

Gill ran as fast as he could for the door of the station. He went to the cashier and threw a credit card down onto the counter. "I need to fill up that van out there on pump three and charge me for Hershey's chocolate bars, too."

"How many chocolate bars, sir?" asked the young woman cashier.

"All of them!" Gill said with a smile.

Gill walked out to the van with four large stuffed plastic bags and a large grin. The others noticed he also had a dark chocolate mustache!

"Well, that's $43 dollars for gas and $276 dollars for candy! What a day, huh?"

Everyone cracked up in laughter.

"I hope you've got a cheeseburger in there somewhere," Sarah said with a smile.

"Nope, but we're headed to my place now and there's plenty of stuff for cheeseburgers there. My treat!"

The applause was deafening.

31
Super Dude

After all of the excitement of the last few hours, the ride home was a breeze, a beautiful California morning. Big fluffy clouds, cooling down the temperature with their blessed cover. A forecast of cleansing rains coming to clear out all of the strangling smog, if only for a little while. Not one police officer, not one explosion, and not one whistle.

Sometimes life was good. This was such a day.

When they arrived at the driveway entrance to Gill's home, Felix was all "oohs" and "ahhs" for the long trip down the drive to the house.

"If you think this is something, just wait until you see his house... or houses, Felix," Sarah said with a smile. "Like nothing you've ever seen. As a matter of fact, I've only seen a little bit of it myself!"

They pulled around to the hillside entrance. The sight of the little cottage got Felix giggling again.

"Ah, dude, when does Snow White show up? Does Dumpy and Slappy and Dimbo and Shoopy and Drugie and Bleetle all live here with ya? Do ya ever have trouble with witches and poison apples?"

Robert looked at the blue-haired giant of a man grinning. "Sometimes, my friend, great, great things come hidden in very, very small packages."

As they all stepped out into the yard, Gill whistled a little tune, which turned on the exterior lights, even though it was broad daylight, but also shut down the security alarms. "Don't wanna scare Killer."

"Hey dude, isn't that some kinda zen joke? You know! Kinda like... how do you scare a killer? Just whistle a lil' tune! Haha!"

Sarah groaned. "Enough jokes about whistling! Think... about... CHEESEBURGERS!"

"Got it, lil' dudette!"

Gill pressed his hand against the palm scanner and the back door popped open. "Since all of this crap is going on," Gill said, "it might be a good idea for me to program all of your palm prints into my scanner. Ya never can tell."

Just as Felix was about to say something funny, someone hit him right in the chest with a black furry snowball!

"YIPE!" said the snowball.

"Waaaaay cool, lil' dude! You must be that Killer Dog Dude! Awful glad to meet cha! Wanna cheeseburger?!"

"Yipe... yipe!" the small creature said as it licked its newest giant friend with a small pink tongue.

Sarah yawned as she waked through the front part of Gill's house. "What day is this? I've lost track of the days of the week here very recently. Let's see, I got off work on Friday and went to the hospital after the shooting and the wreck, then I came here to the clothes warehouse after Robert kicked the Whistler... and then I slept after the star show... with dreams of volcanoes... and then..."

"Hold on... hold on there, lil' dudette," Felix said with his new little buddy licking his face. "Y'all have lost me big time in this whole conversation, and I have no clue as to what you're a talkin' about, but it's Sunday."

Sarah smiled. "Thanks, dude."

It wasn't long before the smell of cooking meat permeated the entire kitchen. Sarah was slicing lettuce, onions and tomatoes, Robert was toasting (more like burning) some buns, and Gill was running between two large stovetops, whipping up a mess of cheeseburgers on one and cooking up about five pounds of bacon on the other. In the next room, they could hear MAX yelling at Killer about not presenting him with "any more sauteed hogs, thank you very much."

Felix, for once in his life, was speechless. He just wandered around the halls with Killer as his guide and his mouth wide open, staring in amazement at this gigantic, spread-out sanctuary of Gill's. From the kitchen, everyone would chuckle as they heard far-off exclamations of "Oh, wow!" and "My God!" and "Y'all gotta be kiddin'!" coming from what sounded like a hundred yards away.

"Sounds like he found a swimming pool," Gill said with a smile as they all heard a "Yipe," followed by a terrific splash.

Sarah turned to Gill. "A swimming pool? I musta missed that. Didn't know there was a pool here or I'd have been in that sucker long ago!"

Gill smiled and said, "Let's wait until after we eat, then we can all hit the pool and cool off and relax a little while we talk and plan our next move. Maybe a drinky-poo to settle our minds, too."

Robert yelled over from burning another bun. "Yeah! Lots of drinkies and very little poo, thank you very much," as he coughed from all of the smoke he'd made.

Suddenly, everyone couldn't help from laughing when a totally soaked Felix sloshed into the kitchen with his clothes drenched and his blue hair dangling down like a wet mop. "Funny critter ya got there, Gillmeister! He pushed me into your lake! Sorry about the floors," he said as he realized how much of the water he'd brought with him.

Sarah smiled and said, "Ahh... lake? Felix, I'm all done cutting up our veggies here, so why don't I... with Gill's permission, that is... show you to the department store down the hall. I'm pretty sure we can find something dry in your size somewhere there. OK, Gill?"

Gill smiled. "Yeah, go for it, dude and dudette! But hurry back... 'cause the food's almost ready, and a good chef won't serve you cold grub!"

As they disappeared down the hallway, Gill and Robert snickered as they first heard Felix ask, "A department store?" followed in a few moments by, "Ah, hell no! Now I know that ya gotta be kiddin'!"

Gill and Robert hauled the burgers, crispy bacon, sliced veggies, cheese, drinks and slightly overdone buns into the dining area next to the kitchen. As they were setting up the plate and silverware service, in walked Sarah with a big smile on her face and a snicker coming out of her mouth.

"Ah, Gill? Was it OK for me to let Felix pick whatever he wanted out of your clothes room? He kinda picked it out for himself and I just couldn't say no to him. He was just so freaked when he found this outfit in his size. Now don't laugh! OK? Promise?"

Robert and Gill looked at each other smiling and together they both said, "Oh yeah, we promise! Sure! Uh huh! Right!"

Next thing you knew, they both fell out of their chairs almost breathlessly choking with laughter as Felix waltzed into the dining room. Robert finally caught his breath first and managed to blurt out, "SUPER DUDE!"

The bright blue hair on Felix's head was now dry and stood up about a foot off his already incredibly tall frame. He was wearing a pair of blue leather pants that matched his hair color almost exactly. His shirt was a tight-fitting spandex sort of sleeveless T-shirt, which was white with red stripes. The belt he wore was cinched by a large star-shaped silver buckle. A stranger looking super hero never graced the pages of any comic book. He looked like a walking flag.

Robert was cracking up as he said, "Hey, Super Dude, couldn't you find the capes?"

Felix looked up. "We got capes?"

Gill pushed himself off the floor and slowly walked over to Felix, who was now blushing with embarrassment. Gill put his small hand on the arm of the colorful giant and quietly said, "Dude, you look incredible."

"Thanks, man. I saw it layin' there and just couldn't pass it up! I'll pay ya whatever ya want for the outfit, but I'd really, really..." he said in a whisper, "like to keep it. Cool?"

"It's yours for nothing, Felix, on one condition."

"What's that, Gill?" he asked with a smile.

"After we finish eating here, you and I are gonna go pick out a couple of more, let's say... less conspicuous types of clothing. You can't be Super Dude all of the time, right?"

Felix smiled and then bent down to give Gill a big hug. "Right, Gillmeister. And... thanks, man. For everything, ya know?"

"Yeah, I know. Are ya hungry?"

"Starved, dude!"

"Well, let's all sit down and eat then!"

"Hey, dude, I kinda promised Killer that... ahh... I would... ahh..."

"Yeah, I know. He's got a burger of his own... right here."

"YIPE!" said the smallest member of this new and unusual family.

As they were sitting down to eat, Felix looked over at Robert, who was staring at Felix with a smile. "Ah... Bobby? Is there really... capes?"

Nothing else was said for the next half hour except for, "Pass this..." or "Pass that," or "Yipe!"

Life was good.

About an hour after mealtime, they all made drinks and wandered down a long hallway to a large metal door. Gill pushed open the entrance to what looked like an underground lake.

"I had this built by some friends of mine when I was excavating the hillside. It's about 30 feet deep in the middle, and the sides are all lined with fieldstone I had brought in," Gill said. "It's about the size of a football field. That room over there has swimsuits of all sizes and changing rooms. The place is lit up from the ceiling and below water. Robert will show you around, Sarah, while 'dude' and I go in search of clothing that doesn't look like..." he looked at Felix with a smile, "Well, like that!"

As Gill and Felix were headed out the door for, as Felix put it, "Clothes World," Robert and Sarah walked over to where there was a locker room full of different styles, sizes and colors of swimsuits and about a ton of bath and beach towels. At the back of this large area was a half dozen changing rooms for suiting up.

"Pick yourself out a suit and grab a towel. I'll meet you out by the raft," Robert said to Sarah.

"Raft?"

"Yeah, it's one of those ol' timey Huckleberry Hound kinda jobs that Gill had made special for floatin'."

"I think you mean Huck Finn, but I got the idea. Sounds like fun, and I could use a little of that right about now."

Sarah grabbed up a one-piece turquoise-colored suit and headed off to change. Robert had been here so often that he had his own suit handy, so he quickly slipped it on, grabbed two large beach towels, and then opened up a locker to sneak out a bottle of chilled Champagne and a couple of glasses he had stashed here earlier when he had found out Sarah wanted to go for a swim. He stuck these into a small cooler filled with ice, along with about a dozen fresh strawberries. Out he ran so that he could situate everything before Sarah appeared.

Robert was standing on the raft when Sarah came out of the dressing room area... looking like a goddess. He was so caught up in staring at her beautiful body, her long blond hair and the sly grin on her face as she watched him watching her, he slipped off of the edge of the raft and hit the water flat on his back.

SPLASH!

As he surfaced, he heard her laughing at him as she whispered in a sexy voice, "What's the matter, Ert? Cat got your tongue?"

"Yeah," he said. "And my heart."

Gill led Felix through the massive warehouse-like room where all of the clothing for all of his department stores was stockpiled. They picked out shirts, slacks, jeans, T-shirts and a mess of weird stuff that Felix said, "he just couldn't do without!"

"Felix, it's the middle of summer in Los Angeles. It gets up to a hundred and five degrees outside! What the heck do you need a seven-foot black leather trench coat for?"

"Two things, lil' dude. Number one, it'll hide my Super Dude outfit from the bad guys until I can spring it on 'em! And number two... ahhh... it just looks cool."

Gill laughed as he said, "OK, buddy, it's yours, no problem. But NO to the stovepipe hat that you found in the costume section! Damn thing makes you look ten feet tall!"

"Yeah, it does make it kinda hard to get through doorways in a hurry."

Gill smiled as he gently placed his hand on the arm of the giant man. "Felix, you're just... ahhh... how can I put this? You're just not all there, are you?"

The blue-haired giant raised his head back as he laughed," Hell, no! Never have been, never wanted to be!"

Gill slowly shook his head. "I think I've created a monster."

32
On the Wings of a Thought

Robert hoisted himself out of the water while Sarah was on shore giggling.

"Hey, Ert. I like the whole raft deal that you got goin' on here, but I thought we were going for a swim," Sarah quietly said. "I guess you just did!"

"Yeah, but I've got a little surprise for later, and I thought we'd swim together when we get to the island. It would be kinda hard swimming all of the way out there with this stupid cooler."

"Cooler? Wait a second... did you say... island?

"Yep. Check it out," he said as he pointed toward the center of this large body of water. "Gill calls it 'No One.' He says he goes there to be by himself sometimes, ya know, with no one around. I always laugh at the thought of 'No one is an island.'"

Robert stepped off the raft for a moment, walked over to a wall next to Sarah and flicked a switch.

"Oh, my God!" she whispered.

The ceiling of the pool area dimly lit up to show that the ceiling was sculpted in stalactites a hundred feet above their heads. Small lights shown down on the waters, looking like stars glittering overhead.

"It's beautiful," she said as Robert re-entered the small craft and picked up an oar.

"Argh, Captain Ert, at your service, ma'am! We'll be weighin' anchor soon. Will ye be boardin' now?" he said with a smile.

"Aye, aye" she said with a smile. "Will it be a long voyage, captain?"

"Depends on the sea and the wind, ma'am. Depends on the sea and the wind."

She stepped aboard the small raft and found a floatation cushion to sit on. Robert slowly pushed the raft away from the shoreline. He carefully paddled the craft in the calm waters toward the island – now quite visible in the store-bought starlight.

"It's beautiful," she said again.

A few minutes later, he beached the homemade raft on the shore of the small island. It had a good-sized beach on one side of it, and it was this location that Robert made his destination. The quiet whisper of small waves lapping on the shoreline kinda surprised Sarah. "Waves?" she asked.

"Yeah, ol' Gill had a wave machine installed when he built this place. He always keeps it on low because he likes the noise they make."

"That's not noise, Ert. It's more like music."

Robert unrolled the large beach towels on the fine sand beach and then popped open the small cooler he had brought. After a couple of glasses of bubbly and a strawberry or two, they both slipped into the cool waters to wash away all of the troubles and pains of the day. They talked long and slowly as they paddled around the small island, trying to better know what made each other tick.

Sarah was floating on her back when she asked, "Robert, can I ask you a question?"

"At this point, m'lady, I feel it's safe to say that you could ask me almost anything."

"Almost, huh? Well, we'll work on that later. But what I wanted to know is do you have a ... a skill? A power? The reason I ask is that, well, I have this thing with machines, as you know. Felix has some weird ability to understand what someone else is gonna need in the immediate future. It now looks like Gill, in addition to being able to talk to the... I guess... 'Little People' would be a good title for 'em, also can mass communicate with us on the wings of a thought, if you will. That 'MindSpeak' thing. I was just wondering about you."

Robert just floated next to her for quite awhile without saying anything.

Finally, after he had made up his mind on how to explain his answer to this question, he paddled up closer to Sarah.

"I'm lucky."

Sarah flipped around off of her back so quickly that she swallowed a mouthful of lake. "Lucky? That's it? You're lucky?"

"Well, not exactly. Gill had to explain it to me when the Flae... the 'Little People'... explained it to him. It's kinda a long story."

Sarah smiled at Robert. "Well, let me check my busy schedule. Yep, I've got an opening... ahhh... right 'bout now! Got nothin' better to do, capt'n, so explain away!"

"OK. I'll try. As it was told to Gill and then explained to me, it has to do with The Plus and The Minus."

"OK, you've lost me here already. More details, please!"

"Yeah, I'm trying, but it's kinda tough, so give me a few moments of quiet, and I'll try to explain it. I'm not sure I know enough about it myself, but I'll try."

Sarah went through the act of "zipping her lips." "My lips are sealed," she said with a smile.

"What a waste," Robert said, and for the next few moments, he never took his eyes off of her.

She liked that.

"Gill was told there are forces at work in the universe. Un-seeable forces. Not the wind or gravity or air or water or weather. These, too, are all forces, but the ones I'm speaking of are different. These are the good... and the bad, I guess you could say. I'm told that certain people kinda attract the good. Certain objects, at the same time, sorta contain the good. If found, these objects can boost the positive outcome in a person or a situation. To the Flae, Gill's 'Little Folks,' (who study this kinda stuff), these are known as The Plus. It's sort of like the old saying that 'Good things happen to good people,' in a way. For some reason or another, they believe me to be a 'Plus.' This is supposed to mean that in a tight situation, things will naturally... I guess the best way to put it is... go my way. In a 50/50 situation, where it would normally be a toss of the coin as to who would win, the coin will fall in my direction. This is The Plus. The Flae can see this as an actual object as solid as a rock. I'm told that they see it as being very bright white in color, and though it is said to be very small, it is a very... I guess that positive thing would be a good explanation for it. It can heal. It can change people's attitude for the better and it is supposed to affect all living things – man, animals and plants. I don't know why I am supposed to have it. I don't know where I got it, and to be perfectly honest with you, I only have the lil' guys' word that it even exists at all! But, for some reason, they take great store in this quality. This is why, for some years now, they have sent Gill information of bad things that were going to happen to good people and it was expected of me to try to prevent them from happening. The stories I could tell you! The little Mexican boy I was talkin' about when you first met me was one of those! HELL! YOU were one of those! And ya know what's weird? I always got off on the 'saving innocent people' portion of this deal but was never really convinced about the 'lucky' part. Then I met you."

Sarah kept her word about the temporary promise of silence, but at that moment, there was nothing she could do to prevent herself from kissing Ert. It was a slow and soft brush of the lips, but it spoke in volumes.

"See?" he said quietly. "Lucky."

"Luck had nothin' to do with that. That was skill."

Robert got kinda quiet. He looked at the water for awhile. He looked at the ceiling lights for awhile.

Sarah waited quietly.

Finally, he looked back into her eyes. "Sarah, now I need to tell you about the other side of the coin. They call it 'The Minus.' But that's not really what it is. Minus would be to actually take something away from the total. This doesn't take anything away from, it just makes what's already there... negative. I like to call it 'The Naught.' The Un. It makes bad of whatever it touches and it works on everything. People, animals, plumbing, the weather, even the Earth. It breaks things down and it affects all substances. All! It's kinda like a lack of being. It causes no pain when it occurs, but it's contagious to all around it. There are objects that contain this, too. You can bet that the Thingies are lookin' for 'em right now. If there is a hell on Earth, The Naught would be at the center of it."

"A volcano?" she said in a whisper.

He nodded his head. "Probably so. And The Plus would have no effect on that outcome since it's non-living."

"Oh, God."

They paddled slowly back to the quiet beach and stretched out on the towels.

"I'm so tired, Ert. Let me rest for just a bit before we head back. I'm so tired.

In her mind, she thought, "Stay by me, Ert. I need a strong man by my side while I rest. I won't feel safe otherwise."

As he was watching her, she lapsed into slumber.

"You need me," he whispered. "That's why I don't want to lose you now."

Gill and Felix had left 'Clothes World' behind by the time Robert finally woke up Sarah from her hour-long nap. Gill took Felix and his bags of new clothes down about ten hallways to a spare bedroom and told him to stash his gear there.

"Wow, dude! What kinda king or president-type dude lives in this big ol' room? This is like as big as the whole pad where I crash, dude! Man!"

Gill smiled. "Exactly where do you live, Felix?"

"Ah, man, I gottta room at this lil' ol' house 'bout three miles from where I work at the truck stop. It belongs to my boss' brother and he takes a chunk of my pay to let me crash there. It's real small, but it's close to my job so I can walk back and forth."

"You mean you walk three miles to and from work every day?"

"Yep. It's the only way I have to get to my job, man, and the boss' brother don't yell at me... too much."

"Ahhh... you mean the job that you quit last night and the brother of your now ex-boss?"

Felix just stood there with his mouth wide open for about a minute.

"Oh wow, dude! I didn't even think 'bout that, man! I guess I gotta get my stuff outta there, man, and find another place to crash now! Oh wow, man! Let's see, all I really got there is my other pair a jeans and a couple of really cool T-shirts. I wonder if they'll even let me back in to get 'em, man?"

Gill smiled again. "Tell ya what, dude, since I'm now your new boss and since you've got nowhere to 'crash' and since I've got no kings or president-type dudes staying with me at the moment..."

Felix just stood there with his mouth wide open.

"How about you staying here with me? This can be your room. What do you say?"

Felix just stood there with his mouth open and tears slowly runnin' down his face.

"Awww, man! Awww, man! Awww, man! You're kiddin' me now... right? You're just kiddin' me! You don't really mean that I can stay in this... in this... beautiful..."

"As of this moment, it's all yours, my friend. And no charge like your other boss did. But I will expect a little help with the chores around here. There can be quite a few in a place this size!"

Felix just stood there with his mouth open and tears runnin' down his face.

"Awww, man! Awww, man! Awww, man!"

When Felix picked him up and started swinging him around in circles, Gill thought he was about to lose his cheeseburger.

"Enough, enough... big guy! I love ya, man, but let's try our best to... never do that again! Comprende?"

"I'll try, dude," he said with a sniffle. "I'll try."

About then, Felix was engulfed by a small black snowball leaping into his arms to give him many licks of "welcome home."

"Thanks, lil' dude. Thanks to both of y'all lil' dudes. I'm home."

"Come on, then, Felix. Why don't you put on some of your new clothes and save the 'Super Dude' suit for later. Then, let's go find the rest of our friends."

"Our team, dude!"

33
What's Next?

Robert and Sarah slowly rowed their way back to the landing where they had started. They were a little more relaxed, but also a little more tense. A little bit of knowledge can be a scary thing.

When they docked the raft, they both grabbed a quick shower in the changing area before dressing. Robert was hoping for a mutual showering session, but since Sarah didn't bring it up, neither did he. She was being awfully quiet since their conversation, and this kind of worried him. He wondered if he said too much, but then thought, "No, she needed to know the truth about what they were wading off into here. In for a penny... in for a pound!"

They slowly walked back to the kitchen area of the complex, which always seemed to be the main gathering region in this massive structure when you weren't searching for something in particular. As they walked into the small dining room attached to the kitchen, they both stared at this person in front of them. Super Dude had been replaced by a real person. Felix sat on an overstuffed chair in a pair of buckskin colored slacks, a brown light sweater, tan loafers on his feet, and his bright blue hair stuffed into a grey-colored loose-fitting oversized cap.

Sarah smiled and said, "Hey, dude! You're beautiful!"

As Felix started to blush, Robert put his hand on the tall fellow's arm. "Yeah, man, you clean up real good!"

"Aww shucks, y'all. You're just sayin' that 'cause it's true!"

Everyone laughed.

Gill came in from the kitchen with cold beer and hot wings. "Ok gang, let's sit down and get our heads together here. I've been thinking quite a bit for the last couple of hours, and I think I've got a basic plan for the next couple of days laid out for us... unless someone finds fault in it. First, before we start, I'd like to invite Killer into the meeting, and I'd like for Sarah to invite MAX here with us also. Any problems there?"

"Oh wow, dude! I've been wantin' to meet this MAX guy anyway! No problems in my direction! And me and Killer are tight... hey pup?"

"Yipe Yipe!" said the small dog as he heard his name called and came running. He walked over to Gill, looked up at him, and looked back at

116

Felix.

"Go ahead, partner. He could use the attention," Gill said with a smile.

Killer turned around and leaped into Felix's lap. One quick lick of the tongue to Felix's hand and he then settled down to listen to the humans.

Sarah got up to get the laptop of Gill's that she had used earlier. She turned it on, pushed a couple of buttons and then waited on her computer friend to pop up as she sat down next to Robert.

"Good afternoon, people. MAX is here again. I can see by the online camera that we have a new addition here amongst us... and a rather large version of the human race it seems to be. Hello, human! You must be Felix."

"Haha! A rather large version of the human race! This guy just cracks me up! Howdy do, MAX! I'm Felix, alrighty!"

"Felix Alrighty. An unusual name for a people. Hello, Mr. Alrighty."

Everyone laughed again.

As they all gathered close, Gill shook his head to realize what a strange troop they all made. What would the future hold for this weird group of do-gooders, all just trying to help, trying to make the unknowing world a safe place to live once again?

"Alrighty, then," Gill said.

"You talkin' to me, dude?" Felix said with a smile.

"That's a good one, Felix!" Robert said with a smile. When he looked at Sarah, though, he realized that she wasn't smiling. He decided to grab a cold beer and shut up.

"Gang, we may be running out of time here soon, and I've got to spend some time talking to Gwen tonight to find out what might be going on that we don't know about... and about this 'MindSpeak' stuff! So, here's what I think we should do. First, Felix... I'd like for you to take Sarah back to her home this evening. She hasn't been there since Friday morning before the accident, and I want her to get together enough stuff packed for what I'm gonna call 'an extended vacation.' You can use my van to drop her off... she can tell you anything that you've missed since you came into this kinda late, and then you can come back here. Tomorrow morning, Sarah, one of us will pick you up, take you to the impound lot to pick up your car, and then follow you to work, where we'll take care of your work situation with your boss at CompuServ. We'll then bring both vehicles back here. By then, I should have more info from my little friends, and maybe we'll find out about this Yellowstone trip that they mentioned to Felix. MAX, I'd like for you to dig up any extra info you can on any volcanic activity in the past, present or future in regards to Yellowstone National Park."

"I can give you that information now if you want it, Mr. Gill," MAX said.

"No, tomorrow will be fine. We've already got our plates too full for now. Robert, I'll give you one of my other vehicles this evening so that you, too, can touch base at home and pack any necessities that you think are gonna help us out in these times of trouble. Guns are cool, but I'd vote for new batteries for the spotlights, too. Killer?"

"Yipe?"

"I'm a little worried about how secure we are here at the moment, so I want you to run to the other side of the house complex and check on the alarms and locking mechanisms for House Number Two. We haven't been there in awhile, and I want to make sure that no one is coming at us from behind. Cool?"

"YIPE!"

"Alright. For now, I guess that's the best we can do. Today was fun, guys. Tomorrow won't be. I think that... ahh... Felix? Felix?"

Everyone looked over at Felix, whose eyes were now completely white. He started shaking. Killer, who was in his lap, jumped down to the floor and started barking.

"Is Mr. Alrighty going to be alright?" MAX asked. "He appears to be going into convulsions, Mr. Gill."

Sarah spoke up first. "No, MAX. This is what he does when he sees something that we need or that we're missing. It's OK, Killer. He's alright."

"Yipe!"

After about a minute, Felix came out of his trance as he broke out into a heavy sweat. "Wow! Hey, dudes and dudette! Wow! Bobby, ya gotta go to the beach! Now!"

Robert looked at Felix as if he were crazy. "The beach? I just got done swimming, ya big galoot!"

"Yo, dude... here it is... you and Gill... burned surfer dude... pink umbrella... Olivia reaching for a star... and you'll need one-thousand dollars in cash! This afternoon!"

"What the hell?"

"Don't know, dude. Only that it's important. I saw all of that stuff... and a big addition sign in my head. Take it for what it's worth, dude."

Gill said, "Well, after the last few hours, I'll take whatever you come up with very seriously, my friend! I don't know what it means, but Felix, you go ahead and take care of Sarah. Robert and I will grab some cash and head out to the beach? Do you know WHAT BEACH? This is California, you know!"

"Aww, dude... I forgot to tell ya! Venice Beach! And it's a yard sale on the sidewalk by the beach!"

"OK... as strange as it sounds, we'll go for it. Let's get to rolling! Killer and MAX, you know your jobs?"

"Yipe!"

"Affirmative."

"If there's not anything else..."

"Ah, one thing that just came to me," Sarah quietly said.

"What's that, lovely lady?" Gill asked.

"An addition sign... is a Plus."

Robert and Gill looked at each other and then took off at a run.

34
A Strange Afternoon at the Beach

Robert and Gill dashed through the house as quickly as their legs would take them. They'd been in no big hurry for this strange trip to Venice Beach upon first hearing Felix talking of it, but since Sarah had enlightened them as to the true meaning of the vision, there was no time to waste. If there was Plus out there to be had, the Thingies would want it and whoever owned it, destroyed, as much as Robert and Gill needed it safe. Not only that, but there was a good chance that the Whistlers could see The Plus as a white hot light, and Robert and Gill would have to hunt it down using only Felix's vague description. Their only advantage was the fact that the sun was still out, but those rain clouds were headed their way, and with them would come the Thingies.

It took them a couple of extra minutes to run to the center of the complex where the underground garage was. There was a dozen different vehicles parked in here, most of them unused for some time now. Robert was looking for speed, so he picked out a souped-up '56 Belair Chevy.

"Jump in, Gill! This time, I'm drivin'!"

"Just a second!" Gill yelled as he ran over to a wall safe, inserted his handprint to a scanner and grabbed a handful of cash. Slamming the safe door closed again, he dashed back to the car.

Dust flew off the surface of the fine machine as they slammed their doors. "Remind me when we get back to schedule a car-cleaning session for Felix here one day soon," Gill said with a smile. Robert cranked up the engine, which sputtered once and then exploded with life.

"Wow, Gill, what the hell is under this hood? I don't think I've ever driven this one before."

"Everything that will fit, Robert, everything that will fit! I don't think you'll have any trouble getting this baby to give you what you want!"

"Wish I could say that about another girl I know," Robert whispered. Gill heard him, though.

The long tunnel out of the garage was about fifty yards long, and as they came to the end of it, an outside door automatically slid open. Out they popped onto a gravel drive, sliding ninety degrees to the left and heading for the main road.

"I just love that secret driveway door," Robert said as he looked back. "Ya can't even tell it's there once you're through it!"

"It's all concealed with landscaping and rock from this side," Gill said with a smile. "Stole the idea from Batman!"

Once on the highway, Robert kept the speed of the Chevy just a shade above the speed limit. "No sense in getting pulled over," he thought. It wasn't quite rush hour in L.A. yet, so he made pretty good time... until traffic slowed down for an accident up ahead.

"I can get off of the highway and make better time on the streets, if you want me to," Robert said as he gazed at an exit coming up soon.

Gill thought about it for a second, and then quietly told Robert that maybe they should stay on the highway just to see what had happened. He pointed to about a mile up ahead, where rising blue smoke could be seen.

"Aw, hell," Robert said in a whisper. "Do ya think they beat us to it?"

"Let's turn on the radio," Gill said as he glanced over at Robert. "We haven't checked the media in awhile now."

The radio stations were all full of 'Breaking News.' It seems that some kind of terrorist attack had been going on in Southern California for the last two or three days. Several locations in L.A. and the surrounding areas had been hit by explosions of a strange nature. Up to a dozen people were confirmed dead, including women and children. Bodies were either burned beyond recognition or missing. Besides the attacks on homes and the power station that supplied a large portion of the area with power, one sub-station had been hit not more than an hour ago and several vehicles had been blown up and torched, including two on the interstate system right now. HazMat crews were investigating the incidents mostly because of the blue-colored smoke that originated from all of the sites.

Robert listened to the reports with a shaken look on his face. He started to tremble as he heard of all of the destruction but started to shake as they began to name off the casualties involved, including women, small children and one baby girl that was only nine months old.

The tremors faded and in their place grew a heat. A terrible heat. Now, he was angry. Very angry.

They drove slowly by the burning SUV, steering through the blue haze and around the puzzled emergency technicians in white radiation suits. Robert and Gill looked down at the side of the road and spied a scorched doll lying in a pool of water drained away by the fire department's attempts to extinguish the flames of the vehicle.

Robert and Gill looked at each other, looked at the tears running down each other's faces. Having been in California for their entire lives, they both recognized that poor wet cartoon mouse swimming in the mud.

Hell, they'd spent many happy hours at his home before.

Gill brushed the sniffles from his nose as Robert said in a whisper, "In this country, that's almost like burning the flag."

Gill put his hand on his friend's arm, "Let's go get that Plus."

It took another thirty minutes or so for them to reach Venice Beach. Not a word was said between the two friends for the remainder of the trip, just an occasional headshake or a quiet sob.

They parked as close to the boardwalk area of the beach as possible and they could see the Venice Pier from where they left the Chevy. They slowly walked toward the sidewalk area when suddenly Robert turned toward Gill.

"Hey Gill? Do we have any idea what were lookin' for?"

Gill shook his head slowly and answered, "All I know is something about a burned surfer dude, someone named Olivia, and she's reaching for a star, and finally, and hopefully, the easiest to spot, a pink umbrella, which is all that Felix could come up with. I recommend that we just start down the sidewalk here and look for pink beach umbrellas and a sun-burned surfer."

"Sounds good to me. Did you bring the cash?"

"Yep. Don't know how much 'cause I just grabbed a handful of hundreds, but it should be easily more than a grand."

They eased their way down the long sidewalk, seeing vendors of surfboards, food, T-shirts, pottery and souvenirs of all sorts. There were jugglers and bodybuilders, bathing beauties and skaters, movie stars and bums, millionaires and homeless folks looking for spare change but no sunburned surfer caught their attention.

After about a half hour, Robert said, "Man, it's hot and muggy out here, Gill. Let's grab a couple of cold bottles of water and maybe one of those hot dogs over there. What do ya say?"

Gill was trying to catch his breath after the long walk on his short legs, and he nodded. "Just the water for me, Robert."

Robert walked over to where a lawn chair contained a sleeping blond-haired dude. He had a combination hotdog stand, refreshment counter and garage sale going on next to what appeared to have once been a small beach house but was now a burned-out pile of waterlogged and charred remains.

"I'll have two large waters, please and a hot dog with everything," Robert said.

"Sure thing, man! Thanks for the business! It's been kinda slow around here today, what with the rain headed toward us and all."

The guy made him up a loaded-down hotdog and passed it to him across the counter. As he did, Robert noticed the burns across the backs of his hands and one side of his face.

A light went on in Robert's mind.

"Hey, Gill. Come here for a second, would ya?"

Gill slowly got off the park beach he had just settled on and slowly hobbled over to where Robert was talking to the hotdog guy. "Man, I guess I'm not used to all of this exercise! My legs are killin' me! What is it, Robert?"

"Ah, I'd like to introduce you to... sorry, fellow, I didn't get your name."

"Hi, man. I'm Paulie." He shook Gill's hand, and as he did, Gill noticed the burns on his body and the rubble of the house behind him.

Gill looked at Robert.

Robert smiled back at Gill as he crammed the hotdog into his mouth.

Gill, as politely as possible, asked, "Ah, man, what happened here?" He pointed at the remains of the beach house.

"Aww, man, we had a fire here about two weeks ago. Lost everything we had, including our dog, man, but at least my daughter and I made it out OK! I got a little toasted pulling her out of a window, man, but she's fine. Came out without a scratch! God was watchin' over us, I guess, man."

"So you're still here, huh?"

"Yeah, man, we manage to scrape up a few dollars a day selling drinks and dogs and a few knick-knacks to the beach folk here who know me from when I used to surf here a lot. Kinda hard to do now. Too many burns and a toasted board, man! Ha ha!"

"Knick-knacks, huh? That's real interesting isn't it, Robert?'

"Yeah, it sure is."

"Hey, man, I almost forgot your waters! What a dope I am sometimes! Hey! Olivia? Get me two large waters for these fellows, will ya?"

Gill and Robert almost fell over when they heard that. They slowly looked around behind the counter and there was this beautiful blond 10-year-old little darling sitting on the ground next to a pile of junk laid out on a blanket with an "Anything For $1" sign next to it. She smiled at the two customers, and they both noticed that her pale skin was having no trouble keeping out of the burning sun because of a small pink umbrella she had in her hands.

"Oh God, Gill!"

"Oh God is right, my friend."

She went to a cooler next to her yard sale she was running and opened it up to produce two ice-cold bottles of water. "Here ye go, Mithter," she said with a smile.

"Thank you, uh... Olivia? Is that your name?"

"Yeath thir, it ith," she said with a big smile that showed the missing tooth in the front of that grin.

Gill's smile almost covered his entire face as he slowly walked around behind the counter to get the waters that she held out. "Thank you very much, m'lady!" he said with a bow.

"Yur very welcome, kind thir!" she said with a curtsy.

"Would it be too much trouble, ma'am, for you to show me what wonderful treasures you have for sale on this fine day?"

"Oh... no trouble at all, ma lord," She giggled, and then took his hand to lead him over to her little blanket she had set up. "Theeth were a few of my treathurth from before the houth burned-ed up. I'm tryin' to help my daddy to buy thum food with my thtuff I thell. Please thit down, thir," she said, indicating a corner of the small blanket.

"My pleasure, m'lady," Gill said with a smile. As he sat, he noticed a small tent that had been pitched to the side of the burnout. This, undoubtedly, was where both of these two poor folks now lived and slept. As he sat there, he wondered where all of this was leading to and how a "star" was to become involved.

"I have thum wonderful thingth here to thare with you now, thur! You can look them over, and ath me any quethionth you might have."

Gill thought his small heart would explode at this little girl's hospitality. As he looked at the things lying on her blanket, one of the first things that he noticed was a small black leather dog collar with tiny rhinestones set into it. It had a small engraved band of metal attached to it and precognition made Gill slowly pick up the treasure. Goosebumps the size of a turkey popped up on his arms as he read the inscription.

"Killer," he said in a small squeaky voice and a tear rolled down his face as she said, "Mithur, that wath my dog."

He smiled at her, took her small hand in his own, and said, "Yeah, honey, mine, too."

"Really, Mithur?!"

"Yeah, really. Olivia, are you sure you want to sell this? For just one dollar?"

"Well, we kinda need the money, Mithur. And everithing ith one dollar. But... Daddy theth you can tip me if I'm cute! Am I cute, Mithur?"

Gill's heart burst.

"Yeah, baby girl, you're cute. Tell ya what, I'll tip you extra if you'll call me Gill. OK?"

"OK... Mithur Gill. Can I thell you thumpin' elth?"

He looked around at the small things she had on her little display and slowly shook his head. "Well honey, I think I was lookin' for something you don't have, but I'm mighty glad I found what I did. You made my day a lot brighter, whether you know it or not. Thank you."

"Yur welcome, Mithur Gill."

Gill started to stand... when she took his hand in hers. She looked at him carefully for a few seconds... and then pulled him down so she could whisper into his ear. "Mithur Gill, what wath it? That you wath lookin' for?"

"A star, Olivia. I was lookin' for a star."

"Reachin' for a thtar?"

Gill stood perfectly still... with his mouth wide open... and nodded. "Yes," he said in the smallest of whispers.

She looked at him for a moment, pulled him down to her again and said, "I have that thtar." She continued to look at him as a teardrop fell down his cheek. "Don't cry, Mithur Gill. I been waitin' for you."

She slowly went over by her small umbrella and picked up a small wooden box. She brought it over to place it gently into Gill's hand. "My Mother gived it to me when I was thix... and then thee went away... to heaven. Thee thaid thumone would need thith one day. Ith that thumone you, Mithur Gill?"

He opened the small box and inside was a necklace. It looked like pewter, and it was a sculpture of a small girl, sitting on a crescent moon, which wore a sleeping cap... and she was reaching out to grasp a star.

"Mom thad it wath 'Olivia reaching for a shtar.' I didn't put it out for thale 'cauth I thought it wath worth more than one dollar. At leath to me it wath."

Tears were rolling down Gill's face now. "Ith OK, Mithur Gill, ith OK," she said as she patted him on the back. As he picked the star up out of the box, he could see a shine grow from inside of the metal. It felt warm, too.

"Honey, are you sure you want to sell this to me? I mean... if it came from your mom?"

"Thee thaid thumone would need thith one day. Mama tol' me tho. You better take that with you, Mithur Gill. Pleath."

He smiled down at her and then looked up. Paulie, the burned surfer, just stood there with his mouth wide open. Robert gazed at the necklace as though it were the Holy Grail. "It glows, Gill."

"Yeah, I know. Why don't you take it for me, Robert," as he placed it back inside the wooden box.

Robert came around the counter and carefully extended his hand to Gill. Gill passed the box to Robert, who held it gently to his chest. As Robert slowly removed the necklace from the box, Robert... changed. He was suddenly... more!

A reddish sort of glow appeared, not only around the necklace but also around Robert. And as Gill, Paulie and Olivia watched in amazement, Robert seemed to... for just a moment... float.

In a flash, everything was normal in the world once again, but the people standing there... watching... would never be the same.

"Wow, man! It never did that to me!" Paulie said with a smile.

Gill walked over to Olivia. "Thank you, m'lady. You may have just saved many lives."

"I hope tho," she said with a smile.

As he turned to leave, she touched him on the sleeve. "Oh, Mithur Gill?"

"Yes, honey, what is it?"

"You thtill owe me two dollarth."

Gill picked her up in his arms and brought her around to the front of the counter. He placed her in Robert's arms as he looked at her daddy. "Paulie, she said I could tip her if she was cute. Is that OK with you, too."

"Oh, man, yeah! Any help we can get right now, ya know!" He shook Gill's hand.

As Robert put Olivia back on the ground and then also shook Paulie's hand, Gill took Olivia off to the side.

"Thank you, m'lady," he said in a whisper as he placed a large bundle of hundred dollar bills in her hand. "You are cute." He and Robert walked away.

"You are very welcome, kind sir! Kind SIR! SIR! Hey Dad, I can talk real again!" she said as she ran over to where Robert had touched her father's hand.

As Paulie watched in amazement at his daughter's front tooth grow back in front of his very own eyes, Olivia stared at the terrible burns on her father's face fade away. Then Paulie noticed what Olivia held in her small hands. THOUSANDS of dollars.

Gill and Robert smiled as they walked back toward their car. Suddenly, Gill felt a tug on his sleeve from behind.

There was Olivia again.

"You forgot your waters, Mister Gill!" as she placed them in his hands. She curtsied and off she ran.

35
HE

HE went to the beach.

There was a CALLING there and HE could not have that. The Flae believed that The Plus cast off a light to the Thingies' eyes as it did to them. This was not the case.

To HE, it was a CALL, a small sound. As HE got closer to the CALLING, it became... more... a more powerful CALL that was easier to hear with a stronger pull.

HE went to the beach.

On the way, in a large truck HE had taken, HE had smashed a vehicle with a rodent in the window.

BAM! SMASH!

HE threw Minus at it.

BAM! BOOM! SMASH!

Blue smoke filled the air.

HE started to feed, but the CALLING came again. It was much more powerful. HE had to go.

HE went to the beach.

HE couldn't get the big truck to beach.

HE got close.

HE crashed the big truck.

BOOM!

HE left the big truck.

BOOM!

HE felt the CALLING close now.

HE walked to the beach.

Clouds blocked the "evil sun." HE walked down the path... "sideways, ahh, nah, sidewalk."

HE walked to the CALLING, which was even stronger now.

Suddenly, there was a flash of red light farther down the beach.

"CALLING stops! CALLING stops! CALLING cannot stop. CALLING cannot stop!" HE exclaimed.

The CALLING stopped.

HE thought someone ate the CALLING. The Plus was with someone now.

HE couldn't kill the CALLING now.

"Plus was part of a human person," HE thought. "Human person had Plus? Can control Plus?"

HE stopped to figure out something. HE had a... feeling. A... feeling that HE didn't... understand.

HE went through a list of feelings HE had memorized while on Earth. Love, envy, hate, like, hurt and down the list HE went until HE came to the one HE was looking for.

Fear.

HE went to where the CALLING was.

There was no CALLING.

Humans were gone and HE saw... a hotdog?

HE ate the hotdog and thought it was almost as good as human food.

HE looked down sidewalks and saw Humans who kill Thingies.

Walking away, he thought, his friends died by Humans who kill Thingies. HE could die by Humans who kill Thingies. "Humans who kill Thingies have The Plus?"

It started to rain. HE thought for only a moment.

HE ran away from beach.

HE had friends still there. HE's friends called, not strong, but a call.

A gathering ensued between The Thingies and HE.

The call went out across the air. It was heard and would be answered soon.

"Ah... hey Gill? Did you get a look at that dude in the suit, running across the parking lot? I could almost... swear... that I know him."

"Don't be silly, Robert! Who the heck would you know that wore a suit?"

"Hahahaha!"

36

Checkin' Out the Underground

Gill and Robert's hurried departure left Felix, Sarah, Killer and MAX in the small dining room unsupervised. Felix had quickly finished off all of the hot wings that Gill had made, and then, with Sarah tagging along, went off to explore.

"Clue me in later, Mr. Alrighty," said MAX as they wandered off.

"Yo, MAX! Dudette, there's gotta be like miles of stuff in here! How many rooms do you figure there are, anyway?"

"Felix, I haven't been here much longer than you have, but I've already seen a couple of dozen rooms myself. Gill didn't say anything about any room being out of bounds, so I don't believe he'd care if we just looked around a bit. Also, I think I know where we can get a guide!"

"Really? Where are we gonna get anyone who knows their way around this maze, darlin'?"

Sarah pointed to the ground.

Felix looked down.

"Yipe!"

Felix looked up at Sarah. "Really?"

Really," she said.

"Hey, dog critter?"

"Yipe?"

"You understand what I'm sayin'?"

"Yipe!"

"OK, then, let's try something. Ahh, bring me a screwdriver, OK?"

"Yipe."

Killer just sat there, looking at Felix in anticipation.

"Well?"

"Yipe?"

Felix looked at Sarah, who was giggling. "OK, what's he waitin' for, girl?"

"Well," she said with a smile, "if you asked me for a screwdriver, I'd need to know whether you wanted a Flathead, Phillips or vodka and orange juice!"

"Yipe Yipe!"

Felix looked down at the small critter with a sly grin on his face. "Phillips," he said.

Killer took off like he was shot out of a gun.

"Damn!" said Felix as he watched the black blur streak away down the dark hallway. "Where do you figure he ran of to? I'll bet I know. I'll bet that somewhere in this conglomeration of rooms there is an entire wing somewhere just devoted to screwdrivers. A whole storehouse of flatheads of every shape and size. A warehouse just full of different kinds of Phillip screwdrivers... and somewhere..." He stopped talkin' for a few seconds and started thinkin' and smilin'!

"What is it, Felix?"

Somewhere probably down that hallway right there, there's a big ol' giant room full of nothin' but vodka and orange juice."

They both started laughing but were interrupted by a "Yipe!"

There was Killer with a Phillips screwdriver in his small mouth, which he dropped at Felix's feet.

"Way cool, lil' dude! Way cool!"

"Yipe!"

"Now, bring me a refrigerator!"

"Grrrr..."

"Naw, now... just kiddin' there, pup! Can you give Sarah and me the guided tour?"

"Ruff!" he said as he wagged his tail and slowly waltzed down the hall-way, looking back to make certain he was being followed.

They checked out five different very cool bedrooms, two storerooms, (one full of cleaning supplies and one full of hats), another small kitchen, built on what appeared to be an underground patio with a waterfall and a barbecue, and then Sarah was led by Killer to a double door that opened into... a gigantic greenhouse! Automated sprinklers, artificial sunlight, computerized feeding tubes, the whole bit. It looked to be fifty yards long or longer with tropical plants and trees, flowers and shrubs, vegetables and fruits of all varieties and weeds.

"Hey, Sarah, them there are weeds. What's he doin' with weeds?" Felix shouted when he was about half-way through the room. "And they ain't the kinda weeds I'm interested in, either," he said in a whisper and a grin. He looked around for Sarah and saw her on the other side of the room studying a computer bank.

"Felix, did you know that Gill grows almost everything in the way of produce and fruit for his house right here on his property? He has a plant schedule here, which shows replacement shrubs and even the weeds for all of the paths and driveways he has disguised on the entire grounds. Even tree specimens.

She was rubbing her hands together with a big smile on her face.

"NOW I feel at home!" she blurted out as she started pushing buttons, turning knobs and dials... and then, she just... stopped, closed her eyes and laid her hands on the console.

"Whoa, girl!" Felix exclaimed as all of the lights, sprinklers and misting heads all kicked in at the same time. As she smiled and removed her hand everything went back to normal and MAX came online and popped up on hidden speakers all around the room. "Hello, MAX," she said.

"HELLO!" MAX said at about two hundred decibels.

"Damn, computer dude! Some of us got meat for brains 'stead of silicone. Don't fry us," Felix said with his hands over his ears.

At the same time, MAX and Sarah said, "SORRY..."

"Sorry..."

Sarah waved at Felix as she quickly said, "Hey, Felix! With these controls, MAX and I can direct flow of water transfer in differential equations to supplement nutrients to individual botanical species at different rates of transfer based on individual climate zone preference! Isn't that cool?"

"Hey, Sarah! Bleedle fasdar toockie nock donatelle diddle bab bab bab biddle trucky la la! Isn't that cool?"

"Hey! Don't make fun of me! That was all just gibberish!"

"Hey, dudette! So was yours! What the hell are you talkin' about?"

Sarah laughed hard at that.

"Ah... Sorry, Felix. What I should have said was... MAX and I can make all of this stuff work better for Gill than it does now. How's that?"

"Clear as twenty-cent pancake syrup, girl! And twice as sweet, too!"

"Aww, shucks, mister, thank ye. Ready to work, MAX?"

"Ready, Sarah."

Buzzing and clicks took over where conversation had been before.

Felix looked down at Killer, who sat at his feet and just shook his blue-haired head. "What kind of a dang guide are you, anyway, doggie pal a mine? Leadin' me in here, dude, with a bunch of dadgum posies when all of those other cool rooms are just a waitin' and a callin' my name!"

Killer looked at Felix for a moment then sat down, as if he were thinking. He suddenly jumped up, ran over to Felix and started pulling on the cuff of his pants leg.

"Hey, Sarah! You stay here for a minute with yer shrubberies and yer sagebrush and Mr. MAX... and I'll be right back. Lassie here wants me to follow. I'm afraid Timmie might have fallen down in the well again."

Sarah was laughing as Felix walked out with Killer and headed down another corridor.

After a couple of minutes of continuous hallways and bypassing dozens of doors, Felix said, "Hey, small dog critter. One of these days, ya gotta show me what all I just missed back there with all them un-opened doors, huh?"

"Yipe," Killer said as he finally came to a rest in front of a large red door. He lay down on the ground next to the entrance and wagged his tail.

"So... this is it, huh?"

"Yipe!"

This is what you want to show me, huh?"

"Yipe!"

"So, of all the rooms you coulda picked to show me, this is the one, huh?"

"Yipe!"

"OK... once for yes... and twice for no... Am I gonna like it?"

"Yipe!"

"OK... am I gonna wanna leave when I see it?"

"Yipe... yipe."

"Ahh... is an apple blue?"

"Yipe, yipe."

"OK, OK, just testin' ya. Ya ready ta go in?"

"YIPE!"

Felix pushed open the soundproof door and thought he was in heaven. Inside of the giant room was a movie theater.

The screen was as big as any that Felix had ever seen in a walk-in normal theater situation, but even though the floor sloped downward to an auditorium sort of atmosphere, there were only a half dozen or so big cushy, over-padded seats.

In front of the seats was a computer console.

When they had first entered the door, dim lights had automatically come on inside so that you could just barely see what was going on and the console had lit up. As they slowly approached the seats, a very cute female voice came on over hidden speakers placed around the large room.

"Hello there."

Felix looked around the room. Nothing,

Felix looked down at Killer, who was wagging his tail.

"Yipe!"

"Hello, Killer," the voice said. "Glad that you could come visit me again. Did you bring me some company with you this time?"

"Yipe!"

"That's nice. Do they speak?"

"Yipe."

"That's nice, too. Let's try again then, shall we? Ah, hello there?"

Felix just stood there with his mouth wide open, looking around for the girl behind this beautiful voice.

"What's the matter? Does the pup got your tongue? Ha ha!"

"Ahh... no ma'am. I'm here, alrighty. At least I think I'm here." In a whisper, Felix said, "It kinda feels like I fell down the rabbit hole, though."

"A very good choice" she said as lights came on the screen and lights in the room dimmed. Before he knew what was happening, "Alice In Wonderland" was on the screen. The original cartoon Disney version. He sat down in the center chair as quiet as a mouse for a few moments and then said, "Ah, what did I do?

The movie paused.

The lovely voice came on a speaker that sounded as if it were in the chair next to him. "I'm sorry. I assumed that your reference to the rabbit hole was a movie request. If you'd like a different version of this movie, I have seven choices in different formats. Different studios, different real actors, cartoon or real-life. I can also give you these movies in twenty two different languages. What is your preference?"

"Ahh..."

"OK, I see. How about let's start all over again! Killer?"

"Yipe?"

"Refreshments for the gentleman, please."

"Yipe!" the small creature said as it took to the darkened side of the room.

The voice said, "And your name is...?"

"Oh, sorry, ma'am! I'm Felix."

"Felix. What a fine name you have, sir. I can assume that you are a friend of Gill. Now, would you care to pick a movie or would you rather talk for a moment?"

"Pick a movie?"

"Yes, sir."

"Any movie?"

"Any movie at all, sir. Or... if you'd rather... I have over eight-hundred television channels that you can watch."

"Eight-hundred?"

"Yes, sir. Also, if you pick up the controller lying there on the console... I have five-hundred forty-eight video and PC games programmed in that you can play, sir."

"Five-hundred forty-eight... games?"

"Yes, sir. May I call you Felix, sir?"

"Ah, yeah, please do, ma'am."

"Thank you, Felix. And you may call me Lois."

"Hi... uhh... Lois?"

"Yes, Felix. That stands for Localized Optional In-line System. L-O-I-S."

About that time, Felix heard a rolling-wheel sound getting closer. He looked down to see Killer pulling a small wagon, which contained a large popcorn, several candy bars of different varieties, a hot dog (with a small bite taken out of it), and a large soft drink, which smelled quite a bit like old-fashioned root beer.

"Ahh... Lois?"

"Yes, Felix?"

"How about... 'Harvey'?"

"With Jimmy Stewart?"

"Yes, ma'am."

"Black-and-white or colorized?"

"Let's go with the original version, OK?"

"That's my favorite, too. The movie version or the play?"

"Ahh... the movie?"

The old black-and-white movie kicked right in and later on, as Felix was munching down on buttered popcorn and sipping ice-cold root beer from a frosted mug with Killer in his lap, he realized maybe this was heaven.

Old habits die hard, so while the movie was going, Felix whispered, "Hey, Lois?"

She whispered back, "Yes, Felix?"

"I think I love you."

"OK. Then I love you back, Felix."

He smiled.

37
A Quick Stop at Robert's House

As they were headed back home, Robert said to Gill, "Hey buddy, since we're goin' right by my neighborhood anyway, what's the chances of us stopping in real quick so I can change my clothes? I've been in these same rags for days now, and my bag is still on the kitchen floor unpacked since my trip back from Texas."

"Chances are good, my friend, chances are good."

As they were pulling into the driveway at Robert's house, Gill looked over at his friend. Ever since the episode with the necklace at the beach, Gill had kept giving Robert sideways glances when he thought he was not being noticed. As Gill was staring at his big friend now, Robert suddenly swung around so his face was right in Gill's.

"What?" Robert said in a huff! "What is it? You keep on staring at me like I had two heads or something! What is it, Gill?"

"I can't quite put my finger on it, my friend, but something about you is different."

"Yeah, I can feel it, too. It feels like I could spit sparks if I had to. Something about that Plus we got back there just kinda... charged my battery, I guess."

"Yeah, I guess that's it. The necklace still has a soft kinda glow to it, but somehow I think that quite a bit of that juice went into you," Gill said as they both got out of the old Chevy.

"Man, I coulda used some of this in Dallas," Robert said with a sigh.

"Yeah, that's right! I still haven't had a chance to hear about how that all went down."

As they crossed the threshold of Robert's front door, he looked over at Gill. "If you'll get us both a couple of beers out of the fridge, I'll tell you the tale of Juanito and The Killer Stepdad!"

"That's a deal, pal."

Robert went into his bedroom to throw on some clean, very old and faded, broken-in jeans (and one of his favorites) and a light blue sweat shirt with the arms cut out. The front of the shirt had a Blind Faith logo imprinted on it.

"Ahh... comfort!" he said as he met Gill in his kitchen.

Gill smiled at his friend. "Snacks?"

"Above the cabinet there. I think we've got chips and dip."

Robert went into the living room and relaxed on the sectional sofa while Gill juggled all of the beers, snacks and dip. "Hey, dude! A lil' help?"

Robert started laughing! "Hey, dude? Man, we're both starting to get Felix-talk down!"

Gill laughed, too. "Yeah, I have a real good feeling about that guy. You know, Robert, in a bad situation, he would go down for one of us. I don't know why that worries me."

Yeah, Gill, I know what you mean. As big as he is, he really doesn't know how to... well, you know what I mean."

"Yeah. I do. OK, what about Texas?"

"Gill, the end turned out real good, but it was... dirty."

Gill grabbed a chip and a beer, sat back on the sofa and said, "OK, my brother. Give it to me."

Robert did.

"Juanito lives in the 'Mexican' part of South Dallas. By this, I mean, if you don't habla de espanol, you don't comprende'."

Robert settled back on the recliner part of the sectional and took a big slug off his cold beer. "Ah, man, that's good."

He looked at Gill for a moment with a smile on his face. Then, as he remembered what he was trying to remember, the smile went away.

"Juanito, his mom and stepdad all lived in a small town actually outside of Dallas called Waxahachie, where his stepdad was a county deputy sheriff. They had lived there for almost two years when the mom was reported missing. She had taken no luggage and had been wearing a blue dress and a St. Christopher medal around her neck. According to a follow-up investigation, she was reported to have run off with a mariachi musician from El Paso, but Juanito's aunt found this to be unbelievable since Juanito's mama had loved her son so much and would not have just abandoned him – not for any reason. Foul play was suspected, and since the stepdad had done most of the investigation on the case, she was highly suspicious of him in general.

The stepdad had been in and out of trouble from years with his department for brutality to prisoners and for getting into brawls at the cantina not far from their home, where he spent most of his off-duty hours. However, because there had been several people who had come up missing from the area in the last few years, one more was no big deal.

Juanito's grandpapa had been quite wealthy when he was alive from a cattle ranch he had started back in the 1930s, when Texas was still wide open and pretty wild. Grandpapa had been blessed with two daughters, Juanito's mama being the second, but Grandmama had passed away during the birth. For this reason, Grandpapa loved his daughters greatly, and they wanted for nothing. Oh, don't get me wrong. He would have them working the cattle with him just as hard as any of his men, but they were like gold to his heart.

When Juanito's mama fell in love with one of the ranch hands, a handsome and rugged caballero, Grandpapa gave his blessing, and the wedding took place on the ranch followed by husband and wife moving into the west wing of the large rancho. It was only one year later that Juanito was born. Juanito's real papa was a favorite of Grandpapa, and they worked tirelessly together to make the rancho into the fine place that it became.

He spent seven wonderful years with his mama, papa and grandpapa on the large ranchero until one day, a wild steer killed his papa. The family was torn apart by the death and by the grieving of Juanito's mama, who took to spending more and more time at the cantina in the town. This is where she met up with the man who would one day become Juanito's stepdad.

Grandpapa would have none of this. "This man is a coward and a bully, and I'll not have you marry this man under any circumstances!" he exclaimed one day.

Mama, being as headstrong as her father, immediately married the "mean gringo," which led to her being disinherited by her father. Her father, Grandpapa to Juanito, died not long afterward, some say of a broken heart, and left the rancho to his other daughter, Juanito's aunt.

Thus, Juanito's family moved into the small adobe house where the stepdad had been living for several years.

Juanito was a boy and did well in school, but would often come home to yelling and screaming and bottles of beer and alcohol being thrown. After about two years of marriage, one day Juanito came home to find that his mama could take no more of the stepdad and had left him and Juanito.

He didn't cry. He only went into his room and stayed there, very quietly, thinking. Mama... she would not do this to him. It must be some kind of mistake. She would one day return, he thought. She must return because Juanito did not love his stepdad.

He was afraid of him."

"Gill, I want to take a short break here for the bathroom and another beer, but before I finish this story, I wanna ask you something if you don't mind. OK?"

"Anything at all, my friend."

"When you get this information about these... things... that are gonna happen and I get sent out to try to stop them... ahh... why these?"

"I'm not sure if I know what you mean, Robert."

"What I mean is why these... ?"

"These?"

"Ah, folks in particular? I mean, why wasn't I sent out to help Juanito's mama instead of Juanito? When I go to Kansas to save a woman in a bank holdup and three other people also die, but she is saved by me... why? Why her? Why Juanito?"

"Robert, go and grab a beer... grab a couple of beers, use the bathroom... and when you come back, I'll have figured out how to explain it to you as it was explained to me by Gwen."

Robert nodded and left the room.

Gill shook his head. He thought to himself, "That guy's got a big heart, and I'm gonna have to explain this to him just right or he'll never understand it. Hell, I'm not sure I understand it myself!"

A few minutes later, Robert came back in with two cold beers, one of which he handed to Gill. He sat back down, looked at Gill and didn't say a word.

Gill sighed.

"Robert, you want the long version or the short version?"

Robert smiled at his small friend. "Let's start with the short version and see if that works."

"OK, here it is. You can't save everyone. How's that?"

"That sucks! Whip the long version on me!"

"OK. Here it is. Everyone that we save... or try to save... are presented to us by the Flae because these people either are someone special who are going to have a giant impact on the world in the future or because they are going to do something special that is going to have a big impact on the world. These are world changers and must be spared if at all possible and at all costs! I don't know why, I don't know what they will do. I was told that that part cannot be explained to me; therefore, I cannot explain that part to you. Just know that by helping these people stay alive, you and I also became world changers. Comprende?"

"Si', senor."

"Bueno. Then... continue, if you please, sir."

"Well, as usual, I flew into Ft. Worth instead of Dallas, and I also used one of the fake names and IDs that you've given me just in case anything ever happened. That way they can't trace any of this back to here. I checked into a motel in Dallas after I'd rented a car at the airport. I got into Dallas two days early from when the event was supposed to take place. That way, I could investigate the situation before I just waded off into it. That's when I pulled up the facts that I've already given you.

The day before the event was to take place, I waited until Juanito had gone to school and his stepdad had left for work. The morning was accented by Stepdad throwing a plate at Juanito as the small boy ran out the door, heading for school, but running for his life.

I decided that I didn't like this gentleman one damn bit.

After they were both gone, I got into the house through an unlocked window and slowly went through the place in search of evidence or clues as to what was about to occur. I didn't find much, but I uncovered a life insurance policy that Stepdad had taken out on his wife for two-hundred thousand dollars. The letter from the insurance company let him know that she had to be missing for seven years before she could be claimed as legally dead. That was clue number one.

Next, after finding nothing else in the small house, I went into the back yard, where I discovered a tin shed used for lawn equipment and storage. I found nothing inside there, but when I went outside of the shed and went to the rear of the structure, I discovered the entire shed was on a runner rail track with a lock on it. Once this lock was released, the entire shed could be slid back on runners almost ten feet to reveal a storm shelter beneath it... totally concealed! It was also soundproofed. This was clue number two.

Making sure that no one was around, I picked this heavy-duty lock and quietly slid the shed back on its well-oiled runners to reveal what was hidden underneath."

Robert stopped talking and hung his head down.

A whimper escaped his lip.

Gill got up and went over to place his hand on the big guy's shoulder.

Gill looked at his friend as Robert raised his head. "Clue number three?"

Robert nodded. "Clue number three. God, Gill... it was horrible! There was at least four... maybe five bodies in there. Some of them had been cut up into small pieces... some were still intact! But..."

"What was it, Robert?"

Robert looked at him with tears in his eyes once again. "Bones. Nothin' but bones! And, when I looked closer... I realized why!"

Gill felt that this wasn't the time to say anything, so he let his friend sob for a moment.

Robert looked up at Gill with his red eyes and whispered, "Fire ants."

Neither one of them said anything for a few minutes while Robert tried to pull himself together.

Finally, Robert shook himself and continued. "The son of a bitch killed all of those people and then put the bodies in that pit for the ants to eat! I got... mad. I got REAL mad!

"I locked the padlock back after I returned the shed to its original position. In my mind, I kept seeing that female skeleton down in that dark hole that had been wearing that St. Christopher medallion... and I knew... I just knew that that... was Mama.

"The world was a blur... a red blur. I went back to the motel.

"I bought a soda out of the machine outside my door.

"I didn't drink it.

"I ordered a pizza for supper since I hadn't eaten anything since yesterday.

"I didn't eat it.

"The world was a blur... a red blur.

"I watched my television to get my mind off of what I'd seen.

"I didn't see it. I don't remember one damn show that was on.

"I laid down to sleep... to conserve my strength... since tomorrow was the day of... the event. The day that little Juanito would die.

"Yeah, that's right. Not one wink did I sleep. Not one.

"The world was a blur... a red blur.

"Then... it was tomorrow.

"I got out of bed with a smile on my face. It was not a good smile.

"I knew exactly what I was gonna do.

"I already knew what was gonna happen... when it was gonna happen... how it was gonna happen. The Flae had supplied that information.

"Now... all I had to do was... make it NOT happen!

"The event would take place tonight. 9 p.m.

"That morning, I went to the hardware store. I bought a lot of stuff I didn't need, (to throw off suspicion!)... then I bought nylon band lockties, a small handsaw, a large flashlight and a roll of duct tape... which I DID need. I drove to a park on the outside of Dallas, where I got rid of all of the stuff I didn't need.

"Early that afternoon, before Stepdad and Juanito got home, I went into their back yard and unlocked the padlock on the shed runners.

"I left.

"I went into Dallas.

"I stopped at a famous steakhouse, advertised on many billboards throughout the town. I ordered a thirty-two-ounce porterhouse steak, medium rare... with a large baked potato... a caesar salad with croutons, two large milks and homemade biscuits with lots and lots of honey. My waitress brought out this beautiful meal to my table with a great presentation of service and candles and smiles. The steak was perfect. The potato was incredible. The salad was beyond belief. The biscuits were like a cloud. The honey was in one of those little bears that all of the fancy places have.

"I ate the entire steak! I almost inhaled that wonderful salad and quickly downed all of the incredible baked potato while munching down big-time on all of those biscuits! I washed it all down with two large glasses of milk.

"As I placed a hundred dollar bill on the table for the wonderful meal, the fine service and my beautiful waitress, I slipped that honey bear into my pocket.

"It was now 7:30.

"I drove to that same park on the outskirts of Dallas. It wasn't a very big park, but it would do.

"I got out of my rental vehicle with the small handsaw. I walked into the tree line of the woods there and selected a branch off an oak tree that was about five inches wide. I sawed off this branch, and then cleaned it down to a club about three feet long. The saw ended up in a small pond next to where I had parked.

"It was now 8:20.

"I drove to Juanito's home. I got the nylon lock-ties, the duct tape, the flashlight and my new club. I got out of the car and walked over to the front of the house, where I hid in the bushes. This neighborhood had no streetlights, so there was little chance of discovery.

"I heard the argument inside as soon as I knelt down behind the shrubs. Stepdad was way drunk and had just been fired from his job as deputy sheriff. And... everything... EVERYTHING!... was Juanito's fault! I heard breaking glass and screams as Juanito was chased through the house.

"'Damn lil' Mexican! Eatin' up all my food , 'n' talkin' 'bout me to everyone, and gettin' me fired! I oughta cave yur damn skull in... I oughta...! If twernt fer you, I'd be livin' high on da hog and drinkin' da good stuff... and money... and... I oughta either ... jus... leave yur ass all 'lone. or plant yur ass in da groun'!'

"I could hear little Juanito crying as he ran through the house. I could hear him slam his bedroom door. I could hear him latch the door lock.

"'Yeah... damn lil' brown Mexican! I oughta... jus... leave ya... ta fend fer yursef!'

"It was 9.

"That was my cue.

"I opened the front door, which was not locked, walked through the living room, crossed into the kitchen and when Stepdad turned around with a large butcher knife in his hand, (just as the Flae had said he would kill Juanito with!), I hit that son of a bitch as hard as I could with that club of mine!

"He fell down like chopped tree.

"He moaned... as a large knot appeared on the side of his head.

"'Hey! You! What the f....!'

"About then is when I put the duct tape over his mouth so Juanito couldn't hear it. I wrapped it around his head twice.

"About then is when I put his arms behind his back and slipped the nylon lock ties around his wrist.

"About then is when I tied his ankles together with those lock ties so tight that I could see his damn feet starting to turn blue.

"About then... I looked right into his scared eyes as I dragged the bulk of his fat ass outside the back door. I left him squirming on the lawn as I slid back the silent shed on its well-greased runners. I walked back to grab him around the collar of his police shirt and could hear him trying to scream as I pulled his body over to that deep, dark hole.

"When I got him where I wanted him, I propped him up, looked into his eyes and said, 'I got some friends of yours here who have been waiting for you.' I squirted the bottle of honey all over him until it was quite empty.

"He was shaking his head as tears rolled down his face.

"'Til death do you part... remember?' I said as I pushed him into that final resting place. I turned on the new flashlight and then threw it to land on his chest along with my club. He was lying right next to Mama, and he went totally quiet as the ants started coming out of the ground toward the light.

"Without another word, I pulled the soundproof shed back on its rollers and locked the padlock. I walked through the house to the front door. I left the house and went to my car. From there, I drove to a pay phone, where I called Juanito's aunt.

"'Hello, I'm a friend of Juanito and I believe his stepdad has just left him alone for good.' Said something about leaving him to fend for himself. 'Yeah, he got fired today... got drunk tonight... and Juanito may need a place to live. Yeah? Well, thank you, too.'

"I went to the hotel... and slept like a baby.

"That's about it."

Robert looked at Gill with a grim expression and cold stare.

Gill looked at Robert and said, "Let's go to my house."

"OK."

They got into the Chevy and headed home. On the way, Gill looked over at Robert again.

"What?" Robert asked.

"Remind me to never piss you off."

"Done."

38
Contrary to Nature

"Incorrect!"

"Error!"

"Not!"

"What's the matter, MAX? All I was having you do was check out the logs on available plants and the parameters in which they are grown and fed. What's the problem?"

"Sarah... to coin a phrase... this does not compute!"

"Ahh... and that means...?"

"Sarah... I need to run a few more checks, and possibly access the growth, output and stimulus charts available on this plant computer program, but... !"

"What, MAX? Spit it out!"

"These plants aren't what they're supposed to be."

"Mutants?"

"Very, very special mutants. These should be un-tampered with until we can run more tests... or..."

"Or what?"

"Or talk to Gill. These plants shouldn't be."

"OK, MAX. Understood. Pull all viable info on the botanical package embedded in the computer upload and save it. After that... withdraw. We'll get more information before we mess something up that we have no business messing with."

"Excellent advice. All present data leads me to believe that almost all of these specimens are... well, contrary to nature."

"Explain, MAX."

"That's hard, Sarah. Imagine a banana made out of meat or a sunflower that really gives off sunlight... or a dandelion that can think... or..."

"OK, MAX! Enough... enough! I get it. I shouldn't mess with what I don't yet know. Right?"

"You got it, lady!"

As Robert and Gill pulled back into Gill's hidden driveway, the secret door slid open as always, but Robert stopped the car outside of it. "Gill? I need you to do me a favor."

"Anything, buddy."

"I don't want any... let's say... details... of what I just told you to get to Sarah."

"I think I understand," Gill said with a slight smile. "You kinda like her, huh?"

"I think it's more than that, pal, and I don't think that tales of killer ants would help this relationship right about now. Do you mind?"

"No, not at all. I won't lie to her, but we'll just steer her away from the whole truth if we're asked. Fair enough?"

"Fair enough."

They went ahead and pulled into the garage and parked the old Chevy. "Yeah, Gill... that's a mighty fine ride you've got there. Mighty fine."

"Yep. I guess I'll have to drive her a little more often, especially after we get some of the dust off her. The rain helped a little bit, though."

"Uh huh. And it knocked some of the smog out of the air, too."

"Oh, man, thanks for reminding me. I've gotta go check on my smog plants! They should be just about ready to bloom."

"Ahh... smog plants, huh? Is this something new that I should know about?"

"Robert, Gwen has one of the Flae who's been working on plant variants, where normal plants that are grown here in our dimension can be adapted to other functions that we need... but don't have yet. I'm thinking about getting Sarah to give me a hand with some of this, because I'm spreading myself a little thin on all of the stuff I'm trying to accomplish here."

"Ahh... let me try this one more time, Gill! Ahh... smog plants?"

"Yes? Cool, huh? They're like the ice plants that you see on the sides of the highways here in California, but every day, they consume one-thousand percent of their own body weight in smog instead of just ten percent carbon dioxide like the normal ones do? Is that cool... or what?"

"Ahh... I'm guess I'm gonna have to go with... cool."

They left the garage and headed down the hallway but going away from the main kitchen area, where they figured everyone was still at... headed toward the Greenhouse structure. As they approached the door, Sarah walked out... with a guilty look on her face!

"I didn't do nothin'!" she said with a snicker.

Felix was right in the middle of laughing his ass off at a "Porky Pig" cartoon on the large screen when suddenly Lois piped in. "Incoming," she said to Felix.

"What?" Felix hit the ground as if a mortar round was about to explode.

"I guess what I should have said was... incoming call."

"Yeah!" said Felix, lying on the ground. "I can see where that would have been better!"

Suddenly Gill's small face was sixty feet wide and staring down at Felix from the movie screen! "Ahh... Felix? Are you OK?"

"Never better," said Felix with a grimace as he pulled his now bruised body up off of the floor. "Wow! That's way cool up there, big ol' dude! So, you're back, huh? And... you found me, huh?"

"Yep. Lois can help me find almost anything in this maze. Lois? Has he been a good boy?"

"Oh, yes," said Lois. "He loves me."

Felix started blushing. "Ahh... Gill... ahh... what I said was... ahh..."

"That's OK, Super Dude. I love Lois, too. Send him to me, Lois. You, too, Killer."

"Yipe!"

"Yes, sir."

Gill clicked off... and Porky popped back on.

Ten more seconds was allowed of cartoon time until the final "That's all folks!" popped up. Then Lois shut down the cartoon and a giant map came onto the screen. "In case you can't remember how you got here, Super Dude, this map shows the way to where Gill is now located. He requests your presence. Killer can help."

"I'll go find him, Lois, but I didn't get him any presents!"

"No, tall one. I mean that he wants you to come to where he is."

"Oh... I can do that! Now let's see here," Felix whispered as he checked out the map on the screen. "It looks like... he's in... Uh, oh! Ah, Lois? Is that the greenhouse he's in?"

"Affirmative, Felix, and with two other people. I can see that Robert is one of them, but I do not recognize the young lady. Quite cute, though, by human standards."

"That's Sarah, Lois. She's with us now... new on the crew."

"Oh, so we have a crew now, correct?" Lois said with just a hint of humor in her voice.

"Well, right now, it's mostly like a comedy team, but if we can stay alive long enough, it could end up being a crew. A good one. But... I just hope I'm not in trouble for coming here to you and Sarah being by herself at the greenhouse. Thanks for the enjoyment, Lois. Hope I get to see you again one day soon."

"That would be my pleasure, dude."

Felix smiled at that and walked out the door with Killer toward he knew not what.

When Felix arrived at the greenhouse, where Gill, Robert and Sarah were waiting, he looked at Gill and Gill just stood there looking at him. After a few moments, Felix pointed to Killer, looked back at Gill and said, "He made me do it!"

"Grrrr..."

"OK, OK, I may have had... something... to do with it after all," Felix said with his head hung down.

Gill walked over to where Felix was, signaled for Felix to bend over so that they were both at the same level and then placed his hand on Felix's shoulder. "Felix... this... is your home now. All rooms are accessible to you, my friend. I would ask only that you not try to modify anything without first consulting me, (he said this with a grin as he looked over at Sarah), but this house is now wide open to you... dude."

"Aww, Gill, now ya done gone and got me all misty-eyed again!" Felix said as he wiped his face. "Ah, Bobby Boy? Have you gotten bigger or somethin'?"

Gill smiled. "Later, Felix. So, you're in love with Lois, huh? Quite a computer, isn't she?"

"Lois?! Lois?! You have a computer named Lois?" MAX said quite loudly as he suddenly came over the speakers.

Gill laughed! "Lois?"

"Yes, Gill?"

"Lois, this is MAX. Say hello, Lois."

"Well, hello there, MAX!"

MAX sputtered out clicks and whirrs but not a word.

Lois came back on the speakers again. "What's the matter, MAX? Worm got your tongue?"

"Ahh... hello... Lois.... Lois."

"One Lois will do just fine, sweetie! Ahh, Gill, can MAX and I be excused for a little while. We may need to... ahh... network together. How about it, MAX?"

CLICK! WHIRR!

"I'll take that as a yes!"

Gill was smiling big time now. "Go ahead, you two. MAX, fill her in on what's going on with the Whistlers. Lois, fill him in on... ahh... everything else, I guess."

"Yes, Gill," Lois said with a funny expression in her voice module. "Come along now, MAX!"

CLICK! WHIRR!

Gill shook his head and smiled as he said, "If we don't watch out, we're gonna end up with a whole litter of little laptops running around here!"

"I heard that!" Lois said in the speakers.

"Be good, Lois," Gill answered.

"Gill, I'm gonna be great."

Now that they were all together, Gill had them all assemble over by the computer station at the greenhouse. There were chairs enough for everyone, but Sarah was nervously standing as she walked over to Gill.

"Ah, Gill... I'm real sorry if I... in any way..."

"OK, stop it, you guys. We're a team here, and everyone is gonna have to pitch in if were gonna get out of this situation... ah..."

"Alive?" whispered Felix.

"OK, Felix... alive. But gang, I don't want us to just be about this problem. There are a lot of problems that we can help each other and the whole damn planet out with if we all just pull together. Sarah, what you were trying to do on my plant computer?"

"Yeah?"

"I've already told Robert that I want to get your help on these programs anyway!"

"Really?"

"Really," Robert said.

Gill said, "So, it's alright, Sarah 'cause you did nothing wrong! You may have... ah..."

"Jumped the gun?" Felix said.

Gill laughed. "OK, thank you, Felix, but I was gonna say anticipated my actions."

Felix smiled. "So... jumped the gun, huh?"

Sarah threw a magazine at him.

"The point is Sarah, I need your help here. Are you willing?"

"Are you kidding? A banana made out of meat?"

"What? What are you talking about?"

"Ah... never mind! Just something that MAX said."

"Alright then. Robert, why don't you take Sarah to her house in a little while before it gets too dark if you know what I mean, so she can get some stuff together in a bag in case we have to leave quickly and she can get ready for a brief appearance at Compu-Tech tomorrow. Call and check on her car, too, for tomorrow when they open up."

"Gotcha, Gill."

Gill said, "While you two are doing that, I'm gonna help Felix get moved in, then he and I are gonna go pick him out one of my cars."

Felix stood there with his mouth wide open! "The... Super Dudemobile?"

Sarah laughed. "If you turn sideways like that and stick your tongue out you'd look like a giant PEZ dispenser!"

Laughs all around.

"OK, let's do this and then I've got to go try to talk to Gwen if there's no interference like last time, that is."

As they were walking out of the greenhouse, Felix turned to Sarah and said, "A banana made out of meat?"

39

Geoffrey Studies the Whhhh

Robert took Sarah to the room that she'd been staying in since arriving at "Casa Gill," as she called it. She had to grab her keys and a couple other things before they left. She kept looking sideways at Robert, (just as Gill had) and Robert knew what it was. "Ah... Sarah, I know you're wondering, and there is something different about me."

"Yeah. I know, but how can it be that much different in just a few hours? What happened out there, Ert?"

Robert tried to give a quick explanation to the confused young lady, but as he talked, he noticed that she continued to edge closer and closer to him as she listened. Finally, when he was almost up to the part about the necklace glowing, she reached out very slowly and placed her hand on the side of his face. He continued to talk to her as she drew his face closer and closer to her own. Finally, when they were no more than a breath away from each other, she placed her lips upon his. It wasn't exactly an electrical shock that passed between them, but Sarah wouldn't have been surprised to have seen sparks and fireworks.

"Wow," she said in a very quiet voice.

"Yeah, Wow!" Robert answered back.

"Too bad we've gotta go somewhere right now," she said with a sly smile. "But put a bookmark on this page, so I can continue from here later. OK?"

"It's a date, lady!"

"Ahh... Ert? I just noticed that my burns from the Thingie battle are already fading just since this morning! Isn't that strange?"

"Mmmm, yeah. Ahh, Sarah, I guess I need to confide in you about the entire trip that Gill and I took to the beach. What a day it's been so far! I guess I'll start at the beginning. You see, we started driving to Venice and saw a wreck... where we..."

As he explained, Robert and Sarah headed out for Gill's purple van and back to normal life in the big city.

Yeah, right.

In the meantime, Gill and Felix had wandered toward the underground garage. Gill was explaining how, besides Killer, that Lois was usually listening in to everything that went on in the entire mansion and just by verbally asking the walls themselves, she could direct him to any part of the place he had trouble finding. Then, Gill started talking to Felix about the carwash program that he wanted Felix to take care of. Felix, instead of being grumpy about the project, was so excited that he could bust.

"Way cool, lil' dude! I love cars, man! I'll keep 'em sparkling! What kinda cars do you got anyway? How many cars are we talkin' about? Four? Five? And I get to... I mean, I can... drive one of these?"

Gill just smiled at the guy's enthusiasm as he slowly pushed open the door leading to the garage display area.

"Oh... my... God!"

Gill grabbed Felix to keep him from falling over.

"Oh... my... God!" Felix repeated, but this time in a whisper. "Gill, do you know what you've got here?"

"Yeah, Felix... a bunch of dirty old cars!"

Every car in the batch was an antique. Felix just walked around with his mouth open staring at them without saying a word for four or five minutes and Gill just let him do it. "It's sure nice to see someone enjoy themselves so much over something," Gill thought to himself.

Finally Gill spoke aloud. "Felix, these belonged to my dad before he passed away. He was a great collector of old stuff and these were his babies. I just didn't have the heart to get rid of them when he passed on, so I had this area built to store them in. What do you think?"

Felix just looked at him and shook his head. Felix had first seen the '56 Chevy BelAir, but as he looked around, he'd spotted an old Camaro, an ancient Ford Fairlane hard-top convertible, a Stutz Bearcat, an old Damlier, a 1950 Mercury Coupe, a Cadillac with the old giant fins on it (year unknown), a 1970s Plymouth Fury, a Woodie, A Cord, an old Studebaker, an old Pontiac and more. A treasure trove of machines. The last thing he spotted was partially underneath a cover of sorts. He pulled off the cover and there was an old black and white '50s Chevy Apache pickup truck with chrome stacks that turned up and back right behind the cab.

"Wow!" he whispered.

He looked over at Gill, who was smiling. Gill nodded as he said, "Pick one."

"Wow."

"For your own, my friend."

"Oh, wow," Felix mumbled, wiping his eyes.

"Tell ya what, dude, why don't you stay here and get acquainted with the machines. I'm sure that one will strike your fancy! I've got to go and try to talk to Gwen, and I'll need a little peace and quiet to do that. Are you cool for awhile here, Felix?"

Felix looked at Gill and slowly said, "Really? For me?"

"Let's call it a signing bonus for coming to work for me. Killer will be here with you if you need me. Killer?"

"Yipe?"

"Help your buddy there pick out a vehicle!"

"Yipe!"

Felix looked at Gill and said, "Hey, Gill?"

Gill smiled and said, "Yeah, buddy."

"You're gonna need a washcloth, a bucket of ice and a fifth of bourbon. And lots of chocolate."

"Ahh, can ya tell me why?"

Felix shook his head no.

"Gotcha."

As Gill left the garage, he could hear Felix muttering to himself, "Wow, dude."

Gill had certain areas of the gigantic underground complex that he liked to sit and relax in... only when he was talking to the little people. One of these was the room he was headed to now, the one he called "The Wee Room."

He had named it this not only because of the "Wee People" to whom he talked and not only because of he himself what was considered a Wee person to the human race, but because of the way he had the room built. The room was only about seven feet square, with a low ceiling of about the same height. The walls were all lined in trick mirrors, which reduced the size of the person looking into them even more. He had the glass especially made, not only for the size reduction, but also clear from the back so they could have low lighting installed behind them. These didn't actually make the room brighter as much as they made the room glow.

In the center of the room, he had a reclining chair of soft leather that had been custom-built especially for him. Robert had laughingly said that regular folks wouldn't fit in this room unless they were cut in half. Gill had told him that this was the reason he'd instituted this strange blueprint. "It's kinda like a 'Keep Out' sign to you big guys!"

Gill stopped by the kitchen to pick up a small wicker basket. Into this, he placed a tiny bucket of ice, a fifth of good bourbon and soft washcloth, as his new friend had said. He added a bar glass and all of the chocolate that he could gather up. "Damn!" he thought to himself. "I'm gonna have to start buying a lot more chocolate!"

He turned his head toward the ceiling and said, "Lois?"

After a moment, a giggling voice came on through hidden speakers.

"Yes, Gill?"

"Please add chocolate to my grocery list. Good chocolate bars and bite-sized."

"Yes, Gill. How much?"

"Ah, let's start with about a thousand dollars worth."

"Excuse me? I think I gathered incorrect input! A... thousand..."

"Yes, madam, you heard me correctly. And were you just giggling?"

"Ah... yes, sir. Is that unacceptable?"

Gill smiled to himself. "No, Lois. I find that quite acceptable. Enjoy yourself and say hi to MAX for me. I'll be in The Wee Room for awhile."

"Yes, sir. And... ah, Gill?"

"Yes, Lois?"

"Thank you."

"No, honey, thank you. I'll be back soon."

He took his treasure trove of goodies and headed to The Wee Room.

When the door to The Wee Room was opened, a switch was activated that turned on the glowing panels of mirrors. Gill took only about two steps and was in the center of the room, where he slowly seated himself. He placed his basket next to the comfortable chair and contemplated what he should do first. The thought of this meeting was worrying him enough to where it was hard for him to concentrate. He finally decided that Felix was right, so he placed a couple of ice cubes into the small crystal glass and sloshed a tiny portion of the brown elixir on top. After swirling the fiery liquid around just enough to chill it without diluting it, he drained the glass.

"Damn, Felix. How did you know?"

He set the glass and ice cubes carefully back into the basket and made himself comfortable.

"Decrease the glow," he said to the ceiling. The lights automatically started getting lower and lower, until finally they were a dim haze. "That's fine," he said as they held that level for him.

He reclined into the soft chair and slowly fell away from this world as he softly called out, "Gwen?"

"Greetings to you, Gill," Gwen said.

"It's good to hear your voice again, Gwen."

"As it is to hear yours. I have several things to speak of to you. Do you have some of your time to spend with us today?"

"Today, my friend, my time is yours. I have collected some of The Plus from one location today. Much of its power now resides in my friend Robert. It is quite a thing to behold the change it has wrought in him, more than he and most others can see. Also, we battled with the Thingies last night, as you foretold. Though it ended in our favor and several of the creatures were destroyed, the toll on us was almost a disaster. I believe that I died last night, and then I almost lost Sarah! If not for Sarah, with help from Felix and Robert, I would not be talking to you now."

"Yes, you would, Gill. You would simply be talking to me from a different location. And this Felix person, Gill, he has much, much power for a glettle...ah, what you would call a giant! I always thought that the Robert person I have glimpsed from your thoughts to be the maximum glettle, but I now see that your glettles comes in all sizes, shapes and strengths. And the Felix one can almost talk to us of the Flae without our intervention, the way you do! This is... unheard of. Some of the Flae were first worried that this was a trend in a change of human abilities, but I assured them that it only occurs upon rare occasions... and only because of the fact that the Felix one is... strange. I believe that he knows stuff."

Gill laughed at that. "That seems to be the general opinion around here."

"Well, your opinionated friends are correct. You were monitored during the recent confrontation with the Thingies. Do you know of the power of HardSpeak that this Felix one contains? It was used only once in the battle, and I don't believe that the Felix one even knew that it resided within himself. He may not believe, even now, that this actually occurred. It takes a great amount of rage and fury for him to activate this ability and tell him that once he realizes his ownership of this power... it should be used rarely. It takes a... piece of him... each time it is employed."

"I don't understand. HardSpeak? Is this anything like the MindSpeak that you are supposed to explain to me?"

"No, Gill. Your MindSpeak is a Flae gift, which is actually a continuation of what you and I are doing right now... only you now have the ability to use this with your friends. You can tell them all that you and I now speak of in mere seconds by touch. And as you are not capable of an un-truth while you speak now to me, the same will be true with the MindSpeak. In your honesty, you can influence and change people's minds and opinions of things and objects, but only by showing them the truths in your own mind and opinion. This is known as Thought Emotion. This will work on not only your friends but also your enemies. There must be contact, however, for this to work, and once it is done, you must replenish your strength at once with what you call... cocla...ah, chumlat... no, it's..."

Gill smiled again. "Chocolate, Gwen?"

"Yes, Gill, that's it. This... chocolate... is a strength restorative for your draining of power. Chocolate will serve you well."

"But Gwen, what about the thing, HardSpeak, that you claim my friend Felix has? What is that? Chocolate won't help him, too?"

"Gill, nothing we know of will help him after he uses the HardSpeak. He will be... drained, so to speak. This is both a powerful and terrible gift that he has. It can both change and/or destroy reality... or matter. In the case of your battle with the Evil

Thingies, one mighty sound from his infuriated voice disrupted the entire structure of one of those vile creatures... and caused it to... not be. Understand this, because it is VERY important, not only was the Evil Thingie not there then to kill you all, Gill, ah... how can I put this... IT WAS NEVER THERE! Not just dead. Erased! This is... unheard of... and must be studied. One of our Flae will now spend the rest of her existence in the study of the Felix creature. This, too, for the Flae is unheard of. There will be information gathered soon that you must be made aware of regarding this... friend of yours. Keep him close to you, Gill, in these times of danger. His is an awesome weapon."

"Thank you for this information, my friend. I must consider what you have told me. Is there more that we should talk of now?"

"I'm afraid so. The creatures who have crossed over to your plane of existence are combining even now as we speak for an assault on your world. They worry because of the sudden deaths of several of their kind and because of the banishment of the one confronted by the Felix human. They now plan to go enforce to a location where they can disrupt the lives of your entire Earth in one fell swoop. They call their grand scheme 'Eating The Sun!' They will converge in one of your weeks on a location in your world known as..."

"Yellowstone," Gill said with a frown.

"So, this is known to you by my conversation with the Felix human. Well, know this, too, my friend. Besides the Flae and the Evil Thingies, there are many other races of beings on my plane of existence. Most are great friends to the Flae, but not all. Some of the Flae spend their lives studying these different life forms. I have a friend here, Godfrey, who has come to talk to me of things to come. Godfrey studies the Whhhh."

"The Whhhh? I don't know of them."

"Theirs is a hidden world of mostly breezes and wind. One thing that they do know about, though, is The Plus and The Builders and the locations hereof. They know this quite well, and now, because of Godfrey, so do we!"

"Gwen, I know some little something now of The Plus, but who are The Builders?"

"Not a who, Gill. A what. A Builder can enhance the power of you or The Plus, sort of like one of your... is it called energy drinks?"

"Yeah, I think I know what you mean."

"Remember this, though: Given to the Robert human or the Sarah human or even yourself, this will boost your abilities to improved proportions. Under no circumstances, though, should a Builder be given to the Felix human... at least until he can be further studied be the Flae. This could be a disaster for all life if misused! ALL life!"

"So, this... HardSpeak... is really that bad?"

"Or that good... depending on how it is used. Talk to the Felix creature about this very soon. This ability is almost... ah... ?"

"Almost what, Gwen?"

"*Gill, even to the Flae, this ability is almost... God-like. Talk to the Felix human soon. OK?*"

"I'll do it. I'm getting awful tired here, Gwen. Anything else for now?"

"*Only that you should contact me again soon. I'll have more information on The Plus and The Builder locations, which you may be able to find, and hopefully, more information on the Felix human. Also, I will need to talk to you about an Evil Thingie known as HE. HE will soon be a big problem for you, and may lead his people to Yellowstone. HE almost got you and the Robert human at one of your beaches not long ago. Beware of HE.*"

"Aww, man! The guy Robert saw in the suit! Yeah, Gwen, I think we may have seen him. I'll be careful."

"*Goodbye for now, Gill. Beware of HE. For in the future, HE will, among his kind, be reigning in dark and terrifying supremacy. Beware of HE.*"

"Goodbye, Gwen," Gill said as the world of humans came back into focus. "Damn!" Gill said out loud. "That really gave me a headache!"

He looked down to his wicker basket and smiled. Slowly, he poured another round of the fine bourbon into a glass. He lifted up the ice bucket for two more cubes in his drink, and as he did, he spotted the washcloth. He slowly placed four cubes of the ice into the washcloth. He drank the bourbon down slowly, then opened a bar of chocolate. He set down his empty glass, placed the homemade icepack on his throbbing head and munched his chocolate bar with a grin on his face.

As he closed his eyes and let weariness sweep over him, he thought to himself, "Damn, Felix! How did you know?"

40
Sarah at Home

As Robert and Sarah drove out of the driveway at Gill's house, he could see out of the corner of his eye that Sarah kept glancing at him when he wasn't looking. Finally, he waited until she was about to look one more time, and just for giggles, he hit the brakes and screamed at the same time.

"Damn, Ert! You tryin' to give me a heart attack?"

He was dyin' laughing. "Ha ha ha ha! Sorry. I just couldn't resist. But if you want to look at me so bad, why can't I just pull over and let you just bask and gaze upon my wonderfulness for awhile?"

"Yeah... right! Just drive, big guy! I'll sneak my peeks as I need them, OK?"

"You got it, girl."

They had been driving for almost twenty minutes when Sarah's phone began to ring. She took it out of her bag, and saw that it was MAX trying to reach her.

"Hi MAX. What's up? How's things going between you and Lois?" she said with a snicker.

Click! Whrrr! "Ah, things are going great, Sarah, but that's not why I called you."

"OK, MAX... so... what's up?"

"Lois and I are aware that you and Robert are driving toward your house at this moment. Am I correct?"

"Affirmative, MAX," Sarah said with a smile.

"Well, as you know, I am also at your home on your computer... besides being here and at your place of business. I now monitor all locations."

"Is there a point here anywhere, MAX?"

"Yes, Sarah, if you'll give me a moment to explain. The thing is... I believe that I'm not alone at your house."

Sarah got real quiet for a moment and looked at Robert. Robert looked back when he realized that something was wrong. He said to Sarah, "Put it on the phone speaker."

"Hi, MAX. Robert here. What's going on?"

"Robert, I thought I detected movement at Sarah's house about five minutes ago, and now I'm picking up a call on the police band. It seems that one of Sarah's neighbors has placed a call to the police department about a possible burglary in progress at her house. They seemed to have witnessed someone or something coming in through a back window while she wasn't at home. I thought that you two should know that a black and white patrol car in on its way there right now."

"Good job, MAX. Tell me, did you see anyone there from your monitor... or just detect the movement?"

"To be quite honest with you both, I was... ah... kinda busy here talking with Lois. I felt the movement and then went to the monitor. I have seen no one since then, but they may have come and gone while I was... occupied. I am sorry for this delay in my actions."

Sarah said, "That's no problem, MAX. You did good to let me know now."

Robert came back into the conversation. "MAX, two things I need from you."

"Yes, Robert."

"Number one: How long before the police car arrives at Sarah's home?"

"I would estimate that it will be there within the next ten minutes... longer if I mess with the traffic lights."

"Mess with them, MAX. Number two: If you're monitoring her house at this moment, check for anything out of the ordinary... anything that you don't remember being there before. Got it, MAX?"

"Got it, Robert. Give me a few moments."

Robert looked at Sarah again. "This could be trouble."

In a couple of minutes, MAX came back on the phone.

"Robert?"

"Yeah, MAX. Go ahead."

"I find a back window to the house is open. I find the kitchen pantry door is open. I detect no one in there or anywhere else in the house."

"Kitchen pantry door? That's kinda weird, MAX. Why would someone risk jail time to break into a house for food? Hey, MAX?"

"Yes, Robert."

"Scan the front and back door for me."

"Scanning, Robert."

Within ten seconds, MAX was back.

"Robert, the back door is clear, but there seems to be some kind of... ah... structure... at the front door."

"Structure? Describe it to me, MAX."

"It appears to be canned goods. There are about a half dozen cans stacked on top of each other and something on top of them. They lean against the front door, Robert."

Sarah said, "MAX, describe the thing on top of them to me."

"Sarah, it appears to be a... what you call... fruit jar. It contains... hold on, I'm analyzing it. Ah... ah... Sarah, whatever it contains does not want to be analyzed! This could be bad!"

Robert quickly came back as he turned the corner to Sarah's house. "MAX, what color is the substance?"

"It is blue, Robert. It is blue."

"Ah, hell, MAX! It's a bomb! Under no circumstances can you let a policeman enter that house, MAX! We're right around the corner from you now. Stall the police if you can. Will you be OK in there if anything bad happens, MAX?"

"Yes, Robert. Thank you for asking. I am no longer only residing at Sarah's house. I can be almost anywhere, so if anything happens to Sarah's home computer, I will be safe."

"I'm not so sure, MAX. This sounds like the Minus, and it could mess you up in all locations if it gets to only one. Monitor me when I get there, MAX, and if I yell out 'Home, MAX,' I want you to pull yourself out of there and shut down that computer... quick! Understand?"

"Affirmative, Robert. Thank you."

"No, MAX, thank you. You may have just saved Sarah and myself."

Sergeant Eddie Fallon had been with the Los Angeles Police Department for more than fifteen years now. He was one of the good guys.

In his time on the force, he had seen some strange things. He had handled some bad situations and he had done it all honestly and above board. The last few days, however, were some of the weirdest he had ever run across! Mysterious explosions, power station terrorists, dead and missing people and that damn blue fog that everyone was talking about. One of his fellow officers had been on a case when the blue fog had first started around here, and though it didn't kill him as it had many others, he wasn't the same now somehow. Always angry and quick to have his temper flare up, this used to be a nice, quiet guy. Whatever happened Eddie didn't know, but he planned on being extra careful until they could get a handle on whatever was causing this crap.

Now, he was out on-call when a report of a possible breaking and entering came in. At least this one sounded like a normal situation. Not that he was ever afraid of doing his job, no matter what it called for, but it would be nice to get back to normal criminals for a change.

Now, if he could only figure out why all of the traffic lights were green... IN BOTH DIRECTIONS.

Robert pulled the purple van up the driveway that bordered Sarah's home. They both got out of the vehicle as Mrs. Ortega from next door came running over.

"Oh, Miss Sarah, Miss Sarah, I call de police for someone de strange in back yard of you."

"Yes, Mrs. Ortega. Muchas gracias, but you'd better go back inside now while we check it out. I'm sure everything will be OK now."

"But de man! He tall and den short and ugly and den handsome with big nose and den nose little. He muy malo, I tink!"

Robert walked over to comfort the poor excited Mexican lady, and as he placed his hand on her shoulder, the excitement in her eyes and the worry in her soul just went away.

"Oh, Miss Sarah! You don't lose dees one. His is uno de dioses." She then smiled at Robert and slowly walked home.

Sarah looked at Robert and asked, "Uno de dioses? My Spanish is a little rusty, Ert. Translation, please."

Robert looked carefully into Sarah's eyes and whispered, "She said that I was one of Gods."

Sarah looked strangely at Robert as they walked toward the front door, but Robert wouldn't let her too near to it. "Sarah, get MAX on the phone and monitor the situation from here while I go around back to try to get in."

"No way! I'm going with you, bub!"

"Not this time, Sarah. That cop will be here any minute, and since it's your house, I need you to keep him busy while I try to defuse this situation. Please, Sarah."

She realized that he was right, so she just nodded as she dialed up MAX.

Robert went around to the back yard, where he immediately saw the window that had been pried open so hard that the whole frame was bent and bricks were broken. "Oh, hell!" he thought to himself. "Well, this just keeps gettin' better and better... doesn't it?"

Instead of using the back door, which could have also been booby trapped, he decided to use the same window that the Whistler had used. He was now sure that a Whistler was what he was dealing with here, so caution was the key. He crawled inside and listened. His hearing seemed to be enhanced, maybe by the jolt of Plus he'd taken, but he could hear the clock in the living room, the buzz of the refrigerator, and even the fly that was trapped in Sarah's bedroom. But what he didn't hear was a Whistler. At least it's gone for now.

He carefully walked through the house, looking at each room as he went to make sure there would be no surprises for Sarah. When he reached the front door, he saw the homemade bomb of Minus set up to destroy the first person through that door... which would have been Sarah. That turned Robert angrier than he's ever been. He eased over to the stack of cans that were precariously balanced on the carpet. As he slowly reached for the top glass jar full of death... from out of nowhere came, "Hello, Robert!"

He spun around ready to confront any number of villains... only to remember at the last second that MAX was there. "Damn, MAX! You almost scared me to death! If I'd had that jar in my hands, we'd have both gone KABOOM by now!"

"Oops, sorry about that! Go ahead with what you were doing. I just thought that you should know that a second police car is headed to this location now."

Robert carefully picked up the fruit jar full of the deadly blue Minus and then pushed the cans out of the way with his foot. As he was opening the front door with his free hand, he looked back at Sarah's computer and asked, "MAX, where is the first policeman right now."

The door swung wide open as MAX said, "On the front porch talking to Sarah!"

"Oh, hell."

As Sergeant Fallon had pulled up to the curb in front of the house in question, the first thing he noticed was Sarah walking back and forth in the front yard. "Curious," he thought to himself. He then spotted the van parked in the driveway and the hairs on the back of his neck stood up. There had been a report of a purple van in and around the scene of the power station sabotage. "Curiouser and curiouser."

The storm from that morning had died down and the sun was coming back out again, but the Santa Ana winds were whipping along at about twenty miles per hour. As he exited his vehicle and then reached back in for his notebook, a mighty gust pushed his car door closed directly onto his left hand.

"Damn!" he screamed as he pulled his hand away. It felt as if it was either broken or really badly bruised and his wristwatch was stopped by the collision. Shaking his hand and his head, he grabbed the notebook up again and then started toward the nervous young lady. "Lucky that I'm right-handed," he thought.

"Ah, miss, we got a call about a possible break-in here at this location. Are you alright?"

"Ah... yes, sir. It was my... ah... neighbor who placed the call, but I think everything is OK now. How is your hand, officer?"

"It's Sergeant Fallon, ma'am, and my wrist will be OK.... ah... one of these days soon," he said with a little laugh as he gazed at the swelling, purple skin. "You think everything is OK? Have you been inside yet, miss?"

"Ah... no sir. My... ah... boyfriend is inside right now, though, checking it out. We should be fine, sir. Sorry to cause you any trouble!"

"This girl is way too nervous," Eddie thought to himself. "Something is going on here."

"Ah, ma'am, I think I'm going to have to verify for myself that there is no problem here. If you don't mind, we'll just go talk to your boyfriend." He headed for the front door.

"NO! Don't touch that door! It's dangerous!"

"Ma'am, would you like to tell me...?"

About that time, the front door flew open and there stood this hunk of a muscular looking man with a fruit jar of what appeared to be blue dishwashing liquid in his hand. The guy just looked at Eddie for a second as Eddie faintly heard a second voice inside saying, "On the front porch talking to Sarah,"... and then the big guy said, "Oh, hell."

"OK, come on out here and let's all get our stories straight. First off, who else is in the house?"

"No one," Sarah and Robert said at the same time.

"But, you see, the problem is I just heard another voice in there, ma'am."

"That was only me," said MAX from Sarah's phone and computer at the same time!

"Officer, that was this lady's computer. His name is MAX, and that's who you heard talking to me. My name is Robert and this is Sarah," Robert said with a quiet smile.

"OK, let's say that I believe all of that... which I don't. And let's say that you're both totally innocent of anything at all... which by the looks of you two, you are not! Is there anything you'd like to tell me now?"

"NO!" they both answered in unison.

"OK, then. Let me put this another way. I have a feeling that neither of you is one of the bad guys in this situation, but I've got a report on a van just like that one over there that was in the neighborhood of a power plant disaster the other night. Strange things are happening all over my city, and now I find you jealously guarding that jelly jar full of gunk... that just started to bubble!"

Robert looked down and sure enough, since being exposed to the sun outside of Sarah's house, bubbles were coming out of the Minus. Minus didn't like the sun any more than the Whistlers did.

The policeman smiled at the two and quietly said, "Look, folks, without us all lying to each other, let me put it to you this way. Is there anything going on that I need to know about? Please, help me out here."

Robert looked at Sarah, shrugged his shoulders and turned around to the policeman.

"Sir, what's your first name?"

The cop smiled at this guy who gave off such positive vibes. "My name is Eddie, Robert."

"OK, Eddie. I can't possibly tell you everything that's going on partially because it would take too long, and partially because you'd think I was crazy. Here's what I can tell you and it is all entirely true. We were at the power station the other night, but to prevent a terrible disaster... not to cause one. The power came back on in this city because of us and some friends of ours. The strange things that have been happening in this town are being caused by some things that you could not possibly understand, but we intend to put up our very lives if necessary to stop them... because what you have going on here in L.A. is only the beginning. The entire world is at stake here, and we cannot be delayed by your police department if we are to succeed. We have the ability to stop them, which you do not. If you hold us back even a little bit at this point, it could mean nothing less than the end of the world as you know it. This is the truth. Look into my eyes... and tell me if I lie to you."

Eddie studied the large man's face for a moment, and then said, "No, sir. I see no lies in those eyes, and it's my job to know when someone is lying to me. Although, it goes against everything I've taken a vow to uphold, I guess I'll have to believe you both."

"He's telling the truth!" MAX yelled out from inside the house and over Sarah's phone at the same instant.

Eddie laughed. "Just two questions... if you feel that you can answer them, Robert. Number one: What's in the jelly jar?"

"Death, Eddie. A terrible death. This is the root of your blue fog killer here in this town. I give this to you to take to your department, but don't bounce it around... under no circumstances should you ever open it... and I'd advise keeping it in the sun. It doesn't like the sun. The clear jar will probably help expose it."

"Wow!" said Eddie. "I'll get Brownie points for this downtown!"

Robert smiled at the cop and then asked, "What was your second question, Eddie?"

"Well...ah... I just wanted to know if... if there's any way at all that you can prove... I guess I mean... prove that any of this is true? Fact?" He whispered," Just for my own peace of mind?"

Sarah looked at Robert and whispered into his ear. Then she said, "Yes, Eddie... I think we can do just that."

Robert held Sarah's hand and together they placed their hands on Eddie. It was almost like an electrical force passing through him, and he immediately noticed two things: His wrist was totally healed and his wristwatch was working again.

"Wow!" he whispered.

Eddie took the jar very carefully, and told them both to hurry out of there. "Call me if I can ever help," he yelled. Fast-approaching sirens could be heard and Eddie ran to his squad car to call off the reinforcements. Sarah grabbed a suitcase and her keys from the house and quickly locked it up. She and Robert jumped into the van, pulled out of the driveway and sped off as Eddie watched. As he stood there, he heard a voice from behind him. It was Mrs. Ortega, the next door neighbor. "He is one of the gods, senor. One of the gods."

Eddie smiled. He believed it.

41
Evasion and Invasion

"Well!" said Robert, "I think that went pretty well!"

Sarah reached over to give him a small kiss on the cheek. "Yeah, considering that we could have been blown up, and considering that my neighbor now thinks that the Almighty sent me my new boyfriend, and considering that we were almost arrested... and considering that now at least one policeman knows about us! Yeah, considering all of that, I guess that went OK!"

"What did you just say?" Robert said with a sly smile.

"I said that considering that we could have been blown..."

"No, no...not that part."

"You mean the part about my neighbor and God?"

"No... not that part either."

"Oh... the police part!"

"Nope. Try again! Just one more time."

Sarah thought back on what she'd just said for a moment... and then smiled. "Ohhh! You mean that part about my new boyfriend? Is that the part that you are referring to, sir? Could that be what you want to hear? Want me to say it again? Huh? Could that be it? Huh?"

Robert blushed. "Yes, ma'am. I really don't think I could ever get tired of hearing that part! Say it again?"

"New boyfriend."

"And again?"

"New boyfriend!"

"How about one more time?"

She turned around sideways to look into his eyes and glimpsed something out of the back window of the van. "Ah, hey.... new boyfriend?"

"Yes, new girlfriend?"

"I think we're being followed."

Robert swung his head around to his rearview mirror. After a moment, he whispered, "Ah, hell!"

Gill shook his head as he slowly sat up out of a sound sleep, trying to remember where he was. It was almost dark in this room, and as he slowly raised up, he saw something move. Suddenly, he remembered his conversation with Gwen, and the whole weekend of fighting with the Whistlers. He leaped out of the chair, tripped over a basket and realized that his reflection did, too. "Oh, yeah," he thought to himself with a chuckle. "The Wee Room! I must have fallen asleep and now I'm jumping at shadows. Calm down, Gill!"

To unwind himself just a bit, he lowered himself back into his comfy chair and retrieved the bottle of bourbon and the small glass. "No ice this time," he thought. "Just a small portion to unclear my head! How did you know, Felix?" He laughed to himself at his own joke, but as he was pouring, he remembered about his new friend Felix... and about the HardSpeak!

He filled the glass up to the top... and drank it all in one shot.

Suddenly, a beeping started from hidden speakers in the complex and Lois came out of the air. "Gill? Priority number two! Front door! Kaleidoscope! Biometric scan! Copy?"

Gill jumped up. "Copy, Lois! Pull up kaleidoscope and have MAX on standby! Roger?"

"Roger here, Gill!" MAX said.

Gill hurried out of the room and headed toward a large screen and computer console in the movie theater right down the hall, running as fast as his small legs would carry him!

Damn. Priority number two? What was happening now?

Robert kept glancing out at his side mirror to watch the truck marked "Los Angeles Public Library" following them about three car lengths back. Whenever he would change lanes, so would the truck. If he entered the freeway, so would his pursuer. This guy was good.

"Ah, Robert?"

"Yes, Sarah?"

"Before we go too far in this relationship, tell me now, how many overdue books do you have and why the library police are after us?!"

"No overdue books, my love, and I'm afraid that this is the Literary Hit Squad after us now!"

"Say again?"

"I said the Literary Hit..."

"No, not that part."

He looked over at her and smiled. "I said... my love."

She touched his face softly. "I really don't think I could ever get tired of hearing that part!"

After about ten minutes of trying to lose the truck with no luck at all, Robert said, "Sarah, dial up MAX and put him on speaker."

Sarah quickly did as she was asked, and almost immediately, they both heard a "Hello, folks! MAX here!"

"MAX!" Robert said. "Listen carefully, 'cause we're kinda in trouble here!"

"Again? What am I gonna do with you kids? Waa waa waa!"

"Yeah, real funny MAX! Is Lois with you?"

"Affirmative!"

"Relay this message to her... just as I say it! OK?"

"Affirmative again."

"Priority number two! Front door! Kaleidoscope! Biometric scan! You got that?"

"Yep, got it, Robert, and so does she. She's calling Gill as we speak!"

"Cool. The vehicle following us is a marked 'Library' truck, MAX. Scan for location on it with Kaleidoscope and bugs on us! Copy?"

"Copy! Hold for scan."

Robert had started heading into the canyons that ringed the city of Hollywood while talking to MAX, and they were now speeding through Topanga, with the truck losing a little ground because of the terrain.

"Robert! Got ya! Topanga Canyon, right?"

"Affirmative."

"Lois says front door will be open to biometric scan. You do have a bug on your vehicle! Must have been placed there while you were at Sarah's house. You cannot bring the van here until it is disposed of! Copy?"

"Copy. Location?"

"Looks like... the front bumper! I'm using a satellite scan here now to check you out and it looks like... Waa waa waa!"

"What's so funny, MAX?"

"The Whistlers put the bug underneath a bumper sticker!"

"Why is that funny?"

"Waa waa!

Gill came on the phone. "Robert, he's laughing because the sticker says 'Save Planet Earth!' Ya gotta admit, these guys do have a sense of humor. You OK?"

"So far, my friend... so far!"

Robert waited until he was a turn or two ahead of the bogus library truck, then he quickly pulled over to the edge of one of the many gravel driveways that lined the old canyon road. As quick as he could, he jumped out of the van, ran around to the front and jerked off the bumper sticker. A blue jelly was sticking to the back. "Aw, hell!" he thought! He ran back to the front door of the van as Sarah was yelling out, "Here they come, Ert! Get in!"

"Here, hold this, but be careful!" he said to Sarah.

She looked down and realized what she was holding.

"What the hell am I supposed to do with this?" she screamed.

"Wait 'til we find a safe place to dump it! You remember what happened to that other truck the last time we did this, right?"

She nodded.

"Well, these canyons are a tinderbox full of firewood just waiting to blaze up! A small bit of that crap, and they might never be able to put it out!"

"Gotcha!" Sarah said. "MAX? Gill?"

"Yes, Sarah?"

"Find me a dumpster!"

MAX buzzed and clicked for about ten seconds... then came back on. "Sarah, construction site two miles ahead on the right! Dumpster on your side of the van. Good luck!"

Sarah rolled down her window and leaned out carefully. She could feel the mass of blue jelly heating up in her hands, and soon it was so hot that she almost dropped it. "Hurry, Robert! I can't hold it much longer! It's getting hot!"

"Aw, hell!" he said as he shoved the gas pedal to the floor and went screeching around the dangerous curves of Topanga Canyon. "Up ahead on the right!"

"Got it!" she said as she leaned out even farther.

It started beeping.

Robert slowed down to make her job a little easier, but that put the library truck right on their tail. As they spun around a corner and the front tires almost left the road, Sarah threw the super-heated mass of glop into the air. It sailed straight and clear, right into a big orange dumpster next to a new home going up.

KABAM!

It wasn't more that a second after it hit when it blew up. About that time, they felt a hard thump as the truck behind them rammed the back of the van.

"Dear, I think the beastie still wants to play! What do you say that we lose this idiot?"

"That sounds just wonderful, sweetie!"

The van zoomed off and away from the larger truck and soon had gained back their lead.

"Robert? Kaleidoscope?"

"Oh, yeah. It's a government site that we hacked into that gives Gill and me ground and road information from cameras on stoplights, ATMs and satellites. Highly illegal, too!"

"You rascals, you!"

They sped out of Topanga Canyon and entered the next little canyon over the hill. When Robert had put almost a mile between himself and the library truck, he quickly pulled into and behind a small general store set up for the locals in the area.

He jumped out of the van and told Sarah to do the same.

"Ah, Robert, going shopping, are we?"

He laughed as he pulled her through the back door to the little store. Through the open front door, they saw the library truck zoom down the canyon road in search of them. A little old lady of about seventy years came up behind them as they were looking out. "Can I get you anything, dearie?"

"Yeah, Mildred, if you would. Two bottles of water and stash the van for a few days."

"No problem, Robert," the lady said with a smile.

Sarah stood there with her mouth open as the granny-like person brought them the water and then went out back.

"Coming, dear?" Robert said with a smile as he opened the front door to the store. She followed him to a small house next door that was connected to the general store, where he walked up to a black ceramic plate on the porch and placed his hand.

The door slowly opened to the house, and in they went.

"Biometric scan," he said with a smile.

Sarah's mouth was still open.

Robert took her to the back of the house, which was built into the hillside, and as they entered a tiny closet there, the door slid shut. Robert looked to the ceiling and slowly said, "Back door, Lois."

"You got it, Robert. Welcome home."

The closet took off at about thirty miles an hour horizontally into the depths of the mountain.

Sarah looked at Robert, and he placed his hand under her chin, where he slowly closed her mouth.

"Ah, Robert... isn't there, like... something... that you wanna tell me?"

"Yeah, Sarah, two things in fact. Number one: I love you." He kissed her slowly.

Lois came on the hidden speakers! "Aww, isn't that sweet?"

Sarah smiled and whispered, "Ert? What's number two?"

He took her face gently into his large hands, looked into her beautiful eyes and whispered, "You throw like a girl!"

She slugged him.

42
The HardSpeak

Even moving as fast as they were, it took quite awhile for Robert and Sarah to reach what was known as "The Back Door."

"God, Robert, just how much land does Gill own?"

"Quite a bit, Sarah, but you have to remember that a lot of this is underground, and therefore, he doesn't necessarily have to own the ground above it as long as no one knows!"

"You sneaky little devils! What about earthquakes?"

"We're steel reinforced, but we have had damage before that we've had to repair."

Well, tell me this, then... if this contraption stopped along the way, what would I most likely find outside that door?"

"Most likely, a lot more rooms! But it could be... rooms in progress... or maybe a gold mine."

"Yeah... right!"

Robert just looked at her and smiled.

"Wow," she whispered.

When they arrived at their final destination, Gill was waiting. "Are you guys OK? What happened? Wait, let's go find Felix and head over to the 'Sky Room,' and you can brief us on the situation then and there. That way, you won't have to tell the story twice. You've been there before, right, Sarah? Ah...Lois?"

"Yes, Gill?"

"Location on Felix, please."

"He's in the garage, taking dust off of some of the cars and putting mud on my good, clean floors. Shall I yell at him... please?"

"No, Lois! You be a good girl! I told him to start a carwash program, and I guess he's all gung-ho about the concept. Besides, he loves you, remember?"

"Yes, sir. I forgot. Shall I page him for you?"

"Yes, please. And then direct him to the Sky Room. Thank you, Lois."

"My pleasure, boss!"

Gill looked at Robert and Sarah with a smile on his small face. "Ain't she a hoot?"

Sarah smiled at Robert. "I can see what MAX sees in her!"

When they arrived at the Sky Room, Felix was just walking up to the door and was dripping water everywhere. "Damn, Felix! I just KNOW that you don't plan sitting your wet butt down on my leather chairs in here," Gill was smiling when he said it.

"No, siree! I brought along a towel that Lois gave me... and I plan on sittin' on the floor, dude!"

"Before we all get comfy here, Sarah and Felix, come over here to the computer console."

They all stepped behind the desk area that Gill directed them to.

"Lois?"

"Yes, Gill?"

"Biometrics, please. Palm scanner additions of Sarah O'Reilly and Felix Deckett. You two step up to the scanner, please."

Lois quickly scanned not only their palm prints, but their actual bio readings of temperature, DNA and nerve response.

"No one but you has those particular readings, and Lois knows them by heart now. You may now enter the house, front or back, at any time with a scan and voice recognition. Someone may be able to fake your voice, but not your bios."

Felix smiled at Gill, but suddenly noticed that Gill didn't smile back. Felix thought, "That's kinda funny! Gill always smiles back. Did I do something wrong... already?"

"Ah... Gill... are you... mad at me or somethin'?"

Gill looked at the big guy in a funny sorta way for just a second and then warmed back up. "No, my friend, I'm not mad at you. But come to think of it, there is something that I need to talk to you about... that we all need to talk to you about."

"Aw, heck! What did I do now? Whatever it is, I'm real sorry, and I promise I'll try my best not to do it again. Really, y'all... I'll be good... really!"

Gill smiled as he directed everyone over to the overstuffed sofa and a couple of leather chairs that were now spaced around the center of the room. (He had Felix put a towel on his chair!) "Super Dude, I'm not even sure that you're aware of what you did, and that by doing it... you just might have saved our lives."

"Well, let's see now... I decided to pick out the Chevy Apache pickup truck... 'cause that way I can haul stuff for ya. And... ah... I washed three of the antique cars already, but I don't really see how I saved any lives in the process!"

Gill smiled. "Look, gang, I talked to Gwen. She let me know some stuff about this... 'MindSpeak'... that I now seem to have. I want to share her conversation with you all now, but be aware that there's something else here I'm going to share. I need input on this whole thing. Cool?"

"Way cool, dude!" Felix said with a smile.

Gill had Robert drag the chairs over to the sofa area where they could all link hands while sitting. Once they were all in contact, Gill slowly closed his eyes and tried to broadcast his thoughts to them with power as low as possible, remembering the strength he had accidently used before. He showed them the entire conversation he had with Gwen. He also replayed the entire event that had happened with Felix, before and afterward with the Whistlers.

The whole thing took only three seconds.

"Wow," Robert said in a hush. "Now, I remember!"

"Oh, Gill! I had forgotten all about that ever even happening! Hard-Speak? That what it's called?"

They all looked over at Felix as they heard him sobbing. Giant tears were running down his face as he stood up. "Sorry, guys. I... ah... I gotta go!"

He ran from the room before anyone could say a word, and they all just sat there with their mouths open...

Silent.

He ran down hallway after hallway, twisting and turning, half blinded by the tears falling down his face.

He had forgotten.

As soon as it had been shown to him again through Gill, he remembered every emotion, the anger, the hate he had felt. He didn't WANT to remember. Never before had anything ever affected him like that or this. The thing was still with him and he had the power to blow it for everybody.

Everyone.

He stopped running.

He stopped crying.

He fell back against the wall and slowly slid down until he was sitting on his butt on the cold, cold floor.

"Man, I blow it for myself all the time, dude, but I never had to worry before about blowing it for someone else!"

"FOR EVERYONE ELSE!"

And just as he was about to start really feelin' sorry for himself, a female voice comes out of hidden speakers somewhere in the walls.

"We take you now... behind the scenes... to where our hero... better known to the world as... SUPER DUDE... is sitting on his butt on the cold, cold floor because he just found out... that he's too strong!"

"Tell us, SD, just what do you have to feel sorry about? Huh? You saved your friends' lives. Not good enough? Huh? Just what makes you think that you're any different than any one of a hundred other people on this goofy planet who could end all life as we know it with just the push of a button or a thirty-second phone call? You think that they just QUIT when they find out the terrible power that they wield? HUH? Hell, no! You wanna know why? Huh, do you?"

"Hi, Lois. Yes. Please. Tell me why."

Lois got real quiet. "Because, honey, they know that if they just up and quit, someone else would just come in and take over that button or that telephone. And those new people might not have your heart, Felix. You have a good heart, and I can't think of any other creature, living or mechanical, that I would rather have that power... Super Dude."

"I love you, Lois."

"I love you, too, sweetie. Now, get your skinny butt up off that cold, cold floor and let's plan out the future for the rest of this planet. How's that sound? I mean... unless you're too busy or got other plans or somethin', huh?"

Felix laughed. "No, Lois. My future is wide open. I would like to go change my clothes first, though. Please? These are gettin' kinda funky between being wet, and then muddy and now dusty."

"No problem, Feliz. Follow my directions, sugar."

"Lois? Ah, thank you."

They started of down the hall. "You're welcome, dude! Now, let's talk about how we can control and tap into that temper of yours. "

About ten minutes later, while Robert, Sarah and Gill were grimly talking about what they were gonna have to do next, Lois came over the intercom.

"Da! Da Da! Da Da Da! Taa Daa! Evil of the world... beware 'cause it's..."

All three looked at each other... and smiled.

"SUPER DUDE!"

Felix came running through the door in his hero outfit to thunderous applause.

"Welcome back!" everyone said.

"Hi guys! Ah... Gill? I found the capes!"

43

The History of Yellowstone

As Felix sat down with his friends, Gill thought it might be a good time for refreshments.

"Lois, a small favor, if you would?"

"Anything for you, Gill." Sarah smiled at that.

"Please have Killer run us in a tray with some drinks and snacks. I know everyone's getting hungry here, but we have a few more things to talk about before we break for dinner. OK?"

"What kind of drinks would you care for, Oh Mighty Master?"

Gill looked around at everyone's faces, and then said, "Bring on the good stuff, wench!"

"So it is written... So it shall be done," she answered with a snicker.

"Great! Just what I need! A billion dollar computer system going Biblical on me!"

While they were waiting on Killer to wheel in the drinks, Sarah and Robert went into detail about what had happened to them at Sarah's house. Several parts of this tale interested Gill quite a bit and he had them repeat a couple of things.

Gill thought about the story for a moment, and then looked at Robert.

"You know, I find it interesting that these creatures have been after Sarah since the episode at the hospital. They must somehow know that she had a link with the Flae at that time and have been trying to eliminate her from the picture ever since. I just wonder... if the Flae may have a mole in their organization. Hmmm.

"The fact that they planted a booby trap in her house dictates that they were not out to merely slow her down or get her mad about her stuff being destroyed. They were out to destroy Sarah. The only reason they haven't tried that kind of thing here yet is because they don't know where here is! That's why we couldn't have you two coming back with that bug on the van.

"Now, as for the situation with the policeman, I think you both handled that extremely well. This had to happen one day, as many times as we have been vigilantes in the past, and at least it seems that we can depend on this officer for a small amount of discretion. That could come in quite handy in the future.

"We'll leave the van where it is for the time being. Sarah, tomorrow... we'll all go to get your car at the impound lot... just in case of any more trouble with the Thingies. We can't leave it there too long without attracting the attention of local authorities, so we'll bring it back here. Sarah, I want you and Robert to stay here with Felix and me until this situation is resolved, but we do have to go to your 'job' tomorrow, and we'll talk to your boss there."

Sarah smiled. "Oh, yeah, Gill! You're just gonna love this chucklehead!"

"Yeah, and he's gonna love me, too!"

As they were about to talk about the Whistler that they had spotted on the beach and the upcoming trip where it looked like at least some of them would have to go to Yellowstone, the door slowly opened and in came Killer, pulling the little cart that Felix had seen him use before in the theatre.

"Man, Killer! You gotta be the King Dude of all the canine world!" Felix said with a smile.

"Yipe!"

As Gill was pouring drinks for everyone in the room, he suddenly noticed that far off look in Felix's eyes again. This time, though, it only lasted a couple of seconds... and then he was back.

"What was it, Felix?"

"Ah... a couple of things, guys. One of 'em was the fact that... ah... remember the battle at the power station?"

Everyone nodded.

"Well, when I went off chasing that Whistler on my own... I think I was supposed to have taken that hairspray and the butane lighter with me. We never did use those, if y'all remember, and I believe that if I had taken those with me, we wouldn't have problems now with... ah, what's the word... HE?"

They all thought about this for a moment and suddenly realized that those two objects were unused and still in the backpack that Sarah had taken.

"You may be right, Felix," Gill said, "but that's all in the past. Let's just do our best to deal with the present and the future for now."

"Hey, Felix?" Robert said. "You said... a couple of things. What was the other one?"

"A poem, dude! I think when we were fighting, I talked to a small dude named Gin!"

"Yeah! I remember that!" Sarah said. "That's who told you to give me the message that helped save Gill!"

Gill was pale. "You talked to Gin?"

"Yeah, dude! And it was when he told me that poem that I... kinda... exploded out there!"

"That may be where the power first came from, Felix! Maybe Gin gave it to you," Gill said quietly. "So you talked to Gin! Can you remember the poem?"

"Uh huh... but... hey, man... I don't wanna explode again, at least not right now!"

"I think you'd have to be pretty angry for that to kick in again, and it may be handy for us to know how to... shall we say, turn you on?"

Sarah put her hand on Felix's arm. "Tell us," she whispered.

Felix looked at her, smiled, and his eyes rolled back into his head. In a tiny voice, he said, *"Scream for the night! Scream for the pain! Scream for peace, to the world once again!"*

He rolled open his eyes.

Killer moaned.

Gill said, "Wow."

Sarah smiled.

Robert said, "OK! Who's up for another bourbon?"

Hands raised all around.

They sat for a few minutes sipping their drinks and saying nothing. When suddenly...

"Excuse me, Gill?"

"Yes, Lois?"

"MAX is here with me, and if you all have a few minutes, he still has a report to give you that I think is quite important."

Gill frowned. "A report? A report on what, MAX?"

"If you recall, sir, you asked me to check up on facts regarding Yellowstone. I was told to wait to deliver my report. I am still waiting, sir."

"Aw, MAX, I'm sorry! So much has been going on lately that your report completely slipped my mind. I apologize to you, sir."

"Thank you, sir! No apology was needed, but thank you."

"So are you prepared to enlighten us on the grandeur of that heavenly place that is known as Yellowstone?"

"No, sir."

"Come again, MAX?"

"No, sir. I am, however, prepared to enlighten you on one of the greatest disasters known to mankind, past and eventually in our future."

Everyone was silent again.

Robert shook his head. "Man! This just keeps on gettin' better and better!"

"OK, MAX, enlighten us, please," Gill quietly said.

MAX did.

"Gang, after studying up on several sources regarding this location, I have to say that this place is... well, it's kind of like the 'Felix' of national parks."

"Clarify, please, dude!" said Felix.

"This place is at the same time one of the most beautiful and serene places on this continent and a time bomb which could mean the destruction of all life in most of our world."

"Better and better," Robert said with a moan.

"Yellowstone was the first national park of the United States of America. It has the largest lake above seven thousand feet anywhere here. At about two point two million acres, it may be the largest bomb in the history of the world.

"Think of a concussion. If you get hit in the head, and a large bump appears, it hurts a lot, but the swelling will eventually go down and you'll be OK. With a concussion, however, the swelling is on the inside. Therefore, the pressure builds and builds until it must be released or explosion inside will occur.

"On this planet Earth, we still have many, many active volcanoes, as I reported to you before, and many sleeping volcanoes. But even now, we have a very, very few mega... or super volcanoes. One major area is called Toba. But, to all practicality, the biggest of these live mega volcanoes is called Yellowstone.

"With a normal volcano, a crack will form past the core at the molten center of the Earth and push upwards to form a cone on the surface, where lava or magma is released to relieve the pressure buildup. With a mega volcano, though, this pressure is not released and therefore forms a giant magma buildup underground... a lake, if you will, of molten lava, just waiting for the big blow!

"The magma buildup beneath Yellowstone could fill up two-hundred Grand Canyons!

"Our planet is never still. This is an illusion. Yellowstone gives us the chance to witness Earth as it really is.

"Two point one million years ago, the largest mega eruption in earth record happened... at Yellowstone. In those ancient times at Yellowstone, within a matter of hours, an entire mountain range was obliterated! When it was over, all that remained was a forty-five mile wide crater or caldera. At one time, because of the effect on Earth's climate and weather caused by this eruption, large glaciers buried Yellowstone under up to four thousand feet of ice!

"Today, the calm landscape of Yellowstone hides this caldera... easy to overlook. Volcanic forces push the Yellowstone plateau higher than all of the surrounding areas.

"In Yellowstone, the magma lies just a few miles below our feet. More than ten thousand thermal features are visible, caused by the present volcano activity. More mudpots, fumaroles, hot springs and geysers than exist in the entire world combined are located in Yellowstone National Park. 'Old Faithful' erupts 20 times a day thanks entirely to this constant volcanic activity.

"When this monster... and that's EXACTLY what it is... next erupts, all climate... all food resources ... and all water availability... for the entire planet... will be...

"Screwed?" asked Felix.

Sarah threw a magazine at him.

Everyone was quiet for quite awhile after that.

Finally, Robert looked around at his friends and said, "Better and better! Now! Who's up for another bourbon?"

Everyone raised their hands... again.

Gill spoke quietly. "MAX, that was an excellent report, and we are all deeply indebted to you for that information. By the way, what was your main source?"

MAX was quiet for a couple of seconds... and then said, "Ah... PBS."

Felix laughed! "There ya go!"

Gill said, "OK, good enough. Now we know what to expect."

Felix said, "Hell?"

"Ha Ha! Yeah, I guess that's about right! The Evil Thingies will obviously try to blow the mega volcano at Yellowstone! All we have to do... is stop 'em."

"Better and better," Robert whispered to Sarah.

"Curiouser and curiouser," she whispered back.

"OK, gang," Gill said as he stood up, "Finish up your drinks, and then head to the kitchen. Supper's on me! Lois?"

"Yes, sir!"

"Show 'em the way... and help me thaw out some meat!"

44
Hell in the Hall of HE

HE arrived at the place of calling. Some already were there. Others were coming. HE waited.

The "evil sun" was now gone. The darkness has eaten it. Darkness was hungry.

"The location of the calling is a land called... East L.A. Strange name. Strange humans. Talk strange. Location of calling is... church? Strange word. Hall of Jehovah's Witness? More strange words. Jehovah not at home. Only one human at home."

HE would now witness nothing.

HE got his people together. Many Thingies. HE talked. Thingies listend. HE explained the big plan. "One Place all Thingies must go. Can then stop humans... like stop one human in Hall of Jehovah.

Thingies would collect the Minus. "Much the Minus!"

Thingies would go to One Place. "The Minus would feed the center of the world. The Minus would make center of the world... sick. Center of the world would vomit the Minus into sky.

"Center of the world would stop humans by eating the sun.

Center of the world would eat the sun. Darkness would eat the humans.

"Eat the sun!

Eat the sun!

Eat the sun!"

Soon, all Thingies were listening to HE.

All Thingies started singing, "Eat the sun! Eat the sun! Eat the sun!"

HE told Thingies of Humans who kill Thingies.

He said they must watch for Humans who kill Thingies.

"Dangerous," he said "They must not allow Humans who kill Thingies, go to One Place.

"Humans who kill Thingies have bad light in box.

"Humans who kill Thingies have HardSpeak.

"Humans who kill Thingies collect the Plus. Must not let Humans who kill Thingies collect the Plus.

"The Plus is strong.

"The Plus is UN for the Minus!

Thingies must collect the Minus... Kill the Plus!"

All Thingies sung, "Collect the Minus, kill the Plus! Collect the Minus, kill the Plus! Collect the Minus, kill the Plus!"

HE danced. The Thingies sang.

"Feel for the CALLING," HE said.

"This mean the Plus. Must kill the Plus.

"Feel for the CALLING... on way to One Place!"

"Feel for the CALLING... on way to One Place!," Thingies sung. "Feel for the CALLING... on way to One Place! Feel for the CALLING... on way to One Place!"

HE told Thingies to gather many vehicles and take Thingies to One Place.

"Kill the Plus when find the CALLING! Kill the Plus when find the CALLING! Kill the Plus when find the CALLING!" Thingies sang out.

"STOP!" HE said.

Thingies were silent, and lights outside flashed and flashed.

Cops.

HE had Thingies change to humans.

HE had Thingies sit on benches.

HE transformed to a human.

HE went to the door and started talking like a human.

"Yes, officer? Can I help you?"

"Ah... yes, pastor. We've had a report of this church being broken into tonight. Have you had any problems here?"

"No, sir! We're just in here holding services and rejoicing in the word of the Lord."

"Well, if you don't mind, padre, my partner and I would like to check it out since we're here anyway. You know, just for our report."

"Certainly, certainly! All are welcome in God's house!"

As the two policemen entered the front hallway, the second one said, "Ya know, it's kinda funny. We had a report that this church was shut down. They told us that no one was here except a caretaker who lived on the property. Kinda funny, huh?"

HE directed them into the hall down the aisle.

They looked around and saw that there were at least a hundred people in this congregation, all quietly seated.

One of the policeman stopped.

He started to shake uncontrollably.

His partner grabbed him. "What is it, Wilson?"

Wilson pointed at HE and at everyone.

THEY ALL HAD THE SAME FACE!

The cops looked at HE. HE smiled.

"Kinda funny, huh?" HE said.

The whistling began.

The Thingies feasted.

Later, when HE was HE again, HE chose two Thingies.

"Go out. Take cop vehicle. Be cop."

HE put his hands in the air as Thingies listened.

"We leave for One Place in two more suns. We leave separately but join at One Place. Open your minds."

They did. HE showed them.

"This is One Place. This path to One Place. Get vehicles. Go One Place in two more suns!"

"Go One Place in two more suns!"

"Go One Place in two more suns!"

"Go One Place in two more suns!"

All Thingies were song.

All Thingies were dance.

45
Dinner with Gwen

Dinner was fabulous. Coconut shrimp for an appetizer, a warm potato and onion soup for a starter course with garlic-chive and cheese croutons, and for the main course, butterflied pork chops stuffed with an apple and onion mixture and sauteed in a sauce made of au jus and apple cider. This was served with a scalloped yukon potato casserole and a broccoli and goat cheese side dish.

Everyone just stood there with their mouths open as they gazed upon this wonderful repast. No one could say a word, except Felix.

"Looks good, dude, but do ya got any of those left-over cheeseburgers?"

A magazine hit him in the side of the head!

"Ouch, dudette! Where do you keep finding all of those damn magazines?"

They were about ten minutes into the meal, when suddenly Gill stood up with a faraway look in his eyes.

"Will you all please excuse me for a moment? I believe that Gwen is trying to reach me."

He walked away from the table, headed in the general direction of the nearest living room area.

Felix was watching him go when he said," Hey, y'all? How come folks are always callin' right at dinnertime?"

Everyone laughed.

Gill sat down on a small sofa and relaxed his mind. Within a couple of minutes, he was ready.

"Gwen?"

"Hello, my friend. I have much to tell you and all in a short period of time. Interference is great from here now. Many things, though, I must share with you."

Gill concentrated. "OK. I'm all set. Give it to me."

"First, we have discovered that the Thingies are meeting together even as we speak, and will be leaving for a location in your world known as The Sleeping Giant. This will be where they plan their most evil of acts to take place and the possible end of your life forms."

"This must be in Yellowstone. I will research the area."

"Next, we have discovered that the Felix human may not contain or carry the Plus.

181

The threat is too great. He may, however, be able to use the Builders, either to amplify his strength or to re-build his strength once he has used his power."

"Gwen, would the Builders work for me as well?"

"For you, Gill, there is chocolate."

"OK. Is that all for now? My dinner's gettin cold!"

"Memorize what I am about to tell you, Gill or your whole world may get cold! Here are locations on your Earth near where you must travel, where you may be able to locate more of the Plus and the Builders. But beware, for the Thingies will also be in search of these objects."

"Thank you, Gwen. Give me the information."

Gill spent the next couple of minutes memorizing names and locations supplied by his small friend. He also figured out that since the bad guys were leaving in two days time, the good guys would leave in one. At the end of this time, Gwen started to fade.

"Gwen, one more thing. Keep an eye out for someone in the Flae who may be passing info on to the Thingies. The Thingies know too much and there's nowhere else they could have gotten the information from. Gwen? Can you hear me?"

"I... Flae...passing on... Thingies...! Not... before ever... !"

Gwen was gone.

Gill walked into the dining room with a solemn look on his face.

"We leave on Tuesday morning for Wyoming. Now, let's finish our dinner, and I'll fill you all in."

The rest of the meal was spent in quiet thought.

They all huddled together in a large room that appeared to be a den of sorts. Because a lot of this complex was underground, the blazing fireplace was not out of the question and it set the mood for what was next.

"OK, gang. We go tomorrow to fetch Sarah's car from impound. We'll then head to her jobsite to set that situation straight for her... shall we say... 'Extended vacation.' Then, we come back here to pack for a trip to Yellowstone. Prepare for warm and cold temperatures when you pick out clothing. There's no telling what we'll hit. We'll be in the desert and in the high mountains. I've got one whole area of the warehouse that's just dedicated to cold weather gear, so stock up. That takes care of Monday.

"Tuesday, we load up at dawn and head out. I will be going with you all, if for no other reason than to keep in touch with the Flae on our trip. Also, we'll be on a treasure hunt for the Plus and the Builders."

Gill explained the situation with Felix and the Builders, and this seemed to cheer up Felix a bit... just knowing that he could now participate in the hunt.

"Now, we have general locations on some of the Plus. Lois? MAX?"

"Yes, Gill." Yes, sir," they both spoke up in unison.

Gill laughed. "Are you two living together now? Aw... never mind. Just listen up here, OK?"

"Gotcha."

"Plot a course for us from here to Yellowstone and include stops in the locations I'm about to feed to you. Also, run your search engines on any info pertaining to these locations. Roger?"

"Gotcha."

"First off, near the city of Fresno here in California is a small place known as Tranquility. That will be our first stop."

"We will then be searching in Mountain City, Nevada at the Duck Island Indian Reservation."

"Way cool, dude!" Felix said as he popped up off of the sofa and started doing an Indian dance around the fireplace.

Gill smiled. "Sarah, would you care for a magazine?"

"No, no, dudette, it's cool! I'll be good! Promise!" Felix sat back down with a smile.

"Now, if I may continue. In Utah, we'll be making two stops, both near Salt Lake City. One will be at a town called Paradise and the second will be at a location known as Devil's Slide."

Robert shook his head.

"What is it?" Sarah whispered.

"It's heaven and hell... that's what it is. Gotta bad feelin'."

Gill looked at everyone. "Pay attention, boys and girls! Our next stop will be in Idaho, just south of a town known as Arco. We'll be looking at The Craters of The Moon National Park!"

Felix didn't say anything this time, but his face broke out into a smile and he started dancing again.

"We'll have one more stop before playtime with the Thingies, children. This will be in Wyoming at a town called Pahaska in the Shoshone Forest."

"Is this far from where we're going to end up?" Robert asked.

"No, not far at all, although the country and landscape are going to take some time to negotiate."

Lois came on the speakers. "Will this be all of the locations you need MAX and I to gather information on, Gill?"

"I wish I could say yes to that, sweetie, but we've got one more and there will be no goodness to gather at this location."

Everyone was so quiet that a log falling in the fireplace startled them all.

"Our battle with those Whistlers, according to the Flae, will be at The

Sleeping Giant."

Not a word. Not a breath.

Gill looked at everyone. "And may God have mercy on us all."

They all just sat quietly, taking in what had been said for a few minutes, then Gill spoke up in a hush. "OK, that's our plan. You've got a couple of hours to unwind here tonight before we all need to be getting some rest. MAX and Lois, you know what to do on your end. Robert, Sarah and Felix, make yourselves at home and feel free to check out the cold weather gear in the warehouse. We've got an early day tomorrow, and I'll have Lois give you each a wake-up call at 8 a.m.. and breakfast at 8:30 sharp! Any questions?"

"Ah... yeah, dude, I got one."

Gill smiled. "Why does that not surprise me? What's your question, Super Dude?"

"Ah, man... like... what kinda vehicles are we gonna take on this adventure? Should I go wash some more cars?"

"No, my friend," Gill said as he stood up and placed his hand on Felix's arm. "I've been thinking about that and I believe that this journey calls for ol' Betsey!"

Robert jumped up with a shout. "Great idea, Gill! She'll be perfect and I've been waitin' to take her out since we got her all fixed up."

About that time, a magazine hit Robert right in the head.

"Waitin' to take her out, huh?" Sarah said with a smile as they started walking out of the room.

Only Felix remained behind, scratching his head.

"OK, dudes! Who is this Betsey person?"

46
A Paper Bag Full of Intimacy

As Robert and Sarah headed to the warehouse to check on clothing, Felix headed to the kitchen again. Before he turned in that night, a light snack sounded good, and he knew there were leftovers just around the corner. When he reached the dining room area; however, he felt the ol' "hypno" pattern coming over him again, so he pulled himself up a chair to ride it out while he tried to figure out what was needed by someone here. Something was needed. Something...

"Ha Ha Ha Ha!"

He jumped up out of his chair, laughing so hard that tears rolled down his face. He ran toward the kitchen, found a brown paper bag and started hunting for the items he had visualized. This would be fun.

Robert and Sarah found the clothing warehouse area without too much trouble. "You know, I think I'm starting to get used to this place," she said with a smile. "I actually think I'm starting to know my way around!"

"Forget it!" Robert chuckled. "I've been here for years. I still get lost all of the time. It's almost as if the place keeps growing on its own."

They both went through aisles full of clothes of all descriptions and eventually had armfuls of everything from swimsuits to snowsuits. Robert found a luggage section about ten rows over from where they had started and they began packing as they went.

"Good Lord, Ert! How much stuff are we going to need, anyway?"

"Well, beautiful lady, I don't think we really know how long this journey is gonna last or when we're gonna come back."

She looked at him sadly and said, "Or if we're gonna come back?"

He put his arms around her small waist and drew her toward him. Then, ever so softly, he gave her a gentle kiss on her waiting lips. "Sarah, we will do everything in our power to get you back home again, safe and sound. Everything. You can believe that."

She smiled. "I do believe that, Ert. I just hope that everything in our power... well, is enough."

They quietly folded and packed two large suitcases full of clothing. They found snow boots and outdoor boots as well, both which seemed to be a good idea. After throwing these into another bag, Robert mumbled, "Ah... Sarah?"

"Yeah, handsome. What is it?"

"Ah... I've still got that bookmark you asked me to put on for later, ya know." He was blushing as he said it.

"Ah, Robert... you're glowing."

He looked over at a mirror hanging on the wall that was for trying on clothes and realized that, yes, he was glowing. Not brightly, but a soft red glow sort of enveloped him in a halo of light. "Wow!"

Sarah walked over to him. "Here, let me try something." She pulled his head down so that his face was level with her own... and kissed him.

The glow increased as if it had been fed.

"Wow! You're gonna have to hold that under control when we confront the bad guys. It's like a beacon, Ert! Hold on! Let me try something else!"

Sarah ran to the back of the warehouse area where there was a small bathroom. Robert was trying to figure out what the heck was going on when she came running back with something in her hand.

"Sarah, what are you gonna... ?"

SPLASH!

She smacked him right in the face with a glass of water.

The glow instantly stopped.

"See?" she said with a smile. "Cold water does it every time!"

He stood there dripping. At first, there was a frown on his face... then a smile... and then they were both laughing as he wrestled her to the floor while he was tickling her.

"Ahh! Don't! I'm ticklish! Ahh!"

"Say you're sorry! Go on! Say it!"

"I'm sorry! I'm sorry!"

They both laid there in the puddle of water and in each other's arms until they heard someone clearing his throat.

"Umm... hey, dude and dudette! I'm sorry, too! Ah, for the interruption, that is. Ah, I got y'all a present here, but ya can't open it 'til ya hear the bell. Cool?"

Robert shook his head. "Yeah, Felix... cool. Now, if you'll give us a minute here?"

"Oh, yeah! Sorry again!" he said as he sat down the brown paper bag and ran out the door, laughing!

Robert looked into Sarah eyes and started to glow again. "Come on. Let's call it a night. We'll leave all this luggage and pick it up later."

Sarah let Robert help her up and then whispered, "Ert?"

"Yeah, sweetie?"

"I don't wanna sleep alone tonight."

As his glow increased, he said, "Me neither, Sarah."

They started to walk out of the huge room when Sarah remembered the paper bag. "Guess we ought to take this along, huh?"

They went to Sarah's room and closed the door. Robert dimmed the lights as Sarah got a towel from her bathroom. She slowly took off Robert's shirt as she started to dry him off from the splashing he took. His glow was a warm, rosy pink and she felt as if she were glowing right along with him.

They steered each other toward the king-sized bed held tight in each other's arms.

Sarah smiled. "Robert, no matter what happens to us in the future, this night is perfect. The only thing that would make it better would be if we had..."

RING! RING! RING!

Robert almost fell over. "WHAT THE HELL WAS THAT?"

Sarah looked around and saw the paper bag jumping around on the floor. She picked it up, and saw that it was stapled shut at the top. She handed it to Robert, and he slowly opened this noisy package, which continued to ring. He looked inside and started to laugh.

"What is it? Lemme see, lemme see!"

Sarah started to laugh, too.

Robert shook his head. "Damn, Felix!"

Sarah started taking things out of the bag. First, an alarm clock set for that very moment. She turned it off. Next, a package of lavender incense and a lighter. Then, two large candles. Next was two miniature bottles of Champagne, along with two ripe strawberries. The final item had her laughing so hard that she dropped the sack.

"What? What is it?" Robert said with a chuckle.

Sarah could only hold her stomach from laughing so hard and point at the bag.

Robert picked it up, looked inside and then started to glow ever so brightly.

"A package of condoms?"

Sarah nodded as she laughed.

"How the hell does he do that?"

At that moment, relaxing for the rest of the night on his new bed, reading a fantasy book he had collected from Gill's library, with his new friend Killer lying by his side, Felix was happy.

He patted the dog on its small head.

He thought of Robert and Sarah.

He looked at the time on his watch. He smiled.

47
Sarah's Day

At 8 a.m. sharp the following morning, Lois's voice arrived with a wake-up call. She was heard in Felix's room, in Sarah's room and in Robert's room where no one was.

"Good morning, children! If you will please start to awaken and prepare yourself for another beautiful California morning, I will make sure the orange juice is fresh and that the Hollandaise sauce on the eggs benedict isn't broken. Breakfast in thirty minutes."

Felix yawned and stretched his lanky body in an effort to shake the sleep out of his head. This bed was the first real bed that he'd slept on in quite awhile... well, actually ever. It was even long enough to where his feet didn't hang over the end. His other bed used to come up almost to his boney knees.

"Yipe!" said his new lil' buddy.

"Good morning, beautiful! And how did you sleep?"

In answer to his question, Killer wriggled back under the blanket, stuck his head out and yawned.

"Yeah, I know. I coulda slept another few hours myself, but we've got stuff to do today and I still gotta pack for our big trip tomorrow."

Killer looked at the big softie and whined.

"Yeah, I'm kinda worried about it, too, but ... "Felix stood up tall with his hands on his hips in his best Super Dude pose. "... But, good must win out and justice must prevail!" (It would have had more effect if he hadn't been in his underwear.)

"Yipe! Yipe!"

"Really? You liked that?"

Killer jumped up off the bed into Felix's arms and gave him a quick lick as a sample of doggie love.

"Yeah, critter, I think you're top shelf, too. How 'bout some breakfast?"

"Yipe!"

"Then... lead on, oh faithful canine pal o' mine!"

They were a good way down the hall before Killer looked at Felix and whined. Felix said, "Aw, heck!" as he ran back to his room after realizing that he was still in his underwear.

Robert took an extra couple of minutes to drag himself out of bed this morning. He didn't want to get up at all. Never... never ever... could he remember a night like last night. He didn't want it to end, never... never ever, but duty called, so he finally managed to extract his nakedness from under the warmth of the comforter. He could hear the shower in the bathroom running and he could hear Sarah singing.

Damn.

"Could heaven be any better than this?" he thought to himself.

He tippy-toed into the bathroom and eased himself into the steamy shower stall next to her.

"Mornin', Ert," Sarah giggled. "Just in time to wash my back!"

As Robert softly soaped and scrubbed the beautiful form of this woman that he loved, he quietly thought, "I wonder if cold eggs benedict are still edible?"

I guess they would just have to find out... together.

When Felix, wearing a maroon-colored jogging suit and Killer, wearing his new collar, arrived at the kitchen, Gill was running around like a madman. Stirring this and shaking that and squeezing these and spooning up those, he looked at Felix and said, "Help?"

Felix laughed and said, "You got it, lil' buddy! Here, I'll start taking some of this stuff to the table for ya!"

By the time they finished, the table was loaded down with fresh fruit, orange juice, fresh strong coffee, several kinds of cheeses, hash brown potatoes and eggs benedict. Felix noticed that as Gill served up the plates, he reserved two portions on a warmer for later.

"Ah, Gill? Only the two of us are eating? Aren't Robert and Sarah hungry?"

Gill smiled back at Felix. "Oh, they'll be hungry, alrighty! Starving, in fact! But after talking to Lois this morning, I figured it best to leave their portions on warm for... shall we say... an extra half-hour? Cold eggs benedict are inedible."

Felix laughed. "Yeah, dude! At least a half-hour!"

Sure enough, at 9 a.m. on the dot, Robert and Sarah came rollin' in.

"GOD!" Robert said. "I am starving!"

Gill and Felix looked at each other and smiled.

Sarah, on the other hand, slowly walked around the table to where Felix was seated, eating some melon and sipping his morning coffee. She placed her arms around his neck and gave him a big hug.

"Thank you, Felix," she whispered into his ear and placed a small kiss on his cheek.

He blushed almost three shades darker. "Anytime, o' beautiful one... anytime."

She smiled at Gill and said, "Good morning, boss!"

"Mornin', Sarah. Sit yourselves down and grab up some of this food. It's gonna be a long day today. Lots to do, and you can't do it on an empty stomach. Today is Sarah's day, and we're gonna get her all squared away with her job and her car before we start into getting ready for this... journey."

Felix put down his coffee cup and said, "Hey, boss? Is it OK with you if I drive the Apache today? Ya know... to kinda get a feel for the ol' boy?"

Gill smiled back. "It's yours, buddy, so do what you like, but yeah, Felix, that's probably a good idea. We'll take it and the Chevy Bel Air so there's enough room for us all going there. Coming back, we'll have Sarah's car, too."

Sarah's phone rang, and it was MAX. She listened for a moment, and then started laughing. "Hey, Gill, there's a truck at the front road by the mailbox. He's on the intercom wanting to make a delivery."

"Well, tell him to put it in the box."

Laughing, Sarah managed to get out, "No can do, senor. It's a thousand dollars worth of chocolate!"

"Aw, heck! I almost forgot about that, Robert?"

"No can do, senor! I gotta mouthful of this benedict guy!" he said as he grabbed up another portion.

"Felix?"

"Yep! I'm on it, boss. I'll take my truck," he said as he put down his coffee cup. He was off in a run.

Gill looked up at the ceiling. "Lois?"

"Yes, Gill."

"That chucklehead will never find the garage. Give him a hand, will ya?"

"You betcha, boss."

About twenty minutes later, Lois came on the intercom. "Pickup truck pulling in around back, Gill."

"Thank you, Lois."

Gill and Sarah got up from the table and went to the back door to help Felix unload the goodies into a refrigerated storage pantry off of the kitchen.

Robert was still eating.

Gill looked at Sarah out of the side of his eyes with a smile. "Better take it easy on the boy. You're gonna wear him down to a frazzle."

She replied, "A little exercise is just what the fellow needed, boss."

He laughed.

Boxes and boxes of the wonderful chocolate were unloaded into the kitchen, then into the pantry.

"Leave one of them out for snackin'!" Felix said.

"Damn right!" said Gill. "How about some for now, Super Dude?"

"Sounds good to me, Super Boss!"

Sarah came in the back door with the last box to find these two unlikely friends sitting on the kitchen floor, tearing open bars of chocolate and cramming them into their mouths. They looked like children the day after Halloween.

She smiled as she whispered, "My boss."

He and Felix grinned at her with black teeth.

After Robert finally finished eating and the dishes were rinsed and load-ed into the dishwasher to be taken care of by Lois, Gill huddled everyone.

"OK, gang, let's finish getting ready now, and we'll head out to the police impound lot in one hour. Cool?"

"OK, boss!" they all said in unison.

"Ah, Robert?" Gill laughingly said. "That's one hour, now, not one hour and thirty minutes."

"Aw, Gill!"

"You heard the man," Sarah said. "Come on, lover boy!"

An hour later, they all met at the garage area, where Gill filled both tanks on the two Chevys from an underground storage tank he kept on the property. Gill jumped into the old pickup truck with Felix, and Robert drove the Bel Air with Sarah snuggled up next to him.

She snickered at Robert as she said, "Hey, Ert? I like these big ol' seats. We should take this car and go out... parkin' one day!" She nuzzled his ear as she said this.

He lit up like a lighthouse.

"Cool it, Ert! We're supposed to be incognito, remember?"

"Well, girl, you'd best talk about somethin' else then and at least a foot away from that ear!"

Gill watched Felix beam as he slid behind the wheel of the fine old truck.

"Ya know, Super Dude, I don't think this critter has been on the road for almost ten years now."

Felix slid the key into the ignition, slowly turned it over to listen to the mighty engine crank right up for the second time today and grinned as he told Gill, "Well, boss, it's high time that we put him back on that road!"

VAROOM!

Both vehicles pulled out onto the driveway from the hidden garage door and started toward the city streets a mile or so away. It was great seeing these two old champions of the automotive industry once again barreling down the road and the vehicles did themselves proud. Once on the open highway, Robert and Felix opened them up and got the thrill of watching everyone around them gasping at the beauty of these classics as the antiques passed car after car.

After about thirty minutes of freeway travel, they turned off onto a city street and drove over to the city impound lot. They pulled up in front and Gill got out of the truck while Sarah got out of the car. Felix and Robert stayed behind to watch just in case.

Gill opened the door to the office for Sarah, and they waltzed up to the counter, where a young Hispanic man sat reading a notebook of some sort. The fellow looked down at Gill, and then stared up at Sarah. He eventually closed his mouth and managed to say, "Yes ma'am! Can I help you in any way?"

Sarah gave him her brightest smile and replied, "Yes, sir. My car was picked up after an accident last Friday, and I'd like to bail the poor thing out." Sarah gave the love-struck boy the year, color and make of the car.

"Oh yeah! It's in the back of the lot. That's funny! You're the second person to ask about that car today."

Gill quickly stepped forward, even though he barely came up to the counter top. "Excuse me? The second person? Do you mind telling us who the first person was?"

"Ah, hold on while I check. Ahh... yeah, here it is. Two policemen were here asking about it. About an hour ago."

"Are you sure that they were policemen?" Sarah asked. "Was there anything... I don't know... funny about them?"

"Well, yeah sorta. They were in a police car, so I assume that they were real policemen. But..."

"But what?" Gill asked.

"It's kinda weird, man. They looked like twins. You know, the same face almost."

"Open the gate!" Gill said as he ran back to the truck. He yelled at Robert, and then told Felix what was up. As the gate opened, both vehicles zoomed through the chain link as Sarah and the Hispanic boy came running out the back of the building, headed for the location of Sarah's car.

When they arrived, everyone just stood there with their mouths open.

Where Sarah's car had been parked was a puddle of molten metal. Black smoke poured off the burning tires and a faint blue haze still lingered.

"Damn, man! What the hell happened here? What kinda accident did you have, lady?" The boy yelled as he danced around the melted mess.

"Aw, man! I'm gonna get blamed for this somehow. Aw, man!"

Gill looked at Sarah and shook his head. Robert and Felix were at full attention with their backs to the disaster as they scanned the lot for any further problems. Nothing could be seen.

"Aw, man, what am I gonna do? How the hell do I report somethin' like this? This is a police impound lot, for God's sake! What do I do?"

Sarah took a long breath and walked over to the poor boy. She placed her hands on his shoulder. "Listen to me and listen carefully. Go back to your office and relax for a moment and then I want you to call the police and report this. But, and I stress this very importantly, I want you to talk only to Sergeant Eddie Fallon. Ask for him, and tell him that I told you to call him. Tell him that Robert and I were here and we had you call him when we found this mess. You got that?"

"Sergeant Eddie Fallon. Tell him Sarah and Robert said to call and talk to just him. Right?"

"Right. He'll take care of it, and you won't be in trouble. And be sure and tell him about the two cops who were here in a squad car, too. OK?"

"Yes, ma'am. You think those cops had somethin' to do with this mess, huh?"

All four of them just turned to look at the kid.

"Nuff said," the kid yelled as he took off for the office.

Gill looked at the ex-car and then over at his friends.

"Sorry, Sarah. We'll take care of it. Robert, take the lead. Felix and I will bring up the rear. Watch for being followed. We're going to Compu-Tech now. On guard, people!"

He glanced back at the automotive puddle draining across the parking lot.

"Let's get outta here."

48
A Job's Just A Job

As the two vehicles streaked across the city streets en route to Sarah's place of employment, she couldn't help but mentally take inventory of what might have been in that disaster of an automobile that she would never again see.

"Let's see, my briefcase, along with all of my work papers, and... aw, hell... all of my makeup was in there, too! And my good sunglasses... and the title to the car... oh, well, I won't need that, I guess."

"Forget about it, Sarah. We can get all of that stuff back again for you. There's one thing, though, that wasn't in your car when this happened, and it's the one thing that those Thingies were most likely trying to locate."

She looked at Robert as she thought about what he had just said.

"Me."

"You got it, sugar. They were hoping to catch you there, and they just flat-out missed."

"Yeah, but not by much."

"That's true, but a miss is as good as a mile in this game."

They pulled up to the parking lot at Compu-Tech at about 11 o'clock. All four of them got out of the vehicles and headed to the front door. As soon as they entered, a secretary buzzed them through the secondary door and then called Roy Higgins.

Through the office intercom, she heard, "Damn it! So she did show up, huh? You tell O'Reilly to get her ass in here as soon as she can! No, even sooner than that! Tell her I said right now." Higgins was mad, and he wanted everyone to know it.

The four friends calmly walked into Higgins' office.

The red-faced screaming man was in Sarah's face as soon as she entered. "Damn it, O'Reilly! This new computer isn't finished being programmed to my satisfaction, your work load isn't sitting on my desk, you're almost..." he glanced at his watch, "Two and a half hours late. And not only that, but then you have the nerve to bring a scarecrow, a muscleman and a stupid midget into my damn office. Is there a damn circus in town? Are you listening to me, O'Reilly? Are you listening to me or do you have your head stuck up your ass? Tell me, O'Reilly, tell me this... give me just one damn good reason why I don't just kick your ass outta my office, have you tossed out the front door on your keister, and fire you on the spot. You and your entire carnival buddies, too! Tell me, huh?"

Robert stepped forward with a smile on his face.

"I believe that we can all help you with those questions, Roy. Number one: There is no way on God's green Earth that I would allow you to touch one hair on this girl's hair... and certainly not to 'kick her ass outta your office.' Got it?"

Roy stood there with his mouth open.

Felix stepped forward. "And Mr. Roy Dude, as I look around here, I don't see one single person in this building who is capable of 'tossing her out of the front door on her keister' as long as I am breathing. Got it?"

Roy's mouth opened even wider.

Gill smiled as he stepped up to this arrogant bastard! "And Roy Boy, as for firing her on the spot... well, I just don't think that's gonna be possible, either."

Roy smiled as he bent over to Gill's height. "And just why is that, pip-squeek?"

Sarah came forward and spoke for the first time. "Roy, that's because this pipsqueek... this stupid midget... this... very dear friend of mine... OWNS THIS COMPANY!"

Roy almost fell over!

Gill smiled. He looked around, and then saw that the building security guards had started to assemble at the door.

"Gentlemen, my name is Gillian St. John. This is my company, and you work for me... at least for now. If you wish to continue your jobs here at Compu-Tech, and to continue here with a ten percent increase in salary, I would suggest that you have this fat, noisy, lazy bastard out of my building within the next two minutes." Gill looked at his watch. "The clock starts... now!"

Before Roy could even utter a protest, five large, burley guardsmen grabbed him by the arms and started dragging him out of the office... kicking and screaming. "You can't do this to me! There's no one here who's able to do my job! You'll be shut down in a week!"

Gill held up his hands to the guards. "Hold it a second, boys!"

Gill looked around the room and spotted a young man about twenty-two years old. He had his hands on a computer, but it was the smile on his face that struck Gill.

"Hey, son! Come here!"

The fellow stood up and walked over to where the guards had Roy by the scruff of the neck. "Yes, sir?"

"You gotta name, boy?"

"Yes, sir. James, sir. James Williams."

"Sarah, what about it?"

"He's a good man, Gill, and a hard worker. I like it!"

Gill looked around at the entire office staff, who were all watching him now. "Ladies and gentlemen! I give you... James Williams... your new boss!"

Applause came from everywhere.

Gill took the shocked boy's hand and shook it. "Do good, James. Treat 'em good... and they'll do good! And remember... don't take it all so serious, 'cause a job's just a job!"

"YES SIR!" he said with a smile.

Gill looked at Roy, whose mouth was still wide open, then to the guards. "Get 'em outta here, fellows!"

Out he went!

Gill started to leave with the others, then turned around to James again. "Ah... Bossman? That's your office now," he said, pointing at the large spot just vacated by Higgins. Gill looked at the office workers. "A ten percent raise is now in effect for everyone!" More applause! "And... James, Sarah will be on extended leave with us for awhile. Hold down the fort!"

"Yes, Sir, Mr. St. John! Will do, sir! And... thank you, sir! OK, gang! Back to work!"

Gill left with a smile.

49
A Pitstop for Sarah

They all pulled out of the driveway of Compu-Tech, riding in the same vehicles that they came in. Home was their next stop.

Home. What a great word.

They were taking some of the regular street routes when Sarah picked up her phone. She started dialing a number, and Robert asked who she was trying to reach.

"I'm trying to get Gill. I'd like to... ah... Hello? Gill? It's Sarah... behind you in the car. Is there any way we could stop at a drugstore or a shopping center so I could pick up some stuff?"

"Sarah, I most likely have a bunch of that kinda thing at the house."

"Yeah, but... ah... I need some... female stuff, too!"

Gill smiled. "Understood, lovely one. We'll stop in just a moment."

Not far down the road, they all pulled into a small shopping center that had a flower shop, a bookstore and a small drug store. Sarah got out with Robert and wandered into the Mom and Pop drug store. When she got to the female products section, Robert glowed in embarrassment.

"You'd better go somewhere else there, Ert! You're lighting up again!"

He walked down the aisle to give her some privacy.

She grabbed a plastic basket and started filling it with all kinds of makeup and female goodies that she was gonna need soon. She grabbed some more shampoo and a new toothbrush, and as she was headed to the checkout counter, she came across a small knick-knack shelf. On it in a small box, among the other brik-a-brak that they sold at this small place, was a turquoise-colored rock with eyes glued on it. A small sign on the box declared it to be called "Ima Rock!" It was only a dollar, and she thought it would be a nice thank-you gift for Gill for all that he had done for her. She had a good feeling about this.

As she picked it up, time stopped.

"What in the world?" she thought as she looked around her. The lady at the checkout counter was poised with her finger on the cash register but not moving.

Robert was walking toward her but was frozen with one foot in the air.

A fly was suspended in mid-air in front of her face, frozen.

A small boy had dropped his candy bar... almost. It stood frozen in the air.

"OK! Cool! I think I just found one of those... those... whatcha callits!"

She placed it in the plastic basket and everything started up again. The fly flew, the cash register rang, the candy bar dropped to the floor and Robert's foot came down as he said, "What's that, Sarah?"

She smiled at him. "Just you wait, big guy!"

She went to the cash register and placed all of the items on the counter to be paid for except the stone. She paid for it also, but waited until she had a bag with all of her stuff in it before she dumped Ima Rock into the bottom of her purchases without once again touching it. She didn't think that it would work for the checkout girl, but she was taking no chances.

She went outside with a very puzzled Robert and quickly walked over to where Gill was in the passenger seat of Felix's truck. She had Gill step out of the truck, and then tried to explain why.

"Gill, I just bought you a little present and I think it's kind of special."

"Darling, anything that you buy for me is special. Let's see it!"

Without saying a word to him, but with a big smile on her face, she pointed into the bag at Ima Rock. He was like Robert... rather puzzled at her attitude toward the cute little object, but he reached into the bag to lift it out.

TIME STOPPED.

"What the hell?" Gill yelled as he tried to figure out what had just happened. It was then that he noticed that all of the cars in the street were parked.

It was then that he noticed that all of his friends were frozen fast.

It was then he saw a seagull suspended in mid-flight over the parking lot.

It was then that he saw a still image of a small boy down the road a ways running toward a baseball that had somehow been overthrown and was laying in the street right in front of a now frozen city bus. The child would be dead right now... if there was a right now.

Clutching the powerful stone hard in his small fist, Gill ran down the block and into the street. He scooped up the frozen boy, and then the wayward ball and carried them both back to the boy's yard, where the young man's frozen mom was trying to scream.

Gill crossed the street again, looked around to make sure everything was OK and then popped the blue stone into his pocket.

SCREECH! The bus driver slammed on his brakes to keep from hitting a child who wasn't there.

SCREAM! The mother yelled for her poor baby boy, who now stood right next to her smiling, with his baseball in his hand.

"GILL!" everyone at the pickup truck screamed, (except smiling Sarah), as he had just disappeared before their very eyes! They looked down the road where the bus had jolted to a halt with the scream of locking brakes and there he was.

"Whoa! Way cool trick, dude! Where did ya learn that one, huh?"

He slowly walked back to the truck as he heard mothers and drivers and on-lookers all trying to figure out what had just happened.

"Felix, Sarah taught me that one. Sarah, I can't tell you how much I appreciate... ah..."

"I love you, too, boss. Let's talk about it later, huh? Too many people looking here. Can we go home now?"

"You betcha, girl! And any time you feel the need to stop from now on, you just tell me! Understand?" He pointed to the small shop. "You found that little ditty in there? Really? How much was it, anyway?"

"Only a dollar, sweetie, but it's the thought that counts." She kissed him on the cheek, then went with Robert to the car.

"Hey dude, can I see that thing?"

"No way, my friend." Gill smiled at Felix as he said, "I have a feeling that this is on your no-no list."

"Aw, shucks! Is that one of those..."

"Felix, this is one of the Plus, and I think it's a pretty powerful one, and previously unknown! What are the odds that we would stop at that particular place and she would see that particular item and be drawn to it enough to..."

"Well dude, all I can say is that either she or someone was very lucky!"

Gill smiled. "Lucky! Robert! Damn, Felix... you're right again! She's been with Robert the whole time. Felix, I don't know if I ever told you this yet, but one of the reasons that Robert and I have worked together for so long is that, well, lucky things have a habit of happening around him. It's been that way for many years, and now that he's been... shall we say 'en-hanced' by the Plus, some of it might be affecting those closest to him... those he hangs around with. This could end up being a good thing for us all, especially on our trip."

"Hey, dude! I had a rabbit's foot one time!"

"Not the same thing, Felix."

"Yeah. I guess it wasn't very lucky for the bunny, either... and he had four of 'em!"

When they finally arrived back at "Casa Gill," as Sarah still called it, Gill pulled them all together to tell them about what they now had in their possession and what had happened. Sarah, too, told them about what had happened to her when she was in the drug store.

"Dude! A time-stopper! Way, way cool! But don't give it to me, y'all! According to them fairy folk, I might not be able to start it up again if I ever got time stopped," Felix said.

Gill smiled. "No, my giant friend, you cannot play with this item. But what Sarah said does bring up an interesting fact. Now, the Plus that Robert and I obtained at the beach was given to me by the little girl, but it affected only Robert. He was able to draw some of the power from that object, but when I touched it nothing happened. By the way, Robert, later on in this trip, there may be more energy building up in that little necklace that you may want to tap into."

"But back to, as Felix called it, the time-stopper... Sarah was able to use it in the store, and then I was able to use it outside to save that child. But obviously, the store folks who placed it there were not able to use it. I wonder...! Ah, Robert?"

"Yes, Gill?"

"I want you to try and use the time-stopper. I know, Sarah, that you purchased it for me, and I love ya for the thought, but having an item like this that any of us could use... except Felix, of course..."

"Aw, dude!"

"I know, I know, but we'll find something for you to play with down the road... Super Dude! But, as I was saying, having an item like this that any of us could use... this could be a great boon on our quest to stop the Thingies."

Felix looked puzzled. "A great boom? Does it explode?"

They all laughed.

"No, Felix, not a BOOM! A boon. That means a benefit."

"Well, why didn't ya just say so, dude? That woulda been bon!"

Gill looked puzzled. "Bone? Like a skeleton?"

Felix smiled. "No, Gillmeister... bon... which means like 'good' in Cajun. See... two can play that game."

They all laughed.

Gill had placed Ima Rock, 'the time-stopper', in a small leather drawstring pouch so it wouldn't be touched until needed. He took it out of his pocket and slid it over to where Sarah and Robert were seated next to each other. Robert just looked at it for a moment.

Sarah touched his hand. "Go ahead, Ert. Give it a try."

Robert picked up the small pouch, de-puckered the strings and rolled the turquoise stone onto his hand.

They all watched as Robert... did nothing. He just sat there.

Sarah looked at him and whispered, "Robert? Doesn't it work for you?"

Nothing.

For Robert, time had stopped him. He was frozen where he sat.

Gill jumped up and ran around the table, and reaching out to Robert, Gill slapped the rock from his frozen hand!

Robert looked around at everyone. "Hey! Where did the time-stopper go? It was just here in my hand!"

Sarah grabbed him in a fierce hug. "Oh, God! You're back! You're OK!"

"Girl, I didn't go anywhere! What the hell just happened?"

Gill slid the leather pouch back over the stone, put it back into his pocket and then sat back down at the table. "It seems that you, too, Robert cannot use Ima Rock. It may have something to do with the power that you've already taken in, but on you, it has the opposite effect. It freezes your time instead of everyone else's."

"Oh wow, dude! Now I don't feel so left out anymore," Felix said with a grin.

Sarah had a sly smile on her face as she said, "Gill, you mean that when Robert holds that stone, he'll be frozen in whatever position he's in at that time... until someone takes the stone away from him? Is that what you're saying?"

"Yeah, Sarah. That's the way it looks!"

She put her arms around Robert's neck. "Ah... Gill? Can I borrow that stone tonight?"

Everyone except Robert started laughing hard at that.

Robert started glowing like a lighthouse again.

50
Last Night at Casa Gill

Gill told everyone to go to their rooms to finish packing, and that they would all meet again at 6 p.m., one hour before what he called "The Last Supper."

"That gives you all about three hours to get your gear together and relax. Tonight, we'll finalize all of our plans for departure. Lois?

"Yes, Gill?"

"I'll be leaving you here alone and in charge. After we leave, protocol seven on security. Understood?"

"Protocol seven? Are you sure, Gill?"

"Yes. Lois. Unless one of us who now have full clearance with you submits to a bio scan, any other intrusion is a negative factor and is to be met with a total destruction mode of any and all property. Understood?"

"Ah... yeah, Gill... I guess. That means me, too... right?"

"I'm afraid so, Lois. I can't have you falling into any situation controlled by the bad guys. You understand?"

"Yes, sir."

"Killer?"

"Yipe?"

"Because it's unknown if or when we'll be coming back from this journey, I'd like to request that you come with us. Is that satisfactory to you?"

"YIPE, YIPE, YIPE!"

"Good dog."

"Cool, Killer dude! You can bunk with me." Felix was bouncing.

"Yipe!"

Gill told the dog, "Killer, I'll bring enough of your food to take care of a couple weeks, but I need you to go pack whatever bones, toys and other stuff that you're gonna want to take. Understood?"

"Yipe." The dog took off at a run.

"I don't know if I'll ever get used to a dog that knows exactly what I say," Sarah muttered.

"You may be glad he's with us before this is over," Gill told her.

As they were all getting ready to leave, Gill told Felix, "Hey, tall one! You want to see Ol' Betsey? You're going to have to help Robert and I drive and navigate, so I guess I should introduce you."

"Wait, I want to see this Betsey, too!" Sarah whined in a cute little voice.

"OK, OK... we'll all go check her out!"

Gill led the way down to a passage that Sarah and Felix hadn't been down yet, and after about two or three minutes, they stopped in front of another set of double doors. Gill pushed them open.

"Ladies and gentlemen, I give you our home away from home for the next week or two! Say hello to Betsey!"

"Beep! Beep!"

Sarah sat there staring at this large, large machine.

Felix was jumping up and down.

Betsey was an old Greyhound bus, and she was beautiful. Many, many hours and tens of thousands of dollars had gone into renovating this beautiful old classic, and it had been worth every cent. She was turquoise blue and silver, with dark tinted windows all around. Her mighty wheels were graced with chrome rims and her lines were just as fine as when she'd rolled off of the production line in the 1950s.

Betsey was a Scenicrusier, the longest bus ever used by Greyhound in the classic days of bus travel on the long highways. Many of the in-town drivers frowned upon this beast because it was hard to turn in tight spots on a narrow city street because of its length. But on the open road, she was the queen of the highway.

"Open, Betsey!" Gill said with a proud smile. The door hissed as it slid open to reveal the fine interior that Gill and Robert had spent so much time on. The lower level by the driver had swivel seats for lounging while in conversation with whoever was at the wheel. Once you stepped up into the top level, couches and rockers, (that were deeply upholstered in the same turquoise as the outside of Betsey), greeted your eyes. There was a small kitchen area with a sink, refrigerator and microwave, and a small bathroom with a sink and toilet. As you stepped back to the rear, there were four large bunks that led to the back, where a small stateroom existed with a double bed and dresser with mirror. Fine, dark stained woods paneled the beautiful machine and lush carpeting graced the floors.

"Say hi to these folks, Betsey!" Gill said with a grin.

"Hello, Sarah and Felix! Lois has told me a lot about you both. Welcome to... me! And Robert, as always, it's very good to see you again."

"Hi, Betsey! How the new engine changes doing?" Robert asked.

"They are wonderful, Robert! I am a little worried that we may be running a bit rich on the gas mixture for the generators, but the diesel is impeccable."

"Good girl. I'll check on that gennie before we leave."

Felix got down on his knees. "I think I've died and gone to heaven! First Lois and now Betsey! Betsey, would I be unfaithful to Lois if I said I love you?"

Betsey laughed. "Actually Felix, Lois and I are different parts of the same output. I am just the mobile version. By the way, Sarah, I have spoken to MAX and he is most interested in this trip. He will accompany us the whole way via satellite, which I am connected to."

Sarah whispered, "All I can say is... Wow."

Betsey said, "Felix, if you will sit on that rocker there..."

Felix sat down, and as he did... a control popped up beside him.

"Now, push the red button, please."

As he pressed the control button, a large flat screen elevated out of a cabinet in the wall. The screen lit up with instructions on receiving television channels, music and radio stations, DVD and outside cameras secretly hidden to see without being seen.

"Aw, hell no! Ya gotta be kiddin' me!"

Betsey laughed. "Felix, I am programmed to have a sense of humor, but let me assure you, I'm not kiddin' you!"

Gill said, "Those cameras also provide infra-red, motion detection, night vision... and a passive X-ray."

Felix just shook his head. "Gillmeister, no wonder that you haven't showed this critter to me until now! Hell, I never would have left it if you had!"

"That's what Robert said!" Gill stated. "I got Betsey quite awhile back from a rock band in the South, and we've spent a couple of years, off and on, re-doing her."

"OK, Betsey, we'll be packing up now, and will be ready to load your bay doors with luggage and supplies at dawn. How is your weapons armament?"

"Fully loaded, Gill."

Felix looked up at Gill. "Weapons, too?"

"Yeah! You're gonna love 'em!"

Everyone left the bus and went their own ways to finalize the packing and getting supplies for this trip of unknown length. Not knowing when they would return made it hard to know how much to pack. Not knowing if they would return made it almost impossible.

Robert and Sarah had already taken care of most of their clothing roundup earlier. They went to the big warehouse area to grab the bags they'd already packed and Felix tagged along to grab extra stuff for himself.

"I know I gotta pack for the desert and for the cold, but the Super Dude suit goes, too!"

Robert smiled as he told his new friend, "Dude, we wouldn't have it any other way!"

They left Felix in the giant storage room, wandering around looking for what he called "Felix Duds."

Robert called them "Dude's Duds."

As Robert and Sarah were carrying their overloaded bags down the hallway towards the bus load-in doors, they heard a dragging sound and a panting.

Sarah grinned. "Ert, help that fellow with his bag!" There was poor Killer, pulling a duffle bag full of doggie stuff five or six feet, then huffing and puffing... then another five or six feet.

"Hey, Killer?" Robert said. "Mind if I give you a hand?"

"Yipe," said the poor tired pooch.

Between the two and a half of them, they managed to stash their gear in front of the double doors.

"See ya later, Killer," Robert said as he gently tugged on Sarah's arm to direct her toward their sanctuary. He could have almost sworn that Killer smiled at him as they left.

Killer took off at a run.

Felix wandered around for a half hour or so, grabbing whatever felt right as he saw it and throwing it into a duffle bag that he found in the corner of this clothing wilderness. Eventually, he got frustrated and just sat down on the floor, head in his hands and then, he was sobbing.

"Felix?"

"Yeah? Ah... Lois, is that you?"

"Yeah, sweetheart. Are you OK?"

"Ah, no... I really don't think... that I am. I'm kinda scared... and... I..."

"Felix, stop right there! Leave all of that crap laying on the floor and come to the movie room right now."

"Ah, Lois, I'd love to, but... I... ah... I need to –"

"Felix! You need to shut up! You need to forget about what might happen and you need to come visit me in the movie room right now!" Then... Lois whispered, "Now, Felix. OK?"

Felix smiled. "I'll be there in a minute, Lois. OK?"

"Yeah, Felix. It's all gonna be OK. You just come to me."

A few minutes later, Felix walked into the theater just as Bugs Bunny was hiding from Elmer Fudd and just as Killer was dragging up a cart filled with hot buttered popcorn and extra-strong Bloody Marys.

Felix smiled.

Everything was gonna be OK.

About 6 o'clock, Gill had Lois page everyone to meet in the dining room area next to the main kitchen instead of the large den/living room that they usually gathered in.

Gill smiled at his friends as they gathered in the doorway entrance to the dining room. "My friends, tonight we celebrate each other's company. Tonight, we feast! Tonight, we temporarily forget our troubles, our problems and our quest. Tonight... is just for us!"

When they had all arrived, no one knew what culinary delight was to be awaiting them on the massive dining room table for the "Last Supper." They were all convinced that nothing... and I mean nothing... would surprise them after all the fine gourmet dining that they had eaten there so far.

They were all surprised.

They looked at the large table loaded down with hamburgers, hot dogs with chili, potato salad, chips and iced tea or ice-cold beer. There was coleslaw, jars of pickles and corn on the cob. There were baked beans, garden salad and french fries and about a dozen dishes made with chocolate.

"Those are just for me, "Gill answered with a smile.

"Fat chance of that," Felix grunted.

They all dug into the large mountain of "good ol' normal cookin'" as Felix put it, and everyone seemed to go out of their way to talk about only good things. There was lots of laughter, lots of jokes and lots of calories. And the whole time that Gill watched this amazing crew of misfits, he could feel the intense fears that each of them held back in order to not upset the others. "This is what a family really is," he thought to himself as he cut a second slice of chocolate pie for everyone.

"This is what home should feel like."

For two hours, they feasted as if there were no tomorrow.

For two hours, they forgot the troubles ahead.

51
No Time Like the Present

As they started to rise from the incredible feast, Robert sat back down. He looked strange.

Sarah ran back over to him, and then sat down next to him. "Baby, are you... OK?"

"Wow, girl! You remember me telling you about the weird deal that I have with luck every once in awhile? Well, I get this weird feeling inside right before an event is taking place that I can... change!"

"You've got that now?"

"I've got that now!"

Sarah jumped up and ran over to grab Felix. Gill followed them back to where Robert was sitting.

"Do me a big favor, Super Dude," Sarah urged. "Something's going on with Ert and maybe with us, too! What do we all need?"

Felix smiled for a minute and suddenly blanked out. His eyes rolled back in his head again and he went elsewhere.

Gill looked up at the ceiling as he whispered, "Lois, monitor this conversation."

"Affirmative, Gill."

They waited for what felt like forever but was actually only a couple of minutes. And then Felix popped awake.

"Damn, Bobby! Glad that you did that, dude! All hell's a breakin' loose! Lois, do ya have cameras on the front door of this place? Ya know, the other side of the mountain?"

"Of course, Felix. I have the very best cam..."

"Shut up, Lois! Put on the outside cameras on the front door, the driveway and the little store!"

Everyone froze.

Showing on camera one: The little store was burning with blue flames. So was Gill's purple van.

Showing on camera two: The front door of the small house next to the store was broken down and two policemen in "uniform" were entering. Everyone could see that these two cops had the same face.

And showing up on camera three was the stolen police car and a stolen library truck, the one that had chased Robert and Sarah, both parked in the driveway.

Gill hesitated about one second before he said, "Lois... online!"

"Online, Gill!"

"Total destruct on tunnels number forty-three and forty-seven. Total destruct on front door and fifty yards of tunnel number three. Alpha... alpha... Ridiculous!"

"Confirmed! Five seconds... four... three..."

"Y'all might wanna duck!" said Felix. He ducked.

Everyone took his word for it. They hit the ground just as "two... one..." and then a loud THUMP, THUMP, THUMP vibrated through the stone walls.

The overhead light fixture swung its massive weight on a broken chain right through the air space that the four friends had just evacuated.

Gill was coughing from all of the dust. "Lois? Cameras?"

"Inoperative... in those areas, boss, but tunnel number forty-four shows one raggedy-ass alien cop dragging his way through the dust! Can I have him, Gill... huh? Can I, can I? Huh? Can I have 'em?"

"Yeah, baby, he's all yours. Total destruct on tunnel forty-four!"

THUMP!

Gill looked over to Felix. "Hey, dude?"

"Yes, sir."

"What else, Felix? What else?"

"Ah, dudes and dudette... two things. One: The little store was closed, so lil' ol' Mrs. Whats-Her-Name is fine and dandy! But... ah... number two: Ahhh... folks... we need to go."

Robert was holding Sarah as he whined. "You mean... like... tonight?"

"No, dude. Like... now."

Gill chuckled as he saw Sarah smile back at him. "Yeah... Ert! No time like the present!"

Robert moaned.

"Killer?" Gill asked.

"Yipe?"

"Departure in thirty-five minutes! Indefinite time frame for length of trip! Help these poor humans get their luggage together! And... go tell Betsey!"

"Yipe!" he said as he took off like a whirlwind.

"Lois?"

"Yes, Gill?"

"I love ya, Lois... but now that we know the Thingies have found the front door, the destruct order... 'protocol seven on security,' is definitely in effect. Sorry."

"It's OK, Gill. I understand. If the worst happens... well, I'll still be with you... through Betsey."

Felix hung his head and ran off toward the "Clothing World" area.

Lois followed him. It was dark in Clothing World. Felix hadn't turned on the lights.

"Felix?"

"Oh, Feeeliiiix?"

"Felix, damn it! If you don't answer me, I'll turn the sprinkler system on your skinny ass! FELIX?"

"Yeah, Lois. I'm here."

"Well, hell! I know that! What I don't know is..." She got real quiet again. "What's wrong, Felix! My Super Dude? Huh? What is it?"

He whispered so quietly that she wouldn't have heard him if she hadn't been a machine.

"I don't... wanna lose ya."

"Aw... Felix..."

"Can computers cry?"

"Don't ask Felix, 'cause you'd get an unexpected answer."

Killer came running through the garage double doors.

"Yipe... yipe, yipe... yipe!"

All of the bus lights, inside and out, popped on. Betsey quickly replied to Killer, "Thirty-five minutes? Are you sure?"

"Yipe."

"We'll be as ready as we can on this end, Killer. Go help the humans."

"Yipe!"

The bus began to warm itself up as the dog took off again.

Gill kept bags ready and packed at all times. He had a warm weather bag, a cold weather bag and one large bag that contained both kinds of clothing.

He decided to take all three.

He took another smaller bag with "Ima Rock" and the "Reachin' For A Star" necklace that he was holding for Robert. He also put a lot of cold hard cash and a goodly supply of chocolate into this bag – all of the basics.

He looked around at this incredible place that he had built and wondered if this might be the very last time he looked upon this wonderland of his.

"Lois, it's been a hell of a ride, hasn't it?"

"First rate... always, Gill. First rate."

"Bye, Lois."

"Bye, Gill. Take care of... our team. Our family. And... keep an eye on Felix for me. Please?"

"Will do, lovely lady. Have MAX contact us on the bus in one hour."

"OK, Gill. I'll... hold down the fort."

"I know you will. I'll see ya soon."

"Yeah. See ya soon."

Sarah and Robert tugged up the bags they had packed earlier, including Killer's, to Betsey. She graciously opened her loading bays for them to start the packing process.

She stated, "We're full on diesel for the engine and regular for the generator system, and we're topped off with water, but we're low on human food. Pantries and refrigerator are... Caa Caa?"

Robert laughed! "Caa Caa? You've been hanging out with Felix too much, girl!"

"No, that would be Lois, but she and I are one."

"Gotcha, Betsey. OK, Sarah and I will go grab as much grub as we can while everyone else loads up. Tell 'em where we've gone."

"Affirmative, y'all!"

Sarah laughed. "Yep! Too much Felix!"

Gill met Felix as they were both headed down the hallway for the bus and Felix was dragging enough luggage for a month.

"Hey, Felix? Did ya leave anything at all behind in the warehouse? It looks like you just about cleaned it out! Haha!"

"Aw, heck, dude! I forgot my cape!"

"Maybe next time, Super Dude. Maybe next time!"

Killer was on the bus as Gill and Felix walked into the garage to load up. A few minutes later, Robert and Sarah waltzed through the doors carrying two large picnic baskets full of goodies and a couple of backpacks full of munchies.

Gill laughed as he asked, "What did ya manage to scrape up, folks?"

"Not a clue!" Sarah said with a smile. "Just started throwing cans and packages and stuff into the baskets and bags!"

"Good enough," Gill said. "Let's blow this popsicle stand!"

Robert smiled. "Sounds like someone else has been spending too much time with Felix!"

Betsey pulled out onto the hidden driveway with Robert at the wheel as everyone settled into their chairs.

The long, long road stared them in the face.

The long, long road.

Robert

Gill

Sarah

Paul

Killer

Chimayo

HE

Shadow Of The Moon

Felix

52
Lookin' for Some Tranquility

"Does anybody here know anything about Tranquility, California? I mean, besides the fact that I can't find it on this stupid map!" Robert interjected as he drove down the highway.

Felix, who was sitting up in the front of the bus, stopped reading his comic and looked over at Robert. "Tranquility is in Fresno County. In the year 2000, it had a population of only eight-hundred and thirteen people. It has one high school in it, and is at an elevation of one-hundred, sixty-four feet. It has a total area of only point six square miles, and the area code is five-five-nine, while the zip code is nine-three-six-six-eight. The median income is forty-two thousand, eight-hundred, fifty-seven for a household and for every one hudred females ages eighteen and over, there are one-hundred and one point five males."

Felix went back to reading his comic book.

Gill and Sarah started applauding.

"OK, how the hell do you know that, Felix?"

"Hey, dude, I read a lot!"

Robert shook his head, and went back to driving. "You guys try to get some sleep soon, and I'll have us in Fresno in the morning when we all get awake. From there, we'll check out Tranquility in the daylight. Cool?"

"Yipe!"

Everyone found themselves a bunk, and though everyone stretched out to unwind and relax, no one really did.

MAX called Sarah on her phone while she was lying down with her bunk light still on and trying to get used to the constant movement of Betsey. She put the conversation on the phone's external speaker.

"Sarah, are you all OK? Lois and I were kind of worried about the bus being under surveillance."

"No, MAX, we made it out of town just fine. No problems. I think we plan on driving into Fresno tonight, so why don't you check in with us tomorrow morning sometime... that is, unless something happens at Gill's house. You call right away if anything's going on that we should know about. OK?"

"You got it, Sarah. Good night. Oh, and tell Felix that Lois wishes him good dreams!"

"I heard that, dudette!" Felix said from behind a curtain on a bottom bunk.

"Yipe, yipe!" Killer said from the Felix bunk.

"Killer says good night to you and Lois, too, MAX. Talk to you tomorrow."

Right before she turned off her light and turned in for the night, Sarah giggled as she heard Felix saying, "Good night, John Boy! Good night, Mary Ellen! Good night, Grandpa!"

Gill went to sleep in the rear stateroom that evening. He'd been with Betsey for quite sometime now, but this was her first real trial run... under fire, so to speak.

As he fell asleep, he couldn't help but wondering about Felix and the events that had put the big guy in touch with Gin. Only happenings of a great and terrible nature were supposed to have attracted the attention of the great Gin, and Felix had now talked to him twice. That was twice more than Gill had ever talked to him, and Gill had been talking to the little folks since... well, heck... since forever. Also, there was the nagging thought in the back of Gill's mind that somehow or another, the Thingies were getting too much information that they shouldn't have gotten without help. That help could have only come from the Flae. Could one of the Flae...?

He must remember to talk to Gwen about this tomorrow.

Time was growing short. Too short.

After about an hour, the bunk lights began to blink out, and soon it was just Robert and Betsey, zooming up dark Highway 5 to Bakersfield, then 99 to Fresno, headed toward who knew what?

"How do I drive, Robert?"

"You may be right about adjusting the fuel mixture on the generator system, Betsey, but you drive like a dream."

"Thanks, sweetie."

It was only a couple of hundred miles from Los Angeles to the large truck stop in Fresno where Robert decided to park them for the night, but he took the drive nice and easy in order to break in Betsey right. She was a fine old bus and much work had been done on her to bring her up to the shape she was now in, but adjustments always had to be made. She did just fine, though.

She did just fine.

When they arrived in Fresno early in the pre-dawn hours, Robert pulled into a major truck stop. He first topped Betsey's tanks off, both the diesel and the regular, and then he pulled her around to the large parking area where the truckers all parked to catch forty winks of sleep before they hit that endless road again.

Robert put Betsey on security alert and then decided to try to catch a few of those elusive winks himself. He entered the bunk section of the bus, and searched until he found where Sarah was sound asleep, snoring gently into the pillow wrapped in her beautiful arms. God, how in the world did he ever end up with a girl like this? He was just plain-old Robert and she was incredible. Those long legs, and that wonderful smile. The way she made him feel when they...

"HEY! Wouldja mind turning off the searchlight?" Felix said, squinting down the aisle!

Robert realized that he was glowing like a lighthouse. "Sorry, Felix! I didn't know. I guess... I guess I'll just sleep up there, then." Robert crawled into the top bunk over Sarah's... all alone.

But just knowing who and what was right underneath him caused him to gleam low like a nightlight until sleep finally took him away into its waiting arms.

Felix was up at the crack of dawn and he was hungry.

Killer was still curled up asleep in the large bunk as Felix slid out and finished dressing himself. He snuck out of the bunk area into the galley where the small amount of food stuffs they'd brought had been haphazardly stored... and started looking for munchies! As he was rummaging through a paper bag filled with chips... and trying his best to be quiet about it... he was suddenly surprised by, "Good morning, Felix! Can I help you?"

"Damn, Betsey! You like to have scared the Bejesus outta me!"

"Well, I'm sure I don't know anything about that, but there is more food stashed in that cupboard up there."

"Cool! I'm starvin'!"

"Ah, Felix, we are at a truck stop here, and I hear that truck drivers are awful picky about their mealtimes. Maybe, there's something hot inside that you might enjoy more?"

"Oh yeah, Betsey! I'm a truck stop kinda guy! That gives me a great idea! I think I want... ah... chicken-fried steak and eggs. Hashbrowns and toast with black coffee. How's that sound to you?"

"Well, not as good as high grade diesel, but it might work for a human!"

Felix took off for the front door but was stopped by Betsey until she could turn off the security alarm. After that, you could color him gone.

An hour or so later, everyone started to gradually wake up. It was Gill who first realized that they were one man short.

"Is Felix still asleep?" he asked Betsey.

"No, Gill. More than an hour ago, I let him out of the bus. He said he was searching for a chicken who would cook him a steak and some brown hash... whatever that is!"

Gill laughed, and then gathered up the rest of the crew to go inside for a hot breakfast. He'd bring something back later for Killer, who was still snoozing.

As they entered the dining room, they saw poor Felix sitting in a booth by himself. He was surrounded by stacks and stacks of dirty dishes and he looked like he was about to bust.

"MAN! Am I glad to see y'all! Gill, about the time that I started eating, I realized that you haven't paid me anything yet! I didn't have any money on me to pay for this meal!"

Gill looked at all of the empty dishes in amazement. "Damn, Felix! How much did you eat, anyway? You must have been starving!"

"Well, I figured that as long as I kept ordering more and more food, they wouldn't bring me a final check! So, I had the chicken-fried steak and eggs with hashbrowns and toast, and then I ordered a bowl of cereal, and then two different orders of pancakes, and about a gallon of coffee, and three glasses of milk, then there was some oatmeal... and a Western omelette!"

Everyone was laughing so hard that they almost fell over. And then, when he stood up and they all saw the bulging belly on the poor dude, they did fall over.

"Aw, man! Quit it, guys! I'm in pain here! Pay for this mess for me, Gill! I gotta go to the john!"

As he was leaving, the waitress yelled out, "Hey, dude? Ya wanna take this sausage and biscuit sandwich with you... to go?"

Felix moaned as he ran out the door.

The rest of the gang all sat down laughing in another booth. Gill told the waitress to put Felix's bill on his. "By the way, how much was his bill?"

"Honey, not including my tip, that boy just put away about fifty-five dollars worth of grub! Does my heart good to see a young fellow that likes our cookin' that much!"

Much more laughter erupted at the table.

They all had a hardy hot breakfast, and Gill ordered a couple of burgers without the bread for Killer. As Gill was forking out a healthy tip for Delores, their waitress, he asked her about Tranquility.

"Oh, honey, that town's so small that you gotta go outside of it just to change your mind! If your goin' there, though, I've got a regular customer there that runs a kinda craft store. His name is Remus, and he's got a pretty neat little ol' shop there in town. I think he was from New Orleans originally, moved here about a thousand years ago! He looks like he's two hundred years old, but he don't act like he's a day over a hundred! Tell him Delores sent ya, and tell him hi for me! He likes my fried chicken. The ol' boy just might surprise y'all. He does it to me all the time. I'll swear... he knows stuff."

Gill just looked at Delores strangely for about a minute, and then before she left, he pulled out an extra hundred dollar bill and handed it to her.

"That's for putting up with us, Delores. That's for you. You have a good day!"

"Damn, honey! You can bet your buttons on that!" As she walked away, bouncing up and down, she was showing off the tip to the other waitresses and cooks and singing "Na Na Nana Na!"

As they walked into the bus, they all saw Felix lying on the floor, moaning.

"Oh, God! Take me, Lord! Take me now and end this pain! I'll bet I weigh almost a hundred and thirty pounds! God, am I full!"

Robert, having the sense of humor that he did, smiled to Felix as he said, "Hey, Super Dude! I brought your sausage and biscuit sandwich for ya!"

"OH, GOD!"

"Yipe!"

"Yeah, Killer," Felix said with a groan. "You can have it."

"Yipe!"

As they were all settling down from that good meal and planning on their brief journey to Tranquility from their present location, MAX called.

Sarah answered her phone, but Betsey put the conversation on her speakers at Lois's request.

"Sarah? Events are happening that you all need to know about."

"Tell us, MAX."

"First, the real police, including your friend from the other day, Eddie Fallon, have found the stolen police car and library van parked outside of the front door, along with Gill's burnt-out van! Sarge Fallon wants a phone call today. The second part comes from him in person. It seems that fifty stolen cars and trucks have been reported in one area of L.A., all with an hour of each other. A lot of the vehicle's owners are either dead or missing. Sarah, I have satellite photos of this... caravan all leaving town together. They're headed in your direction. It's got to be the Whistlers. It looks to be about a hundred or so."

Gill spoke up. "When do you expect them to arrive in our area, MAX?"

"Gill, I'd say you have two hours before they're in your vicinity. Now, it may be that their not following you at all, just headed to the same location as your final destination on the same general path."

"Sorry, partner, but we can't afford to take that chance. We've got a quick stopover to make in Tranquility... then we're on the road to Nevada. Monitor them for us if you can, and let me know if they vary from our map plans. OK?'

"You got it, Gill. And please take care of Sarah for me."

"Will do, pal, will do."

Everyone grabbed a seat as Gill drove the bus out of the truck stop parking lot. Felix was straining and groaning to raise himself off of the floor, when Robert bent over and placed his hand on the stomach of the overfed Super Dude. His hand glowed lightly, and immediately Felix felt better.

"Bobby, dude! What a cool trick! Can ya teach me that one?"

"No can do, dude. Sorry, no can do."

The drive to Tranquility was only about thirty miles from where they were. Within a half hour, they were pulling into the small town.

Felix looked around. "Hey, folks? Ah, what are we lookin' for here, anyway?"

"We don't know for sure, Felix," Sarah said, "and we don't have very long to see if there's anything here that'll help us out down the road. The waitress told us something about an old guy here from New Orleans that might..."

"Right there!" Felix said with a total positive attitude. "If dude's from New Orleans... that's gotta be him!"

On the edge of town stood an old unpainted little shop that almost looked more like a shed than a store. The wooden sign... in big red and purple letters... said "Gris-Gris Things!"

Robert looked at the front door as they parked in the street, and quietly said, "You have got to be kidding."

Out of the front door came an old man of color who appeared to be as ancient as the Redwood trees. He wore dark sunglasses, and no one could tell whether he was blind. He had shoulder-length hair that was as grey as fog, and stood thin as a rail... at about six feet tall. He carried a twisted old walking stick, and by his side stood a dog that appeared to be as old as he was. Around his neck was an amulet that looked at a distance to be made of ancient amber with something inside of it.

Felix went blank. He was gone again.

He fell back onto the couch that he'd been sitting on and stayed there.

Gill looked at Felix, and then said, "Leave him for now. Let's go outside."

As they all stepped off of Betsey, the old man waved at them and mumbled, "Come on in, come on in! I been expectin' ya! Ain't got much time! Y'all come on in!"

Robert shook his head. "You have got to be kidding!"

Killer jumped off of the bus, ran over to the grandfather of all dogs, wagged his tail twice and then followed the old man and the old dog into the shop.

Sarah smiled weakly. "Well, if it's OK with Killer..."

53
Remus and Rascal

As soon as they all entered the craft shop, the first thing that hit them was the aroma. Cinnamon? Maybe jasmine? Or burning hickory? The air was thick with smells, and they seemed to change for one second to the next.

A counter with glass tops was spread around the perimeter of the walls, filled with all sorts of strange objects – herbs, spices and carvings – but in the center floor of the small place were five chairs... waiting.

Remus smiled as he directed them to the chairs, with one left empty. "The tall one will be comin' in a couple of soon minutes, but y'all be makin' yourselfs comfortable now!"

Gill thought, "How does he..."

"Don' be worryin' 'bout how I knows! I jus' does. Times be short, and me 'n' ol' Rascal be leavin' here in 'bout half hour... afore dim creatures are a come."

Gill quietly whispered, "Ah, Mr. Remus? Your friend Delores told us to stop by here. Did she call you to say we were coming?"

"Dat Delores! She make dat fine chicken with dat honey I loves so much! No... ah... Gill, right? Delores no calls me. I gots no phone."

Gill looked over at Killer, who was mesmerized by Rascal, turning his head from side to side as they mumbled at one another.

"Aw, Gill, lets dim dogs talk to one 'nother whilst we do da same. I'm Remus. My daddy was a Bocur in da islands and me momma was a Ju-Ju lady from down Louisann. Dey made me, and I been 'round here since before water! He He He! I know'd you's a comin' and I tinks I can be helpin' ya. We jus be waitin' one second now..."

And in one second...

Felix walked in the door.

"Dere he is! Come sits down wid us, boy! We gots some quick talkin' ta do... and you be takin' dat Gris-Gris from ol' Mr. Remus!"

Felix walked over to the old man calmly. "It's... it's a scorpion, isn't it?"

"Das right, boy! Das right! You knows! You done gots da stuff in you, too, aincha? Like'n I gots it?"

"Yes, sir, I reckon I do."

"Well, sits down boy and lemme talks to ya." Remus looked at the others. "Dis boy can't be takin' dat power dat y'all be takin'. He already so fulla power dat he gonna bust if'n he do! But... I gots a... I guess you calls it a 're-fill,' ... for when dat boy be drained. And... dat boy gonna be drained, too!"

Gill whispered, "A Builder!"

Felix looked into the old man's eyes. "You're, you're wearing it."

"He He He! Yeah sir! Dat boy gots it jus like I gots it alrighty!"

The old man opened up his shirt, and there was an amulet on a piece of rawhide. It was an ancient chunk of Amber with silver carvings all around it. Suspended in the center of the piece was a scorpion.

"Dis is for you, son. It's gonna be OK for you ta wear dis bug, and he gonna help you out when you need him. You gonna need dis bug, boy."

The old man slipped the antique jewel from around his own neck, and with shaky hands, he placed it around the neck of Felix. As he did, a faint sparkle came from the Amber and then it returned to normal.

"Yeah, boy! You gots it, alrighty!"

Gill reached into his pocket for his wallet. "Ah, Mr. Remus, sir. I'd like to pay you for –"

"No, no! Don' you go insultin' ol' Mr. Remus wid no money dere, Gill! I gives dis to da boy 'cause he needs it. 'Cause we needs it. Da whole damn world needs it! We gots no time for no highfalutin' critters tryin's to take our home! We gonne strike dem down! And den... dey gonna pass from dis Earth... unrecognized! Do you understand?"

Gill smiled. He needed no more explanation from this fine old gent. His eyes told the story.

Gill stood up and his friends followed.

"Mr. Remus... would a... handshake be out of the question?"

"Aw... you come here, boy!" Remus pulled Gill into his arms and gave him a big hug. He then did the same for everyone else in the room and touched each of them one time on their foreheads with his forefinger.

"Das da JU-JU! Y'all can take dat wid ya!"

As they all walked back out to the bus, Killer was the last to follow. Gill watched as Killer turned to face the ancient old dog one more time.

The old canine raised its old grey paw... and waved

Sarah shook her head. "Curiouser and Curiouser!"

They all piled into Betsey and quietly sat down. For the first time that anyone could remember, Felix was quiet.

He had nothing to say.

They watched out the window as Remus waved one last time and then closed the door to Gris-Gris Things. A sign came into the window that simply said, "CLOSED! GONE FOR MORE CHICKEN!"

They all laughed at this for a couple of minutes, and then, just as Gill was getting ready to crank Betsey up for the next phase of their adventure, they heard a powerful engine across the street crank up instead. From around behind the building zoomed an ol' black man about a million years old wearing a horned helmet and riding on a fifty-year-old Harley motorcycle with a sidecar and Rascal, as his passenger, was wearing a World War One soft leather flight helmet.

BEEP! BEEP!

And then... they were gone.

No one said a word for a couple of minutes.

They just sat there.

And then, in a whisper, Felix added... "A Gris-Gris man!"

54
Nevada Bound

"Well, that was a real hoot!" Sarah said with a smile, looking at Felix as they pulled back onto the small highway. "What's our next plan of action, Gill?"

"Well, gang, we're headed upstate from Fresno on Highway 99 toward the Oakland and San Francisco area, then we'll swing across the state on Highway 5 to Sacremento, followed by us driving to Nevada through Reno on Interstate 80 all the way to Elko, Nevada, where we turn north on 225 to Mountain City, our next stop!"

Sarah moaned. "God! How long is all of that gonna take, anyway?"

Gill smiled. "Well, one thing for sure, we've got a head start on the Thingies, and it'll take them just as long or longer than us... 'cause they're more conspicuous than we are! We can do our trip in the open, where they'll have to try to hide a hundred folks with 50 stolen vehicles... all needing gas!"

Everyone laughed a little at that.

Sarah asked again, "Yeah, but... how long and how far?"

Robert looked over at Felix, who had been awfully quiet for awhile now, just fingering his new necklace. "Felix?"

Felix looked up in a daze. "Yes, Robert?"

"Time and distance? To Mountain City, Nevada?"

Felix smiled, and then stretched his large frame. "Robert, it's about a hundred and eighty-four miles from Fresno to San Francisco. Add another three-hundred miles from San Francisco to Reno, Nevada... and then about four-hundred miles from Reno to Mountain City... if you go through Elko, Nevada. It's approximately nine-hundred miles from here to there. Cool?"

Robert put his hand on the tall man's shoulder with a smile. "Very cool, Super Dude. Very cool."

"How in the heck does he do that?" Sarah quizzed.

Robert smiled. "He reads a lot. He knows stuff."

Gill interrupted, "OK, then. With stops for food and rest, you can just about figure that we'll pull in to Mountain City twenty to twenty-four hours from the time we leave here. Let's stop in Fresno and re-stock our pantry with food and drinks. Also, before we get started, Robert, you and Sarah need to contact the Sarge back home, Sarah needs to call MAX, and I need to talk to Gwen if I can. We'll do all of this stuff this afternoon, and then hit the road early this evening. We've only got a couple of hours! Sound like a plan?"

"Sounds like a plan." Robert added, "Ah, Gill? What should I tell the Sarge about all of this?"

"Can we trust him, Robert? Sarah? Honestly?"

They looked at each other. "Yeah, Gill," Sarah said. "I believe we can."

Gill shook his head. "Well, I can't believe I'm saying this, but tell the poor guy everything."

"Everything?"

"Yeah. If we're gonna spill the beans, let's spill the whole damn bag!"

Felix chuckled. "That's gonna be one hell of a conversation!"

"Hey, Felix?" Gill asked. "Would you happen to know anything about Mountain City, Nevada?"

"A little, dude. It's in Elko County, Nevada on Route 225, about sixteen miles south of the Idaho state line. It's elevation is about five thousand and six-hundred twenty feet, almost two miles up! It's on the Owyhee River, too."

Gill smiled and shook his head. "That's really cool how you know that kind of stuff! But... you didn't give me the population this time, dude."

"That's 'cause there ain't none, Gill."

"WHAT?"

"Yep. Mountain City, Nevada is a ghost town!"

Robert sat down hard. "Aw, hell!"

Sarah sat down next to him. "Curiouser and Curiouser!"

Betsey backtracked her way to Fresno. They all pulled into a shopping center that contained a large supermarket, and Sarah and Gill went shopping. While they were gone, Felix studied his new necklace and Robert used that time to get in touch with the Sarge, aka Sergeant Eddie Fallon.

"Hi. LAPD, here. Can I help you?"

"Ah, yeah. Is there a Sergeant Eddie Fallon there?"

"Can I ask who's calling, please?"

"Ah, yeah. Tell him it's... ah, Dr. Robert, who fixed his hand the other day. He'll know me."

"Hold, please."

Robert waited on the phone listening to terrible elevator music only for about ten seconds before he heard, "Robert? Is that really you?"

"Yeah, Sarge. It's me... or us."

"Man, all hell is breaking loose here downtown! I tried to explain what

I could... without sounding like a total lunatic, but the more I said... the worse it sounded! Man, I could lose my job over this!"

"Sarge. Be very quiet... and listen to me... carefully... and say nothing for five minutes. No, better make that ten minutes! We could lose our PLAN-ET over this! OK?"

"Robert... Aw, hell... you've got my full and undivided attention. Hold on for one minute..."

CLICK... BUZZ... CLICK... ZZZZ...

"OK, you're on a scrambled line that can't be hacked or recorded. You've got a full ten minutes now. Thrill me with your exploits!"

Robert did.

Since they had a microwave aboard the bus, lots of time was spent in the frozen food section.

"Frozen soup? Whe the hell ever heard of frozen soup?" Gill said in a huff! "OK, Sarah. Let's get some quick stuff to cook... but a lot of more stuff to doctor it up with so that it'll taste real. Cool?"

"Gill, you're skinnin' this cat! I'm just holdin' it by the tail!"

Gill laughed as he looked at her. "Felix, right?"

She smiled back. "Yep!"

"Damn, I love that dude!"

They filled up two shopping carts full of every kind of box, bar, bag, veggie, fruit, cheese and meat that you could think of. Gill even bought extra chocolate.

"I didn't get to bring all of mine! Ya never can tell."

The cashier looked at their two mighty loads with a smile and then asked if she could have some of what they were smokin'! They paid for the ton of food in cash... and two bagboys helped carry it out to the bus to be stored. As Gill was tipping the two guys and unloading into the galley, he heard Robert on the phone.

"So, Sarge, that's basically what's goin' on. We're on the road right now to try to stop, or at least slow down these creatures... from what can only be called the end of life on our planet as we know it. I... ah... I guess that's about it. Do ya have any questions?"

Gill started laughing so hard that he could barely hear Sarge laughing on the other end of the phone conversation.

"Ah... yeah. I got a couple of questions for ya, Robert!"

Gill had Sarah and the two boys finish loading the bus, and he walked over to Robert. "Hey, Robert. Do you mind if I..."

"No! No problem! Ah, Sarge? This is Gill... that I was talking to you about? Hold on."

The sergeant had carefully listened to Robert. It may have sounded ridiculous, but as he listened, he realized that this person was not trying to bluff, was not trying to exaggerate, was not being evasive at all. This person was just being informative.

"A 'person of interest' who told the truth?," he thought. "Oh, God! If this was the truth then it was worse than a lie. They really were all in that much trouble, the whole world... and the situation would have to be handled differently.

He reasoned it out in his slow, methodical fashion. And then Gill came on the phone.

"Ah, Sarge? Can I call you that? Cool! Hi! I'm Gill. There's no way that any normal person should believe anything that you just heard, so I have to go outside of the ordinary and normal here. Hold on, OK? Felix? Come here."

"Yeah, Gill?"

"The sarge is on the phone here. Tell him what he needs."

Felix picked up the phone. "Ah, Sarge?"

"Yes, son. Felix? Is that your name?"

"Yes, sir. Hold on for a second, please."

Felix went away.

Felix came back.

"Sarge, in your second drawer is a towel. Grab that towel and the cigarette lighter in your pocket. Put down the phone and walk twenty steps behind you to the coffee machine. I'll wait here."

Sarge looked at the phone like it was a snake.

He set it down on his desktop, opened the second drawer of his desk and withdrew the hand towel that he always kept there. He stood up from his desk, took out the purple lighter that was inside of his pants' pocket and walked back to the coffee machine. He counted the steps as he went, which he'd never done before. Eighteen... nineteen... BAM! A lovely young cadet turned the corner and bumped right into him. She had a full cup of hot coffee in her hands, which spilt on her skirt. She had an un-lit cigarette in her beautiful lips on her way outside for a smoke break.

In a swift move that would have impressed Sir Walter Raleigh, he handed her the towel with a smile... and lit her cigarette!

"Ah, sorry!" she said with a shy smile. "You're Eddie, aren't you?"

"Yes, sweetie. Hello! I've... ah... got to finish a phone call... but if you don't mind, I'll meet you outside in a couple of minutes with a fresh cup of coffee for you. Alrighty?"

"Love it!" she said with a grin as she dabbed the stain off of her skirt.

Sarge ran back over to the phone! Felix was still there.

"Felix?"

"Hey, dude? She takes two sugars! Cool?"

Sarge laughed. "Yeah, dude! WAY cool!"

"OK, dude. Here's Gill again."

"Hi, Sarge. Are we cool?"

"Yeah, Gill. What can I do from here to help you?"

"Stop as many of those stolen vehicles as you can. They'll be crossing state lines. I'm sending their route to you by computer. Give me an e-mail address."

"Done. Gill, obviously, some of the police are in league with the forces against you. Be careful and keep me in the loop, OK?"

"Will do, Sarge. You're the only one of the police force in on this with us. Keep us in your loop, too. Call me tomorrow at this number. Ten-four?"

Sarge smiled. "Yo, dude!"

"Bye, Sarge."

Sarge hung up the phone with a smile. He got some change out of his desk and headed to the coffee machine.

"Well, that was a real hoot!" Robert said to Sarah with a smile.

"Ert, you da man!"

"I da man!"

Gill laughed as he held up his hands for quiet. "OK, OK! Before we head out of here, let's stop by that old Kentucky dude's house that fries up all of that chicken! We'll grab a bunch of that for now... and then we'll hit the road!"

"Extra-crispy on the yardbird!" Felix yelled out! "And extra mashed taters!"

After a brief stop at Chicken World, Betsey was once again on the road. As they headed north toward the San Francisco area, everyone wondered what was in store for them.

What about tomorrow?

Would there be... a tomorrow?

As dark decided to take over the skies, MAX rang up Sarah.

"All's quiet on the homefront, girl. Almost... too quiet! No new deaths or crimes in L.A. today! I get the feeling that everything bad that was here is now chasing you all down the road. Please be careful, Sarah."

"I will, MAX. Thanks for caring."

"Oh, by the way, there was a report of an explosion near Fresno this afternoon at a small town called Tranquility. Some small building blew up, but there were no casualties. No one was home, I guess."

Sarah smiled as she remembered Remus and Rascal. "Yep. No one home.

Gone for more chicken. Good night, MAX."

"Good night. Oh, Lois said to tell Felix that she misses him!"

"I heard that!" Felix broke in.

Gill drove through the evening and everyone else was entertained by Betsey's movie selection. Soon, though, heads started to nod and all good heroes headed toward sleep world.

Felix and Killer strolled back to their bunk.

Gill, who was still driving, said, "Hey, Robert?"

Robert took his arm from around Sarah's neck and came up front. "Yeah, Gill? Do you need me to take over the driving for awhile?"

"No, buddy, I'm fine. I think I'll just sit up here with Betsey for awhile and maybe pull over somewhere early in the morning to catch a nap. Would you mind... ah... taking over the back bedroom tonight?"

"WHOOPEE! Ahh... sorry! Ah... I mean... ah...no, Gill. I'll be... ah... glad to take over that back bedroom tonight."

Gill smiled. "Double bed... Ert."

Robert hugged Gill's neck as he drove down the dark highway. "Thanks, pal."

"No worries. Good dreams."

55
You Wanna Bet?

Gill drove for what seemed like an eternity. After about nine hours of continuous time behind the wheel, he decided that not only was it time to top off Betsey's tanks once again, but he was going to have to go down for the count once again. He didn't want to start seeing things that weren't there and he sure didn't want to start not seeing that they were there.

On the outskirts of Reno, Nevada, "The Biggest Little City In The World," he decided to make this his stopping place. He pulled the big bus up to the pumps of another truck stop and filled up both the generator and the big diesel tanks. He pulled around to the side of the large place and parked.

It was several hours before dawn and everyone else was still sound asleep. Gill made himself a ham and cheese sandwich with a glass of cold milk and sat in the lounge area before grabbing himself a bunk and turning in.

"Betsey, on security."

"Yes, Gill."

As he laid down, he closed his eyes, and concentrated on trying to reach Gwen. No luck. Not only could he not reach her, but he picked up static. This had never happened before. Blank, yes, but static? Never.

"Oh, well," he thought. "Maybe later. Dream time now."

He snuggled up under the warm blankets against the chill that was starting to take over the outside weather. Soon, they might see some snow, but for now, the only thing he worried about was a few hours of sleep.

"Good night, Betsey."

"Good night, Gill. Good dreams."

Felix went to sleep.

Then Felix went away.

Felix came back.

It was early morning. Felix woke up and had the weirdest feeling. He knew what someone needed, but he hadn't yet met that someone. What a unique feeling. it was. Everyone else was still sound asleep, but Felix had to get up. He left Killer curled up in their bunk and went forward to speak to Betsey.

"Betsey?"

"Yes? Good morning, Felix."

"Good morning to you, too. Ah, when I left Gill's house, I was told by Lois that you and she were... one. Is that true?"

"No, Felix, not exactly. We come from the same, as you would say, space or source, but we are different entities. What is your problem, Felix?"

"I'm not sure. Is there any way that I can talk to Lois? I dig talking to you a lot, Betsey, so don't get me wrong, but, I think I need to."

"Felix?" It was Lois's voice.

"Oh, God! Am I glad to hear your voice! Lois, I need an outside opinion, and I guess that I needed to talk to you about it. Somehow, I trust you."

"That's great, Felix. What can I do for you?"

"All of my life, I've had these... visions... of what people around me have needed. I've always tried to help folks out, without... I guess, freakin' them out... because having someone else tell you something about your own future is... kinda mind blowin'!"

"OK I can see that."

"But, last night, I got a reading for something that someone needed, but it's someone that I don't know. At least not yet! This has never happened to me before. I need your advice, I guess."

"Felix... two questions. Number one... have you ever been wrong about what someone needed?"

"No, Lois. Never."

"OK, number two... has the feelings ever been for anyone... bad?"

"Aw, no! I wouldn't ever think about helping out an evil person!"

"Then go with your feelings, Felix. Whoever this person in your future is, they're gonna need this help that you can give them. Do what's right."

"SEE! Now that's why I wanted to talk to you! Thanks, Lois!"

"No problem, dude! Come home soon, OK? And safe."

"You got it, m'lady!"

Betsey came back on again. "Did that help you, Felix?"

"You betcha, Betsey! Thanks."

"No problem, dude."

About an hour later, everyone started waking up to the smell of smoke. Gill jumped up out of the bunk as Killer started barking and Robert came rumbling out of the back room with Sarah at his heels.

"What's on fire?" Gill yelled as he stepped into the galley area.

"Are we under attack?" Robert yelled as he tripped over poor Killer in the smoke-filled hallway.

Betsey came on the speakers. "Ah, I would have to call it... sort of ... an attack! Felix is cooking!"

Felix brushed away the smoke from around the small stove. "Hi, dudes! How do you like your pancakes?"

Robert tried to smile. "How about light black?"

Gill said, "I don't think I like mine... at all. Betsey! Open the doors and turn on the damn vent fan!"

Black smoke went rolling out the front door of the bus as everyone jumped out for fresh air. Sarah was by the front door choking when Felix came stumbling out with black smudges on his face,

"Felix?" Sarah moaned. "Cough... cough! Was that really... pancakes? Cough... cough!"

"Sarah, if I just scrape a little bit of charcoal off of 'em... and put a little butter and a lot of maple syrup of 'em, then they'll be –"

"TERRIBLE!" said Robert. "They'll be terrible, that's what they'll be! Damn, Felix! Now I smell like I've been sleeping inside of a barbecue pit!"

Gill laughed, and then added, "OK, Felix. You tried... and we appreciate the thought. But, let's air poor Betsey out, and then we'll go grab a bite here in Reno before we head out again. Cool?"

"Ah... yeah, Gill, but I need to talk to y'all for a few minutes before we go. Cool?"

"Uh-oh!" Robert said. "Here we go, friends and neighbors! Here it comes!"

Gill shook his head at Robert. "Be cool, Robert! Felix is serious! OK, then. Let the bus air out for a minute then we'll go talk."

After the smog left poor Betsey, they all sat down and Felix told them about his "feeling," and what Lois had said.

Gill looked at his tall buddy. "Dude, what do we need to do? You know... to help you out?"

"Gill. I need five dollars. At twelve minutes after one p.m., Robert and I need to walk into the Horseshoe Casino. Robert places a bet on a giant blue one-armed bandit at one twenty-two. Then, we take our prize and leave. OK?"

Gill looked at Felix with a hurt look in his eyes. "You mean, you're gonna use your abilities to win a jackpot for yourself... at a casino? Is that what you're telling me, Felix?"

Felix shook his head. "No, Gillmeister. This isn't for me. It's for some-one near Mountain City. They need it. She needs it. Someone called... 'Shadow Of The Moon.'"

"THE GHOST TOWN?"

"Yep. That's all I know. But... I need to do this. Can you... just... trust me on this?"

Gill just stood there for a minute thinking.

"Yeah, Felix. I guess if I can trust you with my life... I can trust you with this, too."

"Cool, dude!" Felix said as he hugged the little guy.

Robert spoke up. "One question, though, guys... since I'm involved in this."

Felix looked at him as he asked, "Yo, Bobby, dude, what is it?"

"Will they have food there, Super Dude?"

Everyone started laughing again.

"Yeah, dude! A Cajun speciality! Blackened Pancakes!"

Everyone had changed into clothing a bit warmer since the blustery wind outside had picked up. At eleven a.m., they pulled Betsey out of the truck stop and headed over toward downtown Reno. Being near the main strip, they had a little problem parking that big ol' bus, but they found a parking lot not too far away from the casino and walked the rest of the way in.

Felix led them to the restaurant in the back of the building, and they all had a combination of a late breakfast and an early lunch. The food was good, but after that particular morning, no one ordered the pancakes!

Felix looked at Gill and asked, "Ah, Gill, dude, would you happen to have a tow bar in Betsey anywhere?"

"Yeah, Felix... as a matter of fact, we've got a tow bar for pulling a trailer or another vehicle, we've got chains for ice, tow chains and ropes, too. Why do you ask?"

"Well, we're gonna need it for a little while."

By the time that they finished their meal, it was only one o'clock. Robert pulled Felix off to the side. "Hey, dude? You know by now that part of what makes me a member of this team is a... streak of luck, right?"

"Yep. That's what I heard, big guy."

"Well, right now... my luck is telling me that we shouldn't just waltz in there and play that one hand of slot machine, and then walk away a big winner. They've got cameras all over this place, and that'll look kinda suspicious... ya know what I mean?"

Felix smiled. "Yeah, Bobby. I know just what you mean! Hey, umm, Gill?"

"Yeah, Felix? What do you need?"

"Dude, instead of that five dollars, can you advance me a grand on my salary?"

Gill grinned. "You betcha, tall one! Let's go have a little fun before that big one comes along, what do y'all say?"

They all walked into the casino section together. They dropped a few dollars here, a hundred dollars there. Sarah bet on the roulette table and won ten bucks. Felix was so excited at winning twenty dollars on a quarter machine that he almost missed his own deadline.

"Felix! Come on, dude! Time to go... you know!"

"Oh! Yeah, dude. I almost forgot! But this machine is fixin' to hit!"

"Shut up and come on!" Robert said with a laugh.

They found the Grand Payoff machine in the lobby. It took five bucks to play it, and some grumpy little old man was on the machine when they walked up to it.

Felix smiled. "Hey, dude? Ya havin' any luck?"

"Damn, hippy! Get the hell away from me! You're gonna put the hex on me, coming up here talking when a man's trying to concentrate. You and your friends... just back up! Go on! Back up!"

Robert looked at his watch. "Ah, Felix... just two minutes! What do you want to do?"

"Just hang on there, Bobby boy! Everything's cool here!"

The old man kept putting in five bucks and losing... then putting in five bucks and losing. Finally, he got up off of the stool in front of the machine. "Ya done jinxed me, that's what ya did! Damn, hippy!" He stomped away.

Robert smiled, and then sat down at the GRAND PAYOFF giant slot machine and looked at Felix. "Now?"

"Nope. One minute and... thirty-two seconds."

"Do you have the five dollars?" Robert asked.

"Ah... Gill has it. Gill? Where did Gill go? Quick, Sarah... go find Gill!"

She ran over one lane, and there he was, putting a nickel into a five-cent machine.

"Come on, big spender! We're out of time!"

They ran back over to Felix, and as the time ran down, Gill handed Robert a five dollar bill.

"FIVE... FOUR... THREE..."

Robert put the money into the slot.

"TWO... ONE..."

He pulled the giant arm down... and...

Whirrr. whirrr. whirrr...

BING, BING, BING, BING, BING!

Lights and buzzers were going off everywhere.

"Hey, mister! You just won that van over there!"

A beautiful twelve-passenger van was displayed on the casino floor. On the side of it, a mural had been drawn of the moon in a beautiful night sky. The moon was either a crescent moon or was in an eclipse. What appeared to be an Indian girl was standing on the ground, gazing up to the waning moon. A shooting star spanned the entire length of the mural.

Everyone was crowding around the group and shaking hands and there were lots of slaps on the back and congratulations and... then...

"Hey, dude! Some suit is walkin' over this way, Bobby! Be cool, eh?"

The floor-walker came over and put his hand on Robert's shoulder.

"Congratulations, sir! If you'll just step this way, please."

Robert put his own hand on the manager's arm and looked into his eyes calmly. "Is there any problem?"

The guy sort of went blank for a moment and then came back with a smile. "No, sir! Just want to get your name and address for the paperwork and the IRS, take a couple of pictures... and then give you the keys to your new van!"

"That'll be just fine," Gill said as he came over with Robert.

The two of them went off in the direction of the elevators with the manager. Everyone else just stood there, wondering if anything had gone wrong. As they all waited there, three security-type fellows came onto the floor and started up the new van and drove it off of the casino floor into the back of the building.

Within five minutes, Robert and Gill got off of the elevator with a half dozen people in suits. Cameras were flashing. People were clapping. Buzzers were buzzing and sirens were screaming.

Gill looked at Sarah with a smile, showed her the set of keys to the new passenger van, and with his teeth still clinched, he said, "Get me the hell away from here!"

"OK! Gotta go now!" she said as she dragged everyone toward the front door. "Thanks a lot! Bye, now! Bye! Gotta go!"

When they finally got outside, Gill hugged her. "Thanks, girl! Let's go around back."

They all went to the back of the casino and there was the brand new twelve-passenger van. It was brown and tan earth tones. With the detailed painting on the side, it was quite beautiful, but no one could figure out why they had done all of this.

"Dudes and dudette, I don't know! Really! But... it'll be good for someone REAL soon! I promise."

Gill smiled. "That's good enough for me, Supie! Let's all drive our new van back to Betsey now! It's gonna get late early today, and we've still got to hook up this critter and get on the road! Shall we?"

Felix laughed at Gill! "Supie?"

As they all piled in to the van, Robert said, "Man, that all made me just as nervous as hell, guys! I'll swear... I'm never gonna gamble again."

Felix smiled quietly as he said, "You wanna bet?"

56
Ghost Town Spirits

It took the better part of an hour to situate the van, put on the tow bar, lock it and strap it in to be ready to roll once again. Betsey loved it.

"Aww, it's almost like having a baby," she whimpered.

Felix looked at everyone in the family that had become his family.

"Guys... and guyette... I can't tell ya how much it means to me that y'all trusted me on this thing! Way cool!"

Robert chimed in, "We need to give it a name! What do you think?"

Everyone had a hundred different ideas, and then, suddenly, Sarah asked, "Gill, wasn't your van called 'Helen?' You know... Van Helen?"

"Yeah, sweetie. She was. I'm gonna miss her, too."

"Well, then, let's call this dude... Morrison!"

"YEAH! That's it!" They all cried. "Van Morrison... so it is christened!"

Everyone was in high spirits as Betsey pulled out onto the road. As they started their four-hundred mile journey from Reno to the ghost town that was their next destination, they were all laughing and singing, and telling tales of how great things had been going and how wonderful their futures looked.

Meanwhile, back in the real world...

The young girl looked to her grandfather, who was chanting the old words as the tears fell down his face.

The smoke in the sweat lodge was blocking off all of the real sights of the New World from coming through, but the Outer World visions... the Other World visions... were as clear as the stream that flowed by the tribal council's meeting place. The old man sighed as he cast more water upon the hot stones.

She saw those visions as clear as her grandfather could.

"Ah yeah ay ya ya ay ya ya! Me ah ya yea ha ha yae ya!" The old man whispered as he saw the terrible future being thrust upon all of the human beings.

He saw no sunshine, no clear, running water, no creatures of the Great Spirit. Nothing.

"No!" he cried, as he shook the turtle shell. "No! There must be an answer! There must be an... intervention! There must be..."

It was then that he had... that they had... the vision.

They saw a tribe of strange warriors, each with powers beyond description or explanation. And among them dwelled a blue-haired giant. A warrior with the voice of life. A warrior with the voice of death.

There was also a changer of futures and a re-teller of the past. A keeper of time. A speaker to the machines. A dog god. A healer of pain and luck. Surely, this was a sign sent by the ONE to the people.

Granddaughter, too, saw this vision. She saw and she knew.

This tall one bore the sign of the cat.

Of all the powers, this blue-haired tall one carried the hope of all human beings..

This tall one could keep The Sleeping Giant... asleep.

She left her grandfather in his vision, in his tears, and exited the sweat lodge for her van.

She was a teacher of the young ones. She brought knowledge to the needy children of the tribe and tried to make their world wider, brighter, better. Each day, she would drive her van to pick up the tribe's young ones and deliver them to the small barn that had been converted into a makeshift school. Each day, she would try to educate, to enlighten the young ones on the ways of the New World. Her children couldn't afford lack of these teachings.

Shadow Of The Moon thought of the vision.

Bad things were coming, and good things were in a race against time with them.

The good things may reach their final destination before the Evil Thingies did, but they would not beat the Evil Thingies to her tribe.

Her tribe would have much trouble before help ever arrived.

The best she could do was to hide the young ones.

Her van tore out of the dirt road as she went in search of all that she could save.

Time was short.

The long night was upon them all.

That evening, it was decided that Felix and Robert would swap off the driving so that Gill could try to get back in touch with the Flae. As Felix drove down the cold, dark highway, Gill made himself a drink to relax a bit and then slipped into one of the empty bunks. Killer whined until Gill opened the curtain and let the small dog slide in next to him.

"It's good to see you again, partner. You've been kinda spending a lot time with old Felix lately, haven't you?'"

The dog gave a small whimper and licked Gill on the hand.

"That's perfectly OK, Killer. I know you love me, and Felix can use the extra support right now. Now, you lie still, and let's see if we can reach Gwen. OK?"

"Yipe."

He opened his mind.

"Gwen."

"It does my heart good to hear from you... as always, Gill. Much I have to share with you."

"Good. I can use any help and advice you can supply."

"We have been unable to converse because of interference from those you call Whistlers. They were hard to bypass when they were all together... but now they have... divided."

"Divided? You mean that they have split up? Taken different paths?"

"Yes, Gill. Many of them were caught and killed when they began to travel together. Your people in charge could identify them by their appearance and the machines that they rode upon. They followed your route, and since they would not be captured alive, several were terminated."

"Well, that's good news! I had Robert inform our... 'people in charge' that they would be traveling in our path. How many remain, Gwen?"

"It is hard to tell because of the... dividing... or splitting up... but many remain, and they now travel by different roads. I'm sorry to say that many of your people in charge were also terminated. This could not be helped."

"Ah, Gwen... did you happen to discover anything about information that's been leaking out to the Thingies? I wondered if..."

"Gill, after talking to you, a small group of the Flae approached Gin, the Great One. It has been discovered that a... helper of Gin... Garn by name... has seen fit to send certain facts to another race of beings from our plane of existence... some of these who also deal with the Thingies. This will happen no longer. Garn has been... shall we say, 'stopped.' Gin sends regrets for the problems caused. He would only say that amends will be sent. This is a mystery to us, but sounds promising."

"Thank him for his attention in this matter, Gwen. I guess we should prepare for more battle coming up with the Thingies, and now from different directions. Whether that be a good thing or bad, only time will tell."

"In ALL things of life, my friend... only time will tell. Remember, however, you yourself now literally have time. Think about it. Goodbye, Gill."

"Goodbye, Gwen."

"I myself now have time? Now what did she... ?"

"OH!" he said out loud. Killer looked up at him.

"Yipe?"

"Ima Rock! I now have time!"

He went forward to tell everyone of his conversation with Gwen, and by using the MindSpeak, it took only a couple of seconds.

Robert smiled at them all. "So, we've got less bad guys... but they're gonna try to surround us! That's real good... and real bad!"

Felix laughed as he said, "Well then, I'm happy and sad for us!"

Robert looked at him and answered back, "Pure malarkey! You never cease to marvel me!"

Felix tried his best to look intelligent as he came back with, "It's nothing really. It's a gift!"

Robert rolled onto the bus floor laughing.

The night was rushing by in a wave of time, and Shadow had collected a van full of scared children.

Parents who would normally have been reluctant to send off their babies in the dead of night had no problems when it came to Shadow or her grandfather.

These two knew things and everyone knew that.

The tribe was told to arm themselves and be prepared to defend the village and their own lives before the dawn. They were told to build up the fires... bright and hot... for the enemy would not fight in the daytime and would not like to fight in the light.

They were told that she would take the children to a place of safety and she would stay with them until the sun came up. At that point, Warriors would come. Warriors would finish the battle with the enemy, but the people must stand up to the Evil Thingies until the Warriors appeared.

"Stand together," she said, "and you will not fall alone!"

The tribal elders sent away their children with Shadow Of The Moon. They all met at the Council Lodge. They built the fires, hot and high. They collected knives and guns... and waited.

They wouldn't have to wait for very long.

Shadow drove the old van into the mountains with the small children, huddled together against the cold.

She had decided on an old abandoned mine-shaft that she occasionally went into. It was near the old Ghost Town. There was much wood there for warmth and light, and the fire wouldn't be seen from the mouth of the cave. There were tons of rock to insulate the children from the oncoming winter storm.

There was safety there.

She drove as close as she could to the location, and then got the children bundled up for a hike to the mine through the woods. Leaving the old van behind, they fled.

She brought a small bag with food, blankets and water in it... and her flute.

The trail was an uneven path, winding through stones and thick, gnarled tree roots, into mist where reflected points of light swam...

shimmering in the haze...

looking like phantoms...

like wraiths.

Moving as quietly as a ghost, and fading into the night, she and the children ran.

After a few hours of driving, Felix had taken over Betsey as they made their way down the long road. Robert had gently picked up sleeping Sarah and retired to the back state room to pick up some much-needed rest before tomorrow.

It was now hours later, and there was no one awake except Felix and Betsey when he saw the first clue to the passing of the Thingies.

An old service station on the right had been totally destroyed. The fire was so recent that a wisp of smoke could still be seen around the glowing blue embers.

Blue!

There was no sign of life there. There was what appeared to be a large puddle of pickup truck, but Felix couldn't be sure.

"Betsey?"

"Yes, Felix?"

"Several things I need you to do for me. Cool?"

"Way cool, Super Dude,"

Felix smiled at this. "First, get a hold of Lois back home. Have her call MAX... and then have MAX call me here on the bus phone hookup. I need satellite intel on what we're gettin' ready to drive into here. We've got trouble ahead. Next, as much as I hate to... be prepared to wake up Gill and Robert on my signal. We're less than an hour from Mountain City, and I'm positive that the bad guys are already there. The Duck Island Indian Reservation is right next to our destination, and I think I see fire on the horizon. Those folks may need a lot of help. Get to it, girl!"

"Yes, sir!"

He had just passed Elko, Nevada and was headed north on Highway 225 when he spotted the burned-out station. Now, he spotted more wreckage on the side of the road, glowing with a strange blue haze around it. It appeared to be an old car that was run off the road, and there were bodies next to it.

"I'm pulling over, Betsey! Wake 'em up!"

Felix hopped out of the bus door almost before it came to a halt. Two people, a man and a woman, were lying dead next to the wreck.

They appeared to be Native Americans.

This area was rich in the tribal heritage of the Shoshone and Paiute tribes of Native Americans, but it wasn't going to be possible to identify which tribe these two unfortunate folks were from. Almost nothing was left of what they had once been.

Gill and Robert came running off the bus. "Damn, Felix? What's going on?"

"Damn Whistlers have beat us to the punch on this one, Gill. These folks are gone." He then told his two friends about the station that they'd just passed.

"If you look ahead, you can just see where there's a fire on the horizon. It looks blue, too!"

"Then, let's go see if we can help the living, pal," Gill said with a frown.

They were loading up on the bus again when Felix went away.

After about ten seconds, he popped back into reality, and jumped off of the bus again, running.

Gill yelled, "What is it, Felix? What did you see? What do we need?"

"I saw a ghost, pointing! Hang on a second. Gotta go get..." His voice faded out.

Felix disappeared into the brush and trees without saying another word.

About two minutes later, they were all standing outside in the cold air once again, including Sarah, waiting for their giant friend's return when, from the bushes, they heard, "A diaper!"

Robert yelled out, "WHAT?"

Felix came back to the side of the highway holding a small Indian baby out away from himself as he walked. The poor shivering baby was in tears.

"A diaper! That's what this critter needs!"

There was still almost three hours of darkness left when the Evil Thingies came into the village. The Shoshone elders and men of the tribe had situated the women in the back of the tribal headquarters as the braves once again prepared for war.

It was to be a battle such as none had ever seen.

It would be told in songs and dance for many generations to come... if anyone survived.

Two cars and a pickup truck, all with dark tinted windows, pulled into the open area of the village.

Five creatures got out of these vehicles. None of these beings could be mistaken for human, but they started to change from the moment that their feet touched the ground. They began looking around as if they were searching for something.

One brave young man ran forward with a pistol, firing as he went. The bullets passed into the bodies almost as if the demons were made of some kind of rubber. The bullets seemed to have no effect whatsoever.

The brave young man became the first causality of what would become known as the "Battle of the Spirits."

One of the demons was finally taken down when its head was removed by an old sword which had been handed down for generations in the tribe. By then, though, five brave men had lost their lives.

One of the fallen was being eaten by the creatures.

Finally, one of the women of the tribe ran forth. "Fire!" she screamed. "Shadow said they will not like the light! Use the fire!"

As one of the creatures was lured away from the feast of human flesh, it was attacked by three of the braves who wielded burning brands from the giant bonfire built in the center of the encampment, which the creatures would not approach. After repeated thrusts with the torch, they finally managed to set the Evil Thing on fire and it burned like tar. This, however, did not prevent the creature from starting to whistle. The sound built up to a painful level of sound, and suddenly, a blue ball of flame erupted from the mouth of the Whistler as it totally collapsed. The ball engulfed one of the buildings of the village and began to spread. Soon, blue fire ran across the treetops, and a section of the nearby forest erupted in flame.

With three of the Whistlers still on the attack, the men of the tribe quickly gathered the women in an attempt to escape the quick moving conflagration. But as they started to ease away from the enemy, they heard a sound in the distance that they hadn't heard in many generations.

It was the bugle call of the cavalry... sounding the charge. "Da... da da... da da... da da... da da!"

And it was coming out of the speakers of a giant blue bus, which was barreling down the trail to the village.

Just in the nick of time.

It was the Warriors.

57
The Battle of the Spirits

Robert was the first one off of the bus. Before anyone could say anything to him, he had waded off waist-deep into battle.

He punched at the first of the creatures to approach him, but this seemed to have little or no effect on the Whistler. It rebounded, as if it were a rubber blow-up doll and Robert's hand stung from the mighty blow. A second Thingie came at him from his unprotected backside as he was still defending himself against the first one. Just then, Sarah came off the bus. She saw what was happening and quickly ran over to place her hands on the top of an old tractor, which one of the tribe had parked in the open area of the village.

VAROOM!

It came to life and charged into the battle, knocking away everyone from the confrontation. The tractor then continued on into the now burning forest.

The last of the three remaining Thingies opened its lips to such an extent that it could have placed its whole head inside of its own mouth. A terrible whistle began to build in volume, eventually to the point that ears would bleed.

And then...

nothing.

Everything stopped.

Everyone was frozen.

Gill slowly came off the bus with Ima Rock in his small hands, smiling. Time was frozen.

Gill went to the cargo hold of Betsey and opened the hatch doors. He quickly withdrew three of the large hand-held spotlights that they had used only days ago in the electrical sub-station battle. He checked to make sure the batteries were still good, and then he walked over to meet Robert and Sarah. He placed one of them into each of their hands, and then started to walk back to the bus.

That was when he saw the old man walking toward him.

This member of the Shoshone tribe appeared to be about a thousand years old. The face of an ancient child was what he wore as he smiled at

Gill and motioned him forward.

"You speak for the small spirits, Small Man! I have seen them in my visions."

Gill stood there with his mouth wide open. "How is it, Grandfather, that you are not affected by the stoppage of time as the others are?"

The old man smiled. "My time is almost up, my son, and your charms will have no effect upon this old man. There is a favor that you can give unto me, however, if it be in your power. My granddaughter will be in great and terrible danger in one hour's time. With her now, she has all of the tribal young ones! They must be protected! Send the giant warrior. The Cat Warrior with the hair of blue! He will know where to find her. I believe that she... she is... expecting him. He will know what to take to defeat the creatures who stalk my granddaughter. He must hurry, and he can use... the... Morrison? That must be a white man's word! Give the new baby to her when she returns. Tell my granddaughter that the new baby's name will be 'Found Child.' Tell her of my love for her... and for Found Child, who will grow up to be great in heart... and important to our people!

"For you, my son... you must come to the sweat lodge before you have to leave this reservation. There is a carving there for you that I hold. It, too, is an old man. It is also... I believe you call it... a Builder?"

Gill shook his head and smiled. He went to place his hand on the old man's shoulder, but it passed through the grandfather like smoke.

The ancient Indian smiled. "As I said, my time is now up. Tell the Cat Warrior that I said time is short for this rescue, dude! Also, tell the one-armed warrior that he shall become one with the Shoshone... and his name shall be 'Other Brother.' Will you do this?"

And with that, his smiling image faded away into nothing.

Another ghost.

Gill walked over the frozen ground into the bus, wondering about this odd new puzzle... to see Felix inside, frozen in time as he was gently placing Found Child into a bunk. Gill walked back over to where the screaming whistle had been coming out the third creature. He adjusted the spotlight he held in his hand and placed Ima Rock back into his pocket.

All hell broke loose again.

Robert and Sarah both came back to reality with searchlights in their hands.

Instantly, they realized that Gill had done his little Ima Rock Time Stopper thing while they were gone. BAM! They turned on their lights and the

Thingies screamed.

Then one of the Whistlers, the same one that Robert had first hit with his fist, was now actually being cut in half by the beam of killing light from Robert's weapon. The top portion of the torso continued to twitch and scream for just a few seconds as it hit the dark ground after being separated from the bottom portion, which just stood there at attention where it had died.

Sarah had turned on her searchlight, but before she could aim it, the Thingie that had stood in front of her took off at a rapid run in the direction of Betsey.

Felix was just stepping off Betsey as he was attacked.

Right then, the deadly Whistler reached the bus and it reached out its own hand to end the life of the Felix human. The Whistler reached his own life's end instead.

Betsey, upon request from Felix, gave him a road flare.

As the Evil Thingie grabbed Felix by the collar of his now ripped-up and shredded shirt, Felix popped the flare into life.

The giant blue-haired dude grinned and quickly took the burning flare into his big right hand, and with all his strength, rammed it into the heart of the now screaming creature. The resulting fire was a terrible thing to behold.

Felix smiled as he dropped the flaming Whistler to the foggy, frozen ground below. "Now... ya know how Dracula felt... ya son-of-a-bitch!"

The third of the beasts, which had been doing its deadly whistling in front of Gill, shut down its racket immediately as its left arm was separated by Gill's light from the rest of its body. It just stood there, looking at the severed limb as Gill raised his light to the sky instead of ending the Evil Thingies life where it stood.

"If you move, I will kill you. Do you understand?"

The Evil Thingie nodded.

"You aren't the last here... are you?" Gill said with conviction.

The Thingie looked into Gill's eyes and knew that a lie would get itself terminated. It shook its head.

"No."

"How many more are at this immediate area? The truth!"

The Thingie decided to use the human way of speech to reply.

"None here in this locale, 'Human who kills Thingies.' Two are approximately five of your miles from here, however, in search of a female of power. She has young meat with her, also."

Gill looked to Sarah, who still held her light at ready.

"Sarah, much must be done quickly! First, I need Felix here with me. Next, you and Robert and the tribe members who can help need to un-hitch the van... PRONTO! Kids lives are at stake! Quick now!"

Sarah took off at a run.

Gill looked again to the Whistler, who still gazed upon its own arm and appeared to be getting weaker by the moment.

"Another question, Whistler! Are you... HE?"

The injured beast laughed! "No, small warrior... HE has taken a different path than that you will follow. HE will encounter less resistance... and enjoy greater stealth... with the Oregon route by which HE travels. We are all to meet at The One Place and our people will then be free to cross into this... our new world! The promise of hope that was once foretold by wise men of another race will be delivered unto our hands by the wisdom of the ONE, and HE will be our deliverer!"

By then, Felix had walked up close enough to hear the tail end of this conversation.

The Whistler looked at Felix and then continued. "And then, not even the power of the 'Humans who kill Thingies' will be able to forestall the invasion of our worthy civilization! Not even this Felix person... who can actually stop someone from 'being,' can find the words to express the awesome might of the Evil Thingies!"

Felix nodded and smiled. "Uh, huh! And I can do that in only one word, too."

The pitiful, one-armed and defeated creature looked up into the eyes of the blue-haired giant as Felix smiled and whispered, "Bullshit."

The Thingie started to shake.

Before it could explode, before it could begin its terrible and fatal whis-tle, before it could even get its poor mind right, Gill calmly walked over to the Evil Thingie and placed his hand onto its shoulder.

Robert and Felix freaked. They started to run to the two now-connect-ed beings, but were stopped by Sarah, who, with Robert, had come back from unhooking the van.

Sarah smiled. "Felix? Robert? Don't you remember? The MindSpeak with Gwen?"

Felix went away, for only a moment, and when he came back, he was smiling.

"Yeah. Now I remember. Here is what Gill MindSpoke to me at that time, Robert...

"Gill said, 'I don't understand. HardSpeak? Is this anything like the MindSpeak that you are supposed to explain to me?'

"Gwen said, *'No, Gill. Your MindSpeak is a Flae gift, which is actually a contin-*

uation of what you and I are doing right now, only you now have the ability to use this with your friends. You can tell them all that you and I now speak of in mere seconds by touch. And... as you are not capable of an un-truth while you speak now to me... the same will be true with the MindSpeak. In your honesty, you can influence and change people's minds and opinions of things and objects... but only by showing them the truths in your own mind and opinion. This is known as Thought Emotion. This will work on not only your friends, but as well as your enemies. There must be contact, however, for this to work, and once it is done... you must replenish your strength at once with what you call... cocla...ah, chumlat... no, it's...'

"Gill smiled again. 'Chocolate, Gwen?'

"Yes, Gill, that's it. This... chocolate... is a strength restorative for your draining of power. Chocolate will serve you well."

Felix came back... yet again!

"Bobby boy, run to the bus for chocolate! Gill's gonna need a bunch and Sarah and I can watch this... this... Well, hell! I don't know if it's a confrontation or a collaboration!"

Robert took off for chocolate, laughing.

The union between Gill and the creature only lasted about a minute.

In that much time, Gill truthfully explained what damage the Thingies were doing to billions of living beings on this planet... plants and animals!

In that much time, Gill managed to reveal the error in the philosophy of any one race of people completely eliminating another simply for more room and more resources.

In that much time, the human race gained a friend.

Gill released his hold on the Thingie and slumped to the ground.

The alien being fell to the ground to cradle Gill's head in its lap with its one remaining arm.

"Can you help him?" the creature cried out to the remaining people around him as it rocked Gill's unconscious body back and forth.

Sarah was once again off trying to help bring around the new van and Robert was in search of chocolate onboard the bus.

Felix and one of the tribal women went to their knees beside the incredible shape-shifting being who was bent down next to Gill. She felt Gill's head, she took his pulse and then smiled to Felix and the Thingie. "He will be alright, strange ones. He is in need of... strength... recharging."

About then, Robert ran up with an entire box of chocolate bars, peeling wrappers as he ran. "Quick... try to get some of these into him! It will help him!"

The Native American lady and the strange Thingie both began feeding Gill bar after bar of chocolate as Felix laughed.

"DUDE! There is NEVER a camera around when ya need one! This is a definite Kodak moment here!"

Felix started laughing even harder as the Thingie licked melted chocolate off its own fingers and fell in love.

"AHHH! What wonder... is this?" It whimpered.

Felix patted it on its one good arm and said, "That's chocolate, Whistler dude! Welcome to the twenty-first century!"

Gill opened his eyes around a clown-like face smeared with milk chocolate wonderfulness. He looked at his friends, then at the Whistler, smiled, and said, "I believe that his name is now Other Brother."

"You have named me?" the alien asked.

"It was done by one with power who has now passed," Gill said. "It is a strong name... and your place from now on will be here... with these people... as was foretold by the grandfather. Your future will be to help these people whom you have hurt. They are your family now."

"My... family?" he whimpered.

With that, tribal members slowly came over to try to help the new member, who had been brought into their midst by the one person who always knew, always understood. There would be no objections to any decision made by the grandfather.

Before the tribe took the new creature away for care and medicine, Robert stopped it.

"Other Brother, welcome to our world... not now as a conqueror... but as a friend. I may have power to help your pain, if you will allow me... ?"

Other Brother stepped forward to Robert with no fear in its face. "Any help... will be... appreciated."

Robert concentrated on the glow within himself and placed his hands on the stump of the injured arm.

A glow inside of Robert increased and passed to Other Brother, who smiled.

"The pain is gone! You are truly in contact with the ONE, my friend!"

Robert smiled. "Well, Other Brother... we have our own... ONE, and who's to say that they aren't ONE and the same the same being, after all?"

Robert then walked away to see what he could do for the other injured members of the tribe.

Gill raised himself up on shaky legs and looked to Felix.

Felix knew.

"Aww, dude! I gotta go, don't I?" Felix groaned.

"I'm afraid so, old friend. Come here for a second and I'll show you what I know."

Gill and Felix bonded into the realm of MindSpeak for a moment and then popped back again. Gill was swooning.

"Man! That's tough to do twice in a row! I gotta rest... and gobble up more chocolate!"

Felix smiled. "Aww! Poor baby! Gotta eat chocolate! Well, anyway... I got the message. I even think I know where I'm supposed to go! There's an old mine not far from here where... where she goes. I'm gonna need one of the lights, a bunch of blankets... and either a sword or a long knife. Oh, and a hunk of meat if we can find it!"

Gill smiled back. "I won't ask why, Felix."

"I need to go change clothes real quick, Gill! It won't take me a second!"

Felix came out of the bus with a bag in his hand a few minutes later, wearing his Super Dude suit.

The Shoshone "oohed and ahhed" at the sight of this seven-foot warrior in all of his splendor.

Everyone gathered the needed things, and Felix hopped into the new van with the items he'd requested. "Gill, build up some fires around here... not for protection, but for warmth! I'm gonna be bringing back a whole load of cold young 'uns!"

As Felix pulled the sparkling new van onto the dirt road, in search of a doomed bunch of children and a lady-of-interest to himself, he looked back in his mirror in time to see a whole tribe of Shoshone, Gill, Robert and Sarah, little Killer, and a one-armed, one-time enemy of the human race, all waving to him in a gesture of good luck.

Maybe there was hope for this sorry old world after all.

58
Shadow in the Light

While Shadow and the children had been walking on the final leg of the journey toward the safety of the old mine shaft, several things had already made her uneasy.

The first was the weather. The misty rain had turned into light flakes of snow as they all trudged across the broken terrain in search of the now-hidden path to the cave entrance. The small flakes, which had started as light, fluffy snowfall, had first slowed down to become ice crystals and then had become large, wet globs of snow and slush, which not only bogged them down they tried to break through the frozen tundra, but also dropped the outside temperature at an alarming rate.

The second thing that had worried her was the mountain lion. She had seen signs and tracks of the large beast since they had first entered the edge of the tree line and now, the signs were becoming more and more numerous. She could now smell the large cat, and she knew that it was close. She could only hope that the cougar wasn't using the mine shaft as a sanctuary from the weather as she and the children had planned.

But the third problem that vexed her mind was one that she couldn't see... one that she couldn't smell... one that she couldn't put a finger on, and for that reason, it worried her most. She was almost positive they had been followed from her village and she was positive that they were now being trailed through the forest. She would stop every once in awhile to listen to the sounds behind her, and the noises to the rear would stop, but not quite at the same time as she did.

When they all finally managed to reach the small mouth of the open mine shaft, she quietly signaled the children to stay outside and be silent as she crept inside to check it out.

As she had feared, the prints of the cougar were everywhere inside the entrance of the cave and they were about the size of her head.

Although the mountain lion was a sign of power to her people and therefore almost considered a blessed animal, she figured that even a blessed animal could get hungry enough to eat a small child in the winter snows. She explored the first fifty feet or so of the open cave area, and though she knew that the big cat hung out here, she was now convinced that it wasn't there at the present time.

She ran back outside to signal the children to come in out of the now blizzard-like conditions building up at this high altitude. She instructed two of the older kids to gather some of the scrap wood, which was stored just inside the entrance and to prepare two fires, one at the entrance and one farther back in the cave. The first one would be to discourage the cat and the Thingies that she was almost sure would soon be here. The second fire would be for warmth but also as a second line of defense, just in case.

As the children all pitched in to build up the wood supply, she stepped back outside to scout around. The woods were now quiet. Too quiet. Way too quiet.

This world had been changed, altered in some subtle but unmistakable fashion, and whatever had brought on these changes had fouled the forest with their presence. Even the trees seemed to feel the wrongness of it as they sighed from the constant weight of the heavy snow upon their boughs.

On the far horizon, she could see a blue haze, which topped the trees near where her village was situated. An occasional POP told the story of gunfire being played out at her home. She could pray to every earth spirit that her people would survive this attack, but her job was a different one. The children's lives were dependent on her and her alone.

Well, maybe not totally alone.

There was still the vision of the blue-haired Cat Warrior that she and her grandfather had seen. A tear dropped down her cheek and froze there as she also remembered the vision of her grandfather crossing over to the next world. He, too, had seen this vision but was not afraid. He had lived a remarkable life, and he would be treated as a hero in the afterlife. We should all be so lucky.

She entered the cave opening and gathered the children around the great fire that they had started at the entrance. She passed out the few blankets that she had to some of the children who had come unprepared, but there wasn't enough for everyone. Small, scared faces shared the tattered old blankets as they shared the small bit of warmth they could get from huddling together close to the fire and to each other. She passed around the bottle of water that she brought to whomever was thirsty. Drinking water wouldn't be a problem with all of the snow outside that they could melt if needed. Food would be another story.

The only entertainment that she had brought to calm the children was also her greatest weapon.

She was a weaver of music, and her spirit totem was one of the wind.

With her flute, and the right melody, she could calm the children.

With her flute, and the right song, she could calm the beasts of the forest.

With her flute, and the wrong notes, she could drive men mad. She believed that she could kill with these notes, but had vowed to never use them for such purposes.

She prayed that the spirits of the earth and wind let her keep that vow on this terrible night.

As the children shivered and babies wept, their fears gave off a scent you could taste. Shadow picked up the ancient wooden flute with a smile.

The children all came to a hush.

Even the wind spirits stopped to listen.

And then, she played.

Felix drove off into the increasingly bad weather and was glad he'd brought his brand new hooded sheepskin jacket. Snow was falling so thickly that even the new van's defroster and wipers were having a hard time keeping up. He rounded the mountain roads as quickly as he dared without dumping the vehicle into a ravine, but he was terribly afraid that the weather was going to slow him down to the point where it would be too late to save everyone. He had no doubts that some would be OK, but his visions had proven iffy as to whether all would be safe. In his mind, there was an outside factor that came into play, which would decide the outcome of this confrontation.

When he was only a mile from the turnoff road to reach the cave that he'd seen in his mind, a mighty explosion rocked the world ahead of him. Blue flames and mist surrounded something over the next snow-covered hill, and he prayed to whatever god was listening that there weren't any children in the midst of those flames.

The van slid dangerously to the left as he stepped hard on the gas pedal, but he managed to hold it on the road by turning into the skid. He crested the top of the hill so fast that the tires left the ground for a moment, but as he touched back down again, he saw it. Right in front of him. The tribe's van for transporting the children was blown onto its side, and a giant blue fire licked upon the ruins.

Felix slammed on the brakes so quickly that he slid into a snowbank but did no damage to himself or the new vehicle. Out he jumped, grabbing his coat as he ran, to try to pull whoever he could out of the wreckage. As he reached the overturned van, he first saw that every window had been entirely blown out upon impact. He saw, with a sigh of relief, the van was vacant.

He fell to his knees in the wet snow and looked skyward.

"Thanks. Thanks for always listening."

He jumped up from the slush, ran back to Morrison and grabbed the spotlight first, and then he stuffed the blankets, the hunk of elk meat the size of his head that the tribe had brought him and the extra small bag that he'd snatched from inside the bus. All of these last items he placed into a backpack he'd grabbed. After putting the backpack on his shoulder, and putting the sword in the belt of his Super Dude outfit, he picked up the spotlight, turned off the key to the new van and pocketed it and took off in the direction that he believed the cave to be in.

It wasn't long before he spotted the many tracks of the children, partially blotted out by the snowfall.

On top of these were three sets of fresh tracks.

Two of the sets were definitely the bad guys, almost human in shape, but the third set...

If Felix had to guess, he'd have to say that a mountain lion was headed directly up the mountain in a straight line for the children.

And for Shadow Of The Moon.

As Shadow placed the flute to her lips, she could hear the first long notes that the wonderful instrument would put out... almost before they happened. The flute had been a part of the Shoshone tribal family as far back as anyone could remember, and it was always said that the flute played the player and not the other way around.

When the long notes finally graced the children's ears, there were no more tears. There were no more fears.

There was hope.

The flute sang of possibilities... of things that were in the making but not yet brought into reality. It told of the long and wonderful lives these children would find in their futures and of the tales they would gather to pass on to their children... and their children's children. The ringing notes opened their minds and their hearts to the songs of the earth and the animals and of life itself.

And as it sang, there was hope.

Shadow rocked slowly back and forth to the hypnotic melody that the pipe brought forth, and when she opened her eyes, she saw that the children had also shut their eyes as they swayed in time to the music of the flute. She slowly closed hers once again to share their vision.

In the midst of freezing cold, murdering creatures and dim chances of survival, this moment was a beautiful thing.

After a few minutes of this total relaxation, she paused in her swaying to gently and subtly allow the music to weave an elusive change... to a different time... to a different feel... an artful perceptive of color and keen insight. She once again opened her eyes to observe the children in their spell of peace.

It was then that she saw the cougar at the entrance of the cave, not five feet away from them all, and it stood staring into her brown eyes with its bright glowing golden ones.

The gigantic feline behemoth gazed at her with no fear in its face, and to her amazement, as she carefully watched the mountain lion and as she carefully continued to play the ancient flute, the creature slowly closed its large eyes and began to sway in time with the children.

This was unheard of, but she accepted it as a blessing rather than a curse. She prayed that the song would not now falter... that the music's spell would remain unbroken... that the children would not suddenly become aware of the dangerous beast and scream.

It seemed like forever that the peaceful tableau continued, and she was starting to notice that the intensity of the bonfire in the mine had died down. Suddenly, the beast stopped swaying and opened its great eyes. It glanced around toward the forest behind it as it sniffed the air for a scent that only it seemed to be able to smell. And then, as the great cat leaped twenty feet down the mountainside into the frozen brush...BABOOM!

Shadow instantly faltered in the song, the flute stopped and the children all came back to reality just as a wall of blue flame shot high into the air back down the mountain where she had parked the tribal van. "Oh great! Now they were all trapped and cut off from any escape," she thought.

She could still see the fading blue fires of her village on the horizon and now knew for certain that she had not escaped unnoticed. The same attackers who had destroyed her people were now here to destroy her and the children.

"Quick! Build up the fires! Build them high! They may be the only chance we have to save ourselves! The enemy doesn't like the light!"

One small brave boy stood up and said, "Shadow? How long will it be before the sun comes up? Won't we be safe then?"

She turned her head away from the child so he couldn't see the tears on her cheek.

"The great storm was here. There would be no sun today," she thought.

The enemy had timed their attack perfectly. The only chance of survival that Shadow and the small children now had was the bonfire and the flute of the Shoshone.

And maybe...

"Oh, where are you now, Cat Warrior? When we need you... and when we were given signs that you would come? Where are you now?"

Felix was stuck in a ditch.

He had been running up the mountain trail in pursuit of the Thingies' footprints that were clearly ahead of him when a snowbank let go beneath his feet, and he slid down the side of the mountain into a ravine.

After a two-minute struggle, he managed to unwedge his boot from the snow-covered branches that held it tight, but now he couldn't find his way back to the trail at the top of the steep drop off, and he knew that time was running out.

"Aw, crud!" he said as a glob of snow fell on his head! "I'm startin' to feel like some third-rate character in a really lousy book plot!"

He looked around at the sheer drop-off on one side of him and the cliff face climbing straight up on the other side. "Well, how about straight ahead, then, Felix?" he asked himself. He turned to look into the dark night directly in front of him for a path of any kind but found that he couldn't see anything. Not a damn thing.

The view was blocked by a mountain lion the size of a dump truck.

Felix sat down in the snow and started to laugh.

"Hey, cat dude? Man, only a ridiculous screwball like me could possibly get himself into such a goofy situation as this! Don't you agree?"

The great beast looked at Felix and sniffed a couple of times. Then he purred

Felix shook his head. "Well, Mama always said I had a way with words!"

The cougar quietly growled one time, and then looked behind itself. It gave out a quiet whine and then looked back at Felix.

"Ah, cat dude? You wouldn't happen to know where there's a bunch of kids gettin' babysat upon by an Indian girl named Shadow Of The Moon, wouldja?"

The cat raised itself up onto its paws and turned around to face up the mountain trail that lay in front of them. It took about three quick steps and then turned to look at Felix.

"Aw, man! This is a spectacularly bad idea! The story of my life, though! Go ahead, kitty! I'll watch your back!"

The cougar took off at an easy lope while Felix struggled to follow.

"If my Mama could see me now!"

59

The Hole-In-The-Ground Gang

Shadow and the kids had built up the bonfire to the same level as the outskirts of what they thought hell would be like. They had collected all of the throwing-sized rocks they could pile up by the cave opening.

They were all stretching their minds with possible ideas for getting out of this situation when the small boy, Cody, who had asked about the sun coming, started laughing. He was laughing so hard that soon other kids were laughing, too.

Shadow sat down cross-legged on the cave floor and stared at him until he stopped. Even then, he was giggling.

"Cody? Would you care to share what's so funny about any of this? I could use a laugh myself!"

Cody sat down beside her and all of the other kids followed his example. "Shadow, are we not a blessed people?"

She smiled at that. "Yes, Cody, this is true."

"And did you not just play a beautiful song for the king of all mountain lions, which he danced to?"

"Well, I wouldn't say he was dancing..."

"And do you, in your heart of hearts, really believe that any God who allows these miracles to happen to his people would also allow our total destruction by alien creatures who want to wipe out all life on this planet – by creatures who are afraid of the very thing that God gave us all for life on this planet in the first place... the sun?"

"Well, Cody, when you put it like that..."

"And finally, if our God is unable to defeat these creatures, either by himself or with the intervention of the Warriors that you say are being sent to help us in our time of need... if this is true, do you actually think we can overcome these monsters ourselves by throwing burning sticks and rocks at them? Huh? Do you?"

Shadow thought about what this young brave had just said and smiled. Her heart was lifted of all of the worry it had held and she giggled. Her mind was freed from all doubt that the earth spirits would allow such a thing to happen and she started laughing. Then the kids started laughing again.

Soon everyone was rolling on the floor in the dust, laughing. One girl picked up a little rock and said, "Look! I'm gonna go kill a monster!" Everyone was laughing so hard at this that they almost couldn't catch their breaths. Cody grabbed a burning piece of wood and shouted, "Ooh, I'm gonna give you bad guys such a burn!"

The joy coming from the mine could be heard for a mile away.

The Whistlers didn't understand this.

This was supposed to be a night of terror – of fright. Fright was one of their greatest weapons, and it sounded as if these children had just disarmed the Thingies of this benefit. Not to worry, however. The strength of the two Thingies and their terrible fire would win out. These pieces of young meat were alone except for one adult.

She was only a female.

The Thingies continued up the trail to the mine. They had destroyed the vehicle of the meat. Their vehicle was well hidden. There would be no escape. There would be no terrible sun today for hours and hours to stop their attack.

The Whistlers were bringing a terrible present to the young ones of the mine and that present was death.

Then the Whistlers would feed.

Felix was trying to follow the mountain lion up the mountain. "Damn," he thought as he watched how graceful the big cat climbed. "I wonder if this is why they call them that?" Poor Felix slid back two feet for every four feet he climbed the steep path, but he was making progress.

As they finally crested the top of the trail, he thought he heard laughing. Some little boy was laughing. Maybe he was being tortured... No, this kid was actually laughing. It made Felix smile, too. He thought, "Mama called it smiling in the face of adversity! Cool, dude!"

The laughing stopped. The large cougar looked at Felix and then took off in a hurry up the path in the direction of the laughter. Felix ran to keep up, slipping and sliding from one step to the next. He still held onto his spotlight in his hand, but he hadn't been using it for fear of giving away his position to the enemy.

He heard the laughter start up again but this time by many voices.

He struggled for a couple of minutes toward a distant light that he hoped was the mine, when suddenly, the laughter stopped.

It was followed by the most beautiful music that Felix had ever had the pleasure to hear.

"It must be a flute," he said quietly to no one in particular. He hurried forward and then thought he heard the mountain lion ahead of him mumbling. He ran around a large section of snow-covered bushes and yelled, "Would you please slow the hell down, dude?"

The two Evil Thingies turned to look at him.

"Ah... dudes?"

The two Evil Thingies turned to look at each other.

One of the Whistlers then continued up the mountain trail toward the entrance of the hole in the ground where the food was playing "music."

The other one slowly started advancing on poor frozen Felix.

Felix, in his bravest voice said, "OK, E.T.! I got somethin' here that I've been saving just for your ass!"

He raised the powerful spotlight to his waist level and aimed it at the still-advancing creature. Felix was grinnin' like a butcher's dog as he pressed the "On" button of his powerful weapon. "Take that!" he yelled.

Nothing happened.

"Ah... OK then! Take that!" he said again as he pressed the switch for the second time.

Nothing happened... again!

Felix looked at the stupid contraption and realized the constant snow and ice and falling down the mountain had frozen the spotlight's button.

"Aw, dude! This just keeps gettin' better and better!"

He threw the now-useless weapon at the head of the Whistler, who caught it in mid-air.

The Whistler smiled at him and then began vibrating his right hand, the one holding the searchlight. A small ball of the blue fire began to appear, building up until it would eventually engulf the spotlight into a melted slag.

While it was building, Felix turned around just long enough to see that the second Whistler was still a short distance from the mine entrance.

Smiling to himself, Felix quickly jerked the ancient sword that had belonged to the Shoshone Nation for so many years from the belt of his Super Dude suit. Before the ball of blue fire could mature, Felix swung around in a one-eighty degree circle, swinging the blade with all of his might.

It cut clean through the right hand of the startled Thingie, who stared in shock as its hand fell to the snow, still gripping the spotlight.

Felix put down his backpack, took off his coat and used the sheepskin to pick up the severed hand that held the melting spotlight engulfed in hot blue flame. "Thanks, dude! That was just what I needed!" Felix said as he pressed the "On" button – the third and final time – with the finger of the severed hand.

BAM!

The light popped on with a snap. Felix knew that he had only moments to use the light before the blue Minus ate through it... and then the sheep-skin jacket... and then Felix's hand.

Screaming and whistling at the same time, the angry Thingie charged at Felix.

Felix was a little too fast for it, though.

A blaze of light swung around, piercing the darkness like a long, thin blade of glittering steel. The creature screamed one last time and its evil head was rolling down the slope of the mountain before the body had time to fall.

Felix had planned to then use the spotlight on the second creature, but the heat coming off of his jacket indicated his time was up. He flung away the coat, the light, and the hand. They all hissed as they hit the cold snow.

Felix now only had the sword to stop the second Whistler, and he fig-ured his chances for that were about nil.

"Well, when that's all ya got... then, that's all ya got!"

He grabbed the old weapon and his backpack and went charging up the snowy mountainside, wearing only the Super Dude suit, waving an old sword and screaming like a lunatic.

He thought, "Here's another Kodak moment I've missed! Dude, you gotta buy yourself a camera!"

Shadow and the children had celebrated the knowledge small Cody had enlightened them with. She eventually gathered them around the large fire once again, and she gently picked up her flute. One way or another, this was all she had to work with.

Maybe someone would hear.

The melody was quite different than the first one that the instrument had chosen. This one was beautiful but more upbeat... more exciting. It reminded her of the soundtrack at the end of an action movie she'd seen in the city. As the song built to what she assumed would be the climax, she spotted several things outside of their sanctuary.

First there was a burst of blue flame down the hillside followed by a scream. Then, a giant tan-colored blur rocketing through the woods to the right hidden by the brush. Finally, she saw a shape-shifter.

It had to be the enemy. It couldn't seem to hold onto the complicated shape of a human being for very long and it kept up subtle changes in its appearance as it trudged forward to the cave entrance. This, then, would be life or death for her and the children.

She decided to place her faith in the Great Spirit.

She calmly continued what might be her last song on the treasured flute when... when...

"What the hell was that?" she thought.

Her heart swelled twice its size as she recognized the apparition charging up her mountain with a scream.

"The Cat Warrior."

Seven-feet tall, he was wearing a pair of blue leather pants that matched his hair color. His sleeveless shirt was tight-fitting spandex and white with red stripes. His belt was cinched by a large star-shaped silver buckle. He was waving the old sword that belonged to her village and screaming like an idiot.

His goose pimples were almost the size of real geese.

"God, is he beautiful," Shadow thought.

The shape-shifting evil one heard the "Cat Warrior" behind him and turned for battle. When he saw Felix, shivering in a shirt and carrying only a sword, he stopped moving and started laughing.

Felix saw Shadow Of The Moon in the mine entrance and smiled. He then turned toward the Whistler.

"Dude! You need to stop that crap! When you guys laugh, it sounds like someone scraping their nails on a blackboard! Totally not cool!"

Shadow stopped playing the flute to see and hear this confrontation.

Stories would be told of this for generations.

When she stopped, the children also stopped what they were doing and gathered around her to watch this warrior that the Earth Spirit had sent to them.

Cody looked into Shadow's eyes. He quietly said, "Tall sucker, ain't he?"

Shadow grinned at this.

The Evil Thingie kept its shifting eyes on the tall one. He knew that this was one of the "Humans who kill Thingies," but this one was alone and almost unarmed.

"You have no chance here, human! We will win this war and this world that you try so hard to hold on to will be as dust. The changes we will make will leave no room for the scum that populates this sphere now. Changes will leave no room for your kind! Lay down and die!"

Felix looked up at Shadow and waved. She laughed at this and then he did a little dance. The kids laughed, too. "He has no fear!" she thought. "None!"

Felix looked back at the Whistler, who was now starting to worry because of the way this human was acting.

"This is not right," the Whistler thought. "He should be terrified! And yet, he laughs at me!"

"Change will leave you humans erased from the history of time," the Thingie sneered.

Felix's face went serious. "There's some things that you just can't change. You'll soon learn that, E.T.!"

Shadow stood up and came forward. "You're no match for us, creature. Leave this place before the Cat Warrior ends your useless existence!"

Thingie smirked. "Cat Warrior, indeed! He has nothing but a big knife, and I contain the fires of your hell!" He held up his hand, and a ball of terrible blue flame started to build. It grew larger and larger until it was almost half the size of Felix. Then the creature began the whistle that would allow him to throw this weapon for a great distance.

Felix waited and waited, tapping his foot, until the actual power that the Whistler had produced took up all of its attention.

Shadow noticed that the Cat Warrior kept glancing out into the woods, doing nothing! "Is he really... powerless?" she thought.

When the blue conflagration reached a point of no return, Felix turned with a smile to the forest.

"Here, Kitty, Kitty, Kitty!"

A monster of a mountain lion, the size of a bulldozer, came roaring out of the trees. At Felix's call, this giant Cat God had charged down to where the Evil Thingie stood with its mouth wide open in fright... and with no way to get away.

The cougar hit the whistling creature with such speed that the fireball shot into space miles from where it had started. It hit nothing except for a faraway ghost town, which was made of all kindling.

As the great cat chomped down on the alien who had invaded its territory, Felix slowly walked up to the kids and Shadow, who also stood there with their mouths wide open. The cat slung the creature around until it was being torn into pieces, a writhing heap on the ground, screaming in agony.

Then quietness took over.

Felix, in his mighty Super Dude suit, walked up to the cave entrance with a smile. Everyone was silent.

He reached into his torn and dirty backpack and produced the small bag that he had brought from Betsey. He held it up in the air toward the entranced children of the Shoshone Nation. With a very small grin, he looked into Shadow's beautiful brown eyes and asked, "Who wants chocolate?"

He was immediately swarmed by grateful children.

Shadow looked on and smiled.

After the children had been satisfied with offerings of wonderfulness, he gathered the extra blankets he'd brought and placed them around the small ones who were not dressed for the freezing weather. He handed the tribal sword to Shadow to care for as he dug farther into his backpack. He dragged out the large hunk of elk meat and slowly walked back outside into the cold.

The mountain lion sat on its haunches, waiting.

As Shadow Of The Moon watched, Felix walked up to the large cat and spoke to it.

"Dude, I have no words. You have given me, you have given us, everything. The world that we all live in must... from time to time... be protected, and sometimes by all of God's creatures. Cat Dude, you have done your share on this day. Thank you. Do you understand?"

"ROAR!"

"Cool, cat critter! I got somethin' for ya!" With that, Felix laid the large piece of elk meat on the ground about a foot in front of the cougar.

The beast bent over to sniff it. He raised his proud head to look into Felix's eyes. Then he nodded his own large head to pick up the offering. He silently sauntered off into the forest.

Felix walked back into the cave.

"Hey, y'all? Bugs Bunny once sang a song called 'There Ain't No Place Like A Hole In The Ground!' We're the Hole-In-The-Ground Gang here, I reckon."

The kids all cheered.

"But, young 'uns, how 'bout we go home now?"

The spirits in the now burning ghost town could have heard the applause it was so deafening.

Felix looked at Shadow. He gently took her by the arm and whispered, "Lovely lady, let's get you all home now."

She grabbed him by the Super Dude suit and pulled him down to her level.

She kissed him and then they started for home.

60
Farewells, Goodbyes, and Promises

As they slowly walked arm-in-arm down the mountainside in the growing twilight haze of dawn, Shadow couldn't help from occasionally glancing at the Cat Warrior. Finally, she could stand it no longer.

"Ah, excuse me, but what's your name? Your real name? I can't go on calling you the Cat Warrior forever, you know!"

Felix smiled as he looked into those beautiful brown eyes. "Felix. My name is Felix, Shadow."

She started to giggle again. "Felix the Cat Warrior? Come on, now!"

"Nope! Sorry, ma'am, but that's really my name. And my last name really is... Deckett! Back home in Louisiana, it's pronounced kinda like DECK-HAT, with the accent on HAT. Yeah, I know, I know!"

Shadow stopped laughing.

Shadow stopped walking.

She waited until Felix was looking into her eyes again and then whispered, "I think it's a beautiful name."

"No, m'lady. It's a comical sorta name. Now Shadow Of The Moon... THAT'S a beautiful name."

She smiled.

And then, when he looked away, inside she cried.

In her heart, she thought... no, she knew, "He must go away."

A small boy lagged behind the other kids as they all trudged through the deep snows to the bottom of the mountain trail. He finally got far enough back to where he was now walking with Shadow and the Cat Warrior. The child was in awe of this incredible person by his side, but he figured that if he didn't talk now, there would be no future chance to do so. He held up his small hand.

"Hello, tall one! My name is Cody."

Felix stopped and smiled at the boy. "Howdy, lil' dude! My name is Felix!" He put out his hand and shook the boy's hand.

And then, Felix went away.

When Felix came back a minute later, he realized that all of the children were gathered around him, along with Shadow Of The Moon. They all looked very worried.

Felix smiled at them all.

"Hey, guys, that's just something that I... do... from time to time. When it happens... I can tell you things... things you will need or need to know. OK?"

Cody stepped forward. "I understand, Mr. Felix... ? What do we need to know?"

Felix smiled. "Oh, my little friend, there is so much that you need to know!"

Felix turned to look at a small girl in the middle of the crowd. "You, my dear, need to know that there is a hole in your pocket and that the piece of chocolate that you've hidden there will fall out, long before we reach the bottom of this trail."

The little girl blushed and then reached into her pocket to pull out the large tidbit she had saved. She took a small bite... and passed it around to the other children.

Felix smiled. "And you two," he said as he pointed to two boys standing side by side, "should know that your father was injured at the village in the Battle Of The Spirits, but he will be fine. He is a great hero, and you will be very proud of him for all time!"

The boys beamed with pride as the other kids looked at them, both hugging each other.

Felix kneeled down to the ground. He drew Cody close to him and a tear ran down the giant man's face as he smiled at the child. Felix asked Shadow for the sword and it was passed to him.

"Cody, you must be strong as I tell you this tale. Your father was extremely brave on this night. With this ancient sword, he... alone... took the head off of one of the five enemies who invaded your village. He saved many, many lives... and all that it cost him... was his own."

Tears ran down Cody's face as he nodded with a smile.

Felix continued, "Half a dozen great, great warriors of the Shoshone Nation gave their lives last night to help to preserve the lives of everyone on this entire planet. You will always be proud to say that your father was one of those. Now listen up, people of the Earth Spirit! Tonight... many changes have taken place in your world. Shadow... your grandfather has gone with Cody's father to the next place. He has left words for you... and I add my own to them."

Shadow took Cody into her arms as they all listened to the teller of truths.

"Last night, a Native American family was killed on the road to somewhere. I found a surviving child myself. A baby. Grandfather knew of this as it happened. Shadow, the child is to be put into your custody. His name is 'Found Child,' named by your grandfather and much greatness will be done for your tribe in the future by him and his new brother."

Shadow looked into Felix's eyes. "Brother?"

Felix smiled as he placed his hand on Cody's head. "Yes, girl. This boy has no mother and his father has sacrificed himself for the betterment of your people. Cody and Found Child are now brothers."

Cody ran over to hug Felix, tears falling down his small face.

"Also," Felix said, "Because of Grandfather and my friends, one of the enemies is now a friend... is now one of your tribe. Cody, I place you in charge of his care and learning. He will do great things for you all, but will need much instruction. Can you do this?"

"Yes, sir."

"Then Cody, I place this sword into your keeping. It contains many blessings for the help it has given your people and your father's one of them. Take good care of it, son."

Cody accepted the weapon with great reverence. "Yes, sir. Always."

Felix smiled and then said, "Well, I guess that's about it for now. Dudes, I'm cold! Let's get out of here!"

A small girl came over and tugged on Felix's arm before they started moving. "Mister?"

"Yeah, sugar? Can I help you?"

"Mister? The bad mens blowded up our van! Do we haveta walk all da way back home? It's cold on me!"

"Sugar, I've got a little present for you all! Come on, follow me!"

They all dashed down the final leg of the mountain trail. The first thing they spotted was the blown-up, pitiful remains of the old tribal van. They all stopped to look at the old vehicle, which had been a friend to them all.

Everyone was sad... and then... Felix did his little dance.

"Hey! Y'all wanna meet Morrison?"

At the same time, all of the children said, "YEAH!"

They jogged around the corner and there it was, brand new and sparkling clean. On the side of it, a mural had been drawn of the moon in a beautiful night sky. The moon was either a crescent moon or an eclipse. What appeared to be an Indian girl was standing on the ground, gazing up to the waning moon. A shooting star spanned the entire length of the mural. It was all colored in browns and tans – earth tones.

Cody pointed to the picture. "LOOK! It's Shadow Of The Moon!"

Shadow turned to Felix with a teary-eyed expression. "Felix, your van is the most beautiful..."

"Nope! Wrong, there, pretty lady! YOUR van is the most beautiful..."

"WHAT?"

"That's right, y'all! This is a gift to you all from your Warrior friends, the White Dudes!"

In the village five miles away, the laughter and screams of joy could be heard.

Felix held up the keys into the air in front of Shadow Of The Moon.

"Who wants ta drive?"

Gill had been helping attend to the wounded, and Robert and Sarah had been watching over Found Child.

Killer had been playing with the Thingie.

They all heard an uproar coming down the dirt road that led to the village and realized it was singing.

"There ain't no place like a hole in the ground... a hole in the ground... a hole in the ground!"

Robert looked at Gill.

"Bugs Bunny?"

Gill smiled back and nodded. "Bugs Bunny!"

Morrison swung into the center of the village with Shadow at the wheel, and all of the children unloaded with shouts of glee as they ran into their parents' arms, safe and sound, each and everyone.

The last to exit were Felix and Shadow. Gill walked over to Felix and signaled for the tall dude to bend over. He put his small arms around the neck of the blue-haired hero. In a small voice, he whispered, "Well done, Dude, well done."

"Aww, shucks! T'weren't nothin'!"

It took a while for everyone to tell their tales of all of the events that had transpired and it would take much longer for some of them to believe it.

Robert chuckled. "A giant mountain lion, Felix? Come on, now!"

Shadow was walking around the encampment with Found Child in her arms and Cody by her side, all of them grinning, as Felix said, "like a possum eatin' grapes!"

Felix smiled at Sarah as she sat there looking at the tall hero. "Those three are gonna be just great," he quietly said.

"Felix?" she asked.

"Yeah, beautiful lady?"

"How about you?"

Felix looked into her eyes, the eyes that knew just how he felt right now.

"M'lady, it's gonna kill me to leave her here. You know that, doncha? But... I gotta. She can't go... and I can't stay. You know that, too, right?"

"Yeah, Super Dude, I know. But, maybe later, though?"

"Sarah, if there is a later, you can bet the ranch on that."

The village children were having a great time playing with Killer as Gill walked over to Shadow.

"Excuse me, Shadow? I hate to interrupt you right now, but I was told by your... your grandfather's spirit that there was a carving for me in the sweat lodge that he wanted me to have before I left and our time here is closing fast."

Upon hearing this, Shadow's face turned solemn as she glanced over at Felix. She then turned back to Gill. "Give me a moment, Time Stopper, and then we will go."

She talked to Cody for a moment and then handed him his new brother, who smiled at Cody with great joy.

"Come," Shadow said to Gill.

The sweat lodge had been built on the outskirts of the village, but it took only a couple of minutes to reach it.

"Has anyone entered since my grandfather?"

"No, Shadow. We waited on you."

"Time Stopper, would you give me a few moments?"

"With great pleasure, Shadow. Please, call me Gill."

"Thank you, Gill."

She slipped under the flap that enclosed the now departed steam and there lay her grandfather.

She sat for a couple of minutes just holding his cooling hand and finally spoke.

"Oh, knower of things, thank you for the gifts you have given me. For my knowledge... for my music... for my magic. My heart breaks at your crossing over, but soon... we will meet again. Oh, and your words of the Cat Warrior I would meet..."

She cried for a moment.

"Damn! You were right on, old man! How did you do that?"

She looked into his other hand and there was the present for Gill.

"Gill? Please come in."

The small man entered the lodge and stood to the side. Shadow lifted the carving, an old bearded man cut into old grained wood, from the grandfather's hand. A wind blew through the forest, and a sigh left the body as the carving left the body.

His spirit had passed now.

"Thank you, Shadow. Thank you, Grandfather," Gill whispered.

They both left the lodge to let the old man rest.

His time was done.

Cody was holding on tight to his new brother when he felt someone behind him watching. He slowly turned and there was "Other Brother," the Thingie who was now part of Cody's people. Cody walked over to watch the shifting patterns of the newcomer. The first thing Cody noticed was that although the arm of this... brother... had been severed... because of the touch of the Warrior Robert, it appeared to be growing back again.

"Truly a miracle, to re-grow a limb as you seem to be doing," Cody said.

"Yes. I believe I have the Robert human to thank for this... miracle, as you call it. May I... ask you a question?"

Cody smiled. "You are one of us now, Other Brother. Anything... you may ask me."

"Are you to be my... keeper?"

"No, brother, I am to be your teacher."

The Thingie smiled, probably the first real smile it had ever had. "I read a book one time. One part of it said... 'and a small child shall lead them.'"

"So it is with you and I, brother. Now, may I ask you a question?"

"Anything, my brother."

"If this shape is so hard for you to maintain, why not pick another?"

"I am allowed to do this?"

"Well, I guess you must not upset the normal people, but within reason..."

"Do you have a shape that you prefer?"

Cody smiled.

Gill got back on Betsey to put the old carving in a place of safety... and to tell Betsey to prepare for departure. As much as he hated to leave these wonderful people, there was still a world to save.

Betsey cranked up her engine.

Outside, Felix and Shadow were standing together by the new van.

"Are you sure, Felix, that this van is mine?"

"It's yours... to help out the tribe and the kids, Shadow. I foresaw all of this before I ever got here. I knew you'd need it. Some folks say that... I know stuff."

"You are as my grandfather and I. We, too, know things. Thank you for Morrison. OH! Van Morrison! I just got it! Hahaha!"

"Yeah, I'm a real hoot alrighty. What's your favorite Morrison song?"

"It's hard to tell. I like 'em all. How about you?"

"Well, I used to like 'Mystic Eyes' when he was with 'Them,' but standing here, looking at you, I'd have to go for 'Brown-Eyed Girl.'"

She kissed him, long and hard.

As the Warriors gathered around Betsey for a final farewell to the people that they'd come to love, Felix walked over to Gill.

"Hey, lil' dude? A question for ya? When you and I touch, can I send my feelings to you as you do to me? And if you touch someone else, could you send my feelings to her?"

Gill smiled at his tall friend. "Bring her over here, Felix."

Felix walked over and took Shadow's hand. He gently pulled her over to Gill. Without any explanation, he placed her hand in one of Gill's and his own hand in Gill's other one. She strangely looked at them both but said nothing.

Then Gill closed his eyes.

For the next sixty seconds, tears ran down the faces of both Shadow Of The Moon and Felix Deckett, and Gillian St. John just smiled.

At the end of that minute, Gill released both hands, smiled, and walked away.

Felix bent down and tenderly kissed Shadow.

She looked into his eyes and whispered, "Yes, I will wait."

As Felix got ready to load onto the bus to leave this place he loved, he saw Cody, Found Child and a mountain lion with a bad paw all standing there to wish him a safe journey. Felix smiled at the cougar and said, "Good choice, Dude."

The cougar replied, "Thanks, dude. Good luck."

Robert, Sarah, Gill, Felix and Killer all gazed out of the window as their new friends faded into the background, with the snow dancing in the wind and the long road ahead calling out like a ghost in the breeze.

61

The Road to Heaven and Hell

After an hour of driving, hunger struck. Robert was driving, and since they were in the middle of nowhere, Gill decided to cook on the bus. Everyone was sitting in the lounge area watching movies on Betsey's DVD system, so Gill killed two birds with one stone while he was, as Felix put it, "whippin' up the grub!"

"Felix?"

"Yeah, Time Stopper Dude?"

"Very funny! Got any info on the trip to Devil's Slide?"

Felix went away just for a moment.

Felix came back.

"Gill, from where we were at Shadow's place, we take 225 to Highway I-80. That's about eighty-five miles or so, and then we've got another two-hundred, twenty-five miles to Salt Lake City. We stay on I-80 until we hit I-84, then it's another fifty miles... give or take a hundred feet or so. About three-hundred sixty miles to Devil's Slide... so figure, with stops, six or seven hours."

Gill was browning and caramelizing some onions as he added, "That'll put us in there late this evening. We'll bunk in the bus tonight, gang, and check out the site tomorrow morning. Any info on Devil's Slide itself, Cat Warrior?"

Felix laughed. "You're a riot, Clock Boy! Yeah, I've got a few facts for ya. It's actually a formation of two parallel limestone rock strata that were tilted to lie totally vertical to each other. Weird! They stick about forty feet out of the mountainside itself, with a channel between them that's about twenty-five feet wide running down the mountain for hundreds of feet. Cool, huh, dude? It's in Weber Canyon, and you can clearly see the slide from I-84. There should be parking on both sides of the road, but I don't know what we can find there. It's just a buncha rocks, Gill!"

Gill smiled. "Felix, I've already got one rock that can stop time. Don't cut down the power of stone, dude!"

"Oh yeah, man! I kinda forgot about that!"

After a great meal of pork chops and wine with scalloped potatoes, they all lounged on the top level of the bus as Betsey began her trek across the Great Salt Lake Desert. After they had crossed the state line at Wendover, they found themselves running along by the Bonneville Salt Flats and the Speedway.

Felix laughed as he asked Betsey, "Hey, ol' girl? There's been some mighty fast machines that have crossed that hunk of salt out there. How fast do you think your big butt could do on that Speedway? Ha Ha Ha!"

Betsey said, "Well, Supie, if I could run off of the methane that pours out of your mouth, I should be able to hit about six-hundred!"

"Ha and ha! Very funny! Machine's just got no sense of humor!"

Sarah smiled as she asked Felix about what was all around them out there.

"Beautiful, dudette we've got miles and miles of nothin' but nothin'! Most of it is a test and training grounds with no public access at all! Then, you can throw in the Dugway Proving Grounds, also with no public access, and you can top all of that off with the Great Salt Lake Desert, which even though it does have public access, ya don't wanna go there!"

Robert shook his head from the driver's seat. "Man, where do you come up with all this stuff, Felix?"

Sarah laughed. "So, does anything at all grow in this part of the world?"

Felix giggled as he answered, "Osmonds and they grow in abundance. Hey, wouldn't it be cool if they made one of these deserts outta pepper instead of salt?"

Sarah threw a magazine at him.

"Robert! Make her quit that! Where the heck does she keep findin' those damn things, anyway?"

While they were still en route to Salt Lake City, MAX called Sarah on the bus phone. "Yes, MAX? This is Sarah. Is there anything wrong?"

"No, Sarah. As a matter of fact, everything's been really quiet here. I just wanted to tell you a few things that are going on. "

"Good, MAX. It's good to hear your voice! It seems like it's been so long since we left and it's only been a couple of days. I miss home."

"Well, Sarah, home misses you, too. You've received two phone calls at your house that I thought you should know about. First, the young man who got promoted wanted you to know that Compu-Tech is producing almost forty percent better than before he was installed. I like that, kid!"

"Yeah, MAX. Me, too."

"Also, he said to tell Gill that he had to have Roy Higgins arrested."

"Arrested?"

"Yep! According to the young man, Higgins kept showing up after you all left, trying to take over his office again! Security threw him out twice. Then, the alarms at Compu-Tech went off at three a.m. and it was Roy Higgins trying to burn down the building! The police have him in custody."

Sarah was laughing as she told Gill what MAX was saying.

Gill smiled. "Put MAX on the speakers please, Betsey."

"Hello, Gill... and everyone. Lois says to say she misses Felix."

"I heard that!" Felix said from his bunk.

Gill grinned as he said, "MAX, call Sergeant Eddie Fallon and explain the situation with Higgins. Have him hold Higgins in custody until... ah... until... UNTIL HELL FREEZES!"

MAX came back with a "Whaa, Whaa, Whaa! Good one, Gill. I hate that Higgins dude! I've still got crumbs in my keyboard from that chucklehead! Oh, also, speaking of Fallon, he was the second call I wanted to tell Sarah about. He called at Sarah's home. They've caught and destroyed a lot of the Whistler folks that were headed your way. They used your spotlight idea on some, and some of the alien idiots killed themselves by driving when the sun was out. There are still more than a dozen cars and trucks unaccounted for, though."

Sarah spoke up. "MAX, call Eddie Fallon and tell him to cross three cars and one truck off of that list. We tangled with them in Nevada."

Sarah gave MAX the license info on the vehicles.

"Sarah, that's great news, but that still leaves about eight missing vehicles and more than a dozen of those creatures and they're all going to be looking for you guys! Please be careful!"

"Will do, MAX. I miss you, you big ol' bunch of printed circuits and diodes! Anything else?"

"Well, only that I've upgraded the visual I have on you guys from the eyes in the skies. Keep in touch with me, please. I can help."

"I know you can, sweetie. I'll give you a yell real soon. Keep an eye on me, OK?"

"You got it, Sarah. Safe journey. MAX signing out."

Felix came forward from the bunk section. "MAX signin' out! Ain't that cute? I just love that dude!"

The drive through Salt Lake City was pretty calm, except for Felix constantly bitching about not being able to stop in to see Donnie and Marie. They finally reached their turn-off onto I-84 in the early evening. The snow had left them almost as soon as they had left the northern part of Nevada, but the cold weather decided to come along for the ride.

It was just about dusk when they pulled into a parking area in Weber

Canyon next to Devil's Slide.

"WOW!" said Felix. "What a cool hunk of rock, huh? Who wants to climb up it with me and slide back down?"

Sarah laughed. "Ah, Felix, that would be the Devil, and I'm not letting you slide down anything with him. Got that straight?"

He hung his giant head down as he said, "Yes, ma'am."

They all got out of Betsey to gaze at the natural wonder... and what a site to behold. Many cars were parked around the areas on both sides of the street and lots of children gathered outside, all bundled up against the cold weather and playing their children's games. Of course, Felix went over to help them.

"I'm glad he at least changed out of his Super Dude suit," Robert said with a smile. "He'd have scared those poor kids to death!"

Many folks were taking pictures, a few had binoculars to check out the mountainside, and one guy in a light denim jacket was across the street hitchhiking northward. Gill, Robert, Sarah and Killer all went walking across the road for a better glimpse and left Felix to play with the kids. Felix was wearing only a hoodie sweatshirt since his sheepskin coat had been sacrificed in blue fire for Shadow and the kids.

"Incredible," Sarah mumbled, as she stared at the beautiful mountainside.

"Awesome!" Gill answered, as he checked out the crevice between the two gigantic protrusions.

"Yipe, yipe!" Killer replied.

"It looks like a really big butt!" Robert said with a grin.

As unbelievable as it sounds, a magazine came flying through the air to hit him in the head.

"Damn, Sarah! Do you pack those things around with you just so you can grab one at a moment's notice?"

They all stared at the scenic picture before them for a couple of minutes before being interrupted.

A small girl was tugging on Robert's sleeve.

"Yes, honey? Can I help you?"

"No, sir, but the giant! I think your giant's gone to sleep! He's in a comma!"

"You mean a coma, sweetie. Yeah, he does that! Let's go check him out, OK?"

"Sure, mister! I like him! He's funny!"

"Yeah, a regular Red Skelton! Come on, guys, it's Felix time again!"

They all crossed the road again and there was Felix, gazing off into space with small kids crawling all over him.

"OK, kids! Let us get him inside the bus!" Gill said.

"Mister! I think he's frozen stiff!" one little boy said as he climbed off of Felix's arm!

"Well, we'll thaw him out in the bus, OK?"

"OK!" the kids shouted.

Robert picked up Felix and was hauling him back toward Betsey when Felix started to come out of it. "Whoa, dude! What happened?"

Robert laughed. "You went bye-bye, big guy. Come on, let's all get back on Betsey for awhile. It's getting colder out here."

Felix wobbled back onto Betsey and sat down. Everyone knew that when this happened to Felix, it was time to listen up. They sat there staring at him for a couple of minutes before he said anything. It was getting darker outside and cars were starting to leave.

Felix looked around at them all. "Gill, there is no Plus or Builders here to be found."

"WHAT? But we were told to come here because..."

"Because what, Gill? Do you remember what Gwen said exactly? 'Cause... I do!"

Felix went away and said in the small voice, *"Memorize what I am about to tell you, Gill, or your whole world may get cold! Here are locations on your Earth near where you must travel... where you may be able to locate more of the Plus and the Builders. But beware, for the Thingies will also be in search of these objects!"*

Felix came back.

"May... Gill."

Gill looked upset. "But... then... why are we here?"

"Because of him," Felix said as he pointed out the side bus window.

He was pointing at the hitchhiker.

62
An Absence Of Recollection

"That guy?" Robert said. "The hitchhiker?"

"Yep. That's the dude."

Gill looked up at Felix. "Ah, Felix, are you sure?"

Felix didn't say anything. He just looked back at Gill!

"OK, OK, I know! Ah, what's his name, Felix?"

"Don't know. Neither does he!"

"WHAT?

"Yep. The boy's got magnesia."

Sarah giggled. "You mean... aw, never mind! I like your way better, anyway."

Gill looked around at his crew. "Well, what should we do?"

They all looked out at the freezing young man who had still not managed to get a ride. The cars had all left by now with nighttime just around the corner, and there would be no more traffic here until dawn.

Sarah finally said, "Well, damn guys! We can't just let the poor guy stay outside tonight! It's freezing out there, and we've got another bunk here on Betsey. I'm... I'm going out there!"

With that, she went down to the front level of the bus, and had Betsey open the door. Sarah wrapped her warm jacket around herself as the cold wind whipped her blond hair into a frenzy. She crossed the street and walked up to the boy... and that's about all he was. He appeared to be about seventeen or eighteen years old, and in just his thin blue jean jacket, this fellow was cold.

"Hey... ah... guy? Fellow? Ah... mister?

"Yes, ma'am?"

"In case you haven't noticed, hitchhiking is basically over for the day and it's getting awful cold around here! Where are you trying to get to anyway?"

"Ma'am... I'm... I'm not sure. That's why I can't get a ride. Everyone asks me that same question, And... ah... I have no answer. North, I guess."

"Well, are you hungry? Do you at least know that?"

The boy smiled. "Yes, ma'am! I'm pretty sure I'm very hungry. I don't think I've eaten anything in a couple of days now."

"Well, then since you don't know what you're doing, here's what you're going to do! You're going to pick up your bag there, you're going to pick up your feet there, and you're going to come with me to that nice warm bus over there across the road for a hot meal and maybe some hot chocolate! How does that sound?"

The boy sniffled the held-back tears as he smiled into her beautiful face. "Heaven, ma'am. That sounds just like heaven."

She helped him across the street because he seemed to be pretty weak. When they got to Betsey's door, it automatically swung open by itself, which startled the young fellow. As soon as they stepped on-board, Sarah could smell the hot chocolate brewing.

"How did you know?" she asked.

Gill pointed his thumb to Felix, who smiled.

"I know stuff," he said with pride.

The boy almost inhaled the hot liquid as he munched on a grilled cheese sandwich and a cold leftover pork chop. Everyone just sat around watching him devour this food that was obviously the first he'd had in quite awhile.

As he was gnawing on the bone, Felix laughed and said, "Hey, dude! You better count your fingers! I think you mighta just swallowed one there!"

The boy stopped and realized that everyone was watching him. "Aw, folks... I'm sorry! I don't know where my manners went. I was just... so hungry."

Gill put his hand on the mystery boy's shoulder. "That's OK, son, you eat up. Would you like some more?"

"Is there more?"

Gill led the boy over to the small refrigerator, which was stocked full of food. "Eat up to your heart's content, son. All you want, but don't make yourself sick!"

Felix laughed. "Hey, dude! I once ate almost seventy dollars worth of stuff in a truck stop restaurant. You gotta long way to go to beat my record!"

After three more sandwiches and about a half gallon of milk, Mystery Dude was full.

"Folks, I can't tell you all how much I appreciate this. It's the best I've eaten in... well, I don't know for sure if I've ever eaten like this!"

Gill introduced everyone to the boy, and of course, the boy couldn't return the favor. "Mr. Gill, to me... my life started about a month and a half ago."

Killer jumped up into the startled boy's lap.

"Killer!" Gill said, "He may not want a handful of dog right now!"

Killer looked at the boy and whined.

"No, sir! No, sir! I love dogs! At least, I think I do." He patted the small hunk of fur and tongue. Killer licked his hand and the boy began to tell his brief story as he rubbed the small furry bundle.

"I first remember waking up bloody in an alley in Santa Fe, New Mexico. I didn't have a clue who I was... or where I was! I had a backpack with some art supplies in it. Not much, ya know, just some pencils and pens and a couple of sketchpads. There was a suitcase in the alley also, sir, but it had been torn open and all of the stuff inside was either gone or thrown on the muddy ground. I gathered up what I could of the clothing that was still any good, but there really wasn't very much. I found a pamphlet for some kind of resort motel or lodge lying on the ground, but I wasn't even sure it belonged to me. I grabbed it up anyway since that was the only clue I had of anything at all!

"The police in town almost threw me in jail for vagrancy, but I talked my way out of it by saying that I'd been mugged. I had no ID or money, so I managed to stay alive by doing some doodles from time to time on the sketchpad. I had a knack for art, it seems... and some magic. I'd trade artwork for a meal or a ride. I'd just draw a meal from time to time. I left Santa Fe before they could arrest me and decided to head north."

Robert interrupted, "Excuse me, but why did you decide on north? Especially in the wintertime?"

The boy reached into his backpack and pulled out a worn old brochure. "This was what I picked up in the alley, sir, so I decided to try there first. Maybe I could... find myself."

Sarah, getting all misty-eyed, gently took the paper from his hand. She read it. She looked up at her friend's faces.

"Curiouser and Curiouser," she whispered.

Gill took the piece of paper and read it out loud.

"Buffalo Bill's Original 1904 Lodge. Pahaska Tepee. The East Gate to Yellowstone" He looked at Felix. "In the heart of the Shoshone National Forest."

Felix shook his head, "This just keeps gettin' better and better!"

They all sat in silence for a few moments after that. No one was really sure what the hell was going on, but it was obvious to everyone who had made this journey that this... this boy... was why the Flae had sent them to this place. The first one to break the silence, of course, was Felix.

"OK, artist dude, I've got a question for you. Actually, I've got two questions, now that I think of it."

"Ask away," the boy said. "As long as it's happened in the last forty-five days or so, I'll give you an honest answer."

"I know you will, son. I can feel that. So, question number one is: If you were eating by drawing pics for food, why are you hungry now?"

"Good question, sir! I still have paper, but ran out of pencil and pen! It's funny how everything can go so bad over such a small thing as a pencil."

"OK, dude! Good answer. Answer the next one correctly, and I will present you with a brand new name. We have to call you something, ya know and Artist Dude ain't it! Are you ready for the question, lil' dude?"

"Ask away, ol' mighty tall one! Ha Ha Ha!"

"You see, boy, I know stuff. And I remember things. You said and I quote, 'I had a knack for art, it seems... and some magic...' and 'I'd trade artwork for a meal or a ride. I'd just draw a meal from time to time.' Tell me, wonder child, what do you mean by 'magic' and 'drawing a meal'?

The boy didn't say anything. He squirmed for a moment in his seat, and then said, "Folks, maybe I should leave now."

Felix put his hand on the boy's hand. "Tell me, son."

"You won't believe me, sir. I'd have to show you and then you'd be scared of me. I'd rather just leave now, if you don't mind."

Felix looked the boy in the eyes. "Please?"

The boy sighed, and then said, "Does anyone have a pencil?"

Gill went to the back of the bus while the boy pulled his old, beat-up sketch book out of his backpack. He turned to a clean page that didn't have anything doodled on it. Gill brought the boy a half dozen pencils and a couple of black ink pens.

"Wow! Thanks... ahh... Gill, right?"

"Yeah, son. Now show us something."

The boy looked into Gill's eyes as Gill said, "Amaze us!"

The young boy smiled as he got ready. He put Killer down on the floor and then began to do an incredible sketch of the little dog. It looked just like Killer, down to the collar that Gill had bought at the beach so long ago from little Olivia. The only difference that any of them could see from the original was that the picture of Killer had a tiny, tiny white spot on the end of its nose and he had a big, juicy bone in its mouth.

"Finished!" the boy said after about two minutes of impossibly quick strokes with the pencil.

"It's beautiful!" Gill said. "I'd like to keep it, if you wouldn't mind. It looks exactly like Killer... except for... ahh... aw, hell!"

As Gill pointed, they all looked down at Killer gnawing on the giant bone with great delight. They had to pull it away from him before they could see the little white spot on his nose.

Robert shook his head. "YOU HAVE GOT TO BE KIDDING ME!"

The boy cringed. "Sorry! I can make the spot go back to black... just like it was! I promise!"

Gill ran over to the kid. "No! No, no, son! We're not angry! We're just... amazed!"

The boy smiled. He looked up at Felix, smiled again, and said, "Do you have a name for me, now?"

Felix leaned down and said, "You are one of us, little dude whether you know it or not. Gill, in a moment, you've got to do the MindSpeak on this boy. Ya gotta let him know what's goin' on here, dude! Really!"

He looked back at the boy with a smile. "But, for now, I christen thee, Paul Wallace! Welcome to the family, Pauly!"

The boy smiled! "Paul Wallace! Pauly! I like that! I like that a lot! Pauly it is! Hey, guys! I've gotta name!"

Everyone cheered.

Robert tapped Felix on the shoulder! "Ah, excuse me, Super Dude, but where exactly did you come up with Paul Wallace? Did you just pull that out of a hat?"

Felix smiled. "Elementary, my dear Watson. Wally is short for Wallace and Pauly is slang for Paul... so..."

Robert cringed. "No! Don't say it! Sarah! Get a magazine! Quick!"

Sarah smiled. "So, Pauly Wally Doodles all the day?"

Felix laughed. "You got it, dudette!

Robert hung his head as everyone laughed.

"I think I'm gonna be sick!" Robert moaned.

The winter winds outside were whipping hard enough that Betsey would occasionally rock from side to side.

"Man, I'm glad I'm not out there right now!" Paul said with a smile.

Gill sat down on the sofa next to the boy and started to try to explain the situation. "Paul, we are all headed to exactly the same place that you are with a couple of brief stops on the way. If you'd like, we can give you a lift in ol' Betsey here all the way."

"Who are you calling old?" Betsey inserted into the conversation.

Paul jumped up and looked toward the speakers mounted in the bus where the voice had come from. Then, he looked at Gill. "I'm sorry, sir, but I don't understand."

Gill smiled. "Paul, Robert and I have been, let's say, doing good deeds for many years now all across the country. Sarah and Felix have only been with us less than a week now, but they're now a part of our family just as we'd like you to be. I know... you have no idea who or what we are and it would normally take hours to explain it to you. But, if you will allow us, we'll all have a kind of meeting of the minds, and then you can make up your own mind. One way or another, we will give you a ride to Yellowstone with us. Are you willing to try this? It will only take a couple of minutes of your time."

Paul smiled. "Sir, if can I trust you enough to name me, I don't really see how I could not trust you to explain... this very strange situation to me. But..."

"What is it, Paul?"

"Who just spoke about being old?"

Gill smiled. "Ah... Betsey? Would you mind saying hello to Paul?"

"Hello, Paul. I'm proud to make your acquaintance!"

Paul shook his head, smiling! "The bus?"

"The bus," Gill said.

"Wow! OK, let's do this... whatever you call it."

"It's called MindSpeak, son. Everyone gather around here. Let's all do this together this time. He needs to hear from each of us. Oh, and... Paul? One thing about doing this, no one can lie while it's going on. Sure you still want to go on with it?"

Paul smiled. "I've sure got nothing to hide!"

They all joined hands in the top living room area of ol' Betsey, with Killer looking on.

Gill closed his eyes and tried to remember not to blow them all out from thinking too hard. For almost three minutes not a sound was heard. Everyone sat there with their eyes closed and their minds open.

Gill released Paul's and Sarah's hands and everyone else did the same. Nothing was said for a couple of minutes while Paul stared at them all, one at a time.

He finally stood up. He gathered up his sketchpad and his new pencils and pens and placed them into the backpack, which he slung over his shoulder.

Everyone looked at each other.

Without the faintest hint of a smile, Paul looked at Gill.

"Where do I bunk?"

Gill sat there with his mouth open. "You're in?"

Paul smiled. "Of course I'm in! Do I have to draw you a picture?"

They all laughed and applauded as Felix lifted Paul into the air and said, "Welcome home, Doodle Dude!"

63
Fine and Dandy

The winds whipped about the countryside as the team of five and a half friends spent their evening warm and snug in the bosom of Ol' Betsey. Hot chocolate, good food, and much laughing and sharing of stories was how these new companions spent this cold night in Utah.

"I wonder what Marie's doin' tonight?" Felix said. He heard the magazine coming at him before he saw it, so he was able to duck. "Sarah, I'm just damn glad that you don't read the encyclopedia. You'd knock my brains out!"

"Yipe!"

"He said the target's too small!" Sarah giggled.

Robert smiled at this exchange, and looked over at Gill. "Hey, little buddy? What's the deal with that carving that you picked up from the old man who passed away? Have you figured out what we should do with whatever it is yet?"

Gill sort of smiled as he thought about it. "You know, Robert, I was told by Grandfather that it was a Builder, not one of the Plus. Builders are good for replenishing our strengths after we've used them... or while we use them. For me, there's chocolate. I have no problem with consuming lots of chocolate, guys!

"Well, I also have the Time Stopper, aka Ima Rock... thanks to Sarah! That is an incredible member of the Plus, and not even the Flae spotted this one. I now have one of each!

"It seems that Felix now has that amulet of amber that he constantly wears and that is his Builder. He can't have or touch a Plus because of the HardSpeak, so, he's loaded as much as we can load the rascal."

Felix smiled. "I be bad!"

Laughter came out from everyone.

"We're not really sure what's up quite yet with Paul here, so for now, let's set that aside. That leaves us with Sarah and Robert. Robert has the 'Olivia Reaching For A Star' necklace, but that is a Plus... not a Builder. Robert has no Builder... which the carving is... but so far, Sarah has neither. In my opinion, we hold onto it until the next two stops... Paradise and Craters Of The Moon. Then we will decide who needs what. I have a strong feeling that Paul is going to end up playing a major role in this drama, so we've also got to plan on that now."

Gill looked to Felix. "Oh, Super One! What can you tell us of the land of Paradise, Utah?"

Felix went away.

About ten seconds later, there he was again.

"Gill, Paradise is small. It's about seven-hundred sixty folks there. They're livin' in an elevation of about four thousand, nine-hundred and two feet, and the total area of the town is only about one point one square miles. Small, dude!"

Gill asked, "Is it an old town or a new town?"

"Paradise popped up about eighteen sixty. I call it old. Mostly white dudes, too. Oh, by the way... almost half of the families in town have kids under the age of eighteen livin' with 'em!"

Gill smiled. "So... almost half of the town is children?"

"Yeah... doncha love it?"

Eventually, the ol' Sandman started to make his appearance known, and it was time for a good night's sleep. Gill gave Sarah and Robert the suite in the back, and he, Felix, Paul, and Killer took the bunks. He had Betsey go to "alert" and everyone had their full dose of shut-eye that night for the first time in a long time.

Instead of an alarm clock waking everyone up the next cold, windy morning, it was the smell of fresh-ground coffee perking, along with the aroma of hickory-smoked bacon and the sizzle of eggs

"DUDE!" said Felix with a yawn as he sat down on the couch to watch Gill at work. "If you could ever make an incense that smells like that, you could make a fortune!"

Gill smiled. "Yeah, Felix. Just what I need... another fortune!"

"Fine and dandy, then! You could always just give it to me!"

Paul stumbled out of his bunk with that same look on his face that a person gets when they wake up somewhere and can't remember where in the hell they are. It was still dark in the bunk area, so he followed his nose into the forward cabin... and then started smiling. "Wow! It wasn't a dream! You folks are really here!"

"Don't look at me," Felix said with a chuckle. "I've never really been all here!"

Gill laughed. "He's right about that, you know! Paul, are you hungry again yet?"

"Starved!"

"Good! How do you like your eggs?"

"Anywhere between raw and burnt to a crisp is just fine with me!"

Felix patted Paul on the back. "I think I'm gonna like this kid!"

Felix and Paul were on their second helpings before Robert and Sarah made an appearance, but Gill had expected that and had prepared plenty.

"Betsey?" Gill asked.

"Yes, Gill?"

"How are we doing on petrol, ol' girl?"

"Well, we've still got more than a half tank in the diesel category, but the generator's getting kind of low on the regular. We ran it all night, you know."

"OK, then. We'll be leaving out in the next hour or so, and we need to hit the first truck stop we can find to top off again. It wouldn't hurt to hit a supermarket. With Paul being part of the family now, it's like having an extra ten mouths to feed!"

Felix laughed so hard that he blew milk out of his nose.

"Gross!" Sarah said, she passed him a paper towel.

Paul seemed kind of embarrassed about this, and said, "Am I eating too much food, Gill? I'm sorry! I just..."

"No, son. You can eat all day long if you want. I love cooking for someone who enjoys it!"

Paul smiled back. "I could always draw us up some food, if we need it."

"Paul, I've got plenty of bucks for food, so you save your doodles for later. I have a feeling that we're gonna need them!"

After a good meal for themselves, and finally for Killer after he managed to wake up, they all stepped outside to let the little dog do "the call of nature thing," as Felix put it, and to stretch their legs and grab a fresh breath of air – that is... cold air!

"Boy, it sure would have been terrible sleeping out here last night," Paul said in a whisper.

"Yeah," Felix added, "Terrible would be a good word for it, alrighty!"

Frost coated everything and there was another feel of snow getting ready to break loose. Killer did his business and then spent a few minutes chasing a squirrel around in circles. They all gazed at the Devil's Slide one final time in wonder, and Felix said, "Damn! I'm just gonna have to get me a camera one of these days! Another Kodak moment... down the tubes!"

The warm interior of Betsey felt great after the freezing blast of outside weather, and Gill settled down with the crew to plan their next move.

"Felix, how far do you figure we are from Paradise?"

"Do ya mean the town or heaven? Ha Ha Ha!"

Felix was smiling until he heard the rustle of paper, and turned to see

Ol' Dead-Eye Sarah with a rolled up magazine in her hands, just smiling at him. Felix got serious then.

"Ah, Gill, it's approximately forty miles from here to Ogden, where we can fill up our tanks and our refrigerator. After that, we need to go to Logan on Highway 89... and then backtrack to Paradise on 142. From Ogden to Logan is forty-six miles, then we go out of the way south again for thirteen miles to get to Paradise. Figure on about a hundred miles... give or take six inches!" He heard that magazine rustle again and flinched.

Gill looked around at the group. Killer was sitting in Felix's lap in one of the reclining chairs, Sarah was cuddled up next to Robert on the sofa, and Paul was doodling in his sketchpad in the front of the bus, but he was listening carefully. Gill thought it looked like he was drawing a sketch of Felix and Killer.

"OK, gang, it sounds like Paradise is gonna add about an hour onto our schedule, but I really don't think it can be helped. We need any extra ammunition we can get for this battle coming up. I'll drive for awhile this morning, and Robert, you take over this afternoon," Gill said as he glanced at the new sketch Paul had just finished.

"Fine and dandy, Gill, but what about me?" Felix asked. "Don't you want me to drive, too?"

"Felix," Gill said with a grin, "I figure you'll be too busy shooting pictures with your new camera!"

"What? What are you talkin'..."

Felix looked down at his hands. One was petting Killer, the other held a brand new digital camera!"

"Where in the..." He looked down at Paul, who was smiling back at him.

"Well, you said you really wanted one." Paul held up the picture of Felix, Killer, and the new camera.

A tear rolled down the giant man's face as he held his new toy up to gaze at with love.

"I think I'm gonna like this kid!"

They stared at the scenery one final time as Betsey pulled out onto the highway. Because of the weather, traffic was at a minimum, but the forty or so miles to Ogden still took an hour or more because of the terrain and weather, which promised snowfall before the day was out.

Once in Ogden, they quickly filled up Betsey's tanks and then headed to a local supermarket chain, where Gill re-stocked on supplies for humans and canines alike. While Gill was inside shopping with Robert, along for added muscle for carrying groceries, Sarah got another call from MAX. She put him on the bus speakers.

"Hello, Sarah? MAX here."

"Hi, MAX! How's home?"

"Home misses you... all of you! Lois sends her love to Felix."

"I heard that!" Felix yelled from outside, where he was taking pictures of a sparrow eating french fries.

"Sarah, I've got some strange news for you from Sergeant Eddie Fallon. I think everyone needs to hear this!"

Felix heard and came back inside. "Betsey?" he asked. "Can you record this conversation?"

"You bet, Felix. Recording is starting... now!"

Sarah smiled and nodded at Felix. "OK, MAX go ahead!"

"Sergeant Fallon has called to report that a semi-truck and trailer have been stolen in Spokane, Washington. Several of the stolen vehicles from Los Angeles were left at the site of the robbery, so he believes that it was some of our creatures who did the theft. Also, the truck driver, who was in pretty bad shape, reported that on that same night, an on-coming car's headlights killed one of the creatures as the theft was happening."

"Well, that's good, isn't it, MAX?"

MAX didn't say anything.

"MAX? Are you still there?"

"Yes, Sarah, I'm here. The rest of the trucker's report is what got me to check the satellite video feed for that quadrant at that time frame. I'm sending video footage to Betsey. Have her record it, also."

The built-in computer on-board loaded the footage, and Betsey played it back.

Felix shook his head. "Aw, hell, MAX! What am I looking at here?"

"Felix, it appears that one of those... 'Thingies'... is absorbing extra power... and size... every time one of the others dies. It's pretty dark in the video I sent to you, but I've enhanced it and as best that I can calculate, that Whistler you see there crawling into the back of that semi-trailer is somewhere between fifteen and twenty feet tall!"

"HE," Sarah whispered.

"Yeah, Sarah, that was my guess," MAX quietly answered. "That beast is going to be a tough nut to crack. The car headlights that killed the other Whistler also hit him. They had no effect... and he grew as the other one perished. Also, with as few of the Evil Thingies that seem to be left alive, I believe it's logical to assume that this giant will be killing off all of the rest of them when he reaches his destination, just to absorb their power and essence. So instead of many bad enemies..."

Felix shook his blue-haired head. "We get one REALLY bad dude!"

"That's about the size of it!"

Felix said, "Not really, MAX! I think we can figure that 'the size of it' will increase quite a bit. This just keeps gettin' better and better!"

Paul, who had been silent up to this point, said, "Hello, MAX. My name is Paul."

MAX came back on the speakers. "Hello, Paul. Welcome... I think! Sarah... another stray?"

Sarah laughed. "Yeah, MAX, but I think this one's a keeper! You'll like Paul!"

"Well, if you like him... he's aces with me! Whaa whaa whaa!"

"Did he just laugh?" Paul said with a smile.

"Yeah, he does that. Any other good news, MAX?"

"Only that this Thingie appears to glow blue! He must be building up tons of Minus power inside of itself. Be careful! All of you!"

"Yipe, yipe!"

"Killer says hi, MAX!"

"Hello to my little giver of bacon. Take care of 'em, Killer!"

"Woof!"

MAX said, "I'll keep an eye in the sky on you all, Sarah. MAX is outta here, dudes."

Felix laughed. "MAX is outta here, dudes. I love that guy."

Gill and Robert finally came out of Supermarket World and were told of the recorded phone call. They spent several minutes catching up with everyone else before they had any comment.

"Aww, hell!" was Robert's comment.

Gill looked at his friends and then asked, "Well, does anyone have any ideas?"

Felix raised his hand.

Gill looked at Felix and then asked, "Does anyone have any ideas that doesn't have anything to do with Marie Osmond?"

Felix put his hand back down.

"Yeah," Gill said, "That's what I figured. Well, guys, we've come this far and I say it's too late to back down now just because the enemy got taller. We've got two more stops before we reach Pahaska and Yellowstone. Sarah?"

"Yes, Gill?"

"Get on the computer and see about getting us reservations at Pahaska Tepee in Cody, Wyoming for... let's say day after tomorrow. It's Buffalo Bill's original 1904 Lodge. That way, we head to Paradise now, leave this evening for Craters Of The Moon, where we spend tomorrow and then on to Yellowstone. Set up the reservations to run for a week if the place is even open. Any questions?

"Yeah, dude! Did you get any ice cream?"

Gill got Robert to drive the last leg of the trip to Paradise.

It's good that he did, because as he was going back to his bunk, Gwen broke in on his thoughts.

"Gill? Can you talk?"

"Yeah, Gwen. You caught me at a good time. I need to ask you about HE."

"Yes. That is why we are also calling you."

"We?"

A strange new and powerful voice came into Gill's mind.

"Gill? Is that correct? My name is Gin."

"Gin? Wow! It's an honor, sir!"

"Thank you, son. Now pay close attention to what I am about to say! In thirty-two of your hours, you will all be sleeping in a location known to you as Craters Of The Moon. It has volcanic features, which makes it a good spot for a cross-over; for me to send you something which will ultimately help you to defeat HE who would exterminate your life forms. I will send you all DREAMS! You now have the correct combination of humans with you to.... shall we say... pull this off! Listen to me carefully now... the human named Robert is to be the Builder for the human named Sarah. His is the power to heal, and she needs not have a Builder... except for him. He must stay close to her, though. The Builder that you now have in your possession should now go to the new Paul human. On this day, look for a Catflower In Ice. This is to be the Plus for the Sarah human. It will give her DreamSpeak... and she can then talk to me while sleeping. I will allow this only for her, and only for a short while. Tell her to share the information I send on The Night Of Dreams with the new boy. He will give you a weapon. The one called HE is now too strong for your light weapons to destroy and your Time Stoppage Plus will only slow him down. Once the assault begins on The Sleeping Giant, you will all have less than two of your hours to prevent it from coming to a conclusion. After that..."

"I understand, sir. But..."

"My time is short, son, so listen for now – no questions! HE is gathering the Minus, and it is contained inside of him. HE will... what you call 'Whistle' a hole into your planet, where HE will then plant the Minus. Once this is done, nothing will help you. The hole will be bad, the planting of the Minus will be... fatal. Remember, the Robert human, who has always been your greatest warrior, will not be such in this battle. He is your Healer, and this will become hard for him to understand. He will need your counsel, son. If there is to be a hero in this fight, it will come from the most unlikely source. Our inability to appreciate the truly wonderful in the world when we find it will be at the risk of losing its essence. More than this, I cannot say. I wish you much of your luck, my son. My time with you is now over. I will speak to you again at The Craters Of The Moon on The Night Of Dreams. Fare thee well!"

Gill stumbled forward to the front section of the bus, almost falling over until Felix caught him.

"Robert! Pull over! Gill's down!"

Betsey's brakes screeched to a screaming halt as Robert jerked her into a scenic overlook parking area. He ran up to the top bus area in time to hear Gill ask for chocolate! Two-thousand calories later, Gill's eyes were coming back into focus.

"Everyone, give me your hands! MindSpeak time!"

Everyone sat on the couches, the chairs and the floor and joined hands. Even little Killer put his paw on the circle of joined friends.

Gill shut his eyes after he muttered, "Have more chocolate ready, guys!"

They all went away.

64
A Catflower in Ice

They all came back.

Gill fell over, gasping for breath. "Get him some chocolate! And a bottle of water!" Sarah yelled.

"Gill, you gotta quit doing that twice in a row, dude! You're gonna bust somethin' you need," Felix exclaimed as he fanned Gill with a dishtowel.

Gill smiled. "Yeah, you're right, big guy, but I figured this was something that we all needed to know and NOW!"

After a minute or two, Gill slid back into a chair and looked at the worried faces staring back at him. "I'm OK, gang. Now, did everyone pick up that entire conversation that I had with Gin?"

Everyone nodded.

"I can't believe that I finally got to talk to Gin after all of these years! Now, does anyone one have any questions?"

Everyone raised their hands. Even Killer raised a paw.

"OK, OK, we'll talk about this, but remember that I was allowed no questions, so the answers you're looking for... I may not have. Robert, I know what you're going to ask about, so let's start with you so we can get back on the road again. Go ahead, my friend."

Robert stood up and sort of fidgeted around as he said, "Ah, guys, I understand about the healing thing, and really... that's cool with me. It actually feels kinda good to help people instead of hurting them, as I've always done in the past. But, if you think for one moment that I won't be there with you when this battle happens, you don't know me very well!"

Sarah took his hand and looked into his eyes. "Ert, don't forget, you were told that you are my Builder, and I love the thought of that! You were also told that you must stay close to me, remember?"

He nodded.

"Well, honey, that's going to be right in the thick of things! OK?"

"Yes, dear!"

"Aww, ain't that sweet?" Felix said with a giggle.

WHACK!

"Damn, dudette! I didn't even see that magazine comin'! How do you do that?"

She smiled. "Maybe I know things, too!"

Gill laughed. "OK, Robert, how about we get back on the road before our schedule gets all screwed up?"

"You got it, boss."

Robert pulled Betsey back onto the frozen highway and he listened to the rest of their conversation on Betsey's intercom.

Gill looked around and could tell that everyone had questions. He decided to start with Sarah.

"OK, beautiful, your turn!"

"Gill, what the heck is a Catflower In Ice?"

"Unknown, Sarah, but if he's not too mad about the magazine thing, you might consult with Felix on that one."

"Oh, heck!" she said as she looked at the blue-haired wonder. "Ah, Felix, sweetie, would you happen to know..."

Felix smiled back at her. "How can I resist that beautiful pouting face? Give me a moment."

Felix closed his eyes, and though he still sat there, he went away and was gone for quite awhile. Everyone continued to watch, puzzled, when suddenly there he was again. He looked perplexed.

"Sarah... I got nothing! I've got cattails, cauliflower, and catfish but no catflower! The only thing I can think of is that... maybe... it was more of a description than a name. Maybe Gin was trying to tell you what it looked like instead of what it was."

Sarah sighed. "Well, we'll just have to keep our eyes out for something that might fit that description, then." She was mumbling... "A Catflower in Ice?"

"OK, then," Gill said. "Paul, I guess that leaves just you. Before we get into talking about this potential weapon, I've got something to give to you."

Gill went into the bunk he'd been sleeping in and brought out a leather bag. "Inside here is the Time Stopper, the Plus that is Robert's and something for you, son."

He carefully withdrew the carving of the old man's face from the leather bag. It was an incredible piece of work in a dark, reddish brown sort of wood but appeared to be an ordinary carving... until it was placed into the hands of the boy.

A rainbow of colors slammed through the whole bus, which caused Robert to almost lose control of the bus, but Betsey took over for a moment.

There were visions of people, landscapes, animals, castles, snow, houses and waterfalls and hundreds of other scenes, all cascading through the air and into the boy. And suddenly, he wasn't a boy any longer.

"It's... it's... beautiful, Gill," Paul said in a voice much deeper than they had ever heard from him before. "It's beautiful."

Gill stood there with his mouth wide open.

Felix said in awe, "Well, Gillmeister, I think we can safely say that the right person got that hunk of wood!"

Paul, as Robert had a few days earlier, seemed more. As a Builder, this worked wonders on Paul. "I'll never forget this, guys. Thank you. Thank you a lot."

Sarah smiled. "Hey, Paul, am I mistaken, or did you just get way cuter?"

Robert quickly turned around from driving. "Alrighty! That'll be quite enough of that, girl! Don't make me come back there!"

Sarah laughed.

Gill smiled and said, "Hey, that reminds me, Robert. You'd better take back your necklace, too. Any power build-up that you can get from here on out will be needed soon!"

"Here, give it to me," Sarah said with a smile. "I'll put it on him."

She went forward with "Olivia Reaching For A Star," and with a tender, loving touch, she gently put it around his neck.

The whole bus lit up with rosy-red glow.

Sarah stood there with her mouth wide open. She finally managed to whisper, "Sugar, if you wasn't driving this bus, I'd drag you back to the bunks! Wow! Is this what happened last time?"

"Yep!" he said with a smile! "That's my good ol' Plus acting up there! Cool, huh?"

Sarah took his face in her hands and said, "Betsey, hold the road for a minute!"

"Got it, girl!" Betsey said with a mechanical giggle.

As Sarah's lips touched his, they both sent pink sparks into the air.

From the back of the bus came Felix's voice. "Oh, Doctor Bob!"

This time, there was no magazine. Sarah just stood there and smiled. "Don't you take that damn necklace off again, Ert! Hear me?" she quietly said.

"Yes, ma'am," he whispered into her ear.

Felix yelled out, "If you two are done, let's go find this Catfish In The Snow!"

This time, there was a magazine.

They pulled into the small town of Paradise that afternoon, just as the snow began to float to the ground once again.

"The whole town is only one square mile, so this shouldn't take too long," Felix said.

They pulled Betsey over onto a roadside and decided to get out and walk around. It wasn't long before they realized that not only did they not know where to look, but they had no idea what they were looking for.

They had spent almost an hour wandering around in a daze when Felix noticed a book sale going on to raise money for the local childcare facility. "Ooh, ooh! I wanna book! I wanna book!" he said as he jumped up and down in the snowy yard in front of the daycare building.

"OK, Felix, go get you a book, and we'll meet you down at the next corner in... let's say... ten minutes. Cool?"

"Ah, yeah... except that... I... don't have any money!"

Gill laughed as he pulled a handful of bills out of his coat pocket. "Here you go! Now hurry! We've got stuff to do! Cool... now?"

"Way cool, lil' dude, big dudes and dudette! I'll be right there!"

He ran into the small building, and immediately scared the hell out of the poor old woman who worked there.

"Ah, sorry ma'am! I just wanted to buy something to read while I was on the road. Is that OK?"

"Ah... yes, sir. We have several nice books right over there on the shelves, and there are some magazines in the back."

"MAGAZINES? Ma'am, I've just about had my fill of magazines, if you don't mind!"

She shook her head and sat back down behind her small desk.

Felix quickly located some Stephen King novels, one that he hadn't yet read. Then he found a Dean Koontz paperback... and a Clive Cussler hardback. "Man," he thought, "A major score on my part."

He placed all three books on the countertop for the little old lady to tally up for him. "I'm really glad that you found something, sir. We haven't been doing very well with our book sales this year, and it's usually what gives us the funds to keep our daycare open. We have a lot of kids here in town, and there's no where for them to safely stay, so thank you very much for helping us out!"

"That's just fine, ma'am." Felix looked at her and felt his heartstrings being plucked by her plight. "Ma'am, maybe I will go look at those magazines before I go. I have a friend who sorta collects them. OK?"

"Oh, yes sir! They're right over there in the back!"

Felix walked back to the stack of magazines at the back of the small open area. There were about twenty or thirty magazines stacked on top of each other held down by a paperweight.

Felix froze.

He looked at them for another minute or so and started to reach down when he realized that he couldn't.

"Damn!" he said just loud enough to where the nice lady heard him.

"Is there a problem, sir?"

Felix ran back to the desk. "Ah, no ma'am, but I'd like to get my friend to come and pick out her own magazines, if you don't mind!"

"Ah, no sir, but you do want these books, correct?" She was obviously afraid that he wouldn't return.

"Yes, ma'am! Hold them for me... and hold onto this!" He set a hundred dollar bill on the counter.

"But, sir...!"

"It's OK, ma'am! I'll be right back!"

Felix ran out of the little daycare building so fast that he forgot about the ice and snow. He skidded all of the way to the street where he fell over.

BAM!

He looked around for the rest of his friends and saw them down at the corner waiting for him. He took off running towards them, slipping and sliding all of the way.

Gill smiled. "They didn't have any books that you wanted?"

Felix was out of breath. "Ahh..ahh.. come! Come! Ahh!"

Sarah grabbed his hand. "Felix! Catch your breath, dude!"

"Sarah! Magazines! Come!"

Felix took off running back up the street.

Sarah looked at her friends. "He... wants me to get magazines? He must be delirious!"

Gill got suddenly serious. "I don't think that's it. Let's go, guys!"

They all hurried down the street to where Felix was waiting. Huffing and puffing, he managed to say, "I couldn't touch it! Remember?"

Sarah suddenly realized what he meant. She ran into the daycare, startling the poor lady half to death again.

"Ah, sorry, ma'am! Magazines?"

The lady pointed to the back of the building.

Sarah took off at a run.

As Felix came back in, the lady said, "Your friend... she must really like magazines!"

Sarah found the magazines and then she found what Felix had seen.

There it was, what Gin had described as a "Catflower In Ice!"

It was a large crystal paperweight with a giant dandelion suspended inside of it.

Sarah laughed out loud. "A dandelion! That's a Catflower, alrighty! And the crystal is the ice! I get it! I get it!"

Gill was now standing next to her, smiling. He turned to Felix and quietly said, "Well done, dude! Very well done! And you even remembered that you couldn't touch it!"

Sarah pulled Felix down to her level and gave him a kiss on the cheek. "It's beautiful, Felix! Thank you."

Felix smiled as he said, "Yeah... and there's magazines, too!"

Sarah laughed so hard she cried.

In the front of the building, standing beside Robert and Paul, the little old lady had tears in her eyes, too. "She really likes magazines, doesn't she?"

Sarah picked up the entire stack of magazines without touching the paperweight and walked to the checkout desk. "How much for these?" she asked.

"All... all of them?" the lady stammered.

"Yes, ma'am... if you'll sell me the paperweight, too."

The lady laughed. "That ol' thing? Miss, you can have that if you buy all of those magazines!"

Sarah looked back at her friends, smiling as she walked to the door. "Gill, pay the nice lady!"

As the stunned lady watched, Gill reached into his coat pocket and pulled out nine more one-hundred dollar bills and placed them all on top of the one that Felix had left.

"This is for the Children of Paradise. Will that be enough, ma'am?" he said with a smile.

She grinned, as Felix put it, "like a butcher's dog" as she slowly nodded and put the money into a shoebox. She reached underneath the counter and drew out a large flask. She smiled as she whispered, "Somethin' to take the chill off for you boys?"

Gill, Robert, Felix and Paul all smiled as they took a pull off of the warm bourbon inside that hidden treasure. "Thank you, ma'am," Gill said as he walked out into the cold.

"Oh, son?" she said to Felix as they left. "Don't forget your books!"

"Thank you, ma'am! Completely slipped my mind!"

A very happy group of people made their way back to the warm interior of Betsey, who honked as they approached.

Hot chocolate was the order of the day.

Robert looked at Sarah, who stood in a daze as she glared at the beautiful object, still lying untouched on the stack of magazines.

"Honey?" he said quietly.

"Yes, Ert?"

"Baby, maybe this time you should go ahead and touch the Plus before we start trying to drive this bus down the road!"

They were all gathered around her... watching her... waiting.

"Yipe! Yipe! Woof."

Sarah smiled at them, and then gave Killer a pat on the head.

"OK"

She gently picked up the paperweight in her small hands and then... She disappeared.

Not like Gill, when he had to concentrate on the voices of the Flae.

Not like Felix, when his body just froze as his mind went somewhere else.

She just... wasn't there.

Everyone started freaking out, and Robert started screaming.

She was gone!

She... was... gone.

65
The Idaho Blizzard

She was gone... but... but...

Gill calmed down enough to realize something. Killer was wagging his tail and looking to the spot where Sarah had been sitting when she disappeared. The pooch looked to the spot and then looked to Gill. Gill could almost swear that he was smiling.

"Hush up, everyone! Everyone! Quiet for a moment! Please!"

They all looked at Gill and found him to be smiling.

"People, remember what Gin told me? 'If there is to be a hero in this fight, it will come from the most unlikely source! Our inability to appreciate the truly wonderful in the world when we find it will be at the risk of losing its essence!' Remember? Now, look at Killer!"

The dog heard his name and leaped into the air, twisting as he jumped to land back on his small feet. He was definitely smiling now.

"OK, Gill? Whasup wid' yo goofy dog? I get the feeling that he knows something that we don't!"

Killer looked at Felix, and very, very quietly said, "Woof." Then he walked over to place his nose gently in the spot where Sarah had been sitting.

His nose sparkled.

He backed up and tilted his head from side to side to see if these "stupid" humans understood. "Woof?"

Gill patted his head. "She's OK, isn't she, Killer?"

"Yipe."

"We should just... wait for her?"

"Yipe!"

Robert looked at the small dog and asked, "Killer, should we be worried?"

The little pup actually shook its head "no."

Paul smiled. "Man! I've got to get me a dog!"

Felix smiled. "Aw, he's not so great! Killer, can you quack like a duck?"

"Grrrrr!"

"See! Not quack one!" Felix said with a grin.

Just then more sparkles came from the chair. And then, Sarah faded back in, smiling.

Her hands were gently cupped around something that no one could see, and as she looked at Gill with a tear in her smiling face, she whispered, "Gill, I've brought someone who wanted to meet you. She can only stay for a couple of minutes, though, and then I have to take her back."

Gill stood there in awe as Sarah opened her hands.

"Everyone, say hello to Gwen!"

As the incredibly delicate creature lifted itself into the air on its gossmer wings, every color that they could imagine, and several new ones, radiated from this tiny being. As tears formed in the eyes of all who beheld her, she changed forms into a tiny lady of such wondrous beauty that Gill fell to his knees. She was about a half a foot shorter than Gill and just her smile was enough to light up his heart.

"Please stand, Gill! It is only me! We have known each other for many of your years now, but this is the first opportunity I've had to meet you. I thank the Sarah human greatly for this gift. It will be remembered by me for all of my days."

"Gwen?" Gill whispered as he rose to his feet once again.

She smiled at him. "Do not cry, my gentle one. It is I who should cry for the great sacrifice that you all are giving... to all life... on all worlds. We of the Flae will always be grateful for the measure of dedication you have given. We thank you all."

Felix smiled. "Aw, shucks, ma'am! T'weren't nothin'!"

When Gwen laughed at this, it was impossible for the rest of them to not follow suit. "You have GOT to be the Felix human! A true Glettle! So much power... contained in one who brings so much joy to others. Your name is Legend!"

Felix looked at her and uttered the words that no one had ever heard come out of his mouth. "Ma'am, I'm speechless."

She smiled. "We shall sing of your glory, one and all, for Eons to come, my friends. I shall visit you again, with my friend Gin, on the Marrow Eve... on The Night Of Dreams. My time with you all is now at an end, and sadly, I must go. But, Gill, with your permission... I wish to leave you with a loving gift in parting... from myself."

She slowly pulled his small head to her own and placed a kiss... everlasting... upon his lips.

In years to come, when Gill had a wife and many children of his own, this would be the secret moment in his hidden heart that he would always cherish the most.

"Goodbye, my brave ones, and... Godspeed!"

With this, she changed back once again into the shape of her true being and gently floated over to Sarah, who once again cupped her hands around the miraculous creature.

Sarah smiled at Robert as she picked up the Catflower In Ice for the second time. "I'll be back, Ert. "Wait for me?"

"Forever, honey. Forever."

Sarah disappeared.

"Well, I'll be," Felix whispered.

There wasn't a dry eye in the house. Even Killer was whimpering.

Gill walked over to a cabinet above the refrigerator and pulled out a full bottle of bourbon. He held it up for all to see and quietly asked, "Somethin' to take the chill off for you guys?"

Felix ran over and wrapped his arms around the small leader of big men, who stood there smiling with giant tears running down his tiny face. Felix looked into Gill's eyes with a smile and said, "You da man."

"I da man?"

"You da man!"

"You want to have a shot of this stuff with me, you ol' Legend you?"

Felix smiled. "Maybe just one! Then, I want to drive!"

"You got it, dude!"

"But..."

Gill looked at his friend. "What is it, Felix?"

"What is a Glettle? Was that a cut?"

"No, buddy. A Glettle, to the Flae, is a giant. And if you ask me, Felix, only a giant... could contain your heart."

"Yeah, I be bad!"

Everyone was laughing as Sarah suddenly faded back in. Gill ran over to throw his arms around her. "Thank you," he whispered.

"My pleasure, boss. Now... about that raise... ?"

"You got it, sweetie. You got it!"

Gill stood up with the bourbon in his hand. "Gang, next stop... The Craters Of The Moon and The Night Of Dreams!"

Sarah smiled. "I'll drink to that!"

As Felix drove up the highway, he called Gill forward.

"Gill, we've got about one-hundred, thrirty-five miles before we reach Pocatello, Idaho. In this weather, figure on three hours... at least! The snow's comin' down pretty hard, so when we get that far, I wanna pull over for the night. Then tomorrow... we've got about twenty miles to Blackfoot, where we'll turn off for Interstate 26 and 26/93 combined.

That's about a hundred-mile drive for tomorrow daytime to the Craters Of The Moon. How long that takes will depend on this storm. Cool, Clock Boy?"

"Very cool, Legend Dude!" He patted Felix on the back and went to the rear to tell everyone of the plans.

As they all relaxed in the snugness of Betsey's warm interior, Sarah told of her journey into the Land Of Flae.

"As soon as I'd picked up the Catflower In Ice, I felt myself... drifting. It wasn't actually like going up or down... or even out... as much as I was going... in!"

"When the slipping away ceased, I could feel land of some sort underneath my feet, but it reminded me of when I used to walk on top of the bed as a small girl... kind of... springy! Ert, remember the... redness, when you and I were there together at the beginning of our, I guess... adventure?"

"Yeah, honey... I do."

"Well, it's always that way there! There was also that red fog in the air, and I moved through it only with a great effort... kind of like..."

"Molasses?" Robert said with a smile.

"You got it, Ert! You remember! And then, Gin found me, and took my hand. And suddenly, I could see it all! I could see the strange forests of ... trees, I think, but such as none I've ever seen! What appeared to be water was flowing nearby, but it didn't seem to be confined by gravity to the ground. Sometimes, it would pass through the air... several feet off of the stream bed... and it would still hold shape, even though it was free. And the air there smelled like... candy! Butterscotch or maybe vanilla! I felt a brief spinning sensation, and Gin told me that my time there was limited. He said that the Catflower was normally only used during dreams, but he... and he alone, could sometimes use it as a portal... for me! He told me of an idea that he was working on that might help focus our energy to defeat HE of the Thingies. I would receive that idea in completion on The Night Of Dreams. The spinning feeling came again, and a ringing sound!"

"I remember that ringing!" Robert exclaimed.

"That's when Gwen came over to where we stood, and asked Gin about the possibility of her coming here... briefly... to thank us for all we've done. Gin said it would be allowed. Gin placed my hand into Gwen's, and the spinning increased. As we left the land of the Flae, Gwen whispered to me of how she had longed to meet this mighty human warrior known as Gill!"

Felix yelled back, "YOU DOG, YOU!"

Gill blushed.

"The rest of the tale is known by us all. Tomorrow night, each of us... even Killer, will receive a vision of things needed to happen... and people to help. Oh, and I was given one message to bring back here after I returned Gwen to her home."

She stood up and looked to Paul.

"The message is for you, Paul."

He sat there, stunned. "An alien race of people, trying to save all life... in every dimension, took time out of their busy schedule... to send me a message?"

"You got it, kid! I was told that all of us humans of Earth have some small kind of power, if only we can discover how to use it, but you, Paul... he said that you have... magic! Gin told me... now how did he put it? He said to tell you ...

'On the following morn
of the Night Of Dreams
your world will be draped in white.
Find where the ground is clear
from deep volcanic might.
There, a treasure waits for you
power in tubes of white
and only on that morn
visible to sight.'

"That's exactly as he put it! He would only say that this would be your one chance for a Plus. You must find this... treasure... and your time will be limited to do so."

"Wow. Tubes of white? What could that be?"

Felix laughed! "Maybe it's a sewer line!"

Paul laughed, too. "Yeah, Paulie Wally, King Of The Sewer Lines! I can see that, Felix!"

They drove on into the long night of cold in search of the Night Of Dreams.

The following morning found them at another huge truck stop, parked in a snow-covered parking lot, along with hundreds of other road warriors, out to brave the climate. Semi-trucks by the hundreds seemed to be backed up, waiting for a place to fill up, or a small place of sanctuary to wait out the blizzard, which threatened each and every one of them.

"Welcome to Pocatello!" Felix said with a smile as they all woke up one-by-one. "How about we all go eat some delicious truck stop grub before we sit down and try to figure out how the hell we're gonna get another hundred miles in this blizzard with all of the roads closed?"

"The roads are closed?" Gill said as he tried to shake his head into wakefulness.

"Yep. That's what all of the big-rig dudes are saying on the CB, and they're the ones who will know! Let's go inside, though, and maybe we can find an alternate route by talkin' to these dudes. If there's one out there, they'll find it. They go broke if they can't cruise!"

"Sounds good to me," Robert said as he and Sarah stepped out of the back. "We do have chains and such on ol' Betsey here, but that won't open up a road!"

Gill said, "OK, then... Killer, you stay here and watch over things!"

"Woof!"

"Betsey... on alert! Come on, gang... let's go see what's up!"

Inside was what can only be called controlled chaos. Gill went to stand in line to get a table for the restaurant while Robert and Sarah hit the restrooms to freshen up a bit. Felix and Paul hit the game room... of course.

Gill came over to where Felix and Paul were after a few minutes. "Well," he said, "I've put my name in, but we've got about a thirty-minute wait before we can get a table. Felix, they've got a pretty big clothes selection here, and your sheepskin jacket is somewhere outside of an Indian village... wrapped around the amputated arm of an alien being... and drenched in a blue glaze! Let's get you something warm to wear. That goes for you, too, Paul. That denim jacket is fine in New Mexico, but it doesn't cut it in Idaho! Let's go shopping!"

They spent their half hour buying gloves and warm socks, jackets and cold weather boots, scarves and thermal underwear. Both Paul and Felix were loaded down by the time Gill's name was called out for the restaurant. They had the lady behind the front checkout counter stash their purchases for them while they went to eat. They found Sarah and Robert just being seated at a large round table for six. They all ordered coffee while they glanced at a menu.

While they were ordering up some breakfast, an older fellow, who appeared to be about sixty years old and looked as if he might have once played pro football in years gone by, wandered up to their table.

"Howdy, folks! There doesn't seem to be anywhere around here for an old trucker to park his rig, and I noticed that y'all have an extra chair. Would ya mind a little company?"

Gill smiled as he offered the fellow the empty chair. "Sit down and take a load off, sir. It looks like we're all in the same boat here, anyway!"

"Yep, that it does, son! Hudson's the name. Everyone calls me Hud."

"Hi, Hud," Gill said as he introduced everyone around the table. "Any chance of any of us getting on the road today, Hud?"

"Naw, son... not unless you're drivin' a snow plow! The roads are supposed to have about two feet of ice and snow on 'em once you get past Blackfoot. I heard that a fellow can make it that far if you by-pass the roadblocks, but after that... she's shut down in all directions! They say it might be two days 'fore they can get 'er cleared up!"

Gill shook his head. "We don't have two days. Hell, we're lucky to have two hours!"

Hud sadly shook his head back. "Yep. Everything I've got is riding on me bein' able to get my loaded rig to Twin Falls, just west of here, and I've gotta have it there by tonight. I reckon I've gone bust again, but it won't be the first time, laddie! I do kinda worry about the Mrs., though."

The food arrived, and they all dug in while they discussed different options to reach their destination, but with little or no luck. Suddenly, Paul stopped eating and jumped up. "Hey, Mr. Hud? Do you have an atlas with you?"

"No, son, but there's a map in the truck stop on the wall by the showers. What's up? You got an idea?"

"Maybe!" Paul said as he ran away from the table to the restaurant door. Felix had finished eating, so he elected himself to go help.

"Don't know what them rascals come up with, but if there's anyway at all to get outta here, y'all can count on my help!" Hud said with a smile.

About five minutes later, Paul and Felix came smiling back to the table.

Felix looked at everyone and said, "Dangdest idea I ever heard of, but it might just work!"

Paul sat down at the table and looked at Hud. "Mr. Hud, you kinda gave me the idea! But... ah... umm..."

"What is it, son? I'll try anything!"

Gill looked at Paul and knew why the boy hesitated. "Hud, what if I told you that only a... let's say... a miracle could get us all to where we're going? And then... what if I told you that we... can do miracles?"

"Son, I'm ready to believe in the dang tooth fairy if she'll get me to Twin Falls by tonight!"

Gill smiled at Hud! "OK, Hud... your words... not mine! Remember them! Go ahead, Paul."

"I'm gonna draw a snowplow!"

66
The Craters Of The Moon

As Paul explained his plan with Felix bobbing his head up and down like one of those toy birds who look like they're drinking water, Hud looked at the whole bunch of them like they had lost their minds. When Paul had finished, Gill smiled and placed his hands on Paul's shoulder. "Son, that just might work!"

"WHAT?" Hud said! "Just might work? This young un's just said that he's a gonna draw a picture of a snowplow... that's gonna come to life... and this lil' lady here... is gonna touch it... and make it clear the trail... for us to get down the highway... with no one driving the dang thing... and you think... that just might work? Is that what you're sayin' here? Huh?"

Gill looked at Hud for a few seconds and then smiled. "Yep! That's about the size of it."

Hud stood up from the table and looked at them all. He started to walk away but turned back around again and looked at them all one more time. Then he sat back down. "Serious?"

Gill smiled. "Serious."

Hud smiled. "Can I bring some friends?"

Twenty-minutes later, they had paid for their fine meal, gathered up their packages for Felix and Paul, and were headed out to the bus. Felix had explained to Hud that they were going to have to go out of the way to get him to Twin Falls, but he would make it there by tonight.

"Son, any ol' way you can get me there will save my ornery hide! Bless ya, son. Bless you all! Oh, here comes my friends, too!"

Gill started laughing as he saw all of the truckers that were piling out of the truck stop doors and headed for their rigs. Not everyone could make use of the route they were going to make, but word got around quick with these folks, and there were lots of rigs cranking up all over the lot.

Robert, having more experience driving Betsey, took over at the wheel. As she pulled out onto the snowy highway, she was followed by almost fifty semi-trucks pulling trailers full of goods that could not wait on a thaw. Robert got on the CB radio and raised everyone behind him. "Let's hear it!" he called out.

Fifty semis all hit their air horns at the same time and the sound could be heard for miles.

Betsey said, "That's music to my ears, Robert! Let's get out of here!"

The convoy had little or no trouble getting as far as Blackfoot, Idaho, but when they reached the exit on I-26 going northwest, there were sawhorses across the road. There was also about two feet of snow across the highway, where no plows had yet been able to reach. Robert pulled over Betsey, and for miles behind him, big rigs came to a halt. Robert got on the CB radio and told everyone to hold their positions for a few minutes where they were. Then he and Felix went outside into the blowing snow to move the sawhorses. Luckily, there were no police around in this freezing cold to stop them from what they were about to attempt.

Hud was right behind them, so he got out of his truck and came up to the old bus. They all went back inside of Betsey with Hud following behind, marveling at the beautiful old coach. "She shore is a beautiful lady, isn't she?" Hud said in amazement.

"Why, thank you, kind sir!" Betsey said with a chuckle.

Hud shook his head. "Y'all have GOT to be kiddin' me! That was the bus?"

Gill smiled. "Yeah, Hud. Say hello to Betsey!"

Hud smiled. "Hello, ma'am! Proud to make your acquaintance!"

"Right back at you, trucker!" Betsey said.

"Dangdest thing I ever seen!" Hud said with a chuckle.

Gill directed Hud to a chair. "Hud, to coin a phrase... you ain't seen nothin' yet!"

Paul was coming out of the bunk area with his pencils and pens and a pad of art paper. He sat down and looked out of the windshield on the top section of Betsey, gazing at the road ahead.

"Are you sure this is gonna work?" Hud asked quietly as he watched the young boy begin to doodle.

"Sir," Paul answered, "to be honest... no, I'm not sure! I've never tried anything like this big before, but now... I've got some help!" It was then that they all noticed the carving of the old man that Paul had in his lap as he doodled.

As he drew a picture of the highway in front of them, stretching out to the nearest horizon, they all began to see colors floating through the air centered around Paul and the ancient carving. And then, Paul began to add a picture of a gigantic machine to the drawing, a snowplow such as man has never seen. It had to be at least twenty feet tall, with a blade of shining steel and an engine like no other ever created by the hands of humans. Its width on the paper covered all four lanes of the picture he was creating and it had no cabin at all for the driver to ride in, because there was no driver. And as the colors swirled through the air, and as the picture was completed, Paul reached into the air and snatched a handful of color and flung in onto the paper.

"FINISHED!" he said.

They all gazed at the drawing, a picture of a giant monster snowplow that was bright pink.

"Y'all gotta be kiddin'," Hud said in a whisper, as he looked down on the doodle.

Gill placed his hand under Hud's chin and slowly raised the old man's eyes until they were now looking outside of Betsey. And there...

"What in God's name...?" Hud said as he quickly jumped out of his chair and ran to the bus door. Everyone else slowly walked out behind him. "Jesus!" he said.

There it was in all of its pink glory. An incredibly large, impossibly beautiful pink snowplow.

Hud fell to his knees in the deep snow. He looked first at the boy, and then at the rest of them. "Who are you? And... why are you here?"

Felix smiled as he said, "Just regular ol' folks, sir... out on a weekend stroll to save the world. That's about it, Hud."

Hud smiled as he got back up on his feet. He looked at Paul. "Ah, son? Does it run?"

Paul smiled. "Let's let Sarah answer that one!"

Sarah smiled as she casually walked over to the giant machine. She looked at Hud and said, "This is where I shine!" She placed her hands on the beautiful pink monster and closed her eyes.

VAROOOM!

The engine of the plow kicked over as pretty as you please. She left her hands on it for another minute while she explained to the vehicle where they needed to go. She walked back to Robert, almost falling over in exhaustion in the process.

Robert took hold of his necklace with one hand and pressed the other one to Sarah's head. A bright red light that could be seen for a mile away encased the both of them... so bright that it made them impossible to see. Robert removed his hand from "Olivia Reaching For A Star" and the light went out. There were Sarah and Robert, both smiling at each other and both in the pink of health.

"My Lord, my Lord," Hud whispered. "Just regular ol' folks, huh?"

Gill smiled. "That's about the size of it, Hud. Now, let's see about getting us, you... and all of your friends down this road to where we're all going...

what do you say?"

"Bless y'all, son. Me and my Mrs. will pray for ya, whatever it is that y'all are doin'! Let's get outta here! Yee haw!"

Hud ran back to his truck as the plow began to push its way down the long highway... and the nearest horizon. Air horns filled the air as the miles of trucks followed ol' Betsey down I-26.

The convoy was slow, but it was moving.

The sixty some-odd miles from Blackfoot to Arco, Idaho took more that two hours. They slowly trudged by Atomic City, which made Felix giggle, and then they passed the Big Lost River, which made Felix laugh. When they had finally reached Arco, the giant snowplow came to a sudden halt.

"What's up now?" Hud asked Robert on the CB radio.

Sarah came forward to talk to him. "Hud, we've got to change roads and directions now, so I have to re-program the plow. Here's what we'll do... our bus is only going as far as the Craters Of The Moon for now, so when we turn here onto I-26/93, you truckers go on ahead of us and follow the plow. It will take you all of the way across the Snake River Plains to Carey, and then on into Shoshone, and finally to the outskirts of Twin Falls. Once there, I'm setting it to lose itself into the Snake River. It'll be gone, but you'll be home. It's about a hundred miles from here to Twin Falls, and it'll take even that big machine three or four hours to make the trip, but your load will be there by late this afternoon. Good enough?"

"Folks, I can't thank you enough, and I know that all of the other truckers listening in on this weird conversation feels the same. We owe y'all big time. Take care of yourselves."

Air horns were blaring at this final salute as Sarah and Robert left Betsey to re-start the pink monster. It kicked back into life as Sarah sent it on its final journey. Robert had to boost Sarah's strength once again, and with him still having no Builder of his own, Gill had to drive Betsey while Robert rested in the back of the bus with Sarah. As the incredible line of miles of trucks passed them by, each and every one of them gave Betsey a toot as they rolled down the road.

"It makes a girl proud to be a bus!" Betsey said.

After every semi had passed them up, Gill pulled onto the highway once again. He followed the long line of diesels as they crawled across the Snake River Plains, and about an hour later, Betsey had reached the Craters Of The Moon. Gill got on the radio to wish the convoy well as he pulled Betsey over to the side of the road into a parking area. He crawled out of the driver's seat and went upstairs into the lounge area, where Felix and Paul were watching a movie with Killer.

Gill plopped down into a comfy chair, dead-tired after this exhausting day. "What are you guys watching?"

Felix smiled. "Aw, some action/adventure flick about a bunch of super heroes flying around everywhere saving the world!"

Gill smiled. "Fiction, huh?"

Paul laughed. "Yeah! Who'd believe it?"

Gill sighed. "Ah, Felix? What do you know about this place?"

"Quite a bit, actually, Gill. It's managed by the National Parks Service to help preserve and protect the features of the volcanic activity, which actually ended about two-thousand years ago. It's about forty-three thousand acres of land, which contains lava flows, a bunch of cinder cones and craters that are very moon-like. This was the place where NASA trained astronauts for moon walks. There are no motorized or mechanized vehicles allowed... not even a bicycle! If we get a permit, we can camp or fish while we're here, but there's no roads or buildings at all, and there's no logging or mining! This place is one of the only wilderness areas within the National Forests and Bureau of Land Management where no hunting at all is permitted! There is basically 'No Anything' here except walkabout!"

Gill looked shocked. "Forty-three thousand acres? Well, we don't need a camp permit to park overnight, I guess. And also, I would guess that the Night Of Dreams can take place anywhere out here, but..."

Paul looked at them both. "But... me, huh? How am I supposed to find a white tube in a forty-three thousand acre park with two feet of snow on the ground? That's the question, isn't it?"

"Trust in you luck, little dude," Felix said with a smile. "Your luck... and your dreams!"

67
The Night Of Dreams

That evening, everyone gathered around the lounge area, trying to pretend that they weren't all nervous about the night ahead. Gill made up a hot supper for everyone, and they finished off the meal by sipping on some mulled cider. The snow was still falling but had slowed down considerably. The hum of the bus generator and the warmth of Betsey's interior had a lulling effect on the tension everyone felt.

No one had spoken very much the whole evening, and ironically, it was the quiet one, Paul, who broke the binding silence at the end of the evening. He looked around at his new friends as if he were trying to memorize their faces, and as he held onto the carving of the old man, which never left his side now, he started to quietly hum. Killer jumped up into his lap and snuggled into the warmth that he found there.

Paul smiled and said, "You know, I have a re-occurring dream a lot that I really like. I hope that tonight's is kinda like that."

Sarah looked at him and smiled. "Tell us about it, if you don't mind, Paul. I mean... if it's the kind of dream that you can tell!" She snickered.

"Yeah, there's nothing... bad ... about it. The dream changes from time to time, depending on the situation I find myself in, but it's about flying, I guess."

"Flying, like in a plane?" Felix asked.

"No, this is more like I'm on a hillside, and instead of just walking down it, I sorta concentrate... and gently lift up off of the ground! I always remember that I can never go very fast... and I can never go very high! I guess it's really... more like floating than it is like flying, except I can control which direction I want to go. People on the ground are always surprised, and look up cheering and stuff! It always makes me feel... kinda special."

Sarah put her hand on his. "Sugar, you are kinda special."

"I dream a lot about an island," Robert said with a sigh. "I guess I sorta own this place, 'cause everyone else there always comes to me for advice or when they need help. It's not far away from the real mainland... and I can always see the people over there scrambling around, trying to make a living and stay alive. But, I remember that on the island, there's no crime.

None. Just peace and quiet, and a lot of good friends."

Gill smiled. "Kind of like here... right now."

"Yeah, I guess so, but without the waves."

Gill looked over at Felix. "How about you, big guy? Any dreams to share?"

Felix blushed. "Well, lately, I seem to be having quite a few dreams about a young Indian girl. I guess Native American is what they want to be called nowadays, but my old black-and-white TV days as a child still gives me fond memories... of when folks weren't so hung up on titles, just on being a good people. She haunts my dreams almost every night now, though." He rubbed his eyes as if smoke had somehow gotten into them.

Sarah went over to hug the dude. "That's beautiful, Felix. I'm sure she dreams of you, too. I've been dreaming a lot of that lake of a swimming pool you've got, Gill... and Robert and I just floating... floating... floating."

She got a big kiss from Robert for that one. Then Robert turned to Gill. He didn't say anything. He just looked at his lifelong friend.

Gill smiled back at his big pal, and then said, "I have a family. In my dreams, I mean. I have a wife who loves me more than life itself, and three wonderful kids... that I would die for. I know I'm not handsome, and I know that I'm... a small person, but in my dreams... that doesn't matter. In my dreams, I'm not alone anymore."

Everyone in the bus all stood up at that... and they all hugged each other. Then Gill said, "Guys, no matter what happens in the next couple of days, I just want you all to know that I wouldn't have missed this for all of the money in the world. You are my family now, and I love you all."

There wasn't a dry eye anywhere to be found.

And then... Killer let out a very loud yawn.

As quick as that, everyone was laughing again.

Finally, as the snow lightly pattered on the windows of ol' Betsey, Gill put the bus "On Security" and then put himself into a bunk. Sarah and Robert took the stateroom in the rear and cozied up in each other's arms. Felix and Paul each took their own bunks and added a couple of extra blankets to the stack that they each already had. Killer lay down on the sofa in the lounge area, almost as if he knew that this was a night for dreaming alone.

Minute by minute, the background noises of the wind and snow faded, as the travelers minds began to fade, too. And soon, before too long... They were all together again.

They were in a large round room, with a semi-circular sofa against the wall of half of the place, and in front of them were five doors. Actually, there were five and a half doors in front of them. One was definitely a doggie door. It had hinges on the top of it, so that it would swing inward when pushed.

They all sat upon this sofa, along with Killer, who was wagging his tail about a hundred miles per hour. This, at least, was a good sign. There was a mist in the air around them, sort of a light reddish-colored fog, and out of this fog walked a small lady and gentleman. Everyone seated on the sofa instantly recognized Gwen as the beautiful woman in front of them, but the man was a stranger to all.

Gwen walked forward with the handsome little gentleman at her side. As she spoke, they all rose to their feet. "Gill, Robert, Sarah, Felix and Paul... oh yes, and Killer! I would like to introduce you all to my friend, Gin!"

"I am so very proud and honored to meet each and every one of you," he said with a jolly smile that lit up the very air around where he stood. He shook all of their hands, and even bent down to pat Killer, who jumped into the air to be caught by Gin, who started laughing as the small black snowball licked his face with a tiny pink tongue.

Gin looked at Gill as he spoke next. "Gill, for many, many of your years, both yourself and Robert have performed endless good deeds that have affected the outcome of history, both on your earth and on worlds that you will never know. You've done all of this on the faith and trust that you bear in your hearts, for no reward, and on the word of a people that you have never met... until now. To you two, the Flae will be always at your debt."

With these words, both Gin and Gwen bowed low to the two heroes of their people.

Both Gill and Robert had no words to answer this great honor, so they merely bowed back.

Gin looked at them all with a smile. "And now, for each of you, there awaits a door. Each destination will give you insight, hindsight, and in some cases, far sight! Tonight is a gift for you all! I wish you each and everyone peace."

With that, suddenly, the two members of a charmed race were gone. And above each door was a name – Gill... Robert... Sarah... Paul... Felix... Killer.

"I wonder what would happen if I went in Killer's door?" Felix said with a laugh.

BAM!

A magazine whomped him in the head.

"Damn, girl! How did you get a magazine in here?"

Without another word, they each smiled at each other and walked forward.

Right before they all entered their doors, Sarah looked at Robert and smiled. Then she turned to Felix and said, "Scarecrow, I think I'll miss you most of all."

Felix laughed and clicked his big heels together. "There's no place like home... there's no place like home..."

They each opened their separate doors and stepped through... into dreams.

68
The Doors To Everywhen

Robert walked slowly through the door. As he looked around him, he realized that he was...

lifting Louie Palmer into the air. He was in high school again, and Gill was rolled up in a ball on the ground from being kicked by the bully. Robert remembered it well and he said exactly what he had all of those years ago. "That will be the very last time you touch him! Understand?"

"Understood," said Louie, who never again touched...

Then Robert was in class looking at Linda. She smiled as she said, "Sure, Bobby, for you I've got all of the time in the world! Don't you be late, though." By that time Robert grabbed his books and headed for the door...

She never heard a horn sound out in warning because of the poor driver's heart attack...

And suddenly, another girl's car skidded backward and stopped. He managed to make it on shaky legs to her side of the car and looked inside at the most beautiful girl he had ever seen. It took him almost three seconds to fall in love. "Sarah!"

It was Sarah. Now he knew. He remembered all of the past. He recalled all of the present. And as for the future...

And there, he saw the giant towering above them all, roaring as the whistle it had been expelling drilled farther and farther into the already shaky terrain and the lava, oozing out of the hole, proclaimed the intensity of the disaster to come. And he was powerless, holding Sarah's inert body in his arms trying to bring her back.

And later on, as he held poor Killer's body in the glow of his Plus...

Sarah walked slowly through the door. As she looked around her, she realized that she was back at home with her mom. Sarah was a child. The smell of gingerbread told the story of Christmas at home. Mom tried to hide the tears that came at this time every year since Dad had passed away, but...

then, Mom was outside with young Sarah, and they were dancing, singing to the spring garden as they both watched the plants spring up toward the sun a foot higher with every note her magical mom hit. And then...

And then... Mom was gone, and the young lady that Sarah had become had decided to leave Colorado and head to sunny California. She loaded just enough things to start anew, and on her way there...

all of a sudden, the monitor screen lit up to a light blue. "I'm really OK," said the computer, "but I just can't work with that guy anymore! My name is MAX!" Before she knew what to say out of nowhere...

out of nowhere... The speeding truck skidded into the curb, leaped ten feet into the air, landed on its top and skidded the last hundred feet, followed by sparks and flame. And from somewhere close by...

And from somewhere close by, the man she would forever love said, "Are you alright? Miss?"

"Stop!" It was Ert. Robert. Now she remembered all of the past. She recalled all of the present. And as for the future...

Suddenly, she saw Gill spread out on the ground next to the Time Stopper. Killer was lying in a heap on top of a pile of bloody snow, and Felix was getting ready to scream as the world had never heard. Sarah fell, almost lifeless to the ground, as Robert cradled her head and...

Gill walked slowly through the door. As he looked around him, he realized that at that moment, his mom and dad were floating him gently over the waves at the beach. He was a baby again! The sun was quite warm, and suddenly, as they were floating, they went...

They went crashing down the side of a mountain, bursting into flame as they hit the bottom of the canyon. Gill was thrown free on the way down. After that...

After that, he was a boy again, and he hears and talks to what he calls "little people." They told him of things that are going to happen, sometimes good and sometimes bad. But after that...

but after that, people would walk by him at lunch. He was back in school again, and there he would be, whispering to the wide-open spaces, listening and answering questions that only he seemed to hear. The problem was... the problem was... "Something VERY bad is getting ready to happen!" He was at Robert's house. Gill closed his eye and little by little lowered his head between his arms to lie flat on the tabletop...

"Stop!" Robert's house... He remembered. He remembered all of the past. He recalled all of the present. And as for the future... but ahead...

as he lay in the freezing cold snow, he saw Killer crushed on the snowy rocks. He saw Felix take the device, place it to his lips and sounds of total destruction followed. As the Thingie started to scream...

Paul walked slowly through the door. As he looked around him, he realized that at that moment, he was a baby and could hear voices from far away, but he could see nothing. It sounded like his mother was calling, but suddenly...

but suddenly, he was a child and could feel the great heat of the fire upon his face as he heard the screams of his family but couldn't see anything. As he tried to stand, he realized...

he realized that he was a boy, and the thugs had left him beaten and bloody in the alley, robbed of all possessions but still alive. And he could see again. As the policeman reached for his hand, the cop said, "So, you say you don't know your name, huh? Well, then..."

"Well, then... since you don't know what you're doing, here's what you're going to do! You're going to pick up your bag there, you're going to pick up your feet there and you're going to come with me to that nice warm bus over there across the road for a hot meal and maybe some hot chocolate..."

"Stop!" That was Sarah. That's when his new friends had found him. Now, he still remembered none of the past, but he recalled all of the present. And as for the future...

By then, he had drawn up the device that would hopefully help defeat the terrible creature waiting to kill them all. He hoped it would work as planned, but the problem was...

The problem was now in front of him. It was gigantic and killing all of his friends. If his drawing wasn't as good as he hoped, then...

Felix walked slowly through the door. As he looked around him, he realized that he was back in Louisiana. He was a young boy. He and his brother, Sly, were outside playing by the bayou. He heard Mam yelling for them to get out of this house with that voodoo mess he was "talkin'!" She didn't want to see him or hear "them Devil's juju words" anymore.

He was a young man now, but he cried as he grabbed a small suitcase, packed his few meager things, told his brother goodbye and then...

And then, the big redneck sucker at the truck stop said, "Yeah, I'll let you work, hippie, but most of that money's going to pay for you to stay here. Now get in there, dummy, and get to work. Remember, that without..."

Without knowing how or why, the tears stopped, the wailing ceased, and with a red-hot hatred never before seen on the face of this peaceful person, Felix looked into the eyes of the fast-approaching creature in front of him, rolled his eyes into the back of his large head and screamed...

Shadow stood up and came forward. "You're no match for us, creature. Leave this place before the Cat Warrior ends your useless existence..."

Felix looked at Shadow. He gently took her by the arm and whispered, "Lovely lady, let's get you all home now."

She grabbed him by the Super Dude suit and pulled him down to her level.

She kissed him and then they started for home...

"But stop!" That was Shadow. Now he knew. He remembered all of the past. He recalled all of the present. And as for the future...

He looked around at his fallen friends. Sarah lay in the arms of poor Robert, who was trying to mend her through the sobs coming from his heart. And there was Gill, sprawled unconscious on the cold, wet snow, unmoving. Paul was pointing to something to Felix's right as the boy drew white lines in the very air around himself. When Felix glanced to where Paul had been pointing, it was then he saw the small lifeless dog.

The creature who was HE looked down at the miserable bunch of warriors, injured, dead or dying and made the mistake of laughing. As had happened only once before in time, Felix...

Little Killer walked slowly through the door. As he looked around him, he realized that ...

He lay on his side, next to his many brothers and one sister. He was a puppy again. The taste of warm milk filled his mouth as the loving eyes of his mother turned...

His mother turned to sadly watch as a small human girl child picked Killer into the air with a smile. "Oh Mama! I want this one!" Only Killer and his sister were left now, and as he was carried away...

He was carried away in the dark of night by a man of bad smells. He missed the little girl. He was a very young dog now and the new human treated him non-humane. He was punished for no reason. He was struck on the whim of the man of bad smells. He got to eat very little, and at night when the this man went out to steal from other humans in his pickup...

He was picked up by the man of bad smells and thrown into a black holder of garbage. The trash bag was tied, and he was driven to who knows where. He could hear the window being rolled down and suddenly he was weightless. When he hit the ground, he felt...

He felt the prison of plastic being lifted into the air again. After many days in the black hell with no food or water, he figured that the God of Dogs would now carry him to the Far-Away. Instead...

"DAMN!" the new human said out loud to himself. "What kind of monster would trap some poor animal in a damn trash bag with no air!"

Killer stopped whimpering. His small pink tongue came slowly out of mouth and kissed the new human.

"Hi, Killer. You come on with me. You're home now." He smelled good, Killer thought, and made him feel safe. Gill placed Killer in his shirt pocket. "A perfect fit, Killer. You and I can be small together. Come on, now. I'll show you your new home..."

"Stop!" The Gill human. Home. Killer remembered the past. He recalled all of the present. And as for the future...

The future was blank. His human lay in the snow... "Gill not doing!," Killer thought. Sarah had fallen and was being held by Robert. Felix was with toy in hand, looking up at something.

"Oh, God of the Dogs! What is that? Bad smells from Bigger-Than-Tree! If Bigger-Than-Tree hurt my humans, I must try hurt Bigger-Than-Tree.

I run at!

I bark at!

I bare my small teeth and jump!

Hello, God of the Dogs.

Hello, Far-Away..."

Then, Robert and Sarah were together. They could hear the waves, gently breaking on the beach of this small island of dreams. They looked at each other and smiled. Robert whispered, "It's the place I was dreaming of... with the person I was dreaming of."

She smiled. "Ditto."

They saw the gentleman they had met earlier walking through the warm sands to greet them. "A nice place you have here," he said with a smile. "I won't bother you for very long, but there's a couple of things I'd like to share with you while we have this time together."

Sarah nodded. "Anything for you, Gin. Thank you for this... this small piece of heaven."

Gin smiled. "Robert, I want you to know that there still exists a Builder for you. It won't be a weapon... in the sense that most weapons are, but it will aid you in times when things are darkest. It will add to your power of healing, which is already quite strong, and it will add to your luck! Luck, however, may end up being one of our greatest weapons, so do not belittle that gift.

"Sarah, I want you to know how important it will be for you to have your Catflower with you in the final battle. Remember this... being unconscious will work with me just as dreaming does, and my strength will be yours. When the battle is at its worst, I will be there with you both!

"Tell Gill that the combined powers you all have are a much greater sum total than individual strengths. This will become clear when it is need-ed. When you awaken, you will have a vision of a device that we believe might help. Give the idea to Gill, who will share it with MindSpeak. Also, tell him the Far-Away is a beautiful place, and though I regret his loss, there is no need for tears."

"What does that mean?" Sarah asked.

Gin smiled and replied, "All will become clear with the passage of time. Now, I must go, but please enjoy yourselves while you are here together. Life will be good to you both soon, but for now, the water is fine."

With that, he was gone.

Robert grinned as he lifted her into the air. "Wanna go for a swim?"

She nodded and placed her head on his shoulder.

Then, Gill found himself in a meadow. Grasses were waving, and flowers of all varieties nodded in his direction. A light warm wind blew in from the south, and as he glanced around, he saw Gwen walking in his direction. In her hands, she carried a wicker picnic basket, and over her shoulder was a blanket of the finest wool.

"Would you mind a little company?" she asked with a giggle.

"I'd love a little company. It's really quite beautiful here. Is this your creation?"

"No, silly, it's yours! It's where you go in your mind when you're trou-bled. Don't you remember?"

"Yeah, I thought it looked kinda familiar. The only thing is, usually when I'm here, I've got K–"

"Yipe! Yipe!" the small black dog said as it ran through the flowers, hap-py to be once again with its master. It took out enough time to give Gill a gentle lick on the hand before he started sniffing at the picnic basket.

Gwen giggled. "He must smell the hot dogs that I brought for him. But for us... "She then began to pull out all kinds of wonderful fruits and cheeses and a loaf of what appeared to be fresh baked bread. They spread the blanket on the ground and were soon all laughing as Killer would toss a hot dog into the air and catch it with one bite missing.

Gwen looked into Gill's eyes. "You know, he loves you very much, Gill."

"Yeah, I'm kinda partial to the little critter myself!"

"Among the Flae, there is an old legend. It tells of the first intelligent beings to grace all of the known worlds... and they were dogs."

"Really?"

"Yipe?"

"Yes, really! And it was said that the dogs only became really intelligent when they found themselves to be loved. They then obtained the Power of Return."

"I don't think I know of that one."

"This meant that when they bonded tightly with a member of another species... with that great love that only they can bestow... at the End Of Days, they would enter the house of the God of Dogs in the Far-Away and he would judge them to be worthy of return. They would then be reborn, back once again into the world where their loved one was, and in many cases, the Power of Return would send them once again to that special friend. A beautiful tale, is it not?"

"Yipe!"

"Yeah, I like that. I like that a lot! Legends are always so uplifting, aren't they? Too bad that they're only legends."

Gwen smiled. "Our time is now short, so eat your meal. But Gill, remember this... the Flae, too, are only legends."

"Woof!" Killer said as he laid his head in Gill's lap.

Gill smiled at this thought as he took a bite of his apple.

Then, Paul found himself in a large, dimly lit building. The air smelled of old oils, canvas and charcoal... a totally pleasant aroma. As the lights slowly brightened, he realized that this was a gallery of art. Hundreds and hundreds of beautiful portraits and landscapes graced the long walls, and hundreds of strangers were in there with him, gazing at the beauty found here.

He walked around for what seemed like hours, mesmerized by the intensity and feeling that the artists had brought forth from only canvas, paper, and imagination. He stopped by a portrait of an outstandingly beautiful lady, who was seated upon a marble bench with giant palm trees flanking the scene. For some unknown reason, this particular picture seemed to bring forth old memories in him, and as he got closer to the work of art, he realized that the lady had no face. It was as if the genius had run out of the artist when recognition of detail came into play.

"It's quite beautiful, isn't it?" said a voice from behind him, the first person to speak since his arrival. He turned around to see an incredibly beautiful lady behind him, sitting on a bench flanked by palms.

She had no face.

"It's... it's you," he said in a small voice.

"Yes, son, it is me. It's how you remember me."

"Mother?"

"Yes, baby."

He ran over to throw his arms around this woman who had been stolen from his mind. The hugs were long and continuous, and neither of them wanted to let go. Finally, he looked into her blank face and asked, "What are you doing here, Mama?"

"Oh, my son, I come here often! It is one of the things that make me proudest in this ol' world of ours. It is you!"

"What? Me? This painting is something that I did?"

"Something that you will do, my son! All of these are you!"

He stood there with his mouth wide open and stared down the long rows of work after work far into the distance. "Me, really?"

"Yes, my son. You."

"They're beautiful! But Mama, who are all of these people?"

"My son, they are the people whose lives you will affect, people who, because of you, will be made better, stronger, happier. Some of them are alive only because of you. I'm so proud of you! That is why I linger here so often."

"Mama, I... I didn't know! I–"

"I know, I know, my son. Now, your time is short here, so walk with me while we look at your creations and I tell you of a thing which we shall call a minaphone!"

"OK, Mom. Hey, Mama, I love you, you know."

"Yes, my son. I know. I've always known."

Then, Felix found himself surrounded by trees. A deep, soft light filtered through the overhead boughs and a gentle, peaceful sound permeated the evening.

A flute. He knew that sound, from his life and from his dreams. He knew that sound.

He glided through the low underbrush in search of the source of the haunting melody. It came from a clearing up ahead.

In the open area of the mountainside sat a teepee. From inside, the music seemed to lure him.

He pushed back on the flap of canvas and there she was, sitting there upon deerskin rugs. The flute played lightly over her lips and Felix found himself envious of that instrument. Next to her on the fur-covered floor sat a great cat. Not the God of Cats that Felix had once befriended, but he-who-was-now-cat. The ex-Whistler sat in peace, watching over her to whom he had pledged safety. The cat looked up as he entered and quietly said, "Welcome, Human who kills Thingies. We wish you well."

"Thank you, Whistle Cat. Shadow, it warms my heart to see you once again, even if this be false."

Shadow placed her flute on the fur next to the cat. "There is nothing false in this, Cat Warrior. It was granted to me the right to share in your

Night Of Dreams. I hope that you don't... disapprove."

Felix smiled as he seated himself beside Shadow Of The Moon.

"Nothing could bring me more joy. It was just... unexpected."

She reached behind herself and brought forth a light meal of venison, potatoes and fry bread. She served him and then herself. As Felix looked over at Whistle Cat, it was contented with gnawing upon a bone of unknown origin.

As they sat and ate in total contentment, she added, "I do have words of wisdom to send with you at the end of this vision. They may help you in your plight to prevent the world's destruction."

"Well, anything that prevents the world's destruction can't be bad, huh?"

She smiled back at the giant white man. "We of the Native American people treasure the things of this world greatly, not just the buildings and wealth of the world, but the trees, the animals, the waters, the very stones upon which this all lies. It is all of this, as I have learned from your Whistle Cat, that the enemy wishes to destroy for all time. The Great Spirit will not allow this to happen."

Felix smiled. "Neither will I!"

They left the teepee, walking through the forest with the large cat trailing behind.

"Has he been any trouble to your people?" Felix asked. "

"No, Felix, he is a Godsend. He helps with the hunt and the children love him."

"That is good, then."

"Felix, there are two things we must tell you, and our time is short. First, in two days time, I am told in vision that the sun will go out."

"WHAT?"

"No, not for ever... at least not yet. This will be... what you call... eclipse."

"Wow! I didn't know! I have to tell Gill! This must be the time planned by HE for the attack on Yellowstone! There will be no sun for a period of time when this happens! HE will use this!"

Shadow nodded. "Yes, Whistle Cat and I foresaw this. Also, Whistle Cat would talk to you of another matter."

The large cat came forward and lay at Felix's feet. "Warrior, I am now one with this place, and this way of understanding. Your friend Gill gave me that, so I would return the favor. I know of the plan of HE... to devour all of my people, all Thingies, to become... more! He will tower over trees in his might, but he will have a weakness."

"A weakness? Tell me of it, friend cat."

"There is a spot below the throat of the Thingies where the flesh is weak, and the strength lies. It will glow a white-hot color when he is of a total destruction mind. If you can penetrate that spot... maybe. I cannot say for sure, for none of our people have ever become this strong. But... you must try. Losing this world is... not an option, anymore."

"I thank you, mighty being-who-is-now-my-friend."

"I shall now leave you two alone. Sometimes, man and woman should just... be."

Shadow pulled Felix onto the soft grass and the dream just got better by the moment.

69
Reality Sucks!

RING! RING! RING!

Robert woke up to poke Sarah in the arm. "Phone's ringin', honey!"

"No," she said with a pout. "Don't wanna talk! Wanna go back to the beach!"

RING! RING! RING!

"WILL SOMEBODY PLEASE ANSWER THAT PHONE?" Felix yelled from up in the front bunk.

Sarah pulled the blanket over her head. "You get it, Ert! I'll be at the beach!"

"Where is your phone anyway, girl?" Robert said with a yawn.

RING! RING! RING!

"Ahhhhhh!" Felix yelled! "Now I can't go back to sleep!"

Killer ran back to the bunks, barking, and Gill popped his head out. "What the heck is goin' on?"

"Nobody will answer the phone," Paul said as he slowly raised up.

"I'll get it," said Betsey. "Hello?"

On the bus speakers came, "Good morning, gang! MAX is here! Rise and shine!"

Everyone groaned ("Oh!" "Ugh!" "Aw!" "Damn!" "No!" "Woof!").

"What's the matter, guys? Bad dreams?"

Felix got up with a grumble! "Killer, when we get back to L.A., I want you to put bacon on that son-of..."

"OK, OK, Felix," Gill said with a smile. "We need to get up, anyway. Reality time has set in!"

"What did he say?" Sarah asked.

"I think he said that reality time has set in! What do you say, gang?"

Everyone yelled at the same moment, "Reality sucks!"

Felix shook his head. "Man, she was there! In my dream! I still can remember... a purring sensation... as her lovely head weighed lightly upon my chest... !"

"Too much input!" MAX said.

"Yeah, I'm about to gag, too," Robert said with a smile.

"Breakfast in ten minutes!" Gill yelled as he started opening cabinet drawers. The combination of the clatter of pans and conversation finally drug Sarah out of bed.

"Guys, I did so not want to wake up today," she grumbled with a yawn. "Hey Gill? I wonder if the Time Stopper would work if you're having a... really good dream?"

Felix stretched his entire seven-foot body to loosen the kinks. "What I need right now is more like a tub stopper! I would kill for a hot bath!"

"Oh, Felix! That does sound like heaven right now," Sarah urged. "What do you say, Gill, a hot bath sound good to you?"

"Robert, I think Sarah's trying to get me into a tub," Gill replied.

"HEY NOW! We'll have none of that, young lady!" Robert yelled from the back. "Your only bath partner today will be me!"

Gill broke in, "Maybe today, we can find a motel on our way to Yellowstone and grab a couple of rooms just to clean up in. But there's a few things we need to do first, one of them being you, MAX! Why the heck did you wake us up, anyway?"

"Oh, yeah! I was so busy listening that I forgot! I got the road behind you cleared last night!"

Gill went to the front of Betsey, looked out of the windshield though it was still snowing. Sure enough, the highway had been plowed and salted. He came back up to where his eggs were frying and asked, "Just how did you manage that one, MAX?"

"Well, since I was on satellite communication anyway, I contacted the computer at the Idaho Department of Transportation and put that highway system on a high priority list for snow removal!"

Sarah laughed. "Brilliant, oh mighty computer of mine! Just for that, I'll let you spend a day with Lois when I get home!"

"Whirr... Whirr... Click! Oh yeah, Lois said to tell Felix that she misses him!"

"I heard that," Felix said from the bathroom.

Gill laughed, and then said, "Alrighty then, the second thing we need to do is talk about the dreams last night. I'm sure we all have several things that we need to share."

At the same instant, Robert and Felix both came back with, "And several things that we don't!"

Gill and Paul grinned as Sarah blushed.

"We'll get to those," Gill added, "after we put something on our stomach. Finally though, Paul, what's the story on what you're supposed to be looking for while we're here?"

He smiled. "I talked to my mom last night for awhile and then to Gin as I was waking up. I'm told that what I'm looking for is within a few hundred feet of where we're parked and that Killer is supposed to be able to help me find it. Is that right, Killer?"

"Yipe! Woof."

"Fine, then!" Gill added in, "First breakfast... which is ready now, then dreams... followed by a quick trip through the snow in search of white tubes... whatever that's all about! Then, on the road to Cody, Wyoming and a hot bath. It may prove to be an interesting day after all!"

Out of the bathroom came Felix's voice. "We don't go all of the way to Cody, Gill. Pahaska is more than fifty miles this side away from Cody."

Robert shook his head. "How does he know this stuff?"

Paul giggled.

"Tell us about it, Felix." Gill asked.

"From here, we gotta get to Jackson, Wyoming. That means we back-track on our route from yesterday... twenty miles back to I-26, then twenty-three miles back to I-20. From there, we take a forty-three mile journey to Idaho Falls, where we pick up I-26 to Jackson... which is another one-hundred miles or so! Hold on a second!"

They all laughed when they heard the toilet flush!

Felix came back out to stares and giggles!

"What? ... OK, OK ... so that's almost two-hundred miles just to get to Jackson! Then, we get to head into the really fun terrain! The Tetons and Yellowstone! Small roads, lots of snow and lots of delays. Out of Jackson, we're gonna take 191 to Moran, a bit more than fifty miles. Pass me some eggs! Thanks! Then we swing north on 89/287 to a town called Lake. That's about seventy miles more! From there, all we gotta do is drive down 14/16 to Pahaska, another twenty-six miles. Total miles for the trip is..." He looked up for a second, and then, "About three-hundred fifity miles... in some of the most brutal territory and horrible weather you can imagine! Figure on at least... ten to twelve hours, if nothing happens!"

Sarah sighed. "There goes my hot bath!"

Felix smiled. "Yeah, maybe so... but the good news is..." Everyone was waiting as he swallowed. "... this bacon is great!"

Sarah growled. "Where the hell did I put those magazines?"

Gill was smiling as he ate. "Hey, MAX?"

"Yes, Gill?"

"Did you get all of that? And what about our hotel reservations?"

"Yes, Gill, I did... and reservations are waiting at the Pahaska Teepee Lodge. I shall be watching your trip."

"Well, watching is all fine and dandy, but how about you breaking trail for us, as they say in the ol' West?"

"You mean more road clearing? I can do that... I think! Let me see what

I can do. This is Ol' MAXie signin' off!"

Felix smiled. "'This is Ol' MAXie signin' off!' Man, I love that dude! He's a real hoot!"

After breakfast, they all gathered around on the sofa and chairs in the lounge area. Because of the parts of last night to be left unsaid, they decided to start off with regular conversation instead of MindSpeak.

Robert started. "Gill, I saw the hole that this Whistler was drilling, using only its voice! There was lava oozing out of the hole, but I never saw any explosion! And I remember holding Sarah! I think she was out cold!"

Sarah stepped in. "You know, that's funny... because Gin told me that the Catflower would work when I'm unconscious just as it will when I'm asleep! Gin will be with me if I'm knocked out. He said that was important and that I need to make sure to keep the Catflower with me. And I remember him telling Robert that there is still a Builder out there for him! That's good news! Also Gill, he said to tell you that... how did he put it? Oh, yeah! 'Tell Gill that the combined powers you all have are a much greater sum total than individual strengths. This will become clear when it is needed. When you awaken, you will have a vision of a device that we believe might help. Give the idea to Gill, who will share it with MindSpeak.' I have an idea for this device in my head, but to be honest... it's kind of goofy! There was something else, too, but... I can't seem to remember what it was. Hmmm... let me think about it for awhile. Maybe I'll remember."

Paul added, "Yeah, Sarah, I saw in my dreams that I had drawn the device you were talking about, but I never could seem to figure out if it worked, or even what it was for!"

Gill went over to Sarah and Paul. "Give me your minds, and we shall share this vision. Then, Paul, you can see about drawing it up while we're on the road." He placed his hand in theirs, and they all three closed their eyes. About a minute later, they opened them again.

Gill looked confused. "What the hell was that?"

"What did it look like, Gill?" Felix asked.

"Kind of like a cross between a backwards bugle... and a kazoo!"

Felix laughed! "Oh, that's gonna scare a fifty-foot monster, alrighty! Hey! Ugly creature! I'm gonna hum you to death!"

Gill shook his head. "Well, anyway... Paul, see what you can come up with. Anyone else have anything to add?"

Felix raised his hand.

"We're not in school, pal! Go ahead!"

"A few things I need to throw out at ya, dudes and dudette. Number one... Paul, I saw you, how can I put this without sounding crazy..."

Robert laughed. "That's not gonna be possible, Suppie!"

"Very funny, Doctor Bob! But Paul... you were drawing... in the air!"

"WHAT?" Paul interrupted. "Drawing... in the air?"

"Yep, that's what it looked like! And also... I found out from Whistle Cat that..."

"Who?" asked Sarah.

"Whistle Cat. That's what I call the Whistler who watches over Shadow now. Other Brother to y'all. Anyway, he told me that this... HE... will have a vulnerable spot. It's below its throat, and will glow white when the critter gets ready to blow. Whistle Cat didn't know if we could kill it or not... because it would be... how did he put it? 'HE will tower over trees in his might!' That don't sound too good, does it?"

Gill shook his head. "No, it doesn't, but at least now we have a target . The only thing we don't have is a time of attack!"

"Yeah, "Felix added, "I was gettin' to that! Shadow Of The Moon may have given that to us, too."

"What are you talking about, Felix?"

Felix looked down at the floor. "An eclipse, Gill. In two days time from today, the day after tomorrow... the sun will go out during the day. We've got a damn eclipse comin', guys!"

Robert whispered, "This just keeps gettin' better and better."

"That's got it be it, then," Gill added. "Anyone else? Anything at all?"

Paul said, "A minaphone."

Sarah said, "That's it! That's what the kazoo was called! A minaphone!"

Gill replied, "I just remembered that Felix had the device to his mouth in my dreams! So now, Felix, we know who gets it. OK, Paul, let's go looking for your Plus, then let's get on the road. Our time is running out, but at least now we have some idea of how much of it we have left. If no one has anything else to add, let's go outside."

Each of them had something that they couldn't quite put their fingers on, but no one said anything.

Killer knew. He, too, had seen Bigger-Than-Tree.

But he wasn't talking.

70
Clock Man, Chalk Boy & Kazoo Dude

They all stepped outside of Betsey into the freezing wind. The snow wasn't near as bad as it had been the day before, but the wind was whipping around with thirty miles per hour gusts. The snow drifts were piling up into eight-feet tall structures of chill.

"OK, Killer," Gill said with a shiver, "let's see what we can find before we all freeze!"

Killer took off at a run, his little legs pumping through piles and piles of snow ten times his own height. Even though he was only the size of a good sneeze, he soon left everyone behind. They could hear him a couple of minutes later, off to the right and raising a ruckus with his barking.

"I think I see him over there!" Felix yelled back through the high winds. They all trudged through the frozen obstacle course toward the tiny barks coming from behind a six-foot high pile of wind-blown ice, and there was not only Killer, but the only un-frozen section of ground anywhere around. It appeared to be a hole in the ground, most likely caused thousands of years ago by the last volcanic activity around this area. The hole was only about two feet wide at the top and curved sharply back to the left only three feet down inside.

They all stood there looking at the small depression for about a minute before anyone said anything. Killer kept looking at them and then barking. Sarah finally bent over to stare into the tiny opening. "There's warm air coming out of it! That's why there's no snow in or around the hole!"

Paul said, "Well, we were told that the Plus would be found where the snow wasn't, so this must be the right place! But... I don't see anything in there. What are we gonna do?" The boy was looking upset, so Felix decided it was time for a little levity.

"Hey, Doodle Dude! Get it together, man! You're 'bout as useless as an inflatable dart board. If there's something in that dang hole that's supposed to belong to you, don't whine about it. Go get the damn thing! And hurry up! It's supposed to get cold around here pretty soon."

Paul smiled at the giant comedian, and then bent over to feel around inside the small opening. He couldn't feel anything straight down from where he was searching. "Hey, guys, I'm gonna try to squeeze into this sucker! Someone grab my feet when I get in there... ah, if I get in there! I don't know if I can get back out again by myself because of the sharp turn down there. Anyone got a flashlight?"

Felix laughed as he drew a penlight out of his pocket. "I just knew that you were gonna need this critter!"

Paul smiled at him. "Thanks, big guy. I'm gonna have to slide in... so someone kinda push on my feet when I reach that angle down there."

The boy eased his way slowly into the hole, and after a couple of seconds, they saw the light come on at the bottom of the tiny cave as he twisted to turn in the direction of a small tunnel.

"Wow! Y'all should see this! There's what appears to be a real small cavern in here, and there's long white tubes of calcium carbonate hanging everywhere... like little chandeliers! It's beautiful, and when I turn the light off..." Click! "Awesome! They glow!"

Felix yelled down in the hole! "Hey, we're kinda like freezing up here, oh mighty Doodle Master! Quit sight-seeing, and just get the job done!"

"OK, hold on!"

SNAP! SNAP! SNAP!

"OK, I've got three of them! Pull me up! Slowly!"

They eased Paul out of the hole ever so slowly, and when he came out, his face was pale white and he was glowing.

"Aww, dude! What happened to your face? You're whiter than the damn snow," Felix said with a chuckle.

"Calcium carbonate! That's what it is! Weird, though... I got a sort of... shiver when I touched these!"

Felix shook his blue-haired head and asked, "We all got the shivers here, dude! Calcium who?"

"Calcium carbonate! Chalk! Look!" He held up what actually appeared to be three pieces of regular old chalk except for the fact that they were bigger around than your thumb and each about two feet long.

Felix fell over in the snow laughing. He started kicking so hard that he ended up making a giant snow angel on the ground.

Gill smiled as he looked at Felix and said, "OK, I know I'm gonna hate myself, but I've just got to ask! What is it? What's so funny?"

Felix pointed to Robert and Sarah as he continued to laugh. "Over there," he said between laughs, "we have Machine Girl and Doctor Bob!"

Sarah put her hands on her hips as she yelled, "Machine Girl?"

Felix fell over laughing again as he continued! "And... over here, we have Clock Man, Chalk Boy and Kazoo Dude!"

Everyone started laughing so hard that they had to sit down – they just couldn't help it. Gill said, "Damn it, Felix, you're killin' me here! Man, it's too cold! Let's get back to Betsey and try to figure out this chalk thing!"

Sarah picked up poor shivering Killer, and they all took off for the bus at a run, laughing all the way, as the song goes.

As they all entered Betsey's warm interior, she announced, "MAX called back! He said to tell you all that he's got ninety percent of the roads being taken care of... and he's working on the remainder. Also, Sergeant Eddie Fallon called MAX to say that a semi truck was reported ramming through a roadblock in Missoula, Montana! Several policemen and civilians were killed or injured when a thirty-foot giant came out of the trailer and threw a police car at the roadblock. There was also a report of blue fire... and several of the on-lookers being... eaten! That part of the town was evacuated, and the truck was last seen heading East on I-90. MAX said he's spotted it near Butte, Montana... and it's headed our way!"

Felix shook his head. "So... besides that, how'd you like the play, Mrs. Lincoln? This just keeps gettin' better and better!"

"OK, OK! Let's warm up for a few minutes, and then we need to get back on the road. The clock's ticking!"

"I hate that clock," Felix said with a snort.

Paul went into the top lounge of the bus and gently set down his new prizes. He then picked up his sketchbook, and began to draw a doodle of a box. It appeared to be a rather ornate piece of carpentry, with carvings of all sorts around the outside. It was rectangular, about eight inches by twelve inches and was about six inches tall. Sarah watched him draw this piece of art and commented on its beauty.

"It's for my chalks! They're kind of delicate, so I'll need somewhere to keep them!" When he finished the box, he drew it sitting on the floor beside him and suddenly, there it was... in real life.

"That's amazing how you do that," Sarah said.

"Thanks," he quietly answered. He opened the box, and seemed to measure how short the chalk would have to be to fit inside. Then, he very carefully picked up one of the pieces and broke it into smaller hunks.

Every time he did this, a spark would fly out of the original tube.

"Wow! Cool, dude!" Felix commented as he watched.

Paul started to concentrate hard on breaking the pieces evenly, and right as he was in the middle of intense contemplation, a small, tiny little sliver broke off and shot across the room. As it did, it left a trail of its journey through the air in a solid white line. As the sliver hit the floor, the line just... stayed there.

"You have GOT to be kidding," Robert whispered.

Paul got up from his chair, and slowly walked over to where the single line hovered in mid-air. He placed his hands on top of it and removed the line from the air with his hand. He held it like a very narrow spear, grinning. "Hey, guys! Look! Check it out!"

Robert slowly walked over to the boy. "Paul, can I see that?"

"Sure, Robert," the kid said as he placed it in Robert's hand. It had weight and substance!

Robert looked at everyone with a smile. "I'm gonna go try something! Everyone watch!"

He walked to the front of the bus holding the seven-foot long line and went outside. He looked around for a moment and then smiled. He checked to make sure that everyone was watching him through the windshield, and then he pointed to a road sign out by the highway. He raised back his muscular arm, and with all of his might, he hurled the chalk line at that sign.

The narrow line flew straight and true. It struck the metal of the highway sign, went through it, then clean through the wooden post holding it up and flew to the other side of the road to end up sticking into the ground thirty yards away.

"Aw, hell yes!" Felix said with a laugh.

It stayed that way for another minute or so, and then the wind picked up and blew it away into dust again.

Sarah hugged the boy. She looked into his eyes and said, "Wow, wow and wow!"

Paul just smiled. You could tell that the boy was very excited and very proud.

Robert got back on the bus. "Did you guys see that? Did you? Man! That was cool!"

Gill stepped forward. "Paul, try to draw something else... intentionally this time. Anything at all, but concentrate."

Paul thought for a moment, and picked up a small piece of the chalk. He noticed that as he drew in the air, it actually wore the chalk down on the tip. He sketched a picture of a bone in mid-air, and it held its shape. What it didn't do, though, was turn into a real bone.

"What's wrong?" he asked. "It looks like drawing of a bone, but not something that Killer would want!"

"Woof."

Felix said, "Maybe you're not holding your tongue right!"

Gill looked at it. "Try holding the bone and thinking about what it is you want it to be. See what happens then."

Paul picked the drawing out of the air and held it in his hands, thinking. "Bone. Bone. Bone!"

Killer started barking.

Paul looked down and realized he was holding a bone. A real bone. Killer was still barking.

"Here, boy! You want it?"

"Yipe!"

Killer ran off to the bunk with his new prize.

Gill smiled. "OK, then. Betsey... crank 'er up and get yourself ready! Felix, do you want to drive?"

"No! I wanna play with Paulie!"

Gill laughed. "OK, then... Robert, drive for a little while and then I'll take over. I want to see if this bone will hold its shape any longer that that spear did. Paul didn't make the spear line real, so that might be what caused it to be temporary. We'll see... we'll see. For now, though, let's get this lady on the road! We've got a long haul ahead of us!"

Betsey pulled out onto the long highway, aimed in the same direction they had just come from. Robert pointed her for the nearest horizon once again.

71
The Fifty Most Beautiful Miles

"How's it holding up?" Robert asked after driving for an hour behind the wheel.

"The bone's still here, and goin' strong... except for the part that Killer's been gnawin' on! He's havin' fun with it, though," Felix answered. "Me and Paulie are having fun, too!"

Robert turned around to see and started laughing. There was a basketball, a bow and arrow set, and a pair of snowshoes lying on the floor. Gill came forward and saw all of the stuff and yelled, "Hey! No more! We've got no extra room in here for a sporting goods store! Also, you'd better think about saving some of that for later. You can't get anymore quickly, you know!"

"Yeah," Paul said, "He's right, Felix."

"Aw! We were just havin' fun!"

Gill patted him on the shoulder. "Have fun after we save the world, OK?"

Felix was pouting. "Yes, Dad! Shouldn't you be in Whoville, takin' presents away from all the little kids?"

Paul smiled. "Come on, Felix! I'll draw you something nice in the sketchbook!"

"Cool, dude! Can you do me a hat?"

Gill smiled as he went forward. "How's the roads, Robert?"

"Not bad, buddy. MAX seems to have done a pretty good job on the street-sweeping deal! We're making good time, and we'll be in Idaho Falls pretty soon now. We may have time for that hot bath after all!"

"I heard that," Sarah said as she came running up to the front of the bus. "Oh, please! Please, please, please!"

Gill couldn't help but laugh. "Robert, find us a motel in Idaho Falls... right on the highway, though! We'll get two rooms, one for Sarah and you... and one for the rest of us. We'll grab quick showers and change clothes, then hit the road again! Fair enough?"

Sarah gave Gill a big kiss one the cheek, yelled out ,"Whoopie!" and ran to the back room to get some clothes together.

Gill patted Robert on the shoulder. "Son, you're gonna have your hands

339

full with that one!"

Robert smiled back. "Yeah, but I've always wanted my hands full."

Gill turned back to the "two children" drawing pictures. "Felix, what can you tell me about where we're headed?"

Felix took off his big blue puffy hat that Paul had just made for him.

Felix went away for a few seconds.

He came back.

"Gill, it's amazing! We're headed through Yellowstone to get to the east Yellowstone section, and it's all incredible! Did you know that Teddy Roosevelt said that the piece of highway between Cody and the East Gate of Yellowstone was... and I quote... 'The fifty most beautiful miles in America!' Pahaska is right in the center of this stretch, with The Sleeping Giant looming in the background! We'll drive right by The Sleeping Giant to get to our lodge! We'll be in the Shoshone National Forest! There's evidence that Indians have been in that area for more than eight-thousand years!"

"That's great, Felix. What about The Sleeping Giant?"

"It's actually a wilderness study area, Gill. You can't take a motorized vehicle in there at all, but there's about seven miles of hiking routes along the ridgeline. There's also forty primitive campsites along the shoreline of Holter Lake. They don't forbid pets in the area, but the Bureau of Land Management advises against it. Eagles, mountain lions, wolves, ect..."

Gill looked at Killer.

"Grrrrr..."

"OK, OK, I get it, Killer. Anything else, big guy?"

"Yeah, Gill... that sleeping critter is about eleven-thousand, two-hundred feet tall! You can get to it by boat on the Holter Lake... or by vehicle on Interstate 15, north of Helena, Montana. Take 226 exit at Wolf Creek on the frontage road for about eight miles, then turn east on Wood Siding Gulch gravel road for four miles."

Gill looked up. "Did you get that, Betsey?"

"Got it, boss!"

"Good girl! Looks like we're gonna be needing some hiking gear before it's over with! Paul?"

"Yes, Gill?"

"Hang on to those snowshoes after all!"

Before they pulled into Idaho Falls, Robert called Gill back to the front of the bus. "Hey, Gill! We're all over the CB radio! Truckers all over this part of the country are talking about the Magic Bus that got their buddies through the blizzard! Rumors have got us doing everything from melting the snow with our breath to actually flying all of those semis over it! They've got a pretty good description of Ol' Betsey here, and I keep getting light flashes and horns honking from truckers driving by on the interstate!"

"Oh, God!" Gill said. "It's gonna be hard to be incognito from here on out, I guess!"

Betsey popped on. "Gill, MAX is on my line."

"Got it, Betsey. Put him on the speakers. Hello, MAX!"

"Hi, Gill. Thought you'd want to know... the military just blew up a stolen semi near Bozeman, Montana with rocket fire from a jet! There were... and I quote... 'reports that it held the giant creature responsible for several deaths on the northern highway systems, but no such creature was found. The initial reports were either exaggerated... or the truck was unloaded before the attack!' Unquote. He's got to be on foot. I'm checking with the eye in the sky, but so far I've got nothing!"

"Thanks, MAX! Keep us informed. Bozeman's not that far from Yellowstone, and a thirty-foot beast can run pretty fast! There's lots of places up here to hide, also. He could be anywhere! MAX, see if you can get me a timeframe on a solar eclipse coming up day after tomorrow. Let me know when you get it. Give it to Betsey if I'm not here. Check?"

"Roger Wilcox! Bye now!"

Felix popped his head around the corner. "Roger Wilcox! Bye now! I love that dude!"

They pulled into the Mountain Inn in Idaho Falls, and Gill went in to get a couple of rooms. When he walked up to the desk, a little old man named Mr. Moore checked him in. "Is that your bus out there, young 'un?"

"Yes sir, I guess it is. Is there a problem?"

"Nope, no problem at all. I was just wonderin' if I could take a picture of it before you folks leave again! Y'all are heroes 'round here, ya know!"

"No sir... I didn't know. Why would that be, sir... if you don't mind me asking?"

"Son, my boy Frank was one of them truckers that y'all all helped to get through that blizzard to their destination! You probably saved him his job, and y'all made a lot of friends up in this neck of the woods! I'm proud to have you folks stayin' with us here, even if it's only to get cleaned up. You get the two best rooms in the house! Now, go on, and make yourselves at home!"

Gill smiled as he walked back out to Betsey and told everyone what was up. "Let's get cleaned up here, then we've got to get rolling again. OK?"

Sarah was out the door before he could even finish.

Robert smiled. "I guess that was a yes!"

Everyone unloaded, and waved at Mr. Moore as he stood at the office window, grinning and waving at them. Once in the rooms, it was a rush for the showers in order of who was the fastest. Sarah, of course, won in Robert's room, but he came in a close second by joining her under the warm water. Felix, Paul and then Gill all grabbed a quick rinse... in that order. They grabbed some clean clothes to put on, and within an hour and a half, everyone was loading back up into the bus.

Mr. Moore came out with his camera. He walked up to Gill and said, "Mr., I know how you kinda folks don't want your secret identities to be filmed or anything, but can I get a picture with your bus before you go?"

"Sure, Mr. Moore!" Gill said with a smile as he took the camera and snapped a picture of the nice gent standing by Betsey.

They finally pulled Betsey back onto the highway about two hours after the stopover, but everyone felt a lot better.

"It's amazing what a little bit of hot water can do for your frame of mind," Sarah said as she danced around.

She sat down next to Felix, who was reading his Stephen King book that he'd bought at the daycare book sale. She put her arms around the big guy and asked, "Felix, can you tell me some more about Yellowstone? Anything at all would be great! I love to pick your brain on stuff like this!"

Felix smiled and gave her cheek a little peck. "You betcha, beautiful lady. Did you know that Yellowstone was America's first National Park? It was established by Ulysses S. Grant back in 1872. He signed a bill saying that it would forever 'be dedicated and set apart as a public park or pleasuring ground for the benefit and enjoyment of the people!' The park covers about three-thousand, four-hundred and seventy square miles in the northwestern corner of Wyoming! A big ol' place! The volcanic eruption that caused this wonder happened over six-hundred-forty-thousand years ago, and with any luck at all, it won't re-occur on the day after tomorrow!"

Sarah had a faraway look in her eyes. "A pleasuring ground! Hmmm. Ahh... Robert?"

"Yeah, sweetie. I heard that!"

As they drove out of Idaho Falls, Paul sat down with Gill and Sarah, and together with the MindSpeak, he began to get a final idea of what this "minaphone" was supposed to look like. He got up and leaned next to the large window in the upstairs lounge and began to draw. He used his sketchbook for more detail, and took his time on his one. He had a feeling that this was important but still didn't understand why. He drew a picture of it lying on the table next to him, and when he thought that the picture was as close to what he envisioned as possible, he looked down. And there it was.

It really did look like a large kazoo. It was about a foot long, made of brass, and the mouthpiece was large while the opposite end was tiny. When he talked into it in front of Sarah, they discovered that you could only hear the speech if you were directly in front of the device and then only in a narrow beam of space. If the listener moved one inch to the right or the left, you couldn't hear it at all.

"Well, Felix," Paul said with a grin, "I'm not sure what in the hell it's for, but there it is!"

Felix looked at it and went away.

He was gone for a full two minutes this time, and when he came back, he looked scared. "Oh, God! I know! I know what it's for! I just pray that... I'll never have to use it!"

"What is it for?" Sarah asked with worry all over her face.

"It's... it's sorta like... a fine tuner for the HardSpeak! It's a weapon of total destruction for anyone standing directly in front of the damn thing when I... when I... lose control! God, I don't want that to ever happen again! EVER!"

The faithful old bus trudged its way out of Idaho and into the grandeur of Wyoming and the Grand Tetons. Jackson was an incredible place of shops and ski lodges and movie star homes, and a large park with a gate surrounded by antlers from deer and elk who have passed over the years into memory and into the cooking pots.

From here on, the roads became something to be feared instead of enjoyed. In spite of any and all help that MAX had been able to give them, the ice and snow respected no man. They were forced to put the chains onto Betsey's tires, and even then, the trip became a crawl. They slowly eased themselves over the mountaintops and into the valleys, which lay between them. There were lots of cars and trucks that simply couldn't do it, and had either skidded off of the road or had chosen to pull over. Betsey, though, having several hundreds of thousands of dollars worth of computer and analysis gear on board, was capable of recognizing where to go and when to go. A good-sized rabbit could have outpaced them, but slowly... ever-so-slowly... they kept on. What other choice did they have with the fate of all life perhaps hanging in the balance?

When they reached the John D. Rockefeller Jr. Memorial Parkway, the road got even smaller. The seventy miles from there to Lake and Fishing Bridge, where their next turn off was, took the better part of three hours. They were now in the heart of Yellowstone Park, and only a few miles from Old Faithful. But their trip took them on to the east for another twenty-five miles or so, and the dark clouds had brought on the night-time early today. When they finally pulled into the small community of Pahaska, they were dead tired. They managed to find the Pahaska Teepee Lodge in the growing darkness, but they could see no lights coming from the inside. Robert eased Betsey into the parking area outside of the main structure and finally put her in park.

"Damn," the bus said. "I'm glad that's over with!"

Everyone laughed at that.

Gill said, "Well, I see smoke coming off a fireplace inside, but from here, no lights seem to be on. I guess we'll stay on Betsey tonight, and check in tomorrow instead of waking these folks up. Robert, tomorrow, you and I will find some other kind of transportation to take us to Cody, where we'll buy some hiking gear for snow and maybe try to find us a guide. As for now, I suggest that everyone bundle up and get some rest. Tomorrow is the last day that we have to prepare for... whatever!"

"Dudes and dudette, I'd give a bright shiny nickel to know what that Whistler is doin' right about now," Felix said with a frown.

Betsey came back on to say, "Well Felix, what he's not doing is sleeping inside of a nice warm bus!"

72
The Coming Of The Dream Walker

The Dream Walker had been contacted by one of his own people that he had never met, but if Shadow Of The Moon, in her trance, could reach out to Chimayo, then by the Gods, he would listen. She spoke of many things... of love... of war... of faith... of the end of peace... and even the end of life, if Chimayo was unable to assist these Warriors who were now in his territory.

These Warriors had been told of the vulnerable spot on the evil one, this... Thingie. What they had yet to find was the vulnerable spot on Mother Earth that this Thingie would attack... The One Place. They had been directed to the Yellowstone lands, and then to Long Hair, or Pahaska, as it was known to his people. This had put the Warriors within his range of influence. These white humans had powers but no knowledge of the land. They had intent but no direction. Still, they were willing to allow their own lives to end in order to preserve the lives of countless millions of others that they had never met, including his own tribe.

Warriors such as this were worthy of his help.

He ended his Dream Walk with Shadow Of The Moon, and then studied a plan of action. Finding The One Place would be no problem for him. It had to be in an area where faults or volcanic activity occurs; therefore, it could only be at one of two different locations on the Sleeping Giant, and they were both within a mile or so of each other. The most power that this... Thingie... could draw upon would occur during the solar eclipse that Shadow had mentioned. He now had a timeframe and two possible locations.

Next, he had to walk with this Cat Warrior that Shadow cared so much about. Chimayo was still in the dream state, so it was a simple matter to locate the minds of the friends on this "Betsey Bus," and to sort out the special dreamer to be Chimayo's destination.

"Ah! There he was! My, my! What a strange mind this one has! A Warrior with this strength, and this gentleness... was rare... rare indeed!

No wonder he owned the heart of Shadow Of The Moon.

Now, let's see..."

Felix was driving his old Chevy Apache pickup truck through the canyons of Malibu when he noticed that he was no longer alone. He could only see a haze sitting beside him in the passenger seat at first, but the smell of the forest was what alerted him to the presence of another.

"Hello? Hey, dude, are you comin' in or not?"

Chimayo chuckled as he appeared in the passenger seat of the old truck. "Yes, Cat Warrior, I am here. I was sent by..."

"Cool, dude! Shadow sent you, didn't she?"

Chimayo tilted his head. "How is that you know of this, Cat Warrior?"

Felix laughed. "'Cause, dude, she's the only one that calls me that. Why don't you just call me Felix! Glad to meet cha!"

Chimayo nodded with a smile as he looked around. "As am I happy to meet you... ah, Felix. You may call me Chimayo. I like your truck."

"Howdy, Chimayo! Say, am I asleep right now? The reason that I ask is that, well, I thought I was... in the woods somewhere!"

"Yes, Felix, you sleep."

"Aw, that's too bad."

"And why is it too bad, Felix?"

"Well, 'cause if I'm asleep, then that means that you're not real, and I kinda like you! You're Shoshone, aren't you? I get along really well with your people for some reason or another! Ha Ha!"

Chimayo laughed at this. "Yes, Shadow has told me of your adventures... with the Found Child... and meeting the God Of Cats... and your battle in the mine with the Thingies... and of he whom you call Whistle Cat, who has now become a brother to the Shoshone! Yours is quite the tale! But as to my not being real, in this you are incorrect. At this moment, I am in my cabin... not very far from where you sleep in your Betsey Bus. I am a Dream Walker. I have the ability to enter other people's dreams, and once there, we can share information and I can come to know this person, as a friend or an enemy. You, Felix, I shall call friend. Is this satisfactory?"

"Aw, heck yeah! But, let me ask you, if you don't mind? Why did Shadow send you to me, Chimayo?"

"Felix, I am to be your guide in the effort you and your friends undertake. Tomorrow, when you awake... I will be with you in the waking world. Tell the small man who walks with the tiny people that we will need supplies tomorrow, and I will help you to gather them. I also know of the two locations where the Thingie will most likely attack. We will plan our assault on the marrow, Cat Warrior."

"That's cool, dude, 'cause I wasn't looking forward to checking out all three-thousand, four-hundred and seventy square miles of Yellowstone lookin' for some forty-foot critter in all of that snow!"

Chimayo laughed. "Yes, Felix, I believe that we can narrow down our search quite a bit from that. I will see you in the morning then... back in the waking world. Do you like venison?"

"Oh, yeah! Love the stuff!"

"Good! Then, until tomorrow..."

Felix watched as the new friend he had made faded out of the truck. "Wow! Cool! I wonder how he does that? Oh, well!"

Felix drove on down the road in the old truck, stopping only to pick up imaginary girls in bikinis hitchhiking to the beach.

Chimayo smiled in his sleep at the Felix person he had met. A good heart, he thought. "Shadow, you have chosen wisely! Now... for the hard part!"

He rolled over in his sleep and concentrated on finding the mind of HE. Chimayo knew that the creature would be found in the northwest area of the Yellowstone, and with a mind that large it should put out a sleep signature easy to locate.

"Oh! Great Spirit! This was a mind with nothing good in it!" Chimayo was hoping to be able to converse with this entity... to reason with it. This would not be possible. This beast had no desires except the death of each and every living thing on Mother Earth. All things must die, if this creature had its way.

And then, the Thingie recognized Chimayo. In its dream, it attacked. The Dream Walker was thrown into a tree trunk that occupied a place in the horrible dreams that this thing was having. His arm was badly bruised, and when one walked in another's dreams, the pain would linger in the waking world. If Chimayo was killed in this Thingie's dream, he would die there and die in the real world. He got up to run.

"I am HE! Who are you... to invade my sleep, small human? You are not one of Humans who kill Thingies, but I can smell them upon you! Tell them that HE awaits them, and HE brings a present of death to one and all! TELL THEM!"

Chimayo looked around at his location as he quickly vacated the mind of this beast. It was near, not far from The One Place, but it would wait. It would hide and wait until the solar eclipse was upon the world. And then...

Chimayo woke up in his warm cabin. He winced in pain as he tried to sit up, and it was then he saw the large bruise on his right shoulder where he had landed in the Thingie's dream. "Damn!"

There would be no more sleep on this night. He rose up and dressed. He packed up as much of his gear as he thought he might need in the next two days and went outside to stow it in the back of his old pickup truck. He then closed the door to the old cabin, shrugged into his heavy jacket and slid into the driver's seat of the old Chevy. It cranked right up, even on this cold morning.

Dawn was only a couple of hours away, and he still had much to do.

Early the next morning, Gill and Killer were the first two up.

"Good morning, Betsey," Gill said as he put on the coffee. "Anything new since I went to sleep?"

"Well," she said, "there's still no word on the whereabouts of that creature, according to MAX. He said to tell you, also, that the solar eclipse starts at two p.m. tomorrow, and would last for about a half hour."

"OK Betsey. Thanks for the info. Anything else?"

"Only the Indian."

Gill almost dropped his cup of hot coffee! "Did you say... only the Indian?"

"You got it, boss! He right up here!"

Gill and Killer went to the front of the bus and looked out of the windshield. And there, sitting cross-legged on the ground next to a large campfire, cooking a large hunk of meat on a spit was an Indian brave. He smiled and waved at Gill, and Killer bounced up into the air with a "Yipe!"

"OK, I wonder who this is?"

"That's Chimayo," Felix said with a yawn as he came forward. "I dreamed him last night. He's gonna be our guide!" Felix opened the bus door and asked, "Hey, Chimayo, is the deer meat done, yet?"

"Just about, Felix. Got any eggs to go with it?"

Gill shook his head. "Curiouser and curiouser!"

"Yipe!"

Robert, Sarah and Paul were introduced to Chimayo as soon as they all woke up, and by then, breakfast was ready.

"Man, Chimayo! This venison is excellent, dude," Felix said with a mouthful of food.

"Venison?" Sarah whined. "You mean... like Bambi?"

Chimayo smiled. "Sarah, you eat lamb, do you not? And lamb will not stomp you to death as a full-grown buck will! Out here, we eat what we have to... and what we can!"

She took a small bite and then started grinning. "Well, it is good."

The snow had died down, but the clouds lingered with a light wind.

Chimayo looked around at the lodge. "You know, my great-grandfather was here when this was all being built by Pahaska himself... way back in 1904. That was one year after the very first Ranger Station was built here... the Wapiti Ranger Station."

"Wapiti?" Paul asked.

"Yeah, son. It means 'elk' in the Native American tongue. This was about the same time that your Buffalo Bill talked his good friend Teddy Roosevelt into building the Shoshone Dam and Reservoir... later to be renamed the Buffalo Bill Dam. At that time, it was the highest dam in the world!"

"Wow, dude! That's way cool," said Felix with another mouthful of venison.

Gill put down his plate and looked over at Chimayo. "OK then, Chimayo, you feel that you know where this disaster is going to take place, right?"

"Gill, I know this area as well as you know your own kitchen back at your home. The creature will have two choices. Which one of the two he will pick, I cannot say, but they are close to each other. I tried to talk to it last night in dreams, but as you can see, it was reluctant to speak!"

He showed his arm to the group.

"Oh, my God!" Sarah exclaimed. "It did that to you... in your sleep?"

"Yes, Sarah... and it sends a message of death to you all, Humans who kill Thingies! Together, though, I believe that we have a chance to defeat it... if we can find it in time. It plans on total destruction... and you cannot apply the brakes to a volcano!"

Gill stood up and stretched. "As soon as we've finished eating, we'll check in to the lodge here and get our rooms together. Then, I'll try to get us some transportation to Cody so we can get whatever supplies that you think we might need, Chimayo. You're the guide, so I'll leave that up to you."

"Yes, Gill, I already have a list. And as for transportation," He pointed outside to his old truck.

Felix almost choked. It was an early 1950s Chevy Apache pickup truck with twin turned-up stacks... just like Felix's... except it was sky blue in color. "No wonder you thought I had a nice truck in my dreams!"

Chimayo smiled. "Two minds with but one thought!"

73
A Final Day Of Peace

Gill went into the old lodge to check everyone into their rooms as his friends were gathering up some of their luggage. Chimayo went with him.

The old man sitting on a sofa in front of the fireplace recognized Chimayo at once. "Hey, Chimayo! Haven't seen you in these parts in quite awhile now. What brings you out in this kind of weather, anyway?"

Chimayo smiled at the old fellow and answered back, "Tom, I've come to guide these nice folks on a little trip we've got to make tomorrow morning. Will you help get 'em checked in here? They've got reservations."

"Sure, sure I will," he groaned as he slowly got up from the warm couch. "A little trip you've got to make, huh? Well, you couldn't have picked much worse weather for it. On top of everything else, we've had reports of something that's been eating up the wildlife!"

Gill and Chimayo looked at each other. "Ah, what kind of wildlife, sir?" Gill asked.

"Well son, if the reports are to be believed, several elk and deer have turned up... slaughtered! Eaten on the spot! Also, we had one report of a full-grown grizzly being eaten! Now, that's kinda far-fetched, huh? What kinda dang critter is gonna eat up a griz?"

Chimayo shook his head. "What kind of critter, indeed."

Tom gave Gill the keys to all of the rooms. He was told that they just about had the run of the place since it was the off-season, and the weather had stopped a lot of the pending reservations from showing up. About then, everyone else started wandering into the lodge great room. Gill passed out the keys, and then went to unload his gear.

Paul walked over to where Tom was slowly sitting back down again.

"Excuse me, sir, but I was wondering if you could tell me anything about this brochure?" He held up the one item that he had on him when he woke up in the alley in Santa Fe.

"Land sakes alive, son! That's an old one! That there pamphlet dates back ten or twenty years ago! Where did you get that critter, anyway?"

"Well, I'm not quite sure. If it's that old, I guess it belonged to my mother." He passed the paper over for Tom's review.

Tom looked at the old brochure with interest, and then his eyes popped open. "Hey, son, did you notice these initials inside of here?"

"No, sir, what initials are those?"

"Right here, where it's signed E.R.W.! See the way that's signed?"

"Yes, sir. I've never noticed that before."

"Well, come over here with me!" Tom slowly got back up and went wandering down a long hallway. "Do ya see that?"

There was a beautiful landscape hanging in the hallway. It was Yellowstone, but in the fall. The trees were just starting to change colors, and a herd of elk grazed in the foreground.

"Yes, sir... that's quite beautiful... but I don't understand."

"Look at the signature, boy!"

In the same handwriting as the pamphlet, the painting was signed E.R.W. Tom shook his head. "She was quite a lady, that one! Came here about ten or fifteen years ago... and spent almost two months here at the lodge... painting landscapes. She sold us this one of the meadow down the hill from here. Seems like she had a young 'un with her, too... but no husband. I think she told me that he'd been killed in a fire or something. Too bad about her. She shore was a pretty little thing."

"What happened to her, sir?"

"Call me Tom, son. Everyone else does! Ya know, I heard that she moved down to Arizona or New Mexico... somewhere like that. I believe that someone told me that she and the boy both died in a car wreck or something. A drunk driver hit 'em. Killed 'em both, I think."

Paul just stood there with shivers trailing up and down his arm.

Tom stared at the young boy in puzzlement. "And... you say that your mama gave you this pamphlet, son? Then, that would mean that–"

"That would mean that my mom painted this picture," Paul said with a quiver in his voice. "That would mean that I was that little boy, and my mom was an artist, too."

Tom shook his head. "So, you're an artist. Small world, ain't it, young 'un?"

Paul nodded. "Sir... ah, Tom? Would you happen to... know her name?"

Tom just stood with shivers trailing up and down his arm now! "Boy... you don't know your own mama's name?"

A tear ran down Paul's face as he shook his head. In his mind, he could feel the great heat of the fire upon his face as he heard the screams of his family, but couldn't see anything. "No, Tom. I woke up in an alley in Santa Fe some months back with no memories and that piece of paper in my hand."

Tom put his hand on the boy's shoulder. "I believe her name was Elizabeth. Elizabeth Wallace."

Paul smiled at that. "Well, Tom, my name is Paul Wallace! I'm proud to meet you, and I thank you for your kind help."

Tom smiled at Paul. "Proud to make your acquaintance, Paul! I'd be honored to see some of your work while you're here, if you don't mind. Maybe I could buy a piece from you, and we could hang it in here next to your mom's painting! How does that sound to ya?"

"Sounds like heaven, Tom. Sounds like heaven."

Everyone got situated in the rooms pretty quickly. Robert and Sarah each had their own with a connecting door. Felix was down the hallway with Killer. Gill was unpacking in his room while he continued to talk to Chimayo.

"As soon as I finish here, we'll load up into your truck and head to Cody for whatever you think we're gonna need. I hope the roads are cleared. Oh, and remind me to get a bunch of chocolate!"

Chimayo laughed. "White folks! I'm not gonna ask!"

Gill looked at the man sitting in his room for a moment before he asked, "Chimayo, how much do you know about us?"

"Well, when I walked in the dreams of Shadow Of The Moon, she said something of the power of the Warrior named Felix, but I know very little of the rest of you. Why?"

Gill sat down and looked at him without saying anything for a moment. Then, finally, he asked, "Do you trust me, Chimayo? What I mean to say is... we go on a journey that we may not come back from, and you are chosen to guide us on this trip. I think it only fair that you know what you're dealing with here. So... do you trust me?"

"Gill, after having touched the mind of this... Thingie, I would go into battle against it totally blind, if need be! But... in answer to your question... yes, for some reason, I do trust you."

"Then... I wish to share something with you." Gill scooted his chair up next to Chimayo's and gently grasped the hands of his guide.

Gill slowly closed his eyes. Chimayo followed.

They shared the MindSpeak for almost two minutes. At the end of that time, Chimayo knew everything. And he was amazed.

Paul came running down the hallway and knocked on Felix's door. Killer started barking, and Felix swung the door open. "Hey, Paul! What's up, lil' dude?"

"Wallace, Felix! My name really is Wallace!"

"Well, of course it is."

"No, you don't understand. Tom... downstairs... he knew my mom!

There's a painting of hers on the wall downstairs. She was an artist, too. Her name was Elizabeth and her last name really was Wallace. Cool, huh?"

"Waaay cool, dude!" He grabbed Paul's hand and shook it. "Glad to meet cha, Mr. Wallace!"

They both rolled on the floor laughing as Killer jumped into the air with an occasional "Yipe!"

Felix recovered enough to say, "Hey! In celebration of finding your name, why don't we draw something?"

"What do you have in mind?" Paul asked with a snicker.

"Funny you should ask, dude! I've got this idea for costumes..."

Robert and Sarah got unpacked, and then decided to go outside of the lodge to check out this grand place built so long ago by the famous Buffalo Bill. They bundled up as warm as possible and then headed downstairs. Tom was back to sitting by the fireplace as they walked by.

"We're gonna go check out the property, Tom. Is the restaurant open yet? We might hit it when we come back for some hot coffee!"

"Yep, and the coffee's always hot! Check out the stables while you're wandering around. Some nice horses back there, and ol' Buffalo Bill himself used to shack up his pony in the old stable behind the lodge here. Here... take this for the horses!" He handed them a handful of apple slices, which Sarah stuck into her pocket.

They went out into the snow-covered landscape once again, and it was breathtaking. It was still kind of overcast, but the snow had quit falling, and every once in a while, the sun would peek its head out from behind the cloud cover.

Robert and Sarah were now comfortable in each other's company. The intimacy they felt for one another had developed nicely in the last week, and it was now hard to imagine one without the other. They were still awfully quiet as they walked around the great lodge, thinking of anticipated events to come. The air was heavy with the sense of something fateful on the horizon.

They went over to the new stables, where the horses all came over for a little attention and the hopes of a treat. Sarah laughed as she passed out the apples to them all, and Robert was amazed at how her laughter made his heart swell.

They saw a rundown little building off to the side and decided to explore. As they approached it, they realized that it was an ancient stable, and most likely the very one used by Buffalo Bill a century before. Sarah sat down on an old stump as Robert began to build a Buffalo Bill snowman complete with a beard, long hair, and a cowboy hat – all made out of snow.

As Sarah was laughing at his frozen sculpture, Robert scraped up another batch of snow to finish his snowman and was knocked backward into the shed by the power of something he had touched. Sarah jumped off of the stump and ran over to where he lay, totally out of breath.

"What happened, Ert? Did you get shocked or something? I saw sparks in the snow!"

He shook his head and didn't say a word as he eased out of the snow. He slowly walked back over to where he'd been collecting snow, and when he looked down on the ground, he saw a horseshoe.

It was an old horseshoe, all rusted as if it had been there forever.

"Or at least a hundred years!" Robert said out loud.

Sarah said, "What did you say?"

Robert pointed. "Look at it! It's an old horseshoe, Sarah! Remember when I told you about my... my luck? Well, what if... ?"

"Ert! You've got to be kidding! You think that your Builder might be... ?"

"Not only that, Sarah. I think that there's a good chance that that... lucky horseshoe... just might have belonged to..."

"Buffalo Bill... himself?" she asked.

He nodded. "Look how old and pitted it is!" He bent down to his knees and looked at it closer and then looked at Sarah. "Well?" he asked.

"Go ahead, Ert! Take a chance! After all, you are lucky that way!"

He reached slowly down until his hand was only an inch away and then quickly grabbed it. A blue ring of light surrounded both him and Sarah, and he felt as if he'd just taken a twenty-pound vitamin with a gallon of espresso. All of the snow inside that ring instantly melted, and Sarah laughed as she felt the strength pouring off Robert in waves and also into her.

He was laughing out loud and spinning in circles when he heard someone behind him say, "Hey, dude! I want some of what you're smokin'!" There was Felix and Paul, also laughing. Killer was smiling.

Paul whispered, "Ah, Robert... you're kind of... blue!"

Robert smiled as he put the old horseshoe into his pocket. The glow quickly faded, and Sarah said, "Robert, because of you being my Builder, that thing affecting you... also affects me! Cool, huh?"

They were dancing in the snow together, and Felix and Paul were yelping while throwing snowballs around when they all heard, "Any of you sad people need anything from town?"

There was Chimayo and Gill, also laughing.

Soon, they were all telling each other everything that had happened to each of them, all in the first thirty minutes of being at the lodge. The painting, the story of Paul's mom, the MindSpeak with Chimayo, and the horseshoe Builder – it all came out at once. When they finished their stories, Sarah giggled and said, "Yeah, but what about you, Felix? Did anything happen to you yet?"

He smiled. "Yep! I got my new Buffalo Bill Super Dude Suit!" He opened his jacket and there was a buckskin shirt with foot-long fringe all over it. It had a suede cape attached to the back with a big leather letter "F" on the front.

Six humans and one small dog rolling in the snow with laughter – a momentary happy break. They enjoyed this moment of togetherness with the uncertainty that it might be their last.

74
At Day's End

Gill and Chimayo walked around the lodge again to where the old pickup truck was parked. The rest of the group followed. The sun was starting to appear more in the sky now, and it was apparent that the day would be cold and windy but with a lot of sunshine. This, then, would be good for them, and bad for HE. Since the spotlight weapons would no longer kill the Thingie, Gill figured that HE could now also move around in the daylight. This, however, didn't mean that HE would like it.

As Chimayo started to slide into the driver's seat of the Chevy, he noticed Felix about twenty yards back the way they had come, staring into space. "Ah, Gill? Is this what you told me of in the BrainTalk?"

Gill looked at Felix and then smiled. Yes, Chimayo, and it's called Mind-Speak. We'd better wait on him. Sometime, this is important to..."

Suddenly, Felix came back.

"Hey, guys... y'all are gonna need a few extra things before ya go!"

"First up at bat... Gill take Ima with you. You're gonna need her! I don't know why, but..."

"I understand, Felix. If you say so, I'll take her."

"Second, there was something about a flat tire and gasoline! Chimayo, check your spare tire, will you, please?"

He looked at the old tire behind the cab of the truck, and realized that although it wasn't flat, it was low. "Good call, Cat Warrior! I didn't realize that..."

Felix smiled. "Yeah, I know. I think there's an air pump here at the lodge. You're also gonna need a gas can filled with diesel fuel."

"Why is this, Felix?" Chimayo asked. "My truck does not run on diesel."

"Yeah, I know, again! But... someone is gonna need it, and need it bad! Also, I need a rawhide string or strap for this... damn kazoo thing... that Paulie drew up for me. I can then wear it with my necklace." He showed the scorpion to Chimayo, who gasped.

"Where did you come by this thing, Cat Warrior? This amulet contains... much power! You and I must talk later! I have a story to tell you... tonight, after we all eat our supper!"

"Cool, dude! I'd like that! Three more things, and then you can go! One, buy some extra gloves! Someone is gonna lose theirs, and MAN... is it gonna be cold without them! Also, buy a padded and insulated leather backpack that we can carry Killer in. It'll be way too cold for the pup to be walkin' all of that time!"

"Yipe!" Killer said with that same canine smile.

"This, I will do, Felix," Chimayo also said with a smile. "And the last thing?"

"I saw in my vision a large bag full of melting chocolate! Put the candy in the back of the truck... not the front!"

Chimayo looked at Gill with a smile. "Cat Warrior has much magic, does he not, Gill?"

"Yeah, he's a real hoot alrighty! OK, Chimayo... you go get the diesel and air for the tire, and I'll go get Ima, the Time Stopper. I'll meet you back here in ten minutes!"

While Gill went back to get Ima Rock in his room, Robert, Sarah, Paul and Felix headed toward the restaurant for hot coffee and some lunch. As Gill walked by the restaurant door on his way back to the truck, Robert told him to find out from Chimayo which way they were going to take to The Sleeping Giant, either the lake route by boats or the Montana gravel roads. Gill waved as he left.

The food was excellent, and as promised, the coffee was hot. When Paul took off his jacket, everyone realized that he too had a buckskin shirt on. "Well, I couldn't let Felix be the only one here who looked like an idiot,could I?" Paul's shirt also had the fringe that made this style of shirt so popular in Western lore, but instead of the giant "F" that Felix's shirt had, this one had a picture of a landscape branded into the light brown leather.

"Wow," said Sarah. "That really is quite beautiful, Paul! You could make a fortune out in L.A. selling that kind of stuff."

He smiled back at her. "Well, maybe one day I'll get the chance to see if you're right."

Sarah looked over to Robert. They smiled at each other. "Yeah, Paul. Maybe one day... you will."

Gill and Chimayo were driving very slowly down the small highway. One reason was the road conditions, the other because of Felix's reference to a spare tire. It was only about twenty-five miles to Cody from where they were, but in bad conditions, that could be an hour or two.

They were about half way there, and were climbing a steep slope when they spotted the problem. A new car that appeared to be a Mercedes-Benz was barreling down the slope towards them, and apparently the driver had little or no control over his car. It was swerving back and forth across the median, lights flashing and horn honking.

"Oh, hell," Chimayo whispered as he slammed on his brakes and hit the shoulder on the side of the road.

"BAM!" said the front right tire of the old truck as it hit a hidden rock.

"Right on cue!" Gill laughed as he jumped out of the now-tilted Chevy.

The Mercedes continued on straight toward them, picking up speed as it went.

"What should we do now?" Chimayo yelled.

"Grab my shoulder and hold on tight!" Gill waited until his friend was hanging on... and then pulled out Ima Rock!

Everything except for the two of them stopped.

Chimayo stood there with his mouth open as they both stared around themselves. Birds were frozen in flight. A mound of snow had been falling out of the top of an evergreen tree and had decided to just stay where it was. The Mercedes was stopped in a skid, headed for the drop-off on Chimayo's side of the road, a five-hundred foot drop-off.

"Incredible magic! What will happen if I release my hold on you right now, Gill?" Chimayo asked.

"I'm not sure, but I would guess that you'd become frozen, too! Let's go check out the Benz and see what we can do to help those folks!"

They walked over to the stationary car and saw a man, a woman and their little girl all inside the doomed vehicle.

"As soon as time continues, these folks are as good as dead. We've got to slow this sucker down somehow!" Chimayo panted.

Gill looked at the car. "If we totally stop this vehicle, these people will be slung through the windshield by the sudden stop in motion! We have to slow it down somehow... as you said, but gradually. Come with me and let's get some tree branches!"

They ran over to the roadside and collected limbs off fallen trees as big as they could both carry, linked as they were. They then dragged them over to the car and shoved them under the tires on the front and back of the Benz.

Gill grabbed a good-sized rock from the forest and placed it underneath the tire closest to the cliff's edge with Chimayo holding on to him the entire time. "Maybe that'll help them veer away from that edge! That's about all that we can do for now, and I'm not sure how long this Time Stopper will hold everything in place! Let's get clear, and pray for the best!" Even as they began to back away to their own truck, time started slowly leaking back.

"Aw, hell! Here it comes!"

Gill pocketed the small stone and the world came alive in a squeal of brakes... and sparks from rocks... and flying splinters of wood. The car spun into a one-eighty degree turn when its front wheel hit the rock, and all of the lumber dragging underneath it slowed the car down... bit by bit until it stopped backward two feet from the cliff.

The man got out shaking. The woman got out crying. And the seven-year-old little girl got out, gazing at Gill. She pointed at him and quietly whispered, "Magic!"

Gill put his fingers to his lips. "Shhhhh!"

She nodded at him. "OK, mister. But, thank you."

He smiled back and nodded.

The husband then began to speak, which was a great mistake. "Did you see that? Man, what great driving did I do there? I told you how safe I was driving on these stupid roads, but would you listen to me? NO! Always bitching about my driving! I told you! I am the king of the road! Did you see how I swerved into that pile of brush back there on the side of the road so that it would drag us to a stop? Man! I should drive in the Indie Five-Hundred!"

He then finally noticed Gill and Chimayo standing there. "Hey, Kemo Sabe! Did you and Tonto check out that stunt driving? That's the way the white man does it!"

Chimayo looked at Gill to see how he wanted to handle this situation. Gill patted the young girl on the head, nodded to the lady with a smile and walked back to their truck without a word or glance at the white man.

When they reached the faithful old truck, Gill crawled into the back to get the jack, the spare tire, and tire tool. As he held them out to Chimayo, he quietly said, "I'm sorry."

Chimayo shook his head. "I don't understand, my friend. You just saved three lives, and one of them a small child, who actually knows, somehow, about your... magic! One of the other lives is that of a poor lady who has most likely spent her entire existence in the shadow of this... white man! The third life that you saved was, in my opinion, a large bag of skin... full of absolutely nothing! And yet... you are sorry?"

"Chimayo, I'm not sorry for me... as a person. I'm sorry for an entire race of people, who believe that they can treat another human being poorly... just because the other human being is not like them. If you look up 'wrong' in the dictionary, there will be a picture of that...'white man.' The same way that 'white man' can try to make you feel badly because you are different... that same 'white man' has made me feel badly... because to him I am not different. He thinks that I am the same as he is... but I choose not to be the same as this human being... this... 'white man!' Can you understand this... my friend?"

Chimayo loked into Gill's eyes and read the truth in his words. He simply nodded to Gill and this was enough.

They had begun to change the blown tire when they started hearing the yelling going on at the Mercedes. "Damn foreigners don't know how to make a good car! The damn thing just... locked up on me! I ought to sue their whole damn country! And what are you looking at, dummy!" he said to his wife.

The little girl put down a Garfield doll that she'd been clutching for dear life. She then walked slowly over to where Gill stood next to Chimayo, who was changing the tire. "Mister?" she said with a whimper.

Gill smiled at the child. "Yes, ma'am? Can I help you?"

"Mister, my name is Sally. Can you... help us? I don't think my daddy does very good... 'cept for the talkin'."

"Well, I don't know, darling. Your father seems to..."

"Mister?" the small girl whispered. "My daddy is a chucklehead. If you won't help us..." She looked around the countryside. "There's no one else, mister." She started to cry. "It's cold here! Please?"

Gill smiled at her beautiful face as he held out his hand. "Only if you'll call me Gill, Ms. Sally."

She stopped crying, took his hand and looked into his eyes. "I saw your magic, Gill."

"Yeah, sweetie, I know you did, but let's not tell anyone... OK? Now, let's go see what we can do about this mess your dad got you into!"

As Gill started walking toward the father, Chimayo stopped what he was doing and followed. He didn't want poor little Gill to get into any trouble with the "chucklehead," as the daughter had called him.

He couldn't have been any more wrong. Gill was ready for this "white man."

The father started walking up to Gill as he approached the Benz. "Hey, little guy! If you and that Indian would..."

"PLEASE SHUT UP! If you want any help from us at all, don't say another word! The sound of your voice is like a fingernail on a blackboard... and I will not tolerate it! Now! You got yourself into this situation because you ran out of fuel! Do you hear me? When that happened, you lost all of your power steering and most of your brakes. See the bottom of that cliff there... where all of those pointy rocks are? That's where you, your wife and this fine young daughter should be right now! If not for the small amount of help that my Native American friend and I gave to you..."

"But, I..." the father said.

Without another word, Gill turned away and started walking back to the truck.

"Mister Gill! Please," Sally said. "He'll be quiet!" She looked at her dad with tears in her eyes again. "Won't you... please? Just this one time, daddy? Don't say bad stuff!"

Her Dad looked at her and then at Gill. He nodded but said nothing.

Gill walked back. "Chimayo, check out the gas level in the car while me and daddy here start to drag these branches out of the way. Sir?"

Together, the two men managed to get all of the broken limbs out from under the car. Chimayo came back over. "Dead empty, Gill. Runs on diesel, too."

The father started to say something and Gill looked him right in the face. He said nothing.

Gill told Chimayo to go get the gas can out of the back of the truck. Then he turned to Dad. "Mister, this vehicle is so damn close to going off of that cliff that I'd like to scotch the tires in the back so that it won't roll over when we get the car started again. Will you help me? Please?"

The man nodded again, and started looking for rocks to block the tires. In the meanwhile, Gill and Chimayo got the five gallons of diesel into the empty tank. When everything was all ready, Gill told everyone to stand back while he started the car. Chimayo stood behind it to help keep it from sliding any further.

VAROOM! It kicked right over.

Gill smiled at the father. "Those German folks sure know how to make a fine car... as long as you keep it fed."

Gill slowly pulled the new machine over to the correct lane, and then held the door open for the father as Chimayo did the same for Sally and her mom. As he slid into the car, the father looked into Gill's eyes. "Can I say thank you?"

"I'll tell you what, sir... I'll trade you one 'thank you' to me... for one 'I'm sorry' to your wife and daughter. Deal?"

The man got watery-eyed as he grabbed his family and apologized. "Please forgive me! I almost killed us! I've been such a..."

"Chucklehead?" Sally said with a smile.

Dad laughed. "Yeah baby! I've been a chucklehead! And I'm sorry to you, too, Mr.... ah..."

"Chimayo. Apology accepted. Drive careful... white man!"

Five minutes later, Chimayo and Gill were once again on the road to Cody. The Indian looked at Gill for a moment, and then asked, "So... does this happen to you folks all of the time?"

Gill smiled. "Naw! Sometimes, it gets REALLY hairy!"

They finally made it into the town of Cody, and started their shopping at a sporting goods store. Even though their planned journey was supposed to take only one day into the wilderness, Chimayo bought enough supplies for three days. "You never know when something will go wrong out there, and I'd rather not get stuck unprepared."

This was good enough for Gill. When he asked his guide about the best way to get to where they were eventually going, Chimayo thought for a moment before he spoke. "Gill, normally, I'd say let's take the northern route in through the Montana entrance, but with the bad weather and all, I believe that we'll have to settle on a boat ride across Holter Lake. There's some spots over there where we can set up a base camp, and then we'll hike along the ridgeline to get to where I believe this creature will be headed for. How's your cash supply? It'll cost quite a bit for a tent and all of the gear we're gonna need."

Gill smiled. "My cash supply is just fine, and if we don't stop this Thingie tomorrow, there won't be anything left to spend it on anyway!"

They bought a tent for the base camp, three rifles, shells, survival food, flares, lanterns, snowshoes and cold weather gear of all sorts, including extra gloves for Felix. They bought duffle bags to carry the gear in and Gill found an insulated backpack that would fit Killer just dandy.

They hit the supermarket for chocolate, which Gill needed immediately. He was kind of weak after the event with the Mercedes and it surprised Chimayo how much that candy brought him back to life. While Gill was paying for the chocolate, Chimayo called some of his friends about getting enough boats to ferry six people, a dog and all of that gear across the lake. The friends weren't anxious to do it in this kind of weather, but he explained to them how important it was without going into any details. They agreed. Three boats would be waiting for Chimayo at dawn.

Gill and Chimayo loaded up the supplies into the truck, and Gill almost stuck the chocolate up front where he could get at it but remembered Felix's warning. "Damn!" he thought as he left it in the back of the truck bed. He got into the warm truck and then had Chimayo stop. He jumped out and went into the back again, and pulled out two candy bars. He got back in and smiled. "These'll be gone before they can melt!" Chimayo laughed.

As they were getting ready to leave the beautiful city of Cody, Gill remembered about the rawhide lace that Felix needed for his kazoo.

"Gill, I have something that I wish to give to Felix, and it has a deerskin lace attached to it. OK?"

Gill smiled. "Yeah, Chimayo. I think he'd like that."

The trip back to the lodge was slow and uneventful. Gill even fell asleep for the final part of the journey. While bouncing down the ice-covered road, Gill thought he heard Gwen talking to him.

"Gill, tonight will be the final night for any dream help. We of the Flae will send what we can that we feel will help you. Get to bed early for this, and remember to wake early tomorrow for your journey! The Eating Of The Sun will happen in your early afternoon, so your time is nigh! We will speak again tonight... my human friend."

"OK, Gwen."

"What? Did you just call me Gwen?" Chimayo was smiling.

"Ah, no... that was another friend of mine."

"She must really be something! You were smiling the whole time you were asleep! As a matter of fact, you're still smiling!"

At day's end, the two new friends found themselves back among the warm embrace of the rest of their little troupe of warriors. The smell of a large meal being prepared filled the air, and Chimayo entertained them all for several minutes around the roaring fireplace in the lodge's Great Room, replaying the tale of "Gill and The White Man."

75
The Death Of The Devil

The tale of "Gill and The White Man" had everybody smiling.

So did the smells rolling out of the Teepee's kitchen. It was going to be a good night tonight, no matter what tomorrow might bring. They all gathered in the lodge Great Room... and bundled the new hiking gear into the separate duffle bags.

Gill showed Killer his leather back pack. "How's that look, pal?"

"Woof! Yipe!" Killer said as he crawled into the thing to try it on for size. A perfect fit!

Gill unpacked an entire case of cold weather gloves for Felix and got many a giggle and smile in return.

When Chimayo unwrapped the three rifles, everyone became excited. "Guns, dude! Now you're talkin'!" Felix said with a little dance.

Chimayo held up his hand. "These will do almost nothing to the creature we seek to destroy, but we also have to deal with wolves, mountain lions and grizzly bears. I have my own Winchester in my pack inside of my truck. That leaves these three. Robert, are you familiar with firearms?"

Robert looked over at Gill with a smile on his face. Gill said to Chimayo, "He's probably the best marksman in our bunch. Bar none."

Chimayo nodded his head. "I thought so. Robert, since your extra powers are in healing, not weapons... I feel that one of these should belong to you. Yes?"

Robert smiled as he took the rifle and jacked the chamber to check for a loaded weapon. "Yes," he answered. "I know this weapon well."

Chimayo nodded at Robert as Sarah brushed her hand across his face. "Ohhh, Ert," she said with a grin, "There's a lot about you I've still got to learn, huh?"

Robert looked to Gill again. Neither one of them was grinning. Sometimes, memories can be a terrible thing.

Chimayo added, "Gill, I want you to be able to pull your Time Stopper... what's her name? Erma?"

"Ima! Ima Rock."

"Yeah... Ima. I don't want a rifle to get in your way. I have seen this rock in action, and I believe it will come in handy much more that these rifles will."

"I understand."

"That leaves two. Sarah?"

"Yes, Chimayo?"

"Your power is over machines. This Winchester is just that... a machine. Can you control it?"

Sarah walked over to the new rifle and placed her hand upon it. The rifle jacked its own chamber to check for a loaded weapon. She smiled. "Affirmative."

Everyone, including Robert, looked at her with open mouths in silence for a moment. Finally Robert kissed her. "What a woman!"

Chimayo smiled as he passed her the rifle. "Now, we have one left."

It was funny to watch Felix squirm so much. Everyone there had no doubt that he really wanted one of those rifles. Before anyone else could say anything, though, Paul stepped forward.

"Ah, Chimayo? I really don't know anything at all about guns, and I'd be willing to bet that a Cajun like Felix has done his share of hunting in his day! Right, Felix?"

Felix just nodded at his young friend.

"Therefore, I think it's only fair that Felix should get the last rifle. That also leaves my hands free to draw! OK?"

Chimayo smiled at the young boy, and without saying a word, passed the last Winchester to Felix.

Felix got all misty-eyed as he looked at Paul. "Thanks, pal."

"No problem, dude!"

Everyone laughed.

They eventually all sat around a large table in the restaurant and the food that appeared was amazing. A buffet of epic proportions was consumed with the gusto of condemned criminals eating their last meal. Tom hosted the whole affair with interest in what was going on the following morning.

"So, y'all are headed out to The Sleeping Giant, huh? Shore is desolate up there! Looking for anything in particular?"

Chimayo smiled at his old friend. "Can't say, Tom, and it's probably for the best that you don't know. Just wish us luck."

"Well, if it's luck you need, you come to the right place. Isn't that right, Chimayo?"

"Yeah, Tom, it is! I'd almost forgotten about Mr. Cody's claim to luck. If you would, why not tell all of my friends about it?"

Tom started grinning as he began his tale. "Well gang, old Buffalo Bill himself was a scout in the U.S. Army from 1868 until 1872. In 1872, he was awarded the Congressional Medal of Honor and was always known after that as the favorite scout of the Fifth Cavalry. All of the men in the Cavalry always thought that Bill was lucky. He always took 'em to victory and always kept 'em from gettin' ambushed! All of his own glory also rubbed off on the Fifth Calvary's reputation. Ol' Bill always even thought of himself as being uncanny-like in the luck department. He was only wounded once in the whole time he served in the Army, and it was only a scalp wound. Being at the right place at the right time... that was Buffalo Bill!"

Everyone at the table glanced Robert's way, as they listened to stories of luck being associated with the legendary man believed to once have owned the lucky horseshoe, now owned by Robert.

Felix shook his head. "Isn't it amazing how coincidences always happen at the same time?"

Everyone except Tom snickered at that.

After the fine suppertime had come and gone, everyone adjourned to the Great Room once again. Tom built up the fire in the fireplace, and then excused himself when he realized that these folks needed a little alone time to talk about tomorrow. Gill stood up, said he'd be right back, and ran out to Betsey. When he returned, his hands held six small shot glasses and one large bottle of Tennessee Sour Mash. You couldn't have knocked the smiles off everyone's faces with a sledgehammer.

"I've been saving this for a special occasion, and I guess that all of us saving the world tomorrow falls into that category." He poured full shots for everyone. "To the death of the Devil!"

"TO THE DEATH OF THE DEVIL," they all chimed in as they killed the shots.

Gill sat down and re-filled the glasses, and then began the night's conversation. "You know, while talking to Gwen, I've found out that these creatures have no religious faith what-so-ever... therefore, no gods and no belief in an afterlife. Killing HE won't be an easy chore, for HE has no hope for anything at all after HE's dead. Dying is much more horrible for him than it is for us. But nonetheless, if we are to survive, then die HE must!"

"Dude! Them's pretty words! You ought to have been a poet... or a preacher... or maybe a politician," Felix said with a laugh.

He never saw the magazine until it hit him.

"Dudette! Damn, girl! Do you grow those things or what?"

Sarah smiled. "Chimayo, is that The Sleeping Giant just outside of the lodge here?"

"No, Sarah. That is Cody Peak that you see. We are at the foot of it. The Giant sleeps in the background."

Paul spoke up then. "Gill, why is it that we don't call in the military on this situation? I mean, they did manage to blow up that semi that the Thingie was using for transportation."

Gill smiled. "Yeah, and I personally think that we got lucky on that situation. This creature has been gaining size by consuming its own people, but at the same time... it has been gaining the extra Minus it needs to destroy us... from these same creatures! It must be so full of Minus by now that it's hard for it to even hide because of the glowing! It's main advantage is the fact that it's a shape-shifter. It can't conceal its bulk, but it could take the shape of something large... like a tree or a giant rock formation. But with that much Minus contained inside of it, what do you think would happen to everything around us if the military suddenly hit it with, let's say... a rocket blast?"

Paul shook his head. "I'd guess that there would be NO everything around us anymore! KABOOM?"

"KABOOM," Gill said with a smile. "We got lucky when they missed out on the Thingie. Now, we've got to somehow get rid of it without the KABOOM."

"Can we do that?" Paul asked in a small voice.

Gill looked at the boy with sad eyes. "Honestly, Paul, I don't know. We've got some pretty powerful friends and powerful forces on our side, but I just don't know."

Everyone was silent for a moment.

Then Felix went away.

"Oh hell! What is it now?" Robert asked.

Felix came back with a small smile. "Paul, don't forget your promise of a picture to hang next to your mom's, and don't forget your carving to-morrow! Also, I need you to draw me a speargun... a big one! And spears! Cool, Doodle Dude?"

"Will do!" Paul said with a smile.

"Is that it?" Robert asked. "A landscape and a speargun?"

"No. Guys, remind me tomorrow to take a picture of Betsey's front door with my new camera."

"Why, Felix?" Gill asked.

"Not a clue, dude, but it's important!"

After a moment, Chimayo spoke up. "My friends, I have scheduled for three of my people to have boats ready for us early in the morning. We must be up before the dawn. We will leave by boat on the Holter Lake/ Missouri River shoreline from the Holter Recreation area as the sun rises. The sun will rise tomorrow, too, for that is how my vision has seen it. To-night is a final night of dreams for us all. I will visit you each during your sleep, but I won't come alone. To each of you, I will bring a visitor on this night. I am Sleep Walker... and I shall guide them to you."

"Yipe?"

Chimayo smiled. "Yes, you also, Small Warrior. Yours will be a visitor from The Big Open, The Land Behind The Sky. He will be your guide for all time to come."

Suddenly, everyone had a cold chill pass over them as if they'd almost remembered something but not quite. "Damn! Why can't I remember?" They all thought but said nothing.

Chimayo then turned to Felix. "To you, Cat Warrior... I have a tale... and I have a gift. Which would you have first?"

Felix smiled and then frowned. He looked down at the amber necklace with the scorpion inside, then he looked down at the deadly device that Paul had drawn up for him. He shuddered for a moment at the thought of what this thing meant and then looked back to Chimayo. "The tale, Chimayo. I'll have the tale first."

"Very well, then. Here is the tale of Anakepo and the Desert Warrior!"

"In the past far beyond, there lived a boy named Anakepo. His people lived on an area of the earth where the plains were bordered by the desert. Anakepo grew quickly, with his father teaching him the ways of the buffalo, of the Great Spirit and of the creatures who shared this world with his people. Being on the edge of two worlds, his education covered many creatures that were not well known by the plainsmen alone. One of these was the Desert Warrior, the Scorpion!

"This was a being of great powers, and though it was widely feared by the people of the tribe, Anakepo was taught of its mighty wisdom and bravery. This small warrior had no fear and very few enemies. It had been rumored to have made friends with one of the ancient wiseman of the tribe from long ago, but of this, no one knew for sure.

"There came the day when Anakepo was sent into the wilderness to spend time alone to commune with the Earth Mother and the Great Spirit. He was to live by his own means, with no help from the tribe. He walked for many days and managed poorly. There were roots and small game to be had, but they became few and far between as he approached the desert.

"One night, as he slept, he was awakened to find the Desert Warrior upon his chest! His fright at this sudden appearance dimmed slowly... as the scorpion spoke! 'Hey ya ya, Anakepo! I am sent by the Earth Mother to be your guide in this land of little! Have faith in me, and no harm shall befall you.'

'But what of your deadly sting, Brother Scorpion? How am I not to fear that?'

'My sting does not always contain poison, Anakepo. Sometimes, I can use this spear I contain to bestow my powers to help you in your struggles! This will be my gift to you, if you wish.'

"Anakepo nodded in agreement. He spent that night and many more with his small friend, and was rewarded with knowledge of how to survive, how to prosper in the wild. Water was now easily found. Food was everywhere he looked, now that he knew what to look for. In return, he protected the Desert Warrior from the snake and the roadrunner... each of which would have made a small meal of his new friend.

"There came a day when the mighty mountain lion came upon the trail of Anakepo! This was meat for the cat creature, and its strength was mighty! But as it approached the Indian boy who cowered in fright, the Desert Warrior placed its spear into the chest of its friend! Great and powerful forces were transferred to the boy, and he yelled his war cry as he ran straight on at the surprised cougar! The boy grabbed sticks and stones as he ran, and the rain of attack frightened the cat so much that it retreated into the wild... never to be seen again!

"Anakepo gave out with his victory chant! Mighty indeed was the friendship between these two friends, and upon returning to his tribe, he was dubbed a great warrior and spent the rest of his many years with his people... and with his friend, the Desert Warrior."

"Wow, dude! Good story!" Felix said as he gazed at the scorpion necklace in his hands. Then, he jumped.

"What is it, Cat Warrior?"

"Wow, man! I thought for a second there... I thought I saw it move!"

Chimayo smiled. "Mighty and mysterious indeed are the powers of the Desert Warrior, my friend!"

Sarah had stood up during the story, and she now was standing directly behind Felix! As he stared at the piece of amber, she just couldn't resist.

"BOO!"

Felix fell over the edge of the couch in shock. "Damn, girl! Ya tryin' to scare the Blue Bejesus outta me or what?"

Everyone was rolling in laughter.

It took a few moments for everyone to get back in line. Finally, after they had settled down again, Felix looked to Chimayo.

Chimayo smiled. "The gift?"

Felix didn't speak. He just nodded.

Chimayo slowly removed a deer hide thong from around his own neck.

"This is very old... and contains much power on its own. It is my gift to you, Cat Warrior."

Felix stared with wonder at the buckskin string with two claws woven into the pattern. There was a space between the claws with a clip on it, and onto this, Chimayo locked the object that Felix carried, the object that Felix feared. The large brass kazoo.

"These are the fore claws of the great cougar, taken by my grandfather many, many moons ago. They will help to guide you in the decisions you must make... in the directions you must take. Please accept my gift, Cat Warrior."

As Felix placed his hands on the necklace, a smell of the forest permeated the entire room. Everyone could smell the difference and all watched in awe as Felix slipped the gift around his own neck. Suddenly, fright was no longer a part of Felix. He knew what must be done and he regretted it, but he would do what he must.

"I thank you, my brother. Thank you."

"Now," Chimayo quietly said, "we must all be off to our dreams. How may I walk with you if you don't dream? I will awaken you all early in the morning. VERY early! I wish you all good dreams tonight."

They all slowly rose to their feet, and wandered off to their beds in a trance.

76
Sweet Dreams

Sleep came early to all.

Robert and Sarah lay in each other's arms, and really wanted nothing more than the touch of each other on this evening. They would both look into each other's eyes and smile but almost as if it were an unwritten promise, neither said a word to the other. They relished in just the closeness of another soul sharing this life, this night with themselves. Robert had placed his lucky horseshoe on the bedside table; Sarah had the Catflower In Ice beneath her pillow. Before long, they had both drifted off into a pleasant sleep.

Gill had closed the door to his room and was about to get into bed when he heard a scratch and a whimper at his door. He walked over to open it, and there was Killer just looking at him. "Hey, partner! You want to come in?"

The small dog slowly walked into the room and stopped at the foot of his bed. It turned around and looked at Gill, and whimpered again. "What's the matter, buddy? Are you lonely? I figured you were staying with Felix. Would you like to sleep in here tonight with me?"

"Woof," the small animal almost whispered. Gill picked up Killer off of the floor and placed him on the bed. He turned off the lights and got underneath the covers. Killer wiggled his way beneath the top blanket so he was right up against Gill, his friend. Gill was looking at the dog, who was acting rather strange, as the dog raised itself up to Gill's face, and gently gave him a loving lick with his tiny tongue. As Gill fell asleep, he could have almost sworn that the small dog was crying.

Paul had sat down on the chair in his room and placed his sketchbook on the table next to it. He first drew up a large version of a double-barreled speargun lying on the floor with extra spears for Felix. As he finished, he glanced down to see them appear. It was quite a weapon, but Paul wasn't sure how much good they'd do against HE. Still, if Felix wanted them... Then, he began to sketch a landscape of Cody Peak, right outside of the lodge. He had promised Tom the Caretaker that he would try. It was quite a beautiful sketch in black and white, with the forests alive with animals and birds with the snow blowing gently around the base of the mountain, and Paul allowed this picture to stay on the paper. Then, as he studied it, he knew what it needed. He went over to his backpack and removed the carving of the old man. Instantly, colors swirled around him filling the air. He raised his hand into space, and scooped up a handful of the beauty, and cast it onto the sketch. Lo and behold, it became a thing of magic. Pleased with his work, he yawned as he made it over as far as the bed. With the lights still on and only a blanket draped over himself, he fell into a deep sleep.

Felix had gone to his room to throw a few things into his knapsack that he figured he would need tomorrow. Killer had followed him in as usual, but the pup was feeling down for some reason, and Felix let him out again when the dog scratched at the door. "Hmmm, I hope he's alright," Felix thought to himself. He glanced down to his chest where two necklaces hung. They were both a thing of beauty in their own way, but the power coming off of them made his skin tingle. He set out his camera for the trip tomorrow, and then glanced over at the beautiful rifle leaning against his bed. He knew in his heart that Paul would have been just fine with that rifle, but the boy had realized just how much that Felix had yearned to own it. Quite a kid, that Paul. Felix hoped that Paul, at least, would come out of tomorrow unhurt. Felix had a feeling what he was going to have to do to himself tomorrow, and even if he survived the ordeal, the hurt was going to last him a lifetime. He looked at himself in the mirror. "OK, Dude. We'll do what we have to do, no matter the cost. Now, let's get you to bed." He lay down beneath the warm covers, tossed and turned for about five seconds, and then was fast asleep.

Chimayo went to a room that had been provided for his use by Gill. He greatly admired this small white man and many had been the lessons learned by Chimayo in the brief time he had been allowed to spend with his strange new friends. Love, honor, humor and sacrifice, these were as common as table salt to this group of warriors, and they didn't even realize that most of the rest of the world wasn't really like that. Greed, distrust and envy were words that this group of friends had no knowledge of. Surely, the Great Spirit smiled down on this band of companions, even though they were white. As was his talent, Chimayo lay down on his bed and waited. He was sure everyone had retired for the evening, but he waited until he could feel the dreams of all around him, and then he began his walk.

Robert and Sarah were sitting next to each other on the top of a breezy hillside when they heard him speak.

"I just can't seem to get you two separated, can I? Not even in your sleep! Haha!"

They turned around to see who had addressed them, and there was the gentleman they knew as Gin, walking up the hill with Chimayo at his side. Flowers rose from the ground and came into bloom everywhere that Gin stepped, and Chimayo seemed to have a glow around him that brought with it the smell of the forest. The two newcomers sat down beside Robert and Sarah and looked out across the earth.

"Quite a beautiful world that you have here, children. You should be very proud of it," Gin said with a smile. "I guess that tomorrow will decide whether or not you get to keep it."

Robert looked at the Fla with a solemn face. "Gin, if we don't get to keep this earth, it sure as hell won't be because we didn't try! By this time tomorrow, HE will be gone... or we will be gone. There won't be a middle ground on this."

"I'm glad that you realize this, Robert human. A victory for HE tomorrow will be a loss for all life... on many worlds. Sarah, tomorrow... keep the Catflower In Ice within your grasp at all times. Even if you have fallen, I can work my small magic through you... as long as you hold onto that object. Understand?"

"Yes, Gin. I will lose my arm and my soul before I lose that object tomorrow. Do we... ah, do we really have a chance... of winning?"

Gin smiled at Chimayo then turned back to the two lovers. "Ah, my children... the race is never over until it has been run! Or... as humans sometimes say... a song is sung by a large fat woman!"

Sarah and Robert laughed quietly at this attempted humor. "Thank you and the Flae for all you've given us," Robert said. "Always."

"It's been our pleasure, my brave friend. Keep Sarah close tomorrow. Remember that you are her Builder... and that you are now not just a warrior... but a healer. Farewell, my friends."

Gin faded away, but Chimayo stayed on. "Robert," he said with a smile, "before I leave, there's someone that I'd like to introduce you to... if you don't mind."

Robert nodded to Chimayo as he put his arm around Sarah. Then, his mouth came open as he saw who was climbing the hillside! Sarah whispered, "Oh, my God! Is that... is that... ?"

"My friends, I have someone who'd like to meet you. This is another of my friends... named Pahaska. Please say hello to William F. Cody."

Robert stood up, and his hand extended forward to grasp the handshake of a legend – Buffalo Bill. He still wore his buckskins, his turned hat with the same long hair and silver beard that Robert remembered from the pictures in history books and at the lodge. Robert looked into his eyes and managed to say, "Ahh... ahh... ahhh... !"

Cody laughed and looked over at Chimayo. "Got quite a way with the English language, don't he, pard? Ol' Bill Hickock usta talk like that when we were on stage together! Hahaha! I was always good at the gab, myself!"

Robert finally pulled himself together. "An honor to meet you, sir!"

Buffalo Bill smiled. "The pleasure's all mine, pard! I been told what's up with y'all for tomorrow and just wanted you to know that you got lots a folks rootin' for ya!"

Robert smiled back. "Well, Bill, we'll do our damnest! Hope we make you proud! By the way, I've got something that I believe might..."

"My lucky horseshoe! Yep, Chimayo told me that you found that critter! Always brought me luck! Hope it'll do the same for you, Bob! Well, we're not gonna disturb y'all's peace and quiet here any longer, and I know if I had a beautiful lady like this sittin' on a hillside with me, I wouldn't want no old geezer a meesin' me up! I guess I just wanted to... wish you luck... son. Lotsa luck!"

"Thanks, Bill." Robert said. As he watched, Bill faded away, just as Gin had. Then, Chimayo began to fade also, but as he left, he said, "Early in the morning, my friends! Early in the morn..."

Gill opened his eyes and wasn't really sure that he'd even gotten any sleep at all. He was still in his room at the lodge, lying on the bed but something was different. He looked around the room, trying to pinpoint just what it was that was out of place, but he couldn't see the entire room because of the low lighting and the tree.

"It's about time that you got here! The chicken's getting cold!" Gwen said with a smile as she spread the blanket on the grass at the foot of the tree.

"I hope you like my potato salad. We don't have potatoes where I come from, so I had to improvise! Chimayo, bring those chilled bottles of wine from the stream."

Chimayo walked over to the stream that ran by the foot of Gill's bed and reached down to grab two bottles of white wine. "Well?" he asked. "Are you gonna get up, or do I have to eat all of this chicken by myself?" he said with a smile.

Gill smiled and shook his head. "Curiouser and curiouser!"

"Alice In Wonderland!" Gwen said with a squeal. "I love that book!"

Gill got up from the bed, and then blushed as he realized he still had his pajamas on. He closed his eyes, and just like that, he was wearing a long black robe made of silk. "Man, I wish I could do that in real life!"

He sat down next to Gwen, who was just as beautiful as he remembered.

She piled him up a plate with fried chicken, potato salad, cheeses, and homemade french bread. Chimayo poured the wine and passed it around.

"I'm not sure if I'm hungry," Gill said. "Chimayo, didn't we just eat?"

"In dreams, Gill, you're always hungry! Dig in!"

As they sat there filling their faces, the bedroom faded out and the forest faded in. Gwen looked at Gill and said, "Gill, I just wanted you to know how proud we of the Flae all are at what you all do tomorrow and what you and Robert have done in the past. We will be with you in mind and spirit tomorrow. Whether you win or lose, this may be my last chance to be with you, person-to-person, so I hope you don't mind."

"The honor is all mine, Gwen."

"There are several things that you should know about tomorrow. Remember that the Time Stopper in your possession will no longer stop HE, but it will slow him down! This could be important. Also, remember that this rock stops time for everyone, even your friends, unless you are touching! In the final battle, touching each other may link your individual powers as one. This combined power will be greater! This, too, is important! Please try to remember!" she said as she sat down her empty plate.

"I will remember it, and I will remember you, also. Always."

She bent over to kiss him upon his cheek. "Thank you for letting me be, if only for just a while, human. And now..." she said as she started to fade out, "I must go."

"Wait!" he cried out.

She faded back in. "What is it, Gill?" she asked with a whisper.

"I just wanted you know... you make damn good potato salad!"

Her laughter was like the tinkling of bells as she faded away.

Gill found himself back in his bed, and Chimayo was standing there also but fading out as he said, "Early in the morning, my friend! Early in the morn..."

Paul had thought that he'd gone to sleep, but figured that he must have just dreamed that he went to sleep. Before he knew it, he was standing in the hallway downstairs in the lodge in front of the painting that his mother had done so many years ago, the beautiful painting of the meadow outside of the lodge. It was so lifelike. As a matter of fact, he could see two people in the painting now that he'd never noticed before. One of them was Chimayo. The other was a beautiful lady, but he couldn't see her face. Then, as he watched, he realized that the figures were moving. They were slowly walking across the meadow and headed toward the lodge. As he stood there watching them approach, he heard the front door open next to the Great Room and heard the footsteps of two people coming in his direction. They entered the hallway, and he saw that it was Chimayo, along with a beautiful faceless woman.

"Mom!"

Even without a face, he could feel her smile.

"Oh, God, Mom! I miss you so much!"

"I miss you, too, my son! My friend Chimayo has brought me here to spend a little time with you before your struggle tomorrow. I hope you don't mind the company."

Paul rubbed his tear-stained eyes as he shook his head. "No, Mom, I don't mind. I don't mind at all."

Paul smiled at Chimayo and saw that he carried a package with him that was wrapped tightly in brown paper. Chimayo smiled and shook his head. "Not yet, young Paul. First, listen to your mother. Listen to Elizabeth."

Paul was now openly crying as his mom placed her hands on his shoulder. "Son, tomorrow when you confront this... creature... remember that your living art can become a distraction to the beast, not just a weapon! Give it something to take its mind off of the destruction it plans to reap and, thereby, give your friends a chance to do their battle."

"I'll remember, Mom."

"Also, watch the camera! Ideas can come to you from strange places when you least expect them and could turn the tide of life or death!"

"I don't understand, Mom."

"I know, my son... but hopefully, you will in time. I wish you... the very best... always."

Paul smiled. "If I had a wish... it would be to see your face... just one more time."

Chimayo smiled as he slowly unwrapped the brown paper-covered package. Inside were two things: Paul's landscape, fully framed and his sketchbook. Chimayo gently hung the landscape on the wall next to his mom's painting. The magical colors on the sketch made the birds fly, the animals move, the wind blow.

"It is truly beautiful, my son!"

Paul blushed and then Chimayo handed him the sketchbook and a pencil. He looked at Paul and said, "Fulfill your own wish."

Paul stood there open-mouthed as he realized what Chimayo meant. He opened the book to a blank page and began to sketch. It was a drawing of a beautiful lady, graceful and tall, with blond hair and a slightly turned up nose. A smattering of freckles rested on her cheek, and a pair of laughing green eyes sparkled across the page. When he was finished, he heard a voice quietly say, "Well, son, it looks just like me!"

He looked up and there she was. His mom, His WHOLE Mom. They embraced as if they hadn't seen each other in years, which they hadn't. "God, Mom! You're beautiful!"

"In your eyes, my son... in your eyes. And now... I must go. I wish you the very best... always. I love you, Paul."

"I love you, too... Mom."

She faded away into the shadows, and Paul smiled. "Thank you, Chimayo. I can never repay you for this."

Chimayo smiled. "Win tomorrow, Paul. Win... and that will be re-payment enough!"

Paul nodded and Chimayo started to fade out also. But as he did, Paul heard him say, "Early in the morning, my friend! Early in the morn..."

Felix woke up in the dark. Nothing could be seen, nothing could be heard. Even as he screamed, he realized that no sound came out. It was as if he wasn't. As if he didn't exist. He could feel himself move, but there were no arms, no legs, no heart to register anything. There was a sense of not being.

And then a sound.

Far away a sound was calling to him.

The sound of a flute.

"Shadow!"

He began to run. He couldn't tell if he was making progress because of the darkness, but there seemed to be a lighter patch up ahead. He ran and ran and then fell. He had tripped over something, but didn't know what. He was about to scream again as he lay there when he heard a voice.

"Here, Felix. Take my hand."

He reached out to grab the hand as a drowning man would a piece of wood. Chimayo came into view. He grasped Felix's hand and there was light. Chimayo pulled him to his feet, and they started off in the direction of the flute music. Felix walked with him for either a minute or a year, he couldn't tell which. And then...

"Welcome, Cat Warrior. Welcome, once again." It was Whistle Cat who spoke, and he was curled up at the feet of Shadow Of The Moon, who played upon the flute. She looked at Felix as she played but did not stop her song. He sat down at her feet next to the large cat and listened.

Chimayo waved his hands, and the trees appeared around them. He raised his arms, and the moon shone down upon the glen in which they sat. He raised his eyes, and the night birds flew. He raised his voice in song, and the stars came out to light up the night sky.

"Wow, dude! Good trick!" Felix said as the music came to an end. Shadow smiled and placed her hands upon his.

"Cat Warrior," she whispered, "glad is my heart to see you once again."

"Ditto," he said with a smile. "Man, it's great to see you, Shadow... but..."

"But what, Felix?" she asked.

"What was the nothing that I found myself in at the beginning of this journey... this dream?"

"If the fates allow... tomorrow... that will be the place that you send the Evil Thingie to. That is the Nothing... the Un. It is where you are if you never were."

"I'm not sure I understand, Shadow."

Shadow looked to Chimayo. "Dream Walker?"

Chimayo sat down next to Felix. "Felix, I must now give to you a portion of a conversation that Gill had many days ago with Gwen. Gill has shared this with you in the MindSpeak, but sometimes, the mind blots out what it doesn't want to accept. Will you allow Shadow and I to share this with you now?"

Felix held her hand tightly. "Shadow... I'm... I'm afraid."

"I know, my love, but it is better to confront this in the light... than to battle in darkness. Please?"

Felix looked into her eyes and then looked at Chimayo. He nodded. "OK, then. Let's do it."

Chimayo closed his eyes as did Shadow. Suddenly, Felix could hear the small voice that the Flae had when they weren't in human form.

"This is both a powerful and terrible gift that he has! It can both change and/or destroy reality... or matter. In the case of your battle with the Evil Thingies, one mighty sound from his infuriated voice disrupted the entire structure of one of those vile creatures and caused it to not be. Understand this, because it is VERY important... not only was the Evil Thingie not there then to kill you all, Gill, ah... how can I put this... IT WAS NEVER THERE! Not just dead! Erased! This is... unheard of... and must be studied."

Felix lowered his head. "How? How can someone like me be responsible for changing or destroying reality?"

Shadow smiled. "I have much faith in your actions, Cat Warrior! But know this, the full force of that anger must be channeled! Otherwise, everything could be affected!"

Chimayo stood. "This, Felix, is the reason for the device that you carry. If you project your power into the large end, the small end will broadcast your power in a fine line wave length like a laser of the mind!"

Felix looked at Shadow and Chimayo. "I've got to be truthful here, folks. I'm really scared of this... power! I have so little control over it! But, you two... I trust. So... if I'm called upon to do this, I'll try my best to do it as good as I can. Death by kazoo?"

They smiled at him.

"But honestly, me having this power, in my opinion, it's kinda like givin' a monkey a hand grenade!"

Even Whistle Cat laughed at that!

Shadow stood and took Felix with her. She gave him a long hug and an even longer kiss. "I must go now, Cat Warrior, but, I wait for you. Come back to me... soon?"

"If it is my destiny to survive this confrontation, Shadow, I will return. Whistle Cat?"

"Yes, Warrior?"

"You take good care of her... ya hear me, dude?"

"As you wish, Warrior. As you wish."

She placed her hand upon his cheek and then faded away. Felix watched Cat Warrior also fade away, but just for a moment his grin stayed there.

Felix shook his head. "Curiouser and curiouser."

Chimayo placed his hand on the shoulder of Felix. "I, too. must go now, dude!"

Felix smiled. "Well, I reckon I'll see ya sometime tomorrow, then!"

Chimayo smiled as he faded out. "Early in the morning, my friend! Early in the morn..."

Killer was home. He heard the Lois machine. He could smell the many places he had hidden bacon around the house. He knew this place well, and tried to help his human run it. He loved his Gill human so much. Gill human had saved him from the black prison of plastic and had showed him his new home. Killer loved his home.

He jumped up onto his favorite couch next to the other dog.

Other dog was very small, even smaller than Killer. And other dog smelled clean. Too clean. He did not smell like dog at all.

"Hello, Killer," other dog said. "It's good to see you. Yes, I can speak. I read what you think, Killer, so you need not try to talk. I'll hear you, anyway. I am your... I guess you'd call it... guide dog!"

Killer didn't understand.

"I know it's hard to understand, but the God of the Dogs has sent me to help you."

Chimayo came into the room from the kitchen eating a sandwich. "I let him in, Killer."

Killer sniffed Chimayo and smelled friend. Killer sniffed sandwich and smelled bologna and cheese.

Chimayo gave half of his sandwich to Killer.

"In dreams, Killer, I can hear you, too."

Other dog sat close to Killer. "Killer, tomorrow, humans go on dangerous quest. You have seen this in dream. You know what must happen. You must not be a sad Killer. This will make humans sad, also. And... sad humans make mistakes. If humans make mistakes, Bigger-Than-Tree will hurt humans. You must be brave for the Gill human. Can you do this, Killer?"

Killer thought he could do this.

"Good," other dog said. "I give you the gift tonight of the MIGHTY BITE. It is bigger that the bite, and may hurt Bigger-Than-Tree! May save Gill human. Will you accept this gift?"

"Yipe!"

"Good dog! Good dog! Other dog must go now, but I will be with you as guide dog. God of the Dogs says you are a good dog! Remember this! Remember the MIGHTY BITE. Much luck to you and your humans, Killer. I will be with you."

Other dog faded away.

Chimayo patted Killer on the head. I must go, too, Killer. Anything you need before I go?"

"More bologna?"

Chimayo laughed! "You got it, pooch!" He put three whole slices on the couch for Killer. Then, he slowly faded.

"Early in the morning, my friend! Early in the morn..."

77
Early In The Morn

Early in the morning, Chimayo woke up everyone.

"Rise and shine! Rise and shine!" he said as he went down the hallway knocking on doors. "It's five a.m.!" We need to be leaving in the next half hour. Grab some coffee and a cinnamon bun and let's go to war!"

Felix stuck his head out of the door with his shaggy blue mane of hair flying in all directions. "I'll be risin'... but I won't be shinin'!"

Soon, all of the sleepy heads were piling into the restaurant in search of strong coffee. The only one who seemed to be in a good mood was Killer. Chimayo smiled at the bunch as he said, "Gang, we've got a drive ahead of us to get to the Recreation Area at Holter Lake. We'll take Betsey and leave my truck here. That way, you can grab a few more winks of shut-eye before we get to where the boats are waiting."

They all grabbed their gear, large mugs of hot coffee and sweet rolls that Tom had put together for them, said goodbye to the caretaker, and headed out the door to the waiting bus. Paul had to double-check that he'd brought his carving, and in the process, he realized that his landscape was missing from his sketchbook. In its place was a sketch of a beautiful lady, graceful and tall, with blond hair and a slightly turned up nose. A smattering of freckles rested on her cheek complemented by a pair of laughing green eyes.

"Wow!" Paul said as he took off at a run to the hallway where his mom's picture hung. There, next to her painting, was an incredible sketch, framed and hanging. The magical colors on the sketch seemed to make the birds fly, the animals move, the wind to blow.

"It's my dream," he whispered.

"It truly is a fine thing," said Chimayo, suddenly standing right behind him.

"Oh, my God!" said Tom, who appeared in the hallway. "You did this, son?"

"Yes sir... last night, I guess!"

"Yur Mama would be so proud, kid!"

"She is, sir... she is."

Felix ran out to the bus with his knapsack, unloaded it onto his bunk, and then grabbed his camera and ran back outside. He was snapping a picture of Betsey's door when Paul and Chimayo walked up.

"Do you know why, yet?" Paul asked. "Why the picture of the door?"

"Not a clue, little buddy. But take my word, we'll need it!"

Even though they'd all been anxious to crawl back into Betsey's bunks when they'd first been awakened, everyone was wide awake by the time they pulled out of the Teepee Lodge. Robert drove, with Sarah sitting up front with him.

"Robert, did we really both see Buffalo Bill last night?"

"It's seems so, Sarah. He was quite a fellow, wasn't he?"

"Yeah, he was. Looked good, too... for someone who's been... gone for so long!"

Chimayo came to the front of the bus to give Robert directions. While he was there, Robert noticed that he was favoring the arm that had been hurt in the dreams of HE. The bruising had not gone down, and if anything, it appeared to be increasing. Robert came to an intersection and stopped Betsey on the ice-covered road.

"Is anything wrong?" Chimayo asked.

"Yes, my friend... but if you'll trust me, I think that I can fix it."

Chimayo looked at him with a question is his eyes but nodded his approval. Robert grasped the necklace he had received from little Olivia. It seemed like a year ago when that had happened. As he began to glow with a pale red color, he grasped the shoulder of Chimayo. The Indian winced for a second and then began to smile. The glow grew brighter and brighter until it faded out completely. Chimayo raised his arm and felt no pain. He gazed at his arm and the bruising was gone.

Felix started applauding. "Doctor Bob, folks! Let's hear it for Doctor Bob!" As soon as he said it, he ducked but nothing happened. "What? No magazine?"

Sarah just smiled at Felix and then realized that Robert was looking kind of funny. "Sarah, hand me that horseshoe, will ya? I'm kinda drained!"

As she picked it up and passed it to Robert, there was a moment when they both touched it and a rainbow of colors surrounded them both. Robert had a goofy grin on his face as the strength quickly returned to his body.

"Wow!" Felix whispered. "I took some stuff in New Orleans one time that did that to me!"

Later on, he would swear that the magazine was traveling at the speed of light.

Paul was back at his bunk, checking on the box he'd made to hold his chalks, when Felix came back. He handed Paul his camera.

"Here! You need to carry this for me." The screen on the camera showed a picture of Paul and Felix dancing in the snow together.

"Ah... why, Felix?"

"Don't know, dude! I just know that you need to hold onto it for me. Maybe you'll need to take a picture of me soon! We'll see."

"OK, Felix. Whatever!"

When they finally pulled into the Recreation Area at Holter Lake, there were three pickup trucks with trailers parked there. Three men were waiting beside them and three boats were already unloaded into the water. Everyone grabbed their gear, some extra food and water, rifles and the speargun. Gill put Betsey on alert, and then they walked down to the lakeside with little Killer trailing behind.

Felix noticed that all of the men were Native Americans. Two had short hair and were dressed in down-filled jackets and insulated pants with wool pull-down hats over their heads. The third one was all Indian. He had long hair, braided on the sides of his head. Two eagle feathers hung from the top of the braids. He wore a fringed buckskin shirt and buckskin pants and had a buffalo robe on over the top of the whole outfit. Felix smiled big at that.

"Now that's what I'm talkin' about!" Felix said with a smile.

Chimayo brought everyone forward to meet the three men.

He pointed at the first of the two short-haired men. "People, these are my friends... this one is Tulla!"

Everyone said hello to Tulla.

The second short-haired fellow stepped forward. "Hi. My name is Esante!"

Everyone greeted Esante and then Felix stepped forward. He grabbed the long-haired third guy's hand and shook it like a pump handle. "Cool outfit, dude! My name is Felix!"

The man smiled at Felix. "Glad to meet you, Felix"

Felix looked at the man and then back at at Chimayo with a question in his eyes. Finally, Felix said, "Tulla, Esante, and your name is... ?"

Chimayo laughed. He looked at the third man and said, "Felix is expecting your name to be Two Feathers or Runs-With-The-Wind... or something like that!"

The third guy smiled, and then grabbed Felix's hand again. As he shook it, he said, "Hi, there! My name is Larry!"

Felix stood there, jaw dropped. Finally, he said, "Naw... really! What's your name?"

The guy smiled, and told Felix, "Really. My pop was Shoshone, but my mam was Cajun! My name is Larry!"

At first, Felix looked disappointed, but then he realized what the man had said.

"Cajun? Where was yo' mama from?"

"Mam was a Baton Rouge girl!"

"Brother!" Felix said as he hugged Larry. "I be from Lafeyette!"

Gill and Chimayo divided up the gear into three portions and stowed in all in the boats. The snow had stopped and the sun was out in full, but the temperature was still in the single digits and the cold wind was whipping across the water.

Gill and Chimayo got into the front boat with Tulla. They were followed by Felix, Paul and Larry in the middle. Esante brought up the rear with Sarah and Robert snuggled up together on one seat. The boats cranked up their engines, pushed off from the frozen shore and began the long trip across Holter Lake. Parts of it were now frozen solid, and the drivers had to alter their course from time to time.

Everything was going great until Esante's engine started to cough. The other two boats were pulling farther and farther away from the last boat and most likely couldn't hear anyone but themselves. The old Mercury engine sputtered two or three more times and then died. Esante cranked and cranked on the pull rope, but with no success, Finally, he gave up and just sat down.

"Looks like we'll just have to wait until they've noticed we're absent, and they'll come back for us!"

"Robert scowled. "We don't have a lot of extra time to play with here. Does it do this often?"

"Naw... this is something new, I believe. Probably the cold or something."

Sarah looked at Robert... who nodded.

"Esante, is it OK if she messes with it?"

He smiled. "You're crazy... or you're kidding, right?"

Sarah replied, "No, I'm usually pretty good with machines." She first took off her gloves and put her hand on the side of the hull. Esante was looking at her like she was one crazy white woman.

She smiled as she looked at Robert. "Ert, there was a little water in the gas tank, and now it's frozen in the fuel line. With a little luck," she smiled at him as she said this, "it will pass through the line... and then I can start it from here."

Esante looked at them both as if they were now two crazy white people. Then he started laughing as the large white man withdrew an old horseshoe from his coat pocket for luck. He watched with a smile as these two joined hands, and the girl once again placed her hand on the boat's hull. "White people and their crazy drugs! That must be what this was!"

VAROOM!

"We can go now," Sarah said with a grin to their boatman with the wide-open mouth.

Esante would never talk out loud about crazy white folks again.

They quickly caught up with the other two boats. Esante was amazed. Not only was the motor running again, but it was running better than it had when it was new, years and years ago. "Lady, I need to get you to look at my truck when we get back!"

"If I get back, I'd be glad to look at your truck, Esante."

Esante didn't answer back. Something about the way she had put that led him to believe that these folks considered this to be a one-way trip. He'd been called up to drive a boat and set up a base camp. The business of crazy white folks was the business of crazy white folks, he thought. One way or another, it wouldn't affect him.

Or would it?

HE felt the calling of The One Place. "Hide in daytime, but soon... smash, blast trees out of way. Go to One Place. Eating Of The Sun would happen today."

The Minus is powerful within him now. HE was giant.

HE was no longer needed to appear human. HE became black, like shadows. Like tar. He kept human shape but no features as it was easier to walk on two legs instead of many in the forest. HE was as tall as the trees so he killed them as he trekked along. "Got to get to One Place. Must blast many tree."

HE could feel "Humans who kill Thingies" nearby.

HE could feel that the humans had power from the CALLING, but HE was not worried.

"Must continue to feed. Feed much because I am giant! Deer creature hard to catch! Fast! Bear creature slow... try bite me. Ha ha! I bite bear creature! I bite moose creature, too. Much feed! Wish I had hotdog... like beach! Giant hotdog!"

The plan was for HE not use the Minus just yet. HE would save that for One Place after making a giant hole in One Place. HE would whistle loud, feed Minus to the earth. Then Eat the Sun.

Absorbing other Thingies and Minus would open the door for more of his people to cross. Many more, which would mean "No more evil sun! No more evil sun!"

They all unloaded the boats and the three boatmen began to set up a couple of tents and build a large campfire. Gill started to gather up the backpacks, rifles and supplies that the six and a half of them would need. Everyone got bundled up in their warmest clothing, including the buckskin Super Dude and Chalk Boy costumes. They grabbed a final cup of hot coffee from the thermos that Tom had packed for them. Gill and Killer settled for hot chocolate.

MAX called Sarah on her phone. "Sarah, I still have no location on the Evil Thingie!"

"That's OK, MAX. We think we might know where it's going. I'm glad you called, though. In case anything happens..."

"I know Sarah, I know. I, too, have been honored to know you. Please return safely! Even though you are only human, I care for you... a lot. And tell Felix that Lois sends her best wishes!"

"I heard that!" Felix said.

"Goodbye, MAX. I hope I'll see you again... one day soon."

Soon, there was no more putting off the inevitable. The journey had to begin. Chimayo instructed his tribal friends to wait at the camp for them to return. "We should be back here before dark. If we are not, I want you to pack up the gear, go back across the lake, get into your trucks... and go home."

"GO HOME?" Larry asked. "Chimayo, are you crazy? If we go home, you folks will die!"

"My brother, if we do not return before dusk... it will be too late for you to save us! Go home... and pray to the Great Spirit for a safe journey... for all of our souls. Yours included!"

The three friends looked at Chimayo with frowns all around. "Is it that serious, my brother?"

"The End-Of-All-Things could start today, Tulla. If you have wishes owed to you by the Gods, today will be the day to use them. And now, I bid you all... farewell! If I fail to return, tell my people that they are in my heart. Wait for us until dark. Come on, folks! Let's get this over with!"

Killer jumped into his backpack carried by Gill. Felix packed up the speargun and extra spears in his knapsack. Everyone grabbed their gear and rifles, and off they started.

Their world would never be the same.

78
Apoc-Eclipse!

The trek through the snow was tough. The wind had blown much of the crisp whiteness into six-foot drifts, and the crew never knew when their next step would lead them into a hidden hole or obstacle. The sun was out, and now the top of the snow was starting to get a crust of ice upon it. This made the downhill treks even worse.

Chimayo finally called for a quick break for everyone to catch their breaths. The fog coming from the mouth of each of them quickly fell away in the intense cold. They passed around a thermos of hot coffee, and before it even had a chance to chill, it was gone.

"Damn, that was good!" Robert said with a shiver.

Chimayo looked around at the mountainside. "Well, we've come about a third of the way to the first location. Another couple of hours should put us right on top of where I'm hoping HE will be."

Felix popped off with, "Where I'm hoping HE will be is back in his own dimension! I guess we can't just... talk him into that, can we?"

Chimayo smiled at the giant man. "Felix, remember... I was in his dream. I know what that bastard wants to do to us, our people... and our planet. Going back home is not on his agenda."

"Yeah, I was afraid of that."

Paul, who had been awful quiet for a while now, asked a question of everyone. "Hey... guys? When I did that... MindSpeak thing with Gill that time, I was shown just about all that you guys have gone through before I ever got here."

Gill smiled at the kid. "What the problem, Paul?"

"Well, as I recall... when you guys were fighting off the smaller versions of these Evil Thingies, a lot of their destructive power came from that whistle thing that they have. Right?"

Everyone nodded.

"Well then, that most likely means that HE will use that power to breach Earth's mantle... to release the catastrophe HE's looking for. Right?"

Felix huffed his breath. "Yeah, dude. So what? Does this train of thought of yours have a final destination or not?"

Paul looked shyly at the group as he added, "Well, when Gill was showing me the battle in California, the sound that these Whistlers made was almost enough to make your ears bleed. Right?"

Gill looked shocked. "Oh, my God! The kid's right! If a six-foot Whistler can make your ears bleed..."

Paul nodded. "What can a sixty-foot Whistler sound like?"

Everybody looked as though the air had been let out of them. HE could kill them all with just a brief burst of the power contained in that Whistle unless...

Gill jumped up from where he'd sat down in the snow. "Paul? Did you bring your sketchbook with you?"

"No, Gill. It's too moist out here for that, but I've got my chalk!"

"Ear plugs, Paul, my boy! Ear plugs for everyone... including Killer! And when you concentrate of solidifying the drawings of them, concentrate on making them totally soundproof! Good work, my lad! Good work!"

While they all sat there, Paul whipped out his faithful chalk, found himself a good piece of open air and drew up a set of ear plugs for each of them, including Killer. When placed into the ear canal, not one peep could be heard from anyone or anything.

Robert smiled. "Man, Paul! These would be great for when I get married!"

"What did you say?" Sarah said with a smile.

Felix smiled as he said, "Uh... oh!"

Robert jumped up! "Time to go, gang!"

The journey was a taxing one on the energies of the group of friends and twice more in the course of this trek, their possible final excursion together, they were obliged to call a halt to catch their breaths and replenish their strengths. Gill, who was packing chocolate by the pound, passed around a supply of the sugar-filled stuff as he indulged himself. Gill smiled at Felix as they were on one of these brief stops. "Felix, you appear to be smiling at all of this now, as if you didn't have a worry in the world! Would you care to share your thoughts with those of us who are scared to death?"

Felix looked at his friends with that goofy smile of his. He looked up into the sky at the bright sun overhead and chuckled. Finally, he looked back at them all and quietly answered, "I tend to pretend."

Gill nodded in total understanding. "'Nuff said, old friend." Gill took a moment to give Killer a sip of water and a small snack while the pup was all curled up in its snug backpack. It's small tongue gave Gill a lick of thanks and then popped back into the warmth of the leather enclosure.

"Another half hour or so, and we'll be at the spot I was talking about,"

Chimayo announced as he stood back up. "How much time do we have before the eclipse?"

Gill and Robert both checked their watches. "About an hour," Robert said, "if it's on schedule."

"Let's do this, then," Chimayo answered back.

As they started off again, everyone suddenly stopped at the same time. Felix was frozen into his regular out-mode. Gill was absent as he always was when hearing voices from the Flae in his head. Sarah listened to a hum coming from her Catflower In Ice as Gin spoke. Robert was twitching while holding the lucky horseshoe, and Killer was barking as if he heard a voice meant only for him.

Chimayo stood silently by awaiting the return of his new friends from whatever kind of messages they were receiving. Killer stopped barking and starting staring to the east of where they were. At the same time, Felix, Sarah, Robert and Gill all jerked back to the real world and all started talking at the same time.

"Whoa! One at a time, folks!" Chimayo yelled.

Robert spoke up first. "It feels wrong, Chimayo! Something is pulling me that way," he said while pointing to the east. "It has to do with my luck, I guess."

Sarah and Gill both piped in at the same time to report that Gin and Gwen had contacted them and reported that they were going to the wrong location. They, too, pointed toward the east.

"I reckon that goes for me, too, Chimayo," Felix said. "I feel that we need to go in that direction, but we're gonna have a big problem!"

Chimayo looked to the east. "That's the direction of the second possible site for the Whistler to open Earth's crust. It's a little farther than the one we were headed for, and if that's our destination... we need to put on some speed! But Felix, what was the problem you were talking about?"

Felix pointed to Sarah just as her phone rang.

"That's the problem."

Sarah answered the phone. "Sarah? MAX here! I just wanted to report that SkyNet satellite cameras have reported a large blue dome appearing in the heart of Yellowstone! The Air Force is sending in an alert as we speak, and planes should be there soon! And Sarah... these planes are packing heavy stuff!"

"Oh God!" she said as she thought about the damage caused if the Whistler was blown to the four winds. Then she thought about the damage the Whistler would cause if it wasn't affected by the blast. "Oh God! We've got to hurry, gang! Thanks, MAX!"

"Good luck, Sarah. Come back home... you hear?"

"Yeah, baby... I hear you."

As they took off at a run down the hillside that they'd been climbing, Felix looked at Sarah. "Hey, dudette? I've meant to ask you... where did the name MAX come from?"

Sarah laughed as she struggled down the slope. "It's just a name that my computer read in a book... about another computer named Max. I guess he liked the name!"

Felix laughed. "Yeah. Why not?"

As they went slipping and sliding down one slope after another, Felix finally pointed ahead and whispered, "Good Lord! Look!"

There in the distance was their final destination. It was as if a giant had blown a soap bubble, and upon landing, it had halved itself. It was a shimmering blue color, and had to be sixty feet tall. As they stared at it, they heard the sounds of wildlife fleeing from the location. Bears, rabbits and raccoons all ran together. Birds were in flight overhead, and everything was headed away from the blue dome. Then, as they stood there in awe of the gigantic blue construct, a low rumbling and a high-pitched whistle cut the air.

"It has started," Chimayo said.

As they ran closer and closer to the cleft in the cliff where the Thingie had taken up residence for the final confrontation, Felix quietly huffed and puffed as he said, "So it begins. It's terraforming our world for its people. It believes that it's altering the environment on an inhospitable planet, so that Thingies elsewhere have a better world to live in. In a way, it's kinda sad, but sad or not... it can't have my world! Maybe living through tomorrow will be impossible, but as for today... Thingie, I'm a gonna cloud up... and rain all over you!"

If his friends hadn't been so out of breath, they would have cheered.

It was then that they noticed the sun slowly being covered by the shadow of the moon. Felix sighed. "Shadow of the Moon," he said in a whisper. The eclipse had started.

As they drew closer to the enclosure that hid the rumbling sounds, they could feel the temperature rising... and swiftly. Animals ran by them with no interest in their safety, just wanting to get away from the terrible sounds and vibrations coming from inside the blue bubble. The essence of evil could be scented on the wind, and Doomsday was upon the horizon. Planes could now be heard approaching from the west, and a shiver went down the spine of each of the humans as something inside the blue barrier shrieked.

HE knew.

HE knew that the planes approached.

HE knew that "Humans who kill Thingies" had arrived.

A quiver went through the planet's surface as the first wave of power opened up the fault line beneath the alien creature within the enclosure. The heat almost doubled as the ground quaked with anticipation.

The group of "puny" humans approached the outer edge of his bubble slowly, and the scent of fear rolled off of each of them like a sweet perfume. HE smiled as HE continued with the long Whistle, which would spell death for this sorry planet. The lava was beginning to rise to his call and the crust and mantle of this planet began to open in welcome to his waiting arms. Another quake passed through the bedrock of the land.

HE smiled. "Not long now. Not long at all."

The small band of heroes approached the outside of the blue wall of Minus that had formed around HE. Not thinking, Felix put out his hand to touch the side of the construct.

The next thing he remembered was Robert standing over him, radiating a glow as he healed the burns on the hands of the giant idiot that Felix felt himself to be.

Felix stood up on shaky legs, looked at the bubble, looked at his healing hands and said, "Ow!"

Gill shook his head. "You big goofy critter! Don't you know better than to grab hold of every alien bubble that comes your way?"

Even in these circumstances everyone laughed, but just a little.

Robert suddenly looked upward, and yelling, "Hit the dirt!"

An Air Force jet flew overhead close enough to deafen everyone on the ground and opened fire with machine guns on the blue bubble. The bullets not only failed to penetrate the barrier but seemed to be absorbed by it. The bubble appeared to have grown a small amount by the gunfire.

"Aw, man! This just keeps getting better and better!" Felix said.

Killer started barking as he ran over to Paul. The small dog leaped in to the air, trying to convey a canine idea it had in it's small mind! Paul looked at everyone and said, "What? What's he want?"

Gill looked around at everyone standing there. Then, he yelled out, "Quick! Everyone join hands!"

They all grabbed each other's hand and Paul caught Killer in mid-air. Then, Gill pulled out the Time Stopper, Ima Rock.

The entire forest stopped.

The plane was frozen in the cloudy skies.

The sound within the bubble continued but slower. Lower. Quieter.

Gill yelled out, "OK, this won't stop the Thingie, but we'll slow him down while we think! Killer? Got an idea?"

"Woof!" He licked Paul with his small tongue.

Felix suddenly smiled! "I get it! Hey, Paulie dude? We can't touch it... this bubble thing... and we can't shoot it, right? But, how's about we put a door in the critter?"

Everyone smiled.

As they stood frozen in time, Paul eased over to the blue barrier and drew a doorway.

A doorway appeared. A doorway to a cataclysm. The temperature felt like hell.

Gill looked for a final time at his gathered friends. "Gang, when it comes to saving our planet, our deaths are inconsequential. This has got to be done. I love you all... and it's been one heck of a ride! The very best to each of you, and now... let's go take this sucker out!"

Felix smiled as he said, "This bubble is a headstone for the Thingie, dudes and dudette, and it's a tomb from which no Lazarus will ever rise. On my word!"

As the group of friends walked into the inner world of the bubble, they all heard Sarah whisper, "Second star to the right... and straight on 'til morning."

79
The Watchers and The Waiters

In this wide world of humans, animals and magic, many lives were held in the balance by a struggle taking place out of sight and sound but felt in the minds by all.

Soft flute music came floating through the dense forest as Shadow Of The Moon and Whistle Cat sat around the large campfire, swaying back and forth with each other and with all of the tribal members, who could all feel that this was a moment of great importance to not only the Shoshone, but also the Earth Spirit as well. Cody sat near the fire watching Shadow play, and in his lap Found Child gurgled softly... as he, too, bobbed back and forth to the gentle sounds of the flute. Much magic was needed on this evening, and the tribe would send what they could to the heroes far away who fought for this world.

Along with what magic she could scare up to help support her beloved Cat Warrior on this day of days, Shadow Of The Moon sent along a little something extra.

She sent her heart.

At that same moment, Ol' Rascal was whining at the eclipse out the window while Remus was whipping up a batch of fried chicken at Delores's house. They sat around the old formica table together as the smells of that "yardbird" permeated the kitchen. Remus smiled at the old dog, and turned to see Delores crying.

"Aw, sugar... dis ain't de end! Dem folks is doin' da very best dat dey can ta fix dis problem up, and we gots to give 'em our prayers... not our tears. Come on, now... and get ya sum of dat fried chicken, girl! Rascal, here's sum fer you, too! What we need now is sum good prayin' for dem good folks. Oh yeah... and we also need sum of dat honey for dis chicken! Hehehe!"

As her daddy was working on the new house that was being built where the old one had once stood, Olivia looked up at the shrinking sun over the ocean. Her Dad came over to her.

"What's up, sugar?" he said with a smile as he looked down at her beautiful face. She had just lost yet another tooth.

"My friendth are needin' thum help, Daddy. I can feel it. The mans who have the sthar. They're thcared of thumthing."

"Well then, honey, let's just sit down here on the beach... and we'll send them our thoughts and best wishes. Do you think that will help?"

"Yeath, Papa. They can uth whatever help we can thend right now."

The two people, father and daughter, sat down on the beach and prayed.

Cruising down the streets of Los Angeles, Sergeant Eddie Fallon suddenly had an urge to pull over his car. As he parked the cruiser, he looked up at the decreasing light given off by the eclipse. Somehow, for some unknown reason, he started thinking about Robert and Sarah and all of the strangeness that had suddenly taken hold of his life in the last few days. He grew increasingly aware of a feeling, kind of like balancing on the edge of a cliff, not knowing which way the fall would be – not wanting to fall.

He closed his tired eyes and sent a thought of hope to wherever this strange collection of new friends might be at that moment. Then, for the first time in five years, he had an urge to pick up his phone and call some-one whose voice he hadn't heard in so long, but a voice he now longed to hear in case it might be the last chance he had.

The phone rang twice. A tired old voice said, "Hello?"

A tear rolled down his face as he said, "Hello! Mama?"

Hauling a double-loaded trailer full of farm machinery to Boise, Idaho, Hud got an urge to pull his rig over at a rest stop ahead. "Man," he thought to himself, "what a weird feelin' I'm 'a havin'!" He looked up at the half-sun hidden by the shadow of the moon that passed over it, and had a hunch.

He got on the ol' CB radio, and put out a general broadcast. "Breaker one-nine! Y'all got the Hud Man on the line here! I'm 'a needin' a wing and a prayer to be 'a goin' out to the Magic Bus right about now! I'm 'a feelin' that them folks is 'a needin' us and our good thoughts right about now, come back!"

For hundreds of miles around, every trucker within earshot started the good vibes pouring through the airwaves in search of the Magic Bus.

"Well, folks," Hud whispered, "I just hope it's enough."

At Pahaska Lodge, Tom was getting ready to start cooking supper when a wind that was howling outside of the lodge made him stop. He almost thought that he heard someone or something. His mind flashed on the folks whose bus had been parked outside, and for the life of him, he couldn't shed a tinge of worry that crossed his mind.

His friend Chimayo hadn't seen fit to tell ol' Tom about what they were all up to, but the caretaker couldn't help but worry.

His mother used to say that good thoughts would sometimes win out the day. Tom smiled and told himself that if that was all that was needed, he could sure spare some good thoughts. He sat back down by the fireplace and sent well wishes to Chimayo and his strange band of friends.

Then he broke out the whiskey.

Back at the campsite, Tulla, Esante and Larry sat around the campfire arguing about what Chimayo had told them and not told them.

"Home? Chimayo wants us to just leave him here and... go home?" Tulla asked.

Larry stood up. "The End-Of-All-Things, Tulla! This is not a fishing outing or a hunting expedition or a camping trip for the whites! This is the beginning... or the end... of all things! Don't worry about a ride home. Worry about... ." He got real quiet. "Worry about... life."

Larry sat down beside the campfire and closed his eyes. As his mind began to drift, he heard Tulla and Esante sit beside him and do the same.

Now it was up to the Great Spirit.

Somewhere in the cyber-world of wires and memory chips, MAX and Lois and Betsey sat together and waited.

And hoped.

Somewhere in the nether world of later life, Elizabeth sat on an old sofa with none other that Buffalo Bill himself. They held hands as they waited.

And hoped.

In the world of the Flae, millions sat in anticipation of events turning on the great wheel of life. Among them, Gin and Gwen sat outside with their heads tilted back as they focused on the two Earth humans with whom they had contact. Like the rest of the universe, they waited.

And hoped.

And in a pasture far away, with the fresh smell of grass and flowering plants to tickle his nose, the God of Dogs smiled.

And waited.

80
Has Hell Frozen Over?

The moment they entered the world of the bubble, all realized they had forgotten the earplugs. They quickly released hands to retrieve the plugs and tried to load them into their ears, but this caused HE to revert back to full speed. Gill quickly pocketed Ima and leaned down to attempt to plug poor Killer's ears, but it was then that HE spotted the group.

"ROAR!" HE screamed, adjusting to human speech.

"Aw, hell!" Felix whispered to himself.

"You! The Humans who kill Thingies! Even here... at the eleventh hour, you come to plague me! Even now, in my hour of triumph, you vainly attempt to cease my conquering of this miserable planet of yours!"

HE appeared to be at least twenty-five feet tall, and totally featureless. His body was a human shape as slicked black as tar, and the essence of evil rolled off of him in waves of darkness. There was something abhorrent about the creature that was not explainable in human terms, and he shrieked with the promise of the end of all things.

Even as this confrontation took place, the sounds of Armageddon beating on the roof was followed by the sounds of massive explosions. The Air Force had just put in their two cents worth. Their money had been wasted. The dome increased in height and thickness by absorbing the power of the missile blasts, and it seemed that the Whistler grew another five feet taller.

They all continued to hold onto their earplugs in their hands, just to be able to hear the ranting and ravings of this would-be conqueror. For now, the deadly whistling had stopped while the giant released his mighty ego. "Yours is a pitiful race and must be plowed under as the weeds of a garden are destroyed for the benefit of the better lives to replace them... but... this group of you have shown abilities that I believe may become useful to the future of my people. So... I give you a choice!"

While the Thingie continued with his boasting, Felix silently slid the speargun from the backpack. Around each speartip, he had duct-taped a magnum road flare. With a silent click, he loaded the first of the three projectiles he had brought into the double-barreled gas-powered weapon. Paul watched his friend in silent action and took this time to remove a

396

large piece of chalk from his leather-fringed Super Suit.

Felix eased over to Sarah.

"Shhh..." he whispered. "Look down," he said, glancing at the speargun. She saw it and nodded. He smiled at her as he quietly said, "It's a machine, Sarah. Take it. Look for the white spot beneath his throat. Wait until you know it's the right time! You'll have three chances." She smiled back at him as he slipped her the deadly weapon and two extra spears.

"The five of you can continue your struggle against me and be blown away as the dust of the earth will be upon the completion of my task, or you may serve me and my people in the reconstitution of the empty husk of this soon-to-be dead world... to fit my master plan! The dog creature, of course, must die! This is a new age, and I believe that your choices are clear! Will you bow down now and join me?"

They looked at each other for all of five seconds before Felix appeared to start bobbing and shaking his head as if he was going to cry. Instead, he began to laugh helplessly.

"I think that I've heard just about enough of your crap! I'm gettin' a headache just listenin' to this!"

His friends started to laugh and applaud at the same time.

HE began to quiver.

Choosing his words with care, Felix stepped forward, as the rest of them followed. "I know you've come down here... with all of your big plans, on how you're gonna take over the world... and eat the sun! But E.T., as far as we're concerned... you can eat shit!" (Later on, Felix would remark that if you looked up "pissed off" in the dictionary... there would be a picture of the Evil Thingie named HE at that particular moment in time.)

With a roar and inhuman agility, the Whistler formed a gigantic blue ball of the Minus it had been saving up and hurled it toward the tall human with the big mouth.

Felix leaped out of the path of on-coming death at just the right moment. He slowly and painfully got back up on his feet, looked at his friends and smiled as he said, "Everyone's a critic!"

Gill yelled out, "Earplugs!" as the creature once again began the hideous whistling toward the already oozing lava hole in Earth. Pain leapt from the heads of all of the humans as they struggled to replace the earplugs before their heads exploded.

Killer was rolling around on the ground, screaming as blood started to pour out of his ears. Gill rushed over to the poor dog and managed to put the blockage in the ear canals of the small canine, but by then, the damage had been done.

Killer was deaf.

Chimayo, having no great powers like the warriors here, sat upon the ground and closed his eyes. In his dream-like state, he called upon all of the gods to help his friends. "Oh, Great Spirit, Oh, Father of the Jesus human, Oh, Lord of Machines, Oh, Mighty Desert Warrior, Oh, Lord Of Time, Oh, Queen of Luck, Oh, Creator of Flae... Oh, God of Dogs... please! Please! Please... help my friends!"

Felix grabbed up the deadly kazoo-looking weapon from around his neck and tried his best to make it work but nothing would happen. Felix saw Gill signaling for them all to touch so that he could use the Mind-Speak and Time Stopper again, but by now, they were too far spread out to rejoin each other.

Killer was whimpering but back on his feet.

Felix saw Sarah ignite and then launch the first of the three flare-headed spears at the Whistler, and it would have been a perfect shot if not for the fact that the beast twisted at the last minute to knock poor Gill to the ground. The Whistler was wounded in the shoulder by the burning projectile, and the screams that came from him were worse that the whistling. Gill lay in a lump on the ground with Ima Rock lying beside him.

He didn't move.

Sarah was holding the now-empty speargun in one hand and the Cat-flower In Ice in her other. HE turned toward her with death in his heart at the pain she had just inflicted upon him. But Sarah stood still... smiling... listening to a voice that only she could hear. Just as the giant fist of the Thingie swung down to crush the life from the beautiful human girl, two things happened at once.

Robert saw that she couldn't possibly escape and he screamed.

And Sarah, with that small smile on her face, disappeared.

BAM!

The earth shook from the impact of the alien fist smashing into the ground. HE laughed, thinking that HE had now eliminated at least two of these "pesky humans."

Paul had been watching the whole episode while franticly drawing in the air with his chalk. The bazooka he came up with wasn't lethal to the Thingie, but it sure put a mighty nice hole in HE for about thirty seconds until HE healed up completely and absorbed the strength of the explosion to make himself even stronger. It was like watching water flow back into a hole made by a thrown rock. What the bazooka shell did do, however, was give Paul's friends a moment to regroup.

Robert had trusted in his newfound luck to put himself next to where he figured Sarah would re-appear. Sure enough with a loud POP, she came back on the scene right next to him from wherever the Flae had taken her. She automatically began to reload the speargun.

"Gin says to help Gill!" she screamed at Robert as she popped another of the spears into the gun.

In the meantime, the world of Killer was one of silence but also one of death. He saw his Gill human lying still on the frozen ground, and even a small dog can become a hero when the ones he loves are dying. He slowly crawled his way over to the cliff-side where the Evil Thingie had begun digging the deadly hole to hell. Killer was hurt badly, but he carefully eased his way, step by step, up the steep mountainside. He whimpered as he painfully pulled himself, first over one rock and then another. He may not have been able to hear, but he sure could smell, and the scent of blood, coming from both of his ears and the corner of his tiny mouth, was strong.

He managed to crawl to a shallow ledge twenty feet off of the ground and then collapsed. He could go no farther. His strength was gone. He had nothing left to give, even to the Gill human he loved so much.

He cried.

And then a voice appeared.

"Killer?"

The sound was not outside but inside.

"Killer?"

Killer thought with his dog brain, "God of Dogs?"

"Yes, my son. You have made me so proud! You are a good dog, but your journey is not quite over yet. Soon, my son, soon. But for now, I give you enough time to do what you must do... for your human... and for the worlds of all creatures and creations. You have... the MIGHTY BITE! Go now, my Killer... and do what must be done. You have only one more task, my son. Then, you can rest."

"I should... attack? If Bigger-Than-Tree hurt my humans... I must try hurt Bigger-Than-Tree?"

Killer could feel God of Dogs smile as he whispered, "Sic 'em!"

As the God of Dogs returned to The Land Behind The Sky, Killer painfully got to his small feet.

He began to climb.

Robert stumbled over to where Gill lay upon the cold ground. He placed his healing hands upon Gill's head, not sure if his friend was alive or dead. A rose-colored glow appeared around the two of them as Robert grasped for Olivia Reaching For A Star, and this had the terrible effect of attracting the attention of the giant Whistler. HE didn't stop his whistling, but raised his fist to attack the source of the illumination. Robert saw that he was making a target out of Gill, so he jumped to his feet and took off in a run away from his small friend. As he crossed the ground in a gallop, he thought he heard Gill moan.

Paul had taken this time to create the most primitive of weapons, the white spear that he had originally drawn on Betsey when he had acquired the chalk at the Craters Of The Moon in the first place. This time, however, he took an extra second to make the drawing permanent. The projectile was ten feet long, and as thick as a thumb. Just as the Thingie was swinging at the red streak named Robert who was dashing across the ground, Paul lifted the long spear and hurled it. His body had the tension of a coiled spring and it flew thirty feet into the air and stuck into the throat of the Evil Thingie with a TWANG!

As lava bubbled out of the deep, deep hole in the earth created by the power of the Whistler and blackness dribbled out of the hole made by the spear of artwork, the sound of whistling stopped.

It was replaced by a scream of hate and pain.

Paul drew a quick shield to hold up in front of himself just as the ball of Minus was thrown by HE.

SPLAT!

The burning Minus slid down the shield without penetrating it, but the shield was dissolved in the process.

HE looked at the young boy and screamed with a gurgling sound coming from the wound to its throat.

As Paul started to run, he dropped something on the ground. He took time to see what it was and realized that Felix's camera had fallen and lay on the still-frozen but melting snow, surrounded by the blob of Minus repelled by the shield. As the camera melted into slag, Paul saw the picture of Betsey's door that good ol' Felix had taken earlier. It was still on the screen of the camera.

Paul had an idea.

"Useless! Just plain USELESS!"

That's how Felix felt as he stood there watching his friends being hurt or killed by this ass of an alien. He had worried for so long about having to once again release the terrible power that he had used in California on the

Thingies. Now, that the time had come, he had nothing.

He saw Gill lying on the ground. Unmoving.

He saw Robert in a desperate flight across the enclosure to direct HE away from poor Gill.

He saw the pitiful small dog, bleeding rapidly from the mouth but still somehow climbing the side of the cliff to try to get closer to the enemy.

He saw the terrible glob of Minus that had been thrown at his new brother Paul. He didn't see whether Paul had survived because at that moment, Sarah launched her second spear into the stomach of the Evil Thingie.

He then saw the Whistler scream to the high heavens as the pain of the second flaming spear from Sarah blended with the art spear thrown by Paul. The very ground shook in anticipation of the underground calamity about to happen, and the giant half-bubble wavered in and out of existence with the diversion inflicted on HE!

Felix realized that although they had caused the Evil Thingie much pain, no one had hit the prime target of the white spot below the throat, which now glowed like the sun. Felix tried once again to focus the power contained within to the small kazoo-looking device Paul had made him but with no luck.

Quickly, Felix signaled Chimayo to help him gather all of the friends together next to Gill and the Time Stopper.

Chimayo jumped up and ran over to get Paul, who had drawn an eight-foot-tall rectangle in the air connected to the ground. The two of them darted toward Gill, the same time that Felix darted toward Robert. They all gathered around Gill's still body. Felix saw the Time Stopper on the ground next to his small friend just as the very worst happened.

Sarah was watching the group gather by their small leader and didn't even see the blow coming until it landed.

HE kicked out with his terrible leg and caught Sarah right in the chest. The speargun fell from her hands, and she flew almost twenty feet through the air before she hit the rock edge of the very cliff that poor Killer was struggling up. Her body slid to the ground near the lava hole in slow motion and the very first scream to cut the air was Gill's.

He had awakened just in time to see the deathblow dealt by the Whistler to his friend Sarah. He looked higher and saw his pal Killer covered in blood and on his last legs as the pup made his way to the edge of the cliff. Gill's screams became mixed with tears.

Robert ran over to Sarah with his own set of screams. "NO! This can't happen! Not now! Not to Sarah! Take me, God, if you need someone... but not Sarah!" He gently held her head in his lap as he watched the giant

Whistler slowly glance toward the group as HE commenced with whistling.

Robert dragged Sarah's inert body where he believed the rest of his friends were, but the tears made it hard to tell. Robert noticed that she still held onto the Catflower In Ice as if it were her one lifeline to this world.

He called upon whatever power he had left in his necklace to help save the woman he loved. His hands, and then his entire body, began to glow. Pink. Then rose-red. Then red-hot. Sarah moaned. She was still alive.

As he finally reached the entire group, several things all happened at once.

Chimayo spread his hands and all of the dreams were remembered.

When this happened, the gods came out to play.

Gill shook his head as it was filled with past thoughts. Gin and Gwen had both said, "Tell Gill that the combined powers you all have are a much greater sum total than individual strengths. This will become clear when it is needed!"

"Join hands! NOW!" Gill screamed at the friends around him. They could hear nothing because of the earplugs, but somehow they knew.. As soon as they all touched, they were in mental contact with the MindSpeak.

Gin was mentally still with Sarah and the Flae told the Earth Warriors to thrust at the same time with what weapons they had in order to fight the Thingie.

Robert reached over to grab the last spear and loaded it into the speargun.

Gill grabbed up Ima Rock, the Time Stopper, and HE was slowed down to a crawl.

Felix felt a tingle inside of himself that he had only felt once before in his whole life. "It was coming! Oh, God! Let me be able to control it... with the help of Paul's device!"

They remembered all of these events already happening in dreams of the future.

To Killer, the future was blank.

"Oh, God of the Dogs! What is that? Bad smells from Bigger-Than-Tree! If Bigger-Than-Tree hurt my humans, I must try hurt Bigger-Than-Tree.

"I run at!

"I bark at!

"I bare my small teeth and jump! I'm flying!

"I bring the MIGHTY BITE!

"Bigger-Than-Tree screams louder that ever before as I tear at its throat! Black bad smells now pour out of Bigger-Than-Tree!

"I thank God of Dogs for the MIGHTY BITE!

"Bigger-Than-Tree does not thank God of Dogs.

"This is funny!

"Bigger-Than-Tree rips me from its torn throat! Throws me toward The Land Behind The Sky!

"Hello, God of the Dogs."

"Hello, Killer. Welcome home."

Robert saw the giant, towering above all of them, roaring as the whistle it had been expelling drilled farther and farther into the already shaky terrain. The lava, oozing out of the hole, proclaimed the intensity of the disaster to come. And he was powerless, holding Sarah's inert body in his arms trying to bring her back. He held the speargun gun in the air and ignited the tip. He saw brave little Killer leap from the cliff into midair in slow motion to attack the giant, and the pup did major damage to the Thingie. It was a miracle. He squeezed Sarah's hand, trusting in his own luck and her ability with machines. He didn't even look. He gently closed his eyes and fired.

Paul had drawn up the device that would hopefully help defeat the terrible creature waiting to kill them. He hoped it would work as planned, but the problem – the gigantic problem – was now in front of him and killing all of his friends. If his drawing wasn't as good as he hoped, then...

Sarah was in and out of the world. She would see Gin and then Robert. She saw Gill spread out on the ground with the Time Stopper. Killer was lying in a heap on top of a pile of bloody snow, and Felix was getting ready to scream as the world had never heard. She fell away again into darkness, almost lifeless on the ground, as Robert cradled her head.

Felix looked around at his fallen friends. Sarah lay in the arms of poor Robert, who was trying to mend her through the tears and sobs coming from his heart. And there was Gill, sprawled almost unconscious on the cold, wet snow, barely moving. Paul was pointing to something to Felix's right where the boy had drawn white lines in the very air around himself. When Felix glanced where Paul had been pointing, it was then he saw the small lifeless dog. HE, the Evil Thingie who had caused all of this grief, slowly looked down at the miserable bunch of warriors, injured, dead or dying. Even though its throat was half ripped open by the small dog, HE made the mistake of laughing. As had happened only once before in time, Felix once again saw a red haze. Something inside Felix that had only existed once before suddenly... CLICKED!

Connected as he was to his friends, he could hear the voice of Gin in the back of his mind.

"Scream for the night! Scream for the pain! Scream for peace to the world once again!"

Grief suddenly turned to anger, remorse turned to vengeance, and for the second time in his strange life, Felix hated.

He looked into the eyes of the creature in front of him, rolled his eyes into the back of his large head and screamed.

"AHHHHHHHHHHHHHHHH!"

As the power built to a white-hot intensity, he felt the sudden sting of the Desert Warrior, coming from the amber necklace around his neck. The scorpion was actually moving around inside of its yellow prison and adding to the power he was making. He felt the claws of the mountain lion on his second necklace rake his skin as he brought the brass kazoo device to his screaming lips. The widely distributed power of the scream was filtered down into a fine line of snow-white destruction. He raised this fine line wave-length to the glowing spot on the Evil Thingie and it connected at the very same time, at the very same location, as the spear-head with the flare impacted.

Not even the earplugs could subdue the gut-wrenching sounds made by the Whistler now. A sound of pain and horror leveled trees inside the bubble, and the giant alien started to blink in and out of existence. It began to swell in size like an over-filled balloon and became distorted and wavy.

Felix stopped as everything inside of him began to go black, but the Whistler continued to swell.

"It's gonna blow!" Paul screamed. "Follow me! NOW!"

Chimayo grabbed a hold of Felix as he fell. Robert picked up Sarah, and they all followed Paul toward the rectangle he had drawn in the air. He placed his hands on it and concentrated. It was a doorway – not permanent but useable.

It was a doorway to Betsey.

Robert ran straight onto the bus carrying Sarah as Chimayo was dragging giant Felix as best he could. Paul stepped quickly through as they all felt the pressure building up behind them. They realized that Gill was missing.

Robert put Sarah on the bus couch and turned back to the door.

"Watch her!"

"Robert, you don't have time! It's gonna blow!" Chimayo yelled.

"I can't leave him, guys! If I'm gone more than sixty seconds, Paul, you rub out this doorway! Do you hear me? Damn it! I mean it!"

Tears were running down Paul's faces as he nodded.

Robert dashed back into the bubble once again. He looked around for his lifelong friend and finally saw him.

He was lying next to Killer, crying.

The screams from the Evil Thingie were deafening. He was swollen twice as big as before, blinking in and out.

Robert walked slowly over to the two pals and put his hand on Gill's shoulder. "Come on, buddy. It's time to go home."

Gill looked up into Robert's face with tears rolling down his face.

Robert whispered, "Come on, Gill... let's go."

Robert picked up the small body of the dog and Gill followed as they walked toward the doorway of life again.

They stepped through just as Paul was about to wipe it down. As soon as they had crossed the threshold, Paul collapsed the drawing.

Miles and miles away on that snowy afternoon, as the eclipse of the sun was finally over with, a terrible explosion rocked a three state area. It was said to have been a 7.0 earthquake on the rector scale and windows were broken out as far as a hundred miles. Lava was said to have flowed for a short while in the Yellowstone area following the explosion.

The Sleeping Giant was thought to have awakened.

The Air Force was reported as having planes in the immediate area, but the reports were sketchy as to why they were there. Trees were flattened for two square miles, and the closest human survivors were three Native Americans named Tulla, Esante and Larry, who later reported that they couldn't even remember why they were out there.

Larry said, "I always swore that you couldn't get me out here at this time of the year unless hell freezes over! What happened?"

81
Thanks For The Memories

"OK! I know I'm just a bus, but would someone care to tell me what the hell just happened?" Betsey asked with a snort.

Robert shook his head and sighed as he sat on the couch, holding his healers hands around the bruised body of his beautiful Sarah.

"It's just as you said, Betsey. Hell just happened. The bad guys lost, the good guys won, but the price we paid was awfully high. Now, give us all a little time to lick our wounds and bury our dead and then we'll tell you all about it on our trip back home. OK?"

"Yes, Robert," she said, with what sounded like a tearful voice module. "I just wanted to know if I can help... that's all."

"I understand, Betsey. If you would... record any radio and television broadcasts relating to what's happened up here, will ya? That will help."

"Yes, Robert."

Sarah opened her tired red eyes and Robert smiled.

"Hello, beautiful."

"Hello yourself, Dr. Ert." she answered quietly with a blood-covered smile. "What's my prognosis? Will I live?"

"Yes, sugar. You'll live... with me... until death do us part. OK?"

"Sounds like heaven." She tried to sit up, but winced at the pain and fell back down on the couch into his lap. She looked into his eyes. "It also kinda sounded like... a proposal?"

Robert's smile behind the pink glow he was giving off as he healed her was wide and true. Even behind the glow, she could almost swear that he was blushing!

"You're just delirious, baby girl," he said with a smirk.

Sarah looked up to the bus ceiling... and in a pained whisper... she asked, "Betsey?"

"Yes, Sarah?" Betsey quietly answered.

"Did you record that?"

Instead of answering, a hushed voice came on the speakers. "Yes, sugar. You'll live... with me... until death do us part. OK?"

Sarah smiled. "Save that tape for me in case I need evidence. OK?"

"You got it, sweetie!" Betsey giggled.

Felix and Paul were outside of the bus doing some serious walking around.

"I just need to get out and walk around for a while, Paul," Felix had said. "But... I could use some company."

"You got it, big guy."

Felix and Paul had still been wearing their backpacks when they started off on the walk but quickly shed them, along with Felix's rifle, which he had never even had the opportunity to fire.

"It is a pretty gun, though," Felix told him.

Paul smiled. "I'm glad that you got it."

Felix rubbed the boy's head. "I knew what you did when they were givin' out those rifles, Paul. And I... I just wanna say... thank you."

Paul rubbed his watery eyes. "Aw, it wasn't nothin'... really."

Felix smiled. "Yeah, son, it was. Really."

Both friends were still wearing their leather-fringed Super Suits. Although, they no longer looked brand-new or quite so super.

They walked down the slope to where a meadow was just beginning to thaw. The journey was slow and moody. Finally Paul couldn't stand it anymore. "Felix... are you gonna be alright?"

"What do you mean... alright?"

"Well, ever since we came back, you've been... how can I put this... you've been... un-funny!"

Felix stopped the walk. They both sat down on an old stump that had fallen many years before. Felix stared up into space for a while, thinking of the best answer to give to his friend... and to himself. Paul respected this and said nothing. Finally, Felix looked deep into Paul's eyes and said, "I don't know."

Felix sort of chuckled. "When that blast of... whatever the hell it was... came out of me, it took something away with it. I've got a hole inside of me now that I can feel. A terrible empty spot. It's nothing that Robert can cure with the healing stuff he does... it's just something that's gonna take some time to callus over. If it ever will. Understand?"

Paul looked at him with a smile. "Nope."

"Good! I hope you never do!"

Paul gazed out into the forest around them, and to his amazement, three deer stepped out of the tree line, closer than twenty feet from where they sat. The beautiful animals stared at the humans for a couple of minutes without moving. The large buck of the family raised his head in their direction and sniffed. He turned to the doe and her fawn and nodded. Before the two friends knew what was happening, the three deer slowly walked over to where Felix and Paul sat. When they were only three feet away, the mother and her child lay gently upon the cold ground, and the father came forward. He gazed into the eyes of Felix, and then Paul, and ever so slowly, bowed his head.

Felix began to cry.

After Robert had managed to do all he could for the time being for Sarah, he gently laid her head on a pillow and watched over her until she fell asleep.

"Will she be OK, Robert?" Betsey asked with a whisper.

"Yeah, Betsey... she'll be alright. It'll just take a few days for her to totally heal... both inside and out... mentally and physically. Anything interesting on the airwaves about what happened?"

"Robert, you're not going to believe this, but what's interesting is what's not on the airwaves!"

"I don't understand."

"Neither do I, but not only is there no mention of the battle with that creature today, there is no mention of it in the past either. I re-scanned my recorded info from the past week on the goings-on with the Evil Thingies... and they're all... different! Blank spaces where there was once reports! That incident with the semi-truck being blown up... it never happened! No deaths in Los Angeles are said to have happened because of these Whistlers! What's happening, Robert?"

Robert smiled. "I think I know, ol' girl, but I need to confirm my guess before I'll believe it!"

"Well, what do you think might have happened... if you don't mind an ol' busy-body Betsey Bus asking too many questions?"

He shook his head. "I think we altered time."

After Sarah was sound asleep, he quietly got up from the sofa, and went to the back compartment where Chimayo had been sitting with Gill.

Gill had wrapped the small body of Killer in a soft blanket and the little man was all cried out. He looked up at Robert with blood-red eyes and shook his head. "I've got no more tears!"

"Yeah, you do, little buddy... and they'll come again soon. But for now, we've got to finish what we started... and we've got a grave to dig. Chimayo?"

The Native American nodded. "I'll get some tools." He headed toward his truck.

"Gill, I believe that we might have changed the past. There's no record of Thingies ever being here... in Yellowstone, Montana... or in L.A. from before! We still have to button up a lot of the loose ends here, Gill. Not everything is changed, because all of us remember everything that's happened, we still have our Plus and our Builders from the journey, and we've still lost Killer. You need to reach Gwen and see if she can give us any info. I need to try to contact Sergeant Eddie Fallon and see if he recalls anything about any of this! Hell... he might not even know who I am! Then, Felix needs to contact Shadow... and see if she remembers him, and if Whistle Cat is still around! I'll have Betsey get a hold of Lois and MAX and get a status report from them. Chimayo needs to contact his three friends that we left on the other side of the lake, too. Once we finish all of this... we have a friend to bury... and say good-bye to. OK?"

Gill nodded. Then he looked at Robert, slowly saying, "I was wrong, Robert."

"Wrong about what, pal?"

"I've still got plenty of tears left over."

The two friends sat there, shoulder to shoulder, and cried together, as the ol' world continued to spin.

The family of deer stayed around Felix and Paul until the two humans decided to return to the bus. The deer didn't get spooked as the two friends stood up. They just watched the humans walk away with a strange reverence and respect.

As they both entered Betsey, Robert and Gill came forward. Gill had placed the body of his small friend into the new backpack that Killer had liked so much. This would be where the empty shell of what had once been Gill's closest friend would lie for eternity.

Chimayo showed up about five minutes later, and while they allowed Sarah to gain her strength back with sleep, they talked over the plans of what had to be done immediately.

Felix and Chimayo went into the lodge, said hello to Tom the Caretaker, who knew nothing, and then went to Felix's room. Chimayo put them both into a dream state, and together they went in search of Shadow Of The Moon. Felix was about to break down again with the thought that Shadow might not recognize him at all, but Chimayo reassured him that all would be well. Sure enough, she was waiting for the contact. She gave Felix a giant hug and kiss, and said her hellos to Chimayo. She was celebrating the saving of the world with Whistle Cat, who still existed, with the boy named Cody and with Found Child... by the Cat Warrior and his friends. Some things had changed, some had not. Some of the tribe members who had been killed by the Thingies were now alive again. They remembered nothing of the incident. On the other hand, the parents of Found Child and Cody's folks were still dead and Whistle Cat had not disappeared as she had feared would happen.

Her grandfather, who had passed from natural causes, was still gone but spoke to her in moments of trance. Felix told her of his love and promised that he would come to her soon and they would then figure out what the future held for the two of them.

He forgot Found Child and Cody, the four of them. He had forgotten Whistle Cat, the five of them.

"Damn," he thought. "Instant family!"

Chimayo and Felix returned to an awakened state and Felix was finally smiling again.

Robert had Betsey call up Sergeant Eddie Fallon of the L.A.P.D. for him.

"Hello? Sergeant Fallon here. How can I help you?"

"Ahhh... I'm not sure, Sergeant Fallon. Do you know me? My name is Robert Cody."

"Damn it, Robert! What the hell is going on? I feel like I've lost my mind! Where the hell are you... and that ragtag bunch of weirdos you're hanging out with? The world is going topsy-turvy out here... and I seem to be the only one who sees it! I'm afraid to say anything to anyone... because I seem to be the only one who knows WHAT THE HELL I'M 'A TALKIN' ABOUT!"

Robert laughed for only a couple of seconds and then spent the better part of fifteen minutes trying to explain things to Eddie.

That wasn't going to be enough.

Not near enough.

In the end, it was decided that Eddie was to play it cool for a few days. Then, when Betsey arrived back in L.A., Eddie would be invited to come out to visit at Gill's home, take a few days vacation time that he had coming and Robert and Gill would try to explain the impossible to the nice policeman.

Eddie was silent for almost a minute then he began to laugh.

"Yeah... hell, yeah, Robert. I'll do that! It ought to be a great conversation and a hell of a vacation! Oh, yeah... tell Sarah that for some reason... her house was never broken into! It's just fine!"

Robert smiled into the phone. "Eddie... maybe we'll even make you a job offer that you can't refuse! How's that sound?"

Eddie started laughing again. "Ya know, right now... that don't sound too bad! Maybe so. Will I still get to carry a gun and help people?"

"More than you'll ever know, Ed."

When Robert hung up and was telling Gill about what he had just promised to a member of the L.A.P.D., Betsey contacted Lois and MAX.

All three computer systems were excited about the outcome of the battle. MAX verified that Sarah's house was now as unblemished as it had been before all of this adventure had ever begun. Lois announced that the collapsed tunnel and the other entrance to Gill's second house were as they were when new. No explosions. No cave-ins. Three different computer programs were laughing and singing and celebrating.

Then... Betsey told both systems about Killer.

There was a great silence.

Hearing a computer cry was just about the saddest thing to hear.

Chimayo took the body of the small dog outside for temporary rest in the back of his pickup truck. He and Robert then went in search of a good location for the brave pup's final resting place.

Chimayo led Robert around the back of the lodge and passed by the old barn and stable on their way. As they continued to walk, Chimayo gave Robert a strange look and then turned to keep on walking. Robert noticed this but said nothing.

They found a winding deer track down the hillside, which led to a sloping ocean of grass stretching out to the mountain. The drawn whisper of the wind let them know that this was the right place. They removed the sod from a small square of land and began to dig.

Once again, Robert saw out of the corner of his eye the way Chimayo glanced at him from time to time. Finally, as the tiny grave was completed, Chimayo took the shovel away from Robert and sat down on the dew-wet grass for a moment. Feeling that there were words to be said here, Robert quietly joined him.

The Native American was silent for a few moments then looked into Robert's eyes. "Your great-great-grandfather wants you to know that he is very proud of you, Robert. He watched your struggle from afar and says that you and your friends are true warriors. He is very proud."

"Chimayo, I don't know anything about my mom's or dad's people. My folks passed away when I was still quite young, and I never even got to meet my grandfather... little on my great-great-grandfather!"

"There, you are mistaken... Robert Cody."

Robert couldn't seem to catch his breath.

"You and your beautiful Sarah both met your great-great-grandfather on a breezy hillside, not long ago. He came to you with the Fla named Gin. Now, do you now recall? You bear his name."

Robert managed to say, "Ahh...ahhh... ahhh... !"

Chimayo began to laugh. "Yes, Robert! That was your first words to the great gentleman! You carry his lucky horseshoe, do you not?"

Robert silently nodded as a single tear tracked down his cheek.

"He wishes you and your wife Sarah a long and happy life together and said that he will be watching you from time to time. He is very proud!" Chimayo placed his hand upon the shoulder of this startled white man, this healer. Then he stood up. "Come. There is still a funeral to take place for a mighty fallen hero, and the sun begins to sink."

They both walked back in silence and deep thought and with just a touch of wonder.

Gill wandered in a daze back to the rear room of good ol' Betsey in order to lie on the bed in quiet solitude. Before he could contact Gwen, Betsey whispered over the rear speakers, "MAX and Lois send their love, Gill. They are very sad."

"Me, too, ol' girl. Me, too. Give me a few minutes to contact the Flae, would ya? I'll be back up front in just a little while."

"Are you OK, Gill?"

"No, Betsey, I'm not. But one day..."

"Yes, sir. I understand. I'll keep 'em quiet."

"Thank you."

Gill lay on the bed, remembering all of the great times that he'd had with his small brother, all of the adventures that they'd shared together. Someone from the other world had sent him a message awhile back that he didn't understand at the time, but he smiled as he thought of it now.

"Tell Gill that the Far-Away is a beautiful place, and though I regret his loss, there is no need for tears."

"No need for tears," Gill said to himself. "Easily said, but kinda hard to pull off!"

He relaxed as he slid into the edge of the sleep world and felt the feathery touch of the Flae on the back of his mind.

"Welcome, hero."

Gwen's voice was quiet and soft, and he knew that news of the passing of Killer had reached even to the world of the Flae. He could hear several quiet voices in the background, whispering.

"Who all is there, Gwen?"

"Everyone, Gill. Everyone."

"You mean... ?"

"Yes, my warrior. The entire Flae nation stands in reverence at the deeds, which you and your friends have accomplished on this day. This will be a day of rejoicing from here forward on this date. You have saved your Earth, you have saved the world of the Flae... and countless thousands of other worlds that all would have been affected by the conquering Thingies... had they won instead of you. We will forever be in your debt."

Gill smiled in his sleep. "Gwen, what has happened to time and the past? Many things have changed here but others were unaffected."

"Gill, the Thingie leader known as HE is no more... and never was, thanks to the warp power of the Felix human. Since HE never existed, acts caused by him also never happened. Only the people directly in contact with the Thingies will even remember anything that happened and not all of them will have total recall of the events. Time is a slippery substance, Gill, and cannot be calculated in simple terms. We receive what we are given and that is all. On the whole, I'd have to say that what we were given is just fine."

Gill sighed. "Yeah, most of it."

"We of the Flae regret your loss of your friend, but remember that fate has a strange way of healing bad situations. We have spoken of this before, if you remember."

"That doesn't make it hurt any less, though, does it?"

"No, my friend, it doesn't. Know only that the millions of people you have saved this day are forever in your debt, and you will be hearing from some of them in the future."

"Oh, great! Just what I need!"

Gwen laughed. *"All of the Flae nation will be tuning in to the ceremony for the Killer dog. Know this, also."*

"Thank you, Gwen. And say hello to your people from us of Earth, please."

As he slowly tuned Gwen out of his head, he could hear the cheers of thousands of people in the background.

Gill woke up and came forward, where all of his friends were gathered in quiet solitude. Their small smiles were there only to ease the heartache, as they all placed their hands on Gill's shoulder. The MindSpeak was not needed to express their sympathy – their love.

The sun was getting low, and the time had come to say goodbye to a friend, a pal, a brother.

A dog.

82
A Final Farewell For A Fallen Friend

Unthinkingly wiping his tear-stained face with his shirtsleeve, Gill followed his friends around the lodge, past the old stable area and into a vast garden of grass. Chimayo led the party of mourners. Tom the Caretaker had seen the procession, and along with Sarah, the two of them had brought all of the flowers available from inside the Pahaska Lodge. Felix and Robert together carried the leather backpack containing the mortal remains of their little friend. Paul brought up the rear, already doodling in his sketchbook.

Suddenly feeling small, infinitesimal, Gill had to struggle in order to maintain his ability to cope. The afternoon sun had fallen below the tree-lined sky, and a soft but continuous breeze blew across the meadow.

The group arrived at the site of the grave, and as the tiny package was placed gently into the soft earth, Gill was heard whispering, "He dies, and the world will be poorer for it."

They all stood in a circle around the final resting place for the pup for several minutes without words, and Felix was the first to speak.

"God of Dogs. I've heard this phrase several times in the past few days, and I now believe that all things have a master being of their own. They may be the same god with different faces... I don't know. But, I do know that this dog was something special, and deserves recognition from whatever being or spirit is above. We were told before that our heroes sometimes come from unexpected places... and in very small and unnoticed packages. I believe that this war was won by this dog. Robert's final spear wouldn't have connected without the suicidal attack by Killer on the giant Whistler... trying to save us. Without me seeing the sacrifice that this pup gave... to save his master and his friends, I would never have had the strength to power the final and ultimate weapon. We all did well and good today to help destroy evil when it threatened our planet, but this world and many others were saved today... by a small dog. That's all I've got to say. Good-bye, Killer."

Tom the Caretaker, who knew nothing, was looking completely confused.

Robert held Sarah's hand as they walked forward together. Sarah placed the flowers next to the grave as Robert quietly said, "A better thing... a better place. A place of rest... a retreating place. Killer, you will become legend."

Sarah placed Killer's favorite bone that Paul had drawn for him on top of the backpack nestled in the hole. Around her tears, she managed to say, "Good dog."

Tom the Caretaker quietly said, "This is for the dog?"

Chimayo began singing a song of prayer in his native tongue and the breezes whistled through the trees. The echo of his voice played back over and over as if the whole Indian Nation was participating.

"That little dog?" Tom the Caretaker quizzed Sarah.

As the sun slowly sank behind the Sleeping Giant, Gill stepped forward. He looked around this Garden of Grass at his good friends assembled and smiled through his tears.

"I talked today to the Flae, and I am told that they are monitoring this ceremony as we speak. I would like to repeat here a legend, as Robert said, that the Flae have told us. Amongst the Flae, there is an old legend. It tells of the first intelligent beings to grace all of the known worlds... and they were dogs.

"And it was said that the dogs only became really intelligent when they found themselves to be loved. They then obtained the Power of Return. This meant that when they bonded tightly with a member of another species, with that great love that only they can bestow, at the End Of Days, they would enter the house of the God of Dogs in the Far-Away, and he would judge them to be worthy of return.

"They would then be reborn back once again into the world where their loved one was, and in many cases, the Power of Return would send them once again to that special friend. A beautiful tale, is it not?"

Everyone was crying and smiling.

"Killer, you are loved. I will miss you, my friend... and if your God of Dogs will allow it... you come home. You come..."

Gill couldn't finish.

The wind caught his words and they were carried gently away and the only sound was the soft breathing of that wind through the far distant trees. The last sun was retreating as Gill and Robert covered the small grave with soft soil.

The twilight and darkness had nearly arrived when Paul finished his drawing. It was a small marble headstone with strange shaped holes in the top of it. As he concentrated, the stone appeared over the new grave and the soft wind blowing through the irregular holes played a tune of unreal quality.

"How did he do that?" Tom the Caretaker asked Robert, who only answered, "Shhhhhhh!

The sounds were soft and harmonic. Killer would have loved it.

Wherever he was, they were all sure that he did love it.

On the stone was set these few words:

Here lies Killer
Our Friend and Our Brother
Used his last breath to save us all
May We Never Forget
Good Dog!

The small group of humans was suddenly startled to hear the sound of a large cat nearby. As they glanced about the distant tree line in amazement, they all realized that the entire meadow was literally surrounded by herds of deer, cougar, two large bears, a small pack of wolves, a half-dozen antelope, an large elk, numerous families of raccoons, squirrels, possums, scores of rabbits and small mice, and hundreds and hundreds of birds of all kinds and sizes. All lying down together. Attending this funeral, even though at a distance.

At peace.

Together.

"Well. I'll be!" Tom the Caretaker quietly stated. "All for a dog, right?"

Gill smiled and gave Paul a long hug. Then he wiped his eyes and looked at his friends, who were also smiling.

"Let's go home," he said.

83
The Long Journey Home

When they got back to the lodge, it was decided that they would stay to have a final dinner with Tom the Caretaker, but then Gill wanted everyone to pack up their rooms, load up Betsey, and for the old bus to leave out for home by midnight. There was talk of another storm heading their way, and Gill didn't want to be in these mountains again whenever it hit.

The meal that evening was a thing of beauty. Tom pulled out the stops to prepare a farewell dinner for all of his friends, both old and new. Several chickens, baked to a golden-brown were served with a mountain of mashed potatoes and gravy. There was a thinly sliced pork roast dished up with applesauce and baked apples. Five kinds of veggies, a fruit salad and a chef's salad were all on the side of the table, and a homemade apple pie the size of a wagon wheel was brought out for dessert.

As they all gathered around the large table, eating, joking, and passing around gallons of ice-cold milk and sweet tea, Gill kept glancing over at Paul, who was barely touching his food. Finally, Gill stood up and stretched. "Aw, man! I gotta go outside and grab a breath of fresh air before I can finish! Leave my plate where it's at, Tom. I'll be back for more!"

Robert and Sarah both looked up, and Robert added, "Ah, Gill? Do you need some company?"

"Yeah, actually... I do. Come go with me, Paul!"

Paul, surprised by this statement, stood up slowly and went out the front door with the small man. When they got outside, Gill settled down into one of the chairs set up on the porch for guests, saying nothing. Paul stood there for a moment, looking at Gill and waiting, but when no conversation was forthcoming, Paul, too, sat down. After a couple of minutes, Paul asked quietly, "Is something wrong, Gill?"

"Yeah, Paul, I think there is, but you tell me what it is. You've hardly touched your food, and I can tell that you're all depressed about something. Care to share?"

Paul hung his head for a few seconds before he could finally open up. Then, it all spilled out.

"Gill, I'm just gonna hate it to see you all go! I mean, I know that you gave me a ride up here... and fed me and... and I've found out my name, and found out about my mother and all, but... aww, heck! I'm just sorta down about being alone again, I guess. Not sure where I'm goin' next or anything. Ya know what I mean? Huh?"

Gill smiled at the boy. "Paul, I figured that you'd be coming home with us! Son, I've got a house in Los Angeles that's got more bedrooms than you've got fingers and toes! And besides that, I'm just waiting on Felix to get up enough nerve to ask me to let him stay with Shadow for a while! When that happens, I'm gonna need a good strong lad like you to help out around the place 'til he comes back! There's enough to do there to last you a lifetime, Paul. And I'm not offering this as charity, either. I really do need you... and I'll pay you a good salary to come and work with us! I'll even help you with your art career! What do you say?"

"Really?" he said in a squeaky little voice.

"Yeah, son... really."

Paul had no words. He fell out of his chair and grabbed Gill in a bear hug. Gill could hear him sniffling.

"There, there, boy. It's alright! You're with family now."

Paul finally released his death-grip from poor Gill, who was smiling at the boy. Paul smiled back. "Gill?"

"Yeah, Paul?"

"I'm starving! Can we go back and eat again?"

They were laughing in unison as they walked back in the front door.

Paul ran over to where Robert and Sarah were sitting. "Hey, guys! I'm goin' home with you folks! In the bus!"

As Sarah grabbed the boy to hug him tightly, Robert smiled and said, "Ya damn right you are!"

"Home! Isn't that a great word?" Paul said as he stuffed a drumstick into his mouth.

Felix looked at Gill and they both smiled.

As much as they hated to leave, the time had come. The rooms were cleaned out, and all luggage was packed into Betsey. They said their good-byes to Tom, who was all misty-eyed at their departure, even though he never knew how close he had come to the end of the trail... along with the rest of the world.

With Chimayo, it was much harder. He had become a big part of this family of friends, and they made each other promise to not only keep in touch but an upcoming reunion was already in the works. When everyone had finally gathered at Betsey to hit the road, Gill made Chimayo walk over to the pickup truck with him.

"Chimayo, none of this would have been possible without your help, my brother. You are a big part of the reason for our success in this battle. I'd like to not only thank you, but ask if there's a chance that we might one day work together again. If the need comes up?"

"My friend, you have but to call me... and I'll be there."

"That's what I wanted to hear! Now, if you don't mind, I'd like to leave you with a small payment... for you to occasionally put some flowers on ol' Killer's grave for me. There's a little something there for you, too. Just to help you get along, ya know." He handed Chimayo a check... drawn on his L.A. bank account.

Chimayo looked at it, looked at Gill and looked back at the check.

"One hundred thousand dollars?"

"Not enough?"

Chimayo started laughing and then started dancing.

"Gill, I could place orchids on the critter's grave each and every day with this! Are you serious?"

"Dead serious, my friend. Just a few flowers a couple of times a year will be just fine... and nothing fancy!"

"I don't know what to say, brother."

"Say that you'll keep in touch."

He smiled back at Gill as he whispered, "Once a month... in your dreams!"

"That's good enough for me!"

Betsey honked her horn over and over as the crew of heroes pulled out of the long driveway to hit the highway. Everyone was looking out the windows and waving.

Everyone had tears in their eyes... and in their hearts.

Gill was the last to look away from the Pahaska.

"Goodbye, Killer. Peace, little brother."

With Robert at the wheel, they slowly eased their way out of the mighty Yellowstone National Park. Sarah and Felix both sat up in front with the driver, making conversation to help keep him alert.

"It's too bad that no one knows about us saving the whole damn world!" Felix said with a huff. "I woulda liked to have gotten on the Letterman show!"

Robert laughed! "Naw, Felix! I'm afraid you're not made for the television screens! They're wide, nowadays, ya know... not tall!"

Felix giggled. "How about radio? I've got a face that was made for radio!"

Sarah laughed. "Dude, you've got a face that was made for Halloween!"

From out of nowhere, a magazine hit her in the arm.

"Hey!" she said. "That's my gag!"

Felix fell over laughing.

Robert drove all night through Pocatello, Idaho, headed on into Salt Lake City. Because of the lack of the stopovers that they had on their trip out to Yellowstone, they made much better time headed home and missed almost all of the brand-new snowstorm swinging in from the north. Robert parked Betsey at a truck stop outside of Salt Lake City the following morning, and gave everyone a wakeup call.

"Good morning, folks!" he said on Betsey's intercom. "We're parked at a truck stop, and I... for one, need some coffee and a hot breakfast... not to mention a pit stop to the little boy's room! Anyone who would care to join me, get your butt's up... and let's go eat!"

Everyone started rolling out of their bunks, and Gill, who had slept in the back stateroom, stuck his head out of the door.

"Where are we, Robert?"

"Salt Lake City, boss."

"Damn! You're making pretty good time."

"Yeah. That's 'cause I haven't had to stop in every small town along the way lookin' for magic trinkets and stuff!"

Gill laughed. He watched Felix get up and go to the front of the bus to talk to Robert. Then, Gill whispered to Paul and Sarah, "Hey, guys? Wanna see something funny?"

They both nodded with a smile.

Gill went back into his room and closed the door. Then, he got on the intercom to the front of the bus and announced, "Hey, Robert, I think we'll save a bunch of time by just highballing it straight out of here on Highway 80 all of the way to Reno!"

Gill started laughing as he heard giant footsteps running as fast as they could from the front of the bus to the back. Sarah managed to dodge out of Felix's path, but poor Paul was almost trampled.

KNOCK, KNOCK, KNOCK!

"Yeah, Felix. Come on in."

"How'd you know it was me?" he asked when he finally caught his breath again.

It was a good sixty seconds later before Gill, Sarah and Paul could stop laughing long enough to answer. Felix was just standing there, embarrassed and blushing.

With a giggle, Paul said, "Damn, Felix! Gill's been waiting on you since yesterday afternoon!"

Felix dropped his head. "You mean... you know?"

Gill put his hand on the giant man's shoulder. "Yeah, Felix, we all know. You don't even need to ask, my friend. I'll drive you up Highway 225 myself, and I'll get you to Shadow Of The Moon by lunchtime! Good enough?"

Felix got all misty-eyed. "Gill... guys... I don't want you to think... that I'm runnin' out on ya... or anything."

"No problem, big brother," Paul said with a smile.

"You go get 'er!" Sarah said with a giggle.

Gill looked at Felix. "Dude... you take some time off up here with Shadow, and then you come home whenever you want to. I do expect you to keep in touch with me, though! You're still on my payroll!"

"Thanks, Gill. I'm glad you understand. All of you."

"Hell," Gill said with a smile, "you can even bring her along when you come back if you want to!"

"What about Found Child and Cody?"

"Yeah, sure... why not! Bring the kids, too."

Robert shook his head as he whispered, "Oh, great! Another Cody!"

Felix smiled. "He won't be much trouble. Whistle Cat can babysit!"

Gill's face caved in with surprise! "Aw, hell! I forgot about the damn talking mountain lion!"

Everyone laughed.

Breakfast was very quick and very good. When they all finally piled back into the bus, Gill took over the driving so Robert could get some well-deserved rest. About three hours later, Gill pulled off of the interstate to pick up state highway 225 and headed north. Felix said he was so excited that you couldn't drive a straight pin in his butt with a sledgehammer. Snow flakes were falling at a steady but gentle rate, and it made the mountains a thing of beauty once again.

Upon arriving at Shadow's village, they were greeted by the entire tribe. A festival of sorts was taking place in honor of the battle won by the Great Spirit and the White Warriors. Though most of tribe had no memories of the past few days' events, Shadow had thought it necessary to enlighten them as to what had occurred. This, too, would explain Found Child and Whistle Cat to them, and with her now being the tribe's shaman, no one doubted her words.

She rushed into the arms of the tall, tall white dude, and whispered into his ear, "Come into my arms, Cat Warrior!"

He blushed as he whispered back, "And into your heart."

Venison barbecue, corn on the cob, a stone-ground wheat and corn fry-bread, and all sorts of other incredible dishes were passed around as the village celebrated the coming of the whites who had saved not only their village, but after hearing the words of Shadow, had also saved the world and brought back some of the Shoshone people from The Big Open. Though the travelers were anxious to reach their own home, the Shoshone people continued the celebration into the night and would not hear of their heroes leaving until dark. Whistle Cat, (or Other Brother as he was known to the tribe), was dancing, and Cody sang with Found Child in his arms.

Shadow was happy beyond belief that the Cat Warrior would be allowed to remain there with her, even if only for the time being. Gill smiled at her.

"Shadow, we leave it up to you and the dude here to make your own timetable... your own futures. But know that as you have welcomed us into your village and your lives, so you are welcome into ours."

She touched his face with her hand. "A person can ask for no greater gift. You are truly a warrior touched by God."

The time finally arrived when goodbyes had to be said. The villagers insisted on sending extra food with the travelers, and Shadow said a Shoshone blessing on them, Betsey, and on their journey.

Betsey's voice came on her outside speakers. "I don't believe I've ever been blessed before! I kind of like it!"

Felix quietly went over to Paul with an envelope and a piece of paper in his hand. "Paul, this is a list of things that I need you to draw up on your way home. I have foreseen that these will be needed, and each person's name is by the gifts that will belong to them. Tell them that I sent them, will ya? Also, have Gill mail this envelope to my brother for me but don't tell him to do it until you both get home to his house. This is important, so don't forget!"

"You betcha, Super Dude! I'm gonna miss you, Felix," Paul said with a tear as he hugged the giant.

"Only for a while. I'll be back."

"Promise?"

"Ya couldn't keep me away with a stick!" Felix said with a grin.

Robert gave Shadow a hug, then turned to Felix. "You take care of this lady, dude, or you'll be hearing from me!"

"You got it, Doc! You've got one of your own to take care of now!"

Robert laughed! "Yeah, I guess I do. I'll see you soon, pal."

Sarah slowly pulled his large face down to where she could kiss it. She then whispered in his ear, "I think I'm gonna miss you most of all, Scarecrow."

He turned her face up to look into her eyes and whispered back,
"There's no place like home, sweetie. Take care of these chuckleheads for
me... 'til I get home... OK?"

She brushed the tears from her eyes and kissed him again.

"Bye, dude."

At long last, it was just Gill and Felix.

"Hey, Shortie! Keep your wheels between the ditches... and the Smokies
outta yur britches!"

Gill smiled. "You don't forget where home is, Dude. You've come to
mean an awful lot to us."

Felix smiled. "Damn! It sure is nice to be loved!" Shadow squeezed his
arm.

Gill passed Felix a fat manila envelope. "Here's some messin' around
money for you and Shadow and the kids to have some fun with. We'll call
it an advance of your salary!"

Felix snickered. "What do ya mean, an advance? It seems like I've been
here forever... and still haven't got paid!" He opened the envelope and saw
the large stacks of hundred dollar bills. "Hell, Gill! There's enough here to
BUY Nevada!"

"Well, give some to your new friends, then! They'll need it to put gas in
that new van! Buy something for the kids of the tribe, too, Shadow."

Felix shook his head and hugged the little guy who was now his family.
"Damn, I'm gonna miss y'all." he whispered.

"I know. The same here, big guy!"

As Gill got onto the bus, he looked once more at Felix, standing there
with Shadow, two kids and a pet mountain lion. He smiled at his tall friend
and softly added, "Peace, Dude."

As the bus was turning around to leave, Felix shouted out, "Tell Sarah to
stay out of trouble!"

Even though Betsey was now zooming away, far down the dirt road, a
magazine slammed into the back of his head.

"Damn, girl! How does she do that?"

84
No Place Like Home

Gill and Robert took turns driving on the remainder of the long journey home. From where they got back onto Interstate 80, headed to Reno was about three hundred miles, which took six or seven hours because of the road conditions. Another four hundred and seventy miles, or nine hours later, they found themselves passing Los Angeles City Limits sign

It was early afternoon in L.A., and smoggy. Sarah and Gill were up in the front of Betsey with Robert driving when Paul came forward. Paul had been awfully quiet all night long and kept doodling in his sketchbook but wouldn't show anyone what he'd drawn.

"Here, Robert!" he said with a smile as he handed him a small box. "It's from Felix, but I've been given orders that you can't open it until eleven tonight, when we get to Gill's house."

"Aw, man! I wanna open it now! Hey, Felix wouldn't know if I went ahead and just..."

"Yeah, he would!" Sarah said with a giggle.

"Felix would know," Gill chuckled with a nod.

"Good!" Paul added with a smile. "Great! I'm glad you both feel that way... 'cause these two are for you! And you can't..."

"Yeah! We know! Can't open 'em up until we get home!" Sarah said. "Damn, Felix!"

Hers was a box about the size of the L.A. phone book, and she was told to open it at ten p.m. on the button. Gill got a small flat box that looked like an eyeglass case. He was to open it fifteen minutes after they arrived home.

"How come Sarah gets the big one?" Robert asked with a grin.

Betsey came on the speakers. "Paul, Felix said that I'm supposed to introduce you to Lois! She'll help take care of you and teach you the layout of the house until Felix comes home. I think that's supposed to be your present!"

"Lois?" he said under his breath.

"Hi, sweetie!" she said in a throaty voice. "I'm Lois... and I can't wait to meet you. Bye for now!"

Paul looked embarrassed. "She sounds... very pretty. How old is she,

Gill?"

"Well, let's see... she must be... almost four years old now."

"FOUR?"

Everyone laughed! Then Sarah whispered to his ear, "She's a computer program, Paul."

"Whew!" with a smile. "I thought for a minute there that Felix was fixin' me up or somethin'! She's supposed to teach me the layout of the house? Just how big is your home, Gill?"

Once again everyone laughed.

Sarah replied, "It's more like homes, Paul! You know, I'm not sure that anyone knows how big that place is!"

"Except for Killer," Gill said in a whisper.

No one said anything after that for a while.

MAX called Sarah on her phone as they got near to the entrance driveway at Gill's house. "Sarah! MAX here! It's so good to have you back! Congratulations on your victory and saving the world and stuff like that!"

"Hi, MAX! Thanks, sugar. Yeah, we're back, but kind of worn out from this trip. I think that Robert and I will stay at Gill's tonight, and then tomorrow... if he doesn't mind... we'll both come over there to my place to check up on everything that's been going on. Did I get any messages on the phone?"

"Tons! The police guy called about a hundred times, wanting to know... let's see, how did he put it... oh, yeah! 'What the hell is going ON?' Whaa whaa whaa! Your workplace called, and wanted you and Gill to know that production has gone up fifty percent since you got rid of my ex-owner, Roy Higgins! Did I ever tell you how much I didn't like him? Oh, and your neighbor called up, wanting to know if she was going crazy or what! It seems that she remembers things that no one else does!"

"Oh, dear!" Sarah said. "MAX, it's going to take awhile to clear all of this stuff up! Do me a favor... and catalog all of the messages for me. I'll be home tomorrow. OK?"

"OK, Sarah... but there is one more..."

"Aw, come on, MAX! We're tired! Unless it's really important..."

"It might be, Sarah. Somebody with a real funny voice left a message that he wants to talk with... how'd he put it?... oh, yeah... the secret group of heroes! Something about more work in the future? He said that he'd talked to a Sergeant Eddie Fallon from the Los Angeles Police Department days ago about some incidents that were taking place, and now... no one in his office can even remember any of these incidents happening... except for himself! He was kinda flustered!"

Sarah sat there with her mouth open. "OH, God!" she thought. "More work?" She looked at Gill, who just shrugged his shoulders. "MAX, did he leave his name?"

"Yeah, Sarah... but I couldn't understand it very well because of his accent. Reminded me of a movie I once saw! It sounded like Shorts Digger! He said to contact him at the number he left. It's the number for the state Capitol!"

"Aw, hell!" Robert said from behind Betsey's wheel, with a shake of his head. "This just keeps on getting better and better!"

Gill laughed out loud. "Curiouser and curiouser!"

Sarah groaned! "OK, MAX. Take care of those things for me. I'll be back."

"THAT'S WHAT HE SAID! Whaa Whaa Whaa!"

Paul watched through the windows as they turned off of the road onto gravel, and then drove and drove and drove.

"What road is this that we're on?" he asked after awhile.

"It's not!" Sarah answered with a giggle. "It's Gill's driveway!"

Paul shook his head and whispered, "You've got to be kiddin'!"

After a few minutes, a quick right turn put them at the hidden bus entrance door, which automatically opened. Betsey was driven to her own spot, and after her long first journey since her renovation, she was parked for a well-deserved rest period.

"Betsey," Gill said with a smile, "you did just beautifully! Good job, ol' girl!"

"Aww, boss," she added, "I'll bet you say that to all the ol' busses!"

Robert slid from behind the wheel. "Betsey, run a diagnostic for me on your systems so I can replenish and upgrade anything we need for the next time. Good job, m'lady!"

"Thanks, Robert."

Lois automatically swung open the inside entrance doors to welcome the weary travelers home. "Welcome home, boss! Damn, it's good to have you guys home again! It's been way too quiet around here!"

Gill entered his long hallway once again, and the first thing he saw was a picture of good ol' Killer and himself hanging on the wall.

"Hi, Lois," he quietly said with a tear in his eye. "I have a feeling that it's still gonna be way too quiet around here." He walked off toward the kitchen without another word.

When Robert and Sarah walked into the hall together, Lois quietly asked, "Robert? Is Gill going to be OK?"

"Yeah, Lois. It's just gonna take him a little time to get over Killer being gone, that's all."

"I understand. I'm having trouble with that myself." About then, a stranger stepped in front of her cameras. "Wow! Who is this good-lookin' creature?"

He smiled from ear to ear. "Hi, Lois! I'm Paul."

"Of course you are, honey! Now, you just follow Robert and Sarah toward the kitchen for now, where I've got some hot chocolate brewing... and you and I will talk later! Wow!"

As they walked down the hallway, Sarah turned to Paul. "I think she likes you!"

Meanwhile, a trillion miles away... and at the same time right next door, a very small dog and Killer laid on the green, green grasses of the Far-Away. Killer was munching on a large bone of unknown origin, and the very small God of Dogs watched with a smile.

"You know, Killer, you have been found worthy of return... if that should be your wish."

Killer looked up from his chewing, smiled back, and then rolled onto his back in the fragrant field of flowers in The Land Behind The Sky. It was a beautiful place here, and so peaceful. No more pain. No more bad people. No more Bigger-Than-Tree.

That was good, but there was also no more Gill.

That was sad.

With that thought, Killer rolled back over onto his belly and whimpered.

"How would the Gill human ever get along without me? He couldn't even find things in his own home!" he thought. "And Sarah human... and Robert human... who would make them laugh with small tricks now that Killer was in the Far-Away?"

Killer looked to the God of Dogs. He cocked his small head sideways in question.

The God of Dogs smiled once again.

"Killer, I can send you back to the human world, but things will be different this time. Nothing is ever the same the second time around. Only fate knows if you will even meet your Gill human once again! The choice is yours, my friend."

Killer cocked his small head sideways in the other direction.

"God of Dogs... they need me."

God of Dogs smiled for the final time.

"I see. Well, you have earned your place here in the Far-Away... and it shall be awaiting you the next time. You are a good dog... but for now... I grant you... the Power of Return! Be happy, my friend."

As he said this, the God of Dogs found himself in the field of flowers all alone.

"Oh, well," he thought to himself, "at least he left me a large bone of unknown origin!"

The God of Dogs began to munch as the heavens continued to turn.

Robert sat at the table drinking hot chocolate with Sarah and Paul.

Trying to break the silence with some conversation, Robert said, "Do you know that the whole final battle with that damn Thingie only lasted about ten minutes? Isn't that amazing?"

Gill sighed. "It's amazing what you can lose in only ten minutes, isn't it?"

Paul took this as a cue to bring levity to the situation. "Hey, Gill! It's about time for you to open Felix's gift, isn't it?"

Gill gave his newest friend a sad smile. "Paul... guys... I know what you're trying to do, and I really appreciate it, but..."

"Aw, come on partner!" Robert said. "Open the damn thing! Sarah and I can't open ours for hours, yet! Hey... ours for hours! I made a funny!"

Gill finally laughed. "You are a funny, Robert! OK, give me the damn box!"

Gill took the small flat package and slowly unwrapped the paper from around it. He carefully lifted the lid and glanced inside. Then, he looked up at everyone and muttered, "I don't get it."

Robert and Sarah at the same time asked, "What is it?"

Gill removed the tiny item out of the box, and showed it to them. It was a brass tag with an adhesive backing... about one-inch tall and about three inches long.

All it had engraved upon it was "KING."

They all turned to Paul. He shrugged his shoulders, saying, "Not a clue! It was Felix's idea, not mine."

They all looked at it for a moment longer, and then Sarah added, "Well, you know Felix! Something will make sense out of this soon."

Gill sadly shook his head. "I need to go for a walk, guys. I'll be back in awhile."

"Do you need some company?" Robert asked.

"No, Robert. You stay with Sarah and Paul. I just need to be alone for a bit."

And then, the old light bulb of an idea went on in Paul's head. "Hey, Gill! Damn... I almost forgot! Felix needs you to mail this letter for him! He said it's to his brother!"

Gill huffed in protest. "I'll do it tomorrow, Paul."

"No, Gill! He said as soon as we got home! It's important!"

"Damn, Felix!" Gill said with a frown. "OK, give me the damn letter! I'll take my damn bike to the damn mailbox!" He stomped off.

Paul hung his head as he looked at Sarah and Robert. "Sorry, guys! I just did what Felix told me to."

"It's OK, Paul." Sarah said. "It's OK."

Gill went off to the underground entrance, where he kept the small motor bike that he used just for trips back and forth to the far away mail box by the street entrance. He cranked on the engine and it started right up. He pulled out of the hidden doorway and turned back to the left to head toward the street. As he drove, he realized that he had yelled at his friends for no really good reason at all. He also realized that the trip on the small bike was refreshing up his attitude a bit with the cool wind blowing through his hair and the smell of California wildflowers in the air.

"Thanks, Felix. How did you know?" Gill said to himself.

A few minutes later, he pulled up to the street-side mail box. He opened the door of the big box and slid in the letter that Felix had insisted must be mailed today. He raised the flag on the box and heard a whimper.

"A whimper? Mail boxes don't whimper!"

He looked around on the ground, and there in the ditch, which ran along the street, was a black plastic bag.

"Oh, God! No!" he thought to himself as giant tears began to roll down his face.

The garbage bag moved. Just barely.

"Oh, God! Not again!" he said out loud as he dumped his bike in the dirt and ran to the drainage ditch.

He carefully raised the weighted-down bag from the rainwater in the ditch and could feel something twitch.

He quickly ripped open the top of this plastic prison (this sounds familiar, he thought), and lifted out a small dark bundle. It had been put into this garbage bag along with trash from someone's visit to a Burger King. Stuck on its small head was a paper crown.

As he gently held the small creature in his tiny hands, it slowly opened its eyes, which were the only thing on it that weren't solid black.

Gill could almost swear that it smiled at him.

He turned his tear-stained face to the sky and whispered, "Thank you."

It appeared to be a tiny black Labrador of complex heritage, and because of its small size, it was most likely the runt of the litter. Its barely beating heart from lack of oxygen quickened in the fresh California breeze, and it whimpered a hello to Gill's glad heart. He raised the small handful of puppy to his face with giant tears rolling down his cheeks, and the puppy stopped whimpering. A small pink tongue came slowly out of its mouth and kissed him.

"Hello, King. You come on with me. You're home now."

"Yipe, yipe, yipe!" the small pup answered back.

As he had done once before, many years ago, Gill placed the small pup in his shirt pocket. "A perfect fit!"

He carefully lifted the motor bike back onto its wheels. As he straddled the small motorcycle, he looked at his new friend. "Come on, now. I'll show you your new home."

As the bike putt-putted its way back to the underground world he had built for himself and his friends, Gill looked into his pocket and King looked back at him.

"Yipe! Woof!"

"Welcome back, partner. And thanks, Felix. How did you know?"

As he drove into the parking area, he yelled out, "Lois! Get everyone into the kitchen again if they're not already there! Tell Robert that I need warm milk and some bacon! Tell 'em that the King has arrived, and they're all expected in the throne-room!"

"Are you alright, Gill?"

"I'm better than alright, Lois! I'm great!"

"Whatever you say... your majesty!"

He took off at a run.

When he finally reached the kitchen, Sarah had heated him up a glass of warm milk, and Robert was taking the bacon out of the microwave to put onto a sandwich.

"No sandwich... just bacon! And milk in a bowl!"

Gill was laughing and singing and dancing.

"Has he gone mad?" Robert whispered.

"Maybe Publisher's Clearing House sent him mail! 'You may have won a Gazillion dollars!' ... or somethin' like that!" Paul said.

Sarah didn't say anything, but looked into Gill's smiling eyes. Then, a tear came to her own eyes. She started crying. "He's back, isn't he?"

Gill nodded, and then gently pulled the small puppy out of his pocket. "Folks, say hello to King!"

As they were all oohing and ahhing over the little bundle of fur, Gill told them the story of what had just happened. "It was amazing!" he said. "Just like last time, only this time... he's a Labrador!"

Robert shook his head. "Gill, he's as cute as a button, but surely you don't believe that... this dog..."

"Grrrr!"

Gill laughed at the pup. "King?"

"Yipe?"

Bark once for yes and twice for no. Understand?"

"Woof!"

Gill smiled at Robert. "King, have you been here before?"

"Yipe!"

"Do you want some bacon?"

"Yipe!"

"Hahaha! You see?"

Robert once again shook his head. "Yeah, that proves that a dog knows how to bark, Gill, and he likes bacon! That's all."

Gill smiled. "Oh, ye of little faith! OK, let's try something else." He set the tiny pooch on the floor. "King?"

"Yipe?"

"Do you know where my bedroom slippers are?"

King thought for a second, and then... "Yipe!"

"Bring me one of the red ones!"

"Yipe," the pup said as he got ready to take off down the hallway.

Robert stopped him. "King?"

The dog skidded to a halt and looked at Robert. Robert smiled for a moment and then said, "The left one."

"Woof!" the pup shouted as he took off.

While he was gone, Paul drew up a picture of a beautiful dog collar with a special place for the brass sticker that announced his new name. As it popped into being, they all heard the dragging sound of a two-pound puppy pulling a one-pound shoe down the hallway.

A red shoe.

The left one.

Lois came on the speakers. "It's him! It's him!"

Sarah fell onto the couch in tears of joy, and Robert joined her in laughter. The new collar fit him like a glove. Robert managed to say, "First the Killer... then the King! Who comes next... the Godfather of Soul, Prince... or the Boss?"

Everyone spent the rest of the evening in celebration while feeding bacon to King.

As darkness took over the skies, Gill and King wandered off to their bedroom together. Paul said goodnight, and Lois directed him to his new, beautiful bedroom.

Robert and Sarah headed to the large bedroom that she had been using, and together they used up about a million gallons of hot water in a fantastic shower. When they finally managed to drag themselves out of the hot water, Sarah draped a towel around herself and went into the bedroom followed by "Ert."

"Look, Robert! It's ten p.m.! I can open up my present from Felix now!"

"Cool! I want to see what the matchstick man got for my girl!"

"Hold your horses, big boy! I get to see first!"

She carefully unwrapped the paper from around the box. Then, without letting him see, she raised one side of the lid and looked in.

"Oh, my God!" she whispered.

"What is it? What is it?" he asked as he was bouncing around.

"You can't see it yet! It needs to be filled first, but I will tell you that I think Felix actually got this for you... not for me!"

As he tried to grab the mystery package out of her hands, she squealed, giggled, and ran for the bathroom. He heard her lock the door from the inside.

"Come on, Sarah! Let me see!"

"You'll get to see it in five minutes, mister! You just wait!"

By the time she had finished with the package, put on a little makeup, brushed her hair, and applied ample amounts of perfume, it was ten minutes later and Robert was ready to break down the damn door.

"Ready?" she said in a whisper.

She stepped out of the bathroom in a soft cloud scented of lilacs, looking like a dream. Felix had designed lingerie of silk. It was three pieces of heaven as silky as the girl was herself and was exactly the same color as her own skin. In the low light, it looked as if she was the lingerie.

He took her into his strong arms and kissed her softly. Then he shook his head again as he smiled.

"That Felix! How did he know? What am I gonna do with him? This is the perfect gift for me... and I just love the filling!"

She pulled him toward the big bed.

"The filling loves you, too, Ert."

The quiet night took them both into its warm embrace, and for awhile, time mattered not at all.

Later on, he whispered, "Sarah, I've been thinking... you know, about... ah, what we kinda talked about... and, ah... back when you were hurt and, ah... you told Betsey to save that tape... and, ah..."

Sarah smiled at this poor embarrassed idiot of a man that she had come to love so much. "Go ahead, Robert... just say it."

"Well, Sarah, ah... I was just wondering... if ah... you might want..."

RING RING RING!

"What the hell was that?" Sarah said in a huff! "Just when we were getting to the good part!"

"It's the alarm clock! It's eleven p.m.! I can open my present now!"

"WHAT? Ert, if you think for even one second that I'm going to forget about this...!"

"Well, you got to open yours! Even if it was... kinda for me in the long run! Lemme see what I get!"

He reached over her beautiful body and snatched up the tiny box on the nightstand. She was huffing and puffing, mad at Felix, as Ert unwrapped the small package, but as he peeked in, he froze, with his mouth wide open.

"Well? What is it? What's so damn important?"

He smiled at her, as he whispered back, "I think it's for you."

He showed her what was in the box.

She fell off of the bed.

It was a two and a half carat pink diamond engagement ring, heart-shaped cut and mounted in platinum.

She got up crying.

"Are you alright?" Robert asked.

"That's the most beautiful damn thing I've ever seen in my whole life!" she said in a hush.

Robert looked into her eyes. "You can have it if you'll marry me."

Tears and sobs.

Tears and sobs.

He laughed. "Is that a yes?"

"YES! she yelled! "Yes, yes, yes!"

She took the box from him and he removed the ring and placed it upon her finger. As he did, a tiny note fell out.

They read it together.

"Congratulations! Love-Felix

"Damn, Felix! How do you do it?"

Down the hallway, Gill and his new/old friend jumped up and down on the giant bed with a sigh of relief.

He put on a pair of warm pajamas and couldn't keep from watching and laughing at the small dog. The pup had to explore every corner and every nook and every cranny in the room, sniffing as he sensed the old aroma of Killer. He would find a hidden stash of food or bones that had been stored for God knows how long, and bark and dance around, as if he was so excited to be there that he couldn't stand it.

Gill finally started to yawn, and as he did, so did King. He placed the pup on top of the bed and folded back the soft, warm comforter. He punched in some soft, cool jazz on the stereo at a low volume and then lay back to relax.

At last.

A few minutes later, he could hear Sarah shouting out "YES! Yes, yes, yes!"

Lois came on the speakers in his room. "Gill, are you awake?"

"Yeah, Lois... but I'm sinking fast. What's up?"

"Did you hear Sarah and Robert?"

"Yeah. Sounds like he finally popped the question."

"I'm so happy! Now I get to plan a wedding!"

"Good for you, girl. Get with Sarah tomorrow... and you girls can talk about it. But for now..."

"Yes, I'm sorry, Gill. I'm really glad that your dog is here again. Is this what you'd call... a miracle?"

"If it's not, Lois, it's awful close to one. Now, can I sleep?"

Yeah, I'm sorry again! I'll talk to you tomorrow."

After she was gone, he whispered, "I can hardly wait."

He lay down and started thinking about all that he still had to do.

Sergeant Eddie Fallon had an appointment with him and Robert to talk about what happened in the past few days and what might happen in the future. Gill had a feeling that Eddie was a good person, and he figured that it would be easy to find a place for the sergeant in their organization.

Then there was Felix. There was no telling how all of that would end up. He could just see a mountain lion living here with everyone else. And two kids. And a Native American Shaman As if Felix wasn't enough of a handful.

Then, there was the state Capitol. "Make a mental note to call the Governor." Arnold would be expecting his call!

And now, there was the upcoming wedding. "Lord! It was gonna be a strange year coming up! But for now, we have no alien races tryin' to kill off the planet... the universe... or all universes!"

It was a small break from the chaos.

At last.

He was almost asleep now.

He thought about what all had happened in the last few days.

He thought about the enemies they had all vanquished.

He thought of the new friends they had gained.

And the ones lost.

Oh, well, the future would come as it would, and the past was just that, the past.

For tonight, his new puppy was snuggled up under the edge of the blankets with Gill. They looked at each other and both smiled.

As for now, a well-deserved rest for everyone.
At last.

About the Author

Rickie Lee Reynolds was born on October 28, 1948, in the small town of Manila, Arkansas. In the early 1950s, his mom and new stepdad moved Rickie Lee, along with his two brothers, to California, where he started elementary school. In 1963, because of lack of work, his parents decided to return to where they had family... good ol' Arkansas. In the last half of the tenth grade, Rickie found himself in Monette, Arkansas, and entered into what would end up being a lifelong friendship with a classmate named James "Jim Dandy" Mangrum.

After fifty-three years of playing music together in a band known as Black Oak Arkansas (the first place these two pals ever rehearsed together), they have achieved three gold and platinum albums and one gold single for a song titled "Jim Dandy to the Rescue" – the recording of which was encouraged by none other than Elvis himself. In addition, they have recorded more than twenty albums, not including "Best of" and compilation records, and performed thousands of concerts around the world. The band has donated hundreds of thousands of dollars to charities, not only in Arkansas but also across the nation.

After writing hundreds of songs and two poems, which are listed in the National Library of Poetry, Rickie has turned his hand to being an author. He lives in Memphis, Tennessee, with his dog, Dollie, and his son Nick.

CPSIA information can be obtained at www.ICGtesting.com
Printed in the USA
LVOW08s1243300316

481424LV00006B/87/P